PRAISE FOR

*The Ashtrays Are Full
and the Glasses Are Empty*

"Kirsten Mickelwait writes down to the very bone of the Lost Generation's artists, writers, and families, revealing a past that was not archaic but a glittering guide to today. Weaving stunningly intricate details with a grandiose sweep, Mickelwait provides a jewel box of a book, illustrating that none of us invented the fight for a singular creative life. The remarkable guide, Sara Murphy, hooked me from the first page, and I've mourned her since turning the last. I loved this book."

—Randy Susan Meyers, international bestselling author of *The Many Mothers of Ivy Puddingstone*

"*The Ashtrays Are Full and the Glasses Are Empty* transports readers back to the Paris and Côte d'Azur of the 1920s, slipping us into the luxury- and adventure-filled life of Sara and Gerald Murphy. Both quickly become dear to us, but it is Sara—channeling her creativity into making life beautiful for others—who captures our hearts. When personal tragedy and history bring an end to this charmed life, we grieve along with Sara and Gerald as they struggle to find acceptance and peace. This novel will inspire, entertain, and move you in equal measure."

—Anne Matlack Evans, author of *The Light Through the Branches*

"Every scene in this well-researched novel is thick with authenticity, and Mickelwait's exquisite attention to detail makes the Jazz Age come alive."
—Iris Jamahl Dunkle, author of
*Riding Like the Wind: The Life of Sanora Babb*

"In her first novel, Mickelwait illuminates the life of a woman who is an afterthought among the outsized personalities of the time, especially Hemingway and F. Scott Fitzgerald, who unflatteringly portray her in their work. (Sara's own abilities are overshadowed as she supports Gerald and creates a rich, loving life for her children, but she unflinchingly embraces the messiness of existence.) Mickelwait's descriptions effectively evoke the time and place: "Paris was a living, breathing organism in which fresh ideas were floating on the air waiting to be grabbed, like drunken birds." Fans of Paula McLain and Marie Benedict will enjoy this insightful novel."
—*Kirkus Reviews*

Also by Kirsten Mickelwait

*The Ghost Marriage*

*The Ashtrays Are Full and the Glasses Are Empty*
by Kirsten Mickelwait

© Copyright 2025 Kirsten Mickelwait

979-8-88824-691-7

All rights reserved. No part of this publication may be reproduced, stored in a retrieval system, or transmitted in any form or by any means—electronic, mechanical, photocopy, recording, or any other—except for brief quotations in printed reviews, without the prior written permission of the author.

HUMAN AUTHORED: Any use of this publication to train generative artificial intelligence (AI) technologies to generate text is expressly prohibited.

This is a work of fiction. The characters may be both actual and fictitious. With the exception of verified historical events and persons, all incidents, descriptions, dialogue, and opinions expressed are the products of the author's imagination and are not to be construed as real.

Designed by Suzanne Bradshaw

Published by

köehlerbooks™

3705 Shore Drive
Virginia Beach, VA 23455
800-435-4811
www.koehlerbooks.com

# *The* ASHTRAYS *are* FULL *and the* GLASSES *are* EMPTY

A NOVEL

KIRSTEN MICKELWAIT

VIRGINIA BEACH
CAPE CHARLES

*For Phyllis Willits*
*. . . and all the other Saras in my life*

## AUTHOR'S NOTE

Sara, Gerald, and many other real-life people appear in this book as fictional characters. However, my goal as a writer was to reflect the actual relationships and events of their lives as accurately as possible, not straying too far from the historical record. The real story of the Murphys' remarkable marriage is so fascinating, and has already been so thoroughly told by their biographers, that I tried to imagine more deeply their emotional lives while remaining true to the facts.

Along the way, I've been grateful for a number of sources to enhance my storytelling. Yale's Beinecke Rare Book and Manuscript Library, holder of the Sara and Gerald Murphy Papers, was an invaluable resource for letters and memorabilia. The definitive Murphy biography, *Everybody Was So Young* by Amanda Vaill, was an essential reference point. In addition, I relied on such biographical works as *A Moveable Feast* by Ernest Hemingway, *Living Well Is the Best Revenge* by Calvin Tomkins, *Sara and Gerald* by Honoria Murphy Donnelly and Richard N. Billings, *Letters from the Lost Generation* by Linda Patterson Miller, *Making It New: The Art and Style of Sara and Gerald Murphy*, edited by Deborah Rothschild, and *Everybody Behaves Badly* by Lesley M. M. Blume.

I used actual letters and interviews to inform my dialogue

and correspondence between characters, sometimes quoting their language verbatim—which is reflected in some odd spellings in this text. In other cases, I rewrote their words slightly, or completely reimagined what they might have said. Taken together, I hope that I have accurately portrayed the exceptional spirit of these singular Lost Generation figures.

And there were afternoons when the snow fell
Softly across the wind and in the mirrors
The snow fell softly, flake on flake, the vague
Reflected falling in the long dim mirrors,
Faint snow across the image of the wind, —
And there were afternoons when the room remembered,
When her life passed in the mirrors of the room.

> Archibald MacLeish,
> *Sketch for a Portrait of Mme. G—M—*

# Prologue
## 1965

"Tuna salad on toast," Dottie was saying. "The closest I'll ever get to the ocean again." She carefully removed the cellophane-frilled toothpick from half her sandwich, then the bread, then delicately placed dill pickle slices on the salad and reassembled the whole thing. Bits of tuna fell onto the plate as she struggled to take a bite. "Goddamn it," she muttered.

I'd ordered a cup of the Manhattan clam chowder. Now I tore my dinner roll and buttered just the broken piece with the smear of butter from my bread plate.

"Look at you, still the debutante," Dottie said. "Even the way you butter your bread is approved by Emily Post."

"To the manor born," I smiled. "Even in the Lexington Luncheonette."

"How the mighty have fallen," Dottie said. "I speak not only of reputations but of arches. And pretty much everything else from the neck down."

Here's my advice to you: if you're going to grow old with another person, choose someone who'll make you laugh. At that stage, when nothing in your body really works anymore and your world has shrunk to a few city blocks, what else is there to do?

In my case, I had Dorothy Parker. In those days, Dottie and I were like soldiers in arms, keeping an eye on each other in our dotage. We were living two floors apart at the Volney Hotel, "a fine residential hotel for older women," at East 74th Street between Madison and Fifth. Here we were, two old broads who had seen much better days. And much worse.

I was eighty-two and Dottie was seventy-two; between my short breath and her bad heart, we couldn't go far. The Lexington Luncheonette was our favored restaurant because it was two blocks away and it served the kind of bland cuisine that didn't wreak havoc with our ancient digestive tracts.

I looked around: the dated venetian blinds, the marbled green vinyl upholstery, the other old diners quietly eating their lunches at eleven thirty. "Such a tiny container after a life without borders," I sighed. "Remember those long, leisurely days when we thought we'd be young forever and that nothing could ever go really wrong?"

"Well, it didn't until you were what, forty-six?" Dottie asked. "Your world was pretty damned good up until then. The 'town and country' life. You were raised to expect that nothing but beautiful things would come your way."

Dottie, always known for her savage wit, once wrote, "If you want to know what God thinks of money, just look at the people he gave it to." That's when I realized that, despite our long and loving friendship, she inwardly begrudged me my earlier good fortune, at least a little bit. I couldn't blame her.

"Did I ever tell you that I once advised Gerald not to marry you?" Dottie and Gerald had known each other since grade school, when she was still Dorothy Rothschild. While her family was hardly penurious, her young life was filled with tragedy. Now she gave me that wicked smile of hers. "I called you a bird in a gilded cage."

"Well, you weren't wrong." I buttered another piece of my roll and then, in a moment of weakness, dunked it into my soup. The combination of melting butter and bread and tomato broth: celestial.

Dottie gave me a shocked look. "Your manners are going to hell," she said, not smiling.

I laughed. "I'm ready for it. For all my sins of wealth and gluttony, I think I've been adequately punished in my lifetime."

---

IT'S A VERY American idea that we can make our luck; that with enough drive and work, we will get the life we so richly deserve. I am here to tell you otherwise. I learned the hard way that, despite our youthful belief that we can design and achieve our best lives, larger forces will inevitably teach us that we're not in complete control of our fates.

Does someone keep track of the credits and debits in our lives? Is there meant to be a final sum at the end? Is life fair or arbitrary? At this point, all I can say is that I've had my share of both. I came to understand that even the greatest wealth can't protect you from tragedy or a broken heart; I've paid the price for whatever good fortune I've had. Instead, I learned that happiness can be found, long after the parties have ended, through bottomless love and a creative spirit.

I dunked another piece of bread and put it in my mouth, then shook my head as if to banish those ugly thoughts. More often these days, I wanted to return to my earlier past. To feel the warm rush of air on my face, to see the approaching train. To be that girl on the subway platform, so unsuspecting, about to jump into an unimaginably wonderful, terrible life.

# PART I

*She quietly expected great things to happen to her,
and no doubt that's one of the reasons why they did.*
—Zelda Fitzgerald

*I am thee and thou art me and all of one is the other.*
—Ernest Hemingway

# Chapter 1
## 1904

It was Ray's idea. Strange how someone else's spontaneous choice can set you on the very path you're meant to follow.

"Let's try the IRT," she said. "Let's go to the Village!" Ray, short for Rachel, was my best friend from the Spence School for Girls.

Manhattan's new Interborough Rapid Transit subway had just opened and ran all the way from 145th Street to the Battery. For the likes of us—twenty-one and still living at home—it was a forbidden pleasure. Our parents would be horrified to think of us mingling with the lower classes, so the idea of taking the public subway was thrilling. And Greenwich Village was likewise frowned upon. Ray lived on the Upper East Side and my family was still living at the Gotham Hotel at Fifth and 55th. The Village might as well have been Romania, filled with gypsies.

"Mother's expecting me at five," I said. "Guests for dinner, so I'll need to dress." It was three fifteen.

We walked to the nearest station and descended to an exotic world of vaulted ceilings, tiled walls, and mosaic signage that spelled out *59th & LEXINGTON*. It felt like a Middle Eastern casbah.

"Are we in Istanbul?" Ray squealed.

The air was thick with coal smoke and grease. Working-class men, women, and school children jostled along a wide, curved platform. We paid a nickel each at the ticket kiosk before a lacquered wooden train rumbled to a stop and the doors opened. We found two seats on a wicker bench and grinned as we squeezed each other's hands. The train propelled us into one dark cave after another—even better than the Dragon's Gorge ride at Luna Park.

Yes, I was twenty-one, but I might as well have been fifty, so rigid was my life. Not a week passed that my mother didn't remind us three girls that we'd descended from such American aristocracy as Civil War General William Tecumseh Sherman and Senator John Sherman. My father came from humbler stock but had made his own fortune manufacturing inks for publishing companies. We had both, Mother always said: lineage *and* money. And we'd moved to New York from Cincinnati to advance our marriage prospects among more elevated American families. Marrying well was the family business and, as the eldest daughter, I was the prize heifer.

Ray and I were three years out of school and my future was clear as mud. Although she was engaged to a promising young man named Dick Lambert, my prospects were still unnamed. A career was out of the question, not for a girl of my means. Any number of eligible young men had been vetted and presented, but I couldn't bear the thought of any of them. The boys of my acquaintance all had about four subjects of conversation: their alma mater, golf, Teddy Roosevelt, and football. They seemed at once chained to convention and yet somehow unmoored, like puppies that hadn't yet grown into their own big feet. I wanted something different but what that was, I couldn't say. For today, Greenwich Village would have to do.

Twenty minutes later, we emerged back into the sunlight at the West 4th Street station, pushed up the stairs by the dense crowd. Washington Square. Bohemia! Food carts and sweets vendors and busking musicians. A woman brushed by me in a faded smock and a floppy velvet beret. Another strolled by in coveralls with a man's shirt underneath. Laundry hung low across streets from one window to another. The smell of roasting coffee brought me back to Rome—rich espresso, not that watery stuff that Mother served from a silver urn.

We wandered down MacDougal Street into the Washington Square Bookshop, a tiny breadbox overflowing with books as well as pamphlets on socialism and the International Woman Suffrage Alliance. A broad table stacked with bright-jacketed new volumes. Shelves upon shelves of used books, five for a dime. And around us moved a collage of young men and women in various shades of black, brown, and gray.

"The intelligentsia," Ray whispered, and made a face.

"The cognoscenti," I whispered back, and we giggled.

We concentrated on blending in, but our Bergdorf dresses and Lord & Taylor hats gave away the fact that we were foreigners to this place. From a shelf of used books I plucked a copy of *Les Fleurs du Mal* by Charles Baudelaire, its plain white cover spotted with mildew. I'd heard of the author, of course, but had never read him. Here, in the original French, was the work that was said to have shocked a generation.

I skimmed the contents, the descriptions of Parisian scenes, the themes of decadence and eroticism. From behind the counter, a long-haired gent with tiny spectacles looked up and smirked. "That's not the kind of book your mother would approve of," he said. "You'll find some Dickinson at the back."

I froze. He was absolutely right about my mother. But I caught sight of a suffrage flyer posted behind him and I boldly placed the Baudelaire on the counter. "I'll take it," I said, heart pumping.

"Well done, madam!" Ray said as we scampered back to the street and turned left onto Waverly Place. We wandered down the block and were passing a tobacconist's when she got a devilish look in her eye.

"One more act of rebellion?" she asked.

"Ray, no. We can't!" But she darted in and emerged a few minutes later, palming a packet of Black Cat cigarettes and some matches.

"They arrested a woman just last week for smoking on Fifth Avenue," I said. "You will *not* get me arrested today!"

"But this is the Village!" Ray said, pulling me down the sidewalk. We ran left on Fifth and ducked into Washington Mews, the little alley of stables just north of the park.

Sheltered in the recess of a carriage house, I held Ray's purse as she tore at the wrapper, pulled a machine-rolled cigarette from the package, and fumbled to light it. She took a big puff and exploded into a fit of coughing. "Jeepers!" she gasped.

"Give that to me," I said, and took a cautious inhale. It felt like a hot poker down my windpipe, but I managed not to cough. Hideous.

When we'd recovered our breath, Ray took another puff, examining her reflection in the glass of a window.

"You do affect the suffragist," I said, and tried the cigarette again to see how I looked, striking a dramatic pose.

"Just a couple of femmes fatales," she said, and we laughed hard before dropping the butt onto the cobblestones and rushing back to the station.

---

YOU MIGHT SAY I was overprepared for a life I had no interest in. Along with my sisters, Hoytie and Olga, I received lessons in singing and piano. We were fluent in French, Italian, and German. We learned to ride horses, but also that newer invention, bicycles.

And we traveled, relentlessly. Every year, like clockwork, we embarked on some new spectacular itinerary. Father was often left at home to attend to business, but Mother was determined to make us girls as worldly as possible. In Berlin, we visited Kaiser Wilhelm II aboard his imperial yacht. In Paris, there were operas to attend and dress fittings at Worth or Poiret. In London, the theater and calling upon one and all in Belgravia kept us bustling. After a while, all the castles and estates began to blur, one into the other.

It was very amusing, of course: a life full of applause and compliments and novelty. It was hardly misfortune to be a Miss Wiborg. But there was that specific goal ahead—the task of marrying each of us to the richest, most noble bachelor we could find. And while part of me dreaded the conventionality of my prescribed future, I also eagerly awaited a time when I could at least plan my own dinner parties or foreign itineraries. I longed for independence. For *agency*.

---

THAT EVENING, BACK home in my room at the Gotham, I snuck the volume of Baudelaire out of my bag and lay on my bed thumbing through it. Here were lustful thoughts, obsessions with death, disgust toward evil and oneself. The violence and decadence of the poet's language did shock me. But then I came upon this passage:

> *It's Boredom!—eye brimming with an involuntary tear*
> *He dreams of gallows while smoking his hookah.*
> *You know him, reader, this delicate monster,*
> *Hypocritical reader, my likeness, my brother!*

In my head, a bell rang. I wasn't dreaming of gallows or smoking a hookah, but I was so *bored* with my comfortable, safe, traditional life. Here we were, at the beginning of a brand-new century, and the road before me was so well trod. The Wiborgs of Cincinnati were still arrivistes in Manhattan. Our success was built upon my father's self-made wealth, but the future of that success depended on how well we learned the rules of New York aristocracy.

For me, the eldest of three cosseted daughters, the prescribed future was simple: a good marriage to a boy from the right family. Many children. Baptisms, teas, coming-out parties, weddings, anniversaries, funerals. Wearing the right dresses with the right hats. Speaking, in hushed tones, of private clubs and guest lists. It was all preordained.

IN OUR FAMILY albums, I'd stared at faded photos of my mother as a young woman, so pretty and coy, and wondered how someone so fetching could have turned into such a matronly figure, seemingly carved in marble. All the married women in our circle were like that: as if the minute you wed, you gained fifty pounds and turned into Queen Victoria. The inevitability of that future made me sad and itchy at the same time. My greatest dread was to become my own mother.

In the Village that afternoon, we'd passed a café in which a couple sat talking in the window. The woman's hair was a tumbleweed of brown curls, secured with a chopstick in an unruly topknot. She and her male friend leaned close, their heads together, as if planning some great scheme. I stopped on the sidewalk to stare: how did one find a union like that, so passionately aligned, so interested in what the other had to say? At our family's dinner table, my parents conversed as if giving minutes at a board meeting. I never once saw them in such a unified, conspiratorial pose. *This* was the kind of marriage I wanted: filled with wit, imagination, laughter, passion, and unguarded conversation.

Now my eyes roamed across the pages of the Baudelaire until I came to "L'invitation au Voyage," in which the poet invites his mistress to dream of another, exotic world, where they can live together. The poem ends with the lines *Là, tout n'est qu'ordre et beauté / Luxe, calme et volupté.*

"There, all is beauty and symmetry," he wrote. "Pleasure, calm and luxury." And in that moment, a lifelong credo was crystalized. *Luxe, calme et volupté.* Not the material luxuries with which I'd been raised; I craved the luxury of experiencing life with fresh eyes and ideas.

Here we were in a brand-new century. I could picture myself living in the Village among the bohemians, raising a flock of curly-headed children by day and holding some kind of salon by night. But the face of the man beside me—that was completely blurred. There was no one in our set who fit the bill.

# Chapter 2
## 1904-1912

Yet another tea dance at the Maidstone Club—vast wooden porches and rolling lawns. It was summer, I remember, because all the women were a sea of white louisine and crêpe de chine. The band was playing "In the Shade of the Apple Tree" and I stood watching as couples danced the three-step. It felt as if the season would never end. How many tea dances had I racked up in my short life?

"Refresher?" a male voice asked, and I turned to find myself looking at a young man, a boy really, poised with the punch ladle ready to refill my glass. He was tall and beautifully appointed, with a high starched collar and vested blue serge suit. His light brown hair was slicked back off a high forehead. I nodded and we turned to face the dance floor, a wooden platform set on the grass. I snuck another glance at him: the picture of diffidence. An old man in a young man's body.

"Have we met?" I asked. Chances were good that we had, as tight as the East Hampton social circle was, but I couldn't place him.

"Gerald Murphy," he said, and then quickly, "Fred's brother."

"Oh, Fred! Why didn't you say so? We love Fred."

"Everybody does."

"Well, I'm Sara. Sara Sherman Wiborg."

"I know who you are. 'The ravishing Wiborg girls.' I've seen you perform."

Not surprising. My sisters and I were often urged to sing at parties. We had a repertory of American folk songs that we sang in three-part harmony (I was contralto, Hoytie tenor, and Olga soprano). Our finale always earned an ovation: Standing behind a translucent curtain meant to suggest mist, we would shrug off the straps of our evening gowns, undulate our arms, and sing the Rhine maidens' theme from *Das Rheingold*. Mother was never in such fine fettle as after we'd performed like prancing ponies and she could bask in the compliments.

"Well, what did you think?"

"You didn't disappoint." His restraint was remarkable for a boy his age. Sixteen, as it turned out. His solid brown eyes surveyed the scene, but it was his mouth—full lips poised in a half smirk—that drew my eye. He'd be a perfect match for Olga, or even Hoytie—though I wouldn't wish that girl on him. He was five years my junior, too young for me.

Still, I had nothing better to do. As I couldn't muster up the energy for another dance or croquet game, we found a bench and talked some more. He was a lower middle-form student at Hotchkiss. Loved the arts and animals. Had been to Europe only *once*! But he had such interesting things to say about paintings, plays, museums. Sports didn't come up at all, except that we both occasionally played golf in Sag Harbor. Every summer my family rented a cottage in Amagansett. The Murphys had rented a place in the more socially established Southampton, but I loved East Hampton because it remained a bit rustic—you could still find a few artists and writers about.

We gazed out at the women in their pigeon-breast silhouettes and the men in their Arrow collars.

Gerald sighed. "God, how I hate 'fashionable.'"

I turned and assessed his face more closely. What a remarkable thing to say!

We girls had grown up in Cincinnati, I told him, but were now in residence at the Gotham Hotel on Fifth Avenue. I'd been enrolled at Miss Spence's school, "an elite academy for young ladies," where my curriculum covered everything from Latin to household accounting.

"At least you can live at home in the city, not the wilds of Connecticut," Gerald said. "Have you graduated?"

"In a manner of speaking," I said with a shrug. "There was a prep course for college-bound girls, but I declined. I found the whole place a den of snobs, filled with gossip and boy talk. My performance was deemed 'indifferent,' so I got only a certificate of completion. What would I do with a diploma, anyway?" I looked at him now, barely wrinkled in his blue serge, so composed. "I just want to get out and live. Really *live*, Gerald. See something other than the musty insides of grand houses and estates."

"If it meant traveling the world, I'd put up with a few grand houses," Gerald said. "My father goes abroad for half the year to scout ideas for his company. He took me along once, but I was too young to appreciate it."

"What's your father's business? Have I heard of it?"

"The Mark Cross Company—it's a former saddle and bridle maker that he's turned into a luxury goods business. Fifth Avenue and 34th Street."

"Oh, yes! Fred mentioned that."

For a moment, Gerald seemed to show a reluctant pride in his father's ingenuity. "He observes the habits of the European aristocracy, then brings those ideas back to sell to rich Americans."

"Such as?"

"Such as Scottish golf clubs or Minton china. Pigskin luggage. English driving gloves." Gerald smiled. "He even writes his own advertising slogans."

"Oh, do tell me one!"

"'A woman with a Cross bag wishes to be seen by two people—the man she likes best and the woman she likes least.'"

"Ooh, that's clever."

"Yes, his wit is probably his best feature." With a dry laugh, Gerald shifted and looked out across the lawn. The sea was ablaze with the late afternoon sun. The band had started playing "Where the Morning Glories Twine 'Round the Door." I suddenly felt oppressed by the plink-plink of the repetitious piano melody, the couples bobbing politely to the prescribed beat.

I jumped up. "Let's get some saltier air," I announced. "I can't take another minute of morning glories, can you?"

Gerald looked up in surprise but followed me down the wooden path to the beach, where the sun was beginning to set. He turned his back as I removed my shoes and stockings and laid them on a puff of dune grass, then followed suit. We raced along the sand to the very edge of the water, shrieking as the cold Atlantic met our ankles, drenching the hem of my white linen skirt and his blue serge trousers.

"Let's see who can spot the first star," I said, and we scanned the sky.

An hour later, we rejoined the other guests as we all hailed our carriages in the drive. Gerald and I said our goodbyes, and how lovely it was to have met. I must have extended an invitation to visit, because he soon became a regular at our cottage—"Cousin Jerry"—and his manners were so impeccable that even Mother couldn't object. "Think of me as a wise old aunt," I told him. And I started dating Fred—his older, slightly more appropriate brother.

---

THAT YEAR PASSED in a whirl of leisurely, laconic hours. Dressing three or four times a day. Consommé and aspic and puddings. Music lessons and art classes. And always our retreats to East Hampton, where my summer romance with Fred died a natural death. As I approached twenty-two, I found myself chafing even more at the narrow confines of my social position. If you were expected to act a certain way, dress a certain way, speak a certain way, where was the opportunity to define oneself? How could I break out of the mold of Miss Sara Wiborg to present to the world my own, true self? The upper-class life began to feel less like a privilege and more like a prison.

---

WE RETURNED TO Cincinnati in December of 1905 to hold my coming-out to society with a masked ball at the country club. I was carried into the ballroom in a sedan chair, dressed to the teeth in eighteenth-century court dress and a powdered wig crowned with flowers. Guests came attired in costume: shepherdesses, hussars, or samurais. Understatement was not Mother's particular gift.

A few years later, my father purchased six hundred oceanfront acres in East Hampton. With thirty rooms, our new "cottage," The Dunes, was said to be the largest house in town, and our formal gardens and grounds were the subject of much local chatter.

Mother, ever the ambitious hostess, held fetes and tableaux and other people's weddings all summer long. She "could turn a drawing room into a bower of enchantment," wrote one society columnist. Before long, the summer season had melted into all the other seasons, and we lived at the Dunes nearly year-round.

---

AS I GOT older, I was slowly becoming aware of how ridiculously removed this life was from the way the real world worked. I'd always considered our household staff to be family, so well did they know us. Now I realized that they didn't see us that way at all—our lives and our roles were of completely different worlds. Now when I was out in the city, I noticed all the people who made everything run: the deliverymen and the shop vendors and the chambermaids. Would I ever be one of them? Of course not. But I saw them with a new kind of dignity, even gratitude.

I was also still haunted by the memory of that glimpse into Greenwich Village I'd had with Ray. Our life at the Dunes began to feel hollow—as if we were missing the point of life. What would it feel like to wake up and not know exactly how your day would be prescribed?

At least here there was the surf, which echoed in every room. From the stables, we rode along the shore; on warm days, we bathed in the ocean. The beach became our private playground, where we could picnic or lounge in canvas chairs with our friends. The light and the foam and the fresh salty air revived me—made me feel somehow more *human* than the Miss Sara Wiborg who was being groomed to be a member of American royalty.

As the years passed, even that became tiresome. I was twenty-three, still single. Then twenty-four. Many days, I couldn't even rouse myself from bed before noon. I would look over at my cluttered vanity table where, hanging from the oval mirror, was the corsage of chrysanthemums and daisies I'd worn at my coming-out, now gray and shriveled in its gold satin ribbon.

Hoytie's and Olga's dance cards were still full, but I couldn't muster the energy. I'd had my share of beaux, both here and on the Continent. The last one was Chandler Bailey III, third-year at Harvard with a father in the oil business. I was initially charmed by his irreverent humor and his bottomless brown eyes, but the novelty soon wore off. The small talk during a castle-walk dance. The dull narratives of weekly letters. I yearned for a meeting of *minds*. That was apparently an impossible goal in this crowd.

Over time, Mother seemed to be increasingly fine with the idea of my spinsterhood. While all my friends were starting new lives of their own with husbands and children, she enjoyed having a companion to attend to her complaints and accompany her abroad. Honestly, there were days when I struggled not to resent her. With each passing year, she seemed to believe more in a world that catered only to her.

My hope for independence was desiccating, and the word *melancholia* frequently found its way into my diary. Here I'd thought

I was just being choosy, waiting for the perfect husband to appear, but suddenly it seemed my chances had run out. I'd missed the boat entirely. But I simply couldn't muster the *esprit* to play the game of society belle any longer.

In July of 1910, my cousin Sara Sherman was married at The Dunes, an event whose preparations had occupied Mother for the entire previous year. Never have you seen so many gladioli and white tulle in your life. Although I loved my cousin, the fact that we shared a name made it that much more annoying.

"Here, you try it," Sara said, fixing the crown of her eighteen-foot veil into my hair as I helped her dress before the ceremony. I looked at my twenty-seven-year-old face in the mirror and burst into tears. At the wedding, when the cake was cut, I found the toy ring in my piece—an omen that meant I would marry next. But to whom? There were no contenders, none at all.

"Well, for goodness' sake, get out there!" Ray said. "What man can even *find* you locked up in that massive estate?" I began taking more advanced art classes, drawing from a live model every morning. I visited the studios of some of the best painters in Manhattan. I began to volunteer with the Junior League.

Weather permitting, I'd escape to the beach on my mare, Calliope, and canter her as fast as she'd go. Or I'd flirt my way onto a friend's sailboat, maybe even talk the captain into letting me take the wheel. My favorite photograph of myself from those years shows me at the helm of the *Lorelei*, my wavy hair loose and wild and my expression one of rapture, as I steered the craft into Gardiners Bay. I looked like a pirate queen. Would that spirited girl ever break free?

---

THROUGH THE FOG of my malaise came letters from Jerry, written in his careful, elegant hand. He had followed his brother, Fred, to Yale and, like me, was a mediocre student. But he had such an eye for beauty, and such a mind to describe it: the sandy stones of the campus chapel illuminated by the late afternoon sun. The etched shadows of bare trees on snow, like a pen-and-ink drawing. The exact color of a lady's cashmere coat in a shop window. Through his letters, I was able to imagine the world as a bigger place, a place of imagination. I loved our growing friendship, if only for that.

I wrote him back. About how liberating it felt to ride Calliope on the beach in the late afternoon, the waves licking her feet and the gulls soaring overhead. How Cook had made a roast lamb with fresh mint that tasted as if the garden itself had come alive in my mouth. I added tedious snippets of small talk from the latest function at the Maidstone Club. *The monkey parade is as weary as it ever was,* I reported after another tedious tea. *Are we doomed to become exact replicas of our parents?*

*You will never be a replica of anyone on earth, dear Sal,* Jerry replied. *You're the most original, unpredictable person I've ever known.* At about the time he became "Cousin Jerry," he'd begun calling me "Sal." I loved the unpretentious nickname as much as my mother hated it.

---

BY JERRY'S JUNIOR year in 1911, I considered him my best friend, the only person who truly saw the world through the same aesthetic lens as I did. In January, I accepted his invitation to the junior prom. Mrs. Murphy came along as chaperone, of course, but we always managed to linger a few steps behind her or otherwise find a few moments of unguarded conversation.

"Just ignore them," Jerry said, guiding me past the other Yale dates—shrill girls barely out of high school with dresses that seemed far too revealing for a winter dance. I saw the way he looked at me and realized that my age and nonchalance were *positive* things, in his eyes. While other beaux had admired my blue eyes, my upturned nose, and—unspoken, but surely thought—my Nordic curves,

Jerry expressed admiration for the full article: not just my physical attributes, but my whole self. My sense of style. My animated face. And he loved the tiny gap between my two front teeth, which I'd always considered a flaw. "The French call it *dents du bonheur*, lucky teeth," he told me. "But in your case, I think it's where the truth leaks out. You're simply unable to tell a lie." He was right about that.

There were luncheons and teas and a glee club concert, and at the prom itself I danced until three in the morning—not just with Jerry, but with a card full of boys' names from his fraternity. "You're the sweetheart of DKE," Jerry said, and squeezed my hand. I began to remember the happy, fierce girl I used to be.

Such exuberance didn't last long, once I'd returned to Manhattan, where Mother was in bed with her usual complaints. But even she soon rallied for the next Continental tour, this time to attend the celebrations around the coronation of King George V. In Paris I visited Rodin's sculpture studio (*The Kiss!* I wrote to Jerry. *The most frankly erotic thing I've ever seen!*) and attended classes at the Académie Julian *(When Mother learned that we were drawing from a nude model, all hell broke loose!).* Then London, where we stayed with the marquess and marchioness of Headfort. Lady Headfort—the boisterous former showgirl, Miss Rosie Boote—wore her opera-length pearls dangling down her back. Was it too late for me to find a life where I could be so openly unconventional?

We returned to good news about Jerry: in his senior year at Yale, he was voted "Best Dressed Man" and even elected to the secret senior Skull & Bones Society. He was reluctantly headed to Mark Cross in September to work for his father, but during the summer he and Fred were regular visitors to The Dunes. The two of us took every chance to escape the planned golf matches and card games, instead wandering along the shore or into town to talk freely away from familial ears.

—

"I KNOW!" I said one evening. "Let's camp out on the beach!" It had been a sultry, warm afternoon. A cloudless sky, a still sea.

Jerry gave me a quiet look of surprise before glancing over at my father.

"I am *not* a camper, Sara," Father said.

"Well, then we can go without you." I winked at Jerry.

"You know that won't do," Father grumbled. His affection was unspoken but usually assured. He rarely refused me.

So the three of us collected a pile of wool blankets and trudged down to the shore. We bundled up—Jerry, me, and my father each spaced a few feet apart—and lay back, looking up at the sky. For the longest time we watched damp clouds pass across the stars, like sugar spilled from a bowl, and I felt the dew settle on my face and wool cap before falling asleep.

I awoke as the sun was just beginning to warm our blankets and the gulls were starting to cry out. Jerry was still asleep beside me, but my father had gone. He'd probably waited until we'd dozed off, then hustled back to his warm bed.

I lay there staring at Jerry—his rosy complexion made rosier by the early sun, his relaxed mouth, as innocent as a child's. I thought of the *Metamorphoses*, the tale of Cupid and Psyche, but I banished that romantic image from my mind. He really was so nice, always game for any of my wild ideas. So different from all the other men I'd known.

Then, suddenly worried that he'd wake up to find me staring at him, and feeling awfully embarrassed about the whole thing, I gathered up my blankets and ran back to the house.

# Chapter 3
## 1912-1915

Come fall, Jerry was working for his father at Mark Cross. He told me once of a walk they'd taken in Central Park when he was a child. Somehow Jerry had fallen through the ice of the lake, and his father still insisted that they complete the intended walk. By the time they'd arrived home, Jerry's underwear had frozen to his skin. Now he was forced to work for the very man who'd shown such cruelty to him. When I heard such stories, my heart bent toward him, not in any romantic way, but out of a sort of maternal impulse. How could any person behave so barbarically toward another human, let alone their own child? And how had Jerry emerged such a sensitive, caring person himself? Perhaps our own personas were stronger than the things we experienced?

When we set sail on our annual trip to Europe in March, it was Jerry, rather than any beau, who came to the pier to see us off. *I shall see your saddened face to my dying day,* I wrote to him later. *Such human emotion amid so much chaos and machinery and forced sentiment. You are a dear.* Yes, he was firmly in my heart. But I still couldn't allow myself to think of him as anything but a cherished friend.

THE LONDON SEASON of 1914 was an endless agenda of social proprieties; you could practically see Mother ticking her list as we met one member of the nobility after another. I was more amused by our newfound alliance with Mrs. Patrick Campbell, Mother's cigarette-smoking actress friend, the toast of Covent Garden. She said what she thought, and her wit always hit the mark. One day I accompanied her as she shopped in Mayfair for a gala. Modeling one ensemble she asked, "Sara, darling, does the dress walk? Or does it just make me look like a cigar?" So confident, so self-aware! I wanted to be just like her. I started smoking cigarettes, too—on the sly, of course.

Another night we attended Serge Diaghilev's new ballet, *Le Sacre du Printemps*, which had created an uproar in Paris. It was so raw and sensual, the Stravinsky score a heavy tribal drumbeat. *Nijinsky's modern movements prompted hissing and screaming in the audience,* I wrote to Jerry. *One critic wrote, "musically and choreographically,* Sacre *bid adieu to the Belle Epoque." To which I say, Hooray!*

*It must be sublime,* Jerry wrote back, *to be doing so many new things. It feeds the spirit, doesn't it?*

In our absence, he was spending time with Father at The Dunes, having dinners, enjoying a few of those new moving pictures, even riding all day on horseback to the Montauk lighthouse. *Pretty Sal, I have so much to relate to you,* he wrote. *I find myself wondering exactly what your opinion might be on so many subjects. I will ask you endless questions when we are together—which cannot come soon enough.*

ONCE WE'D RETURNED, Jerry and I resumed our conversation during long walks or sitting on the wide porch at The Dunes, our feet propped on the railing. But we had only the weekends; Jerry was "in trade" now, so his workdays were occupied. And by the spring, Mother was planning yet another trip, this time to India and Ceylon. I carefully proposed that Jerry take a furlough from Mark Cross and come with us. "He would learn more than in years of business," I argued, but Mr. Murphy wouldn't hear of it. Instead, Jerry presented me with the dearest parting gift: a black leather case for my drawing supplies. I carried it with me everywhere, even using it as a pillow on long train rides. And as the leather softened and became glossy with use, my thoughts of him grew fonder.

Nothing I'd experienced in our travels could have prepared me for India. The smells alone—from raw sewage to musky incense—were an assault on the senses. We traveled nearly as far as the Khyber Pass on the swaying backs of elephants. And the elegance of the natives, in their brightly colored silks and ropes of jewels! It was an absolute enchantment, the whole thing.

But, despite Mother's efforts to keep us confined to polo clubs and palaces, there were times I glimpsed the outside world, and it was a cruel shock. The wretched poverty, the crippled beggars, the children with flies on their faces. It threw my own opulent life into an even starker contrast to the world around me, and I felt a deepening sense of shame for the giddy, thoughtless way my family lived. When the opportunity arose, when Mother's back was turned, I would hand out coins or a pastry from breakfast into an outstretched hand. It wasn't nearly enough to make me feel better about my place in life.

―

JERRY AND I continued corresponding with growing frequency. His letters, inscribed in his beautiful hand, arrived nearly every other day, and I wrote back. *Asia is the most marvelous experience!* I wrote. *Kipling and Bakst and Dulac, all made manifest.*

*It is dawning on me,* he replied, *how few men there are with whom I can hold more than a five-minute discourse. The Panama situation, or*

*Wilson, or the 1914 Cadillacs vs. the Fords. Any mention of some new exhibit or book or thought is dismissed as effeminate. I long for company in which I can discuss, without shame, the things that do not smack of the pavement.*

But such personal concerns were shortly overshadowed by worldly events and a brush with actual danger. During our return crossing on the SS *Lusitania*, war was declared between France, Britain, Germany, and the Austro-Hungarian Empire and our ship was fired upon. We convoyed with another vessel to Halifax and, when we finally returned to Manhattan, I couldn't have been more relieved—or more excited—to see Gerald waiting for us at the dock. For somehow, over the previous nine months, Jerry had become Gerald again. Now, instead of a freshly matriculated college boy, he was a gentleman. A professional. A polished young bachelor whose name was on the guest lists of all the most coveted parties in town. As I rushed to hug him, my lips somehow found their way to his cheek. We both pulled back, red-faced but all smiles.

Now there was a pulsing in my ribcage as I prepared to meet Gerald for our outings. I would take his arm and hold it tight around his bicep. I could comfortably lay my head on his shoulder. And one night, he ventured to kiss me full on the mouth. I kissed him back.

"Come here, you," I said, and gently pulled him in for another. All the feigned indifference, the enforced platonic friendship, the thinking that Gerald was merely a friendly placeholder until I met my future husband—it had all drained away and I felt as if I would explode with this new feeling, my heart exposed and pulsing on the sidewalk. *He* was the one. *He* had been right there in front of me all along, waiting for me to comprehend, waiting patiently until I finally saw the light. Now, as far as I was concerned, he hung the moon.

"How differently I feel about things seen and done *with* you," I said. We'd just seen a production of Euripides' *Trojan Women* at the Belasco, and we walked down West 44th Street under the bright marquee lights of the theaters. "It's as if, without you, only half of me enjoys them."

But the moment I let myself feel how fully I loved Gerald, I also understood what lay beneath my previous denial. As upper-class as the Murphys were, they were "in trade." Add to that Gerald's relative youth, and he was simply not in the league of young men that my parents deemed suitable for my hand. Now that I'd finally embraced my own true feelings, I realized that the real hurdle still lay ahead. My father greeted Gerald as if he were just a local boy, stopping by. My mother barely noticed him.

Nevertheless, we began spending every weekend together, exploring all the richness Manhattan had to offer. We stole kisses in the most unlikely places—library nooks, the rear galleries at The Met, even once on a public fire escape. And we developed a sort of manifesto between us: that we would eschew the superficial and the gaudy for the handmade, the authentic, and the deeply felt.

We were a league of two, rebelling against the rigid thinking and traditionalism of our upbringing. I felt as if someone had sprung the lock on my birdcage and I'd flown through the open door with my wings at full span. Everyone kept commenting on how well and *fresh* I looked.

And we still wrote to each other faithfully.

*The other day you asked me if I thought you feminine,* Gerald wrote. *My own dear girl, if you only* knew *how I thought of you!*

*You live in my innermost heart & mind & soul—places where I never thought I'd admit another,* I wrote back. *And to say I love you seems a tiny, ridiculously faint expression of the truth. We simply* are *each other.*

Our new, deeper alliance was still known only to us. Mother and Father were so oblivious to anything outside their own orbit, they didn't notice the frequency with which I casually announced that I'd be meeting Gerald, or of his visits to The Dunes. Olga and Hoytie barely inquired about my social life.

On February 8, nine years after our first meeting at the Maidstone Club, Gerald and I sat in front of the fire at my parents' club in Manhattan. We'd dined on oysters Rockefeller and *omelette a l'orange* and my head was pleasantly light from the pink champagne. He took my hand and gently kneaded it, trying to find his words.

"My Sal," he began. I searched his face for a smile, but he was somber. "In the past, I've pretended to feel affection for many people."

*Where was this going?* I waited, as his kneading grew more insistent.

"But in my heart, I've cared for but a few."

Okay, this was better. Gerald was looking down at our hands, his voice quavering.

*Look up! Look at me!*

"My regard for you is so different, it's so much more *real* than anything I've ever known." Was his voice breaking, just a bit?

"Oh, Gerald." Weeks seemed to pass.

"I only know that, for the first time, I'm ready to give it all to one person." He finally raised his eyes to mine, as I smiled and nodded. "You're simply everything to me, Sal. I can't imagine life without you. And every bit of me is yours. I am *yours*."

A long, expectant pause.

"Is there something you'd like to ask me, Gerald?" The suspense was excruciating. *How long would this overture continue?*

He cleared his throat. "Marry me, Sal. I want to ask you to hitch your life to mine, though I don't even know what that'll look like. But I want to do it all with you, side by side. Could you do that?"

I exhaled. I hadn't realized how long I'd been holding my breath.

"Yes!" I said. "Of course, I could, darling G. I can't imagine any other kind of life. Yes!"

We kissed, and I can still feel the pure bliss of that moment. My future twinkled in the distance.

My happiness was tempered only by the knowledge that we couldn't yet share our brilliant news with anyone else. My parents, we knew, would strongly oppose the idea—especially Mother. We'd face months of maneuvering and breaking them down. But we'd come so far over the years, I assured Gerald, we could manage this final lap. Through our letters we planned a life together, ripe with beauty and friends and new experiences. Perhaps one day we'd have a little farm in the countryside, we thought, where we could be partners on some grand creative endeavor. We felt invincible.

But Gerald's patience soon wore thin. "I'm disappointed that it's not known *today*," he argued.

"Our waiting will pay off, darling," I said. "You'll see. If we stumble in our approach, we'll botch the whole plan."

But there was one thing I had no patience for, either. One evening, after an early supper, we checked into the Yale Club downtown as Mr. and Mrs. Cole Porter, a college classmate of Gerald's. The rooms were plain, but we spent little time assessing the decor.

Gerald had made it clear that he was as innocent as I was on the subject of sex, but he had nothing to prove to me—I wanted this as much as he did. We fumbled and laughed and kissed and, within minutes, our fine clothes were in a heap at the foot of the bed. For so many years, I'd fiercely protected my virtue, but now, at the ancient age of thirty-one, I was ready to fling it away in the hands of this man I loved so dearly.

I remember my friend Celeste Wentworth talking with disappointment about her wedding night. "I felt like some primitive creature," she'd said. "Just lying there while he became a kind of animal on top of me. Afterward, he asked me if I'd liked it, and I burst into tears."

My consummation with Gerald couldn't have been more different—tender and slow and full of giggling whispers. And then how our bodies seemed to merge together and we were one pulsing heart, one brain, one torso with eight tangled limbs. It felt like riding Calliope on the beach. That night was the true officiation of our marriage, even if no one else could know just yet. I felt an impeccable union with this man and knew absolutely that we would think, act, and create as one being, once we were allowed.

The next day, Gerald's letter let me know that he felt the same way. *I feel as if some supernatural power has whispered to me all of life's* secrets. *As I held you, my spirit was weeping for joy. We two—who had not yet been given to either man or woman—are now given only to each other. I have been under the spell of it all day.*

But the frustration and pressure to keep our marvelous secret soon took its toll, again.

One evening, as we took a ride to Central Park, the wheel of our carriage came loose, taking the last thread of Gerald's patience with it.

"I've never driven a hansom cab in my life, and even *I* would know to check the axles before taking on passengers!" he shouted at the driver as we stood by the road awaiting a repair.

I gently squeezed his arm, and he softened at my touch.

"I'm sorry, Sal. These moods of mine are terrible," he said. "I call them 'the Black Service.' They're small, and I *hate* the small. The way you behave in the face of my ravings is such a better example."

"But we can be our true selves with each other, remember?" I said, squeezing his hand. "The noble *and* the wicked. Without fear of blame or reprisal."

The look Gerald gave me was that of a small child who's been given a reprieve from a spanking. He gently kissed my palm.

The next day, Gerald sent me a scowling photo of himself on which he'd inscribed: *The Surly Kodiak in its native haunt.*

---

FINALLY, I AGREED that we could wait no longer. Gerald would come to The Dunes to *"ply my suit with your respected male parent."* But I knew I had to tell Mother first and, after all my caution about waiting for the perfect moment, I couldn't have handled it more clumsily.

I listened at her bathroom door until I heard her preparing a bath and then, once she was in the tub, I yelled through the door, "I'm marrying Gerald!" and ran away before I could hear her screams. But her hysterical reaction came soon enough: she strictly forbade us from announcing our engagement publicly. And Gerald's mother refused even to see me, accusing Gerald of making me complicit in a suicide pact.

The two fathers met to discuss our foolish idea of marriage, then summoned us to deliver the verdict. Never mind that I was thirty-two and Gerald was twenty-seven. Because they'd provided our lives of privilege, we were forevermore children in their eyes.

I sat in my father's study feeling as if I'd been sent for by the headmaster. The dark-paneled walls, the heavy damask drapes weighed upon me like the lining of a tomb. My whole life had been a contract—I could live in luxury and be as frivolous as I wished, but now the time had come to pay up. I had to become just like them—even if it meant I'd end up a spinster.

"Our main concern is Gerald's inability to support you in the manner—or manor—to which you were born, Sara," Gerald's father said.

"And the five-year age difference is unorthodox," my own father added. Such a gap wouldn't even have been noticed if Gerald had been the older one.

Even though Father could easily have given me a comfortable dowry, he was suddenly reluctant to give me that comfort, given my poor choice of a husband. He'd always been so indulgent with me. How quickly his affections were reversed!

Later, Gerald reported that his father was even more harsh. "He believes that I've failed to grasp my fundamental duty in life—financial independence," he sneered. "He blames himself for having supplied me with 'the crutches on which I walk'—namely, money that I don't earn. He said I don't deserve to be married."

Even if we *were* allowed to marry, would I ever learn to love that cruel man?

Despite such resistance, we held firm—it just made our love feel more important, more resolute. And soon our fortitude paid off: the parents capitulated and, although we were still sworn to secrecy, Gerald was allowed to buy me a simple diamond solitaire ring. When the salesclerk at Black, Starr & Frost asked which finger to measure, I could feel the blush rise up my neck and face like a bad rash. Of course, I could wear it only in private, but I never tired of looking at my left hand, especially when the little diamond winked and grinned at me in the sunlight.

---

NO SOONER HAD we rejoiced in our modest achievement than I was called back to The Dunes for a new family crisis. I'd secretly known that Olga had agreed to marry Sidney Fish—of the very rich, very political New York Fishes—but I hadn't anticipated her timing, when Mother and Father were just recovering from my announcement. Mother had again taken to her bed amid much whining and moaning.

"*What* do I know of this boy?" she cried, as if she hadn't read about the Fishes nearly weekly in the social pages. "Nobody could expect me to be *pleased* with this news!" After all her efforts to marry us off, it now seemed that no man would be good enough.

Olga and I clucked and fussed over her while Hoytie stood, arms crossed, in the corner. She was increasingly ambivalent on the subject of marriage.

"Mother, just think how long we've enjoyed living together," Olga reasoned. "*Much* longer than most families."

Mother sniffled. "Well, it hasn't seemed that long to *me*."

Still, Olga and Sidney were allowed to go public with their engagement and before long Mother was planning the wedding of the century at The Dunes. I would have to stand as maid of honor as Olga became Mrs. Sidney Fish at a wedding to rival anything at the Court of St. James's, and I wondered anew if my marriage to Gerald would be doomed. The injustice of it prompted more visits from Gerald's Black Service, while I could offer only small comfort and apologies on behalf of my family.

Finally, in July, Mother grudgingly agreed to let us announce our news, and we set an announcement date for September. Father would provide me with a trust of $15,000 per annum, and Gerald was earning $3,000 a year at Mark Cross. While the total sum was probably no more than I was used to spending on clothes and shoes, we felt as if we'd won a spectacular prize. And Gerald's father surprised us by offering us a lease on a small townhouse at 50 West Eleventh Street in the heart of Greenwich Village, where so many artists and writers had settled.

We'd hardly digested all this good fortune when Father announced that, after looking for months for a new winter residence in the city, he and Mother had found a suitable mansion at the corner of Fifth Avenue and Eleventh Street—literally half a block away. Well, we would just ignore them.

Gerald and I began sketching out our life together, planning our new home. On weekends we scavenged secondhand shops and tag sales, finding treasures among other people's castoffs. We bought American country furniture and raw pine pieces—so different from the dark woods of our upbringing. Painted eighteenth-century Sheraton chairs, old portraits, antique traveling cases, Venetian glass, Japanese woodcuts. We stored our booty in the garage at The Dunes and eagerly awaited the day when we could install it at Eleventh Street.

One Saturday as we walked along Wiborg Beach, we were both so giddy with prenuptial bliss that we broke into a jig right there on the sand. Then we moved into a waltz, Gerald singing the words to an old English tune in his fine tenor voice.

> *Drink to me only with thine eyes*
> *And I will pledge with mine.*
> *Or leave a kiss within the cup*
> *And I'll not ask for wine.*

Bliss, bliss, bliss!

At Mother's insistence, my engagement photo—a gauzy, Gibson

Girl profile—appeared on the cover of *Town and Country* magazine. For our honeymoon, we'd hoped to sail to Europe, but the new war made that impossible. Instead we would sail south to Panama to see President Roosevelt's magnificent new canal with stopovers in Havana, Jamaica, and Costa Rica and a trek into the rainforest. None of Mother's trips had taken me into this wild and natural world—it would be exotic new territory for both of us. We started buying khakis and puttees for jungle life and applied for passports along with our marriage license. Mrs. Gerald Murphy. It looked so fine in print.

---

FINALLY, THE DAY arrived. On Wednesday, December 30, 1915, just a few family and close friends gathered in the drawing room of Mother and Father's new Fifth Avenue house. Gerald sent me my bouquet of orange blossoms, with a loving note.

Olga and Hoytie looked like Greek muses in their teal brocade gowns, their hair held by coronets of silver paper leaves. My gown—white satin with a square neck and lace cowl trimmed with pearls—was offset with a tulle veil and eight-foot train that made me feel like Queen Mary herself.

The organ, cello, and harp struck up the wedding march from Wagner's *Lohengrin*. I could feel my father walking woodenly beside me, but all I saw was Gerald in an aura of candlelight, regarding me with what seemed like frozen awe. It was all I could do not to hitch up my dress and gallop toward him.

Father Martin of St. Patrick's led us through our vows, but our smiles overrode the words. At 2:20 p.m. we were declared husband and wife. Partners for life. My story thus far had been just a preamble. Now the real story would begin.

# Chapter 4
## 1916-1919

"Happy New Year, darling Sal," Gerald said. We'd pilfered a bottle of Heidsieck champagne and two flutes from our reception in anticipation of this moment.

"Happy new life, dearest Gerald." We clinked glasses. It was midnight on New Year's Eve, 1916, and we stood on the deck of the SS *Pastores* as she sailed down the Hudson River, the Manhattan skyline twinkling especially brightly in our honor.

"When you take your first sip of champagne, you must always look at the treetops," I said. I believed it made the taste better, the bubbles more sparkly. But there were no trees, of course. We looked instead at the wooden water tanks that crested most of the city's downtown buildings and clinked again.

Far from the first-class Cunard vessels I'd been accustomed to, the *Pastores* was a United Fruit Company freighter. The ship, and our entire honeymoon, was so different from any experience I'd ever had, despite the many stamps in my passport. With Gerald beside me, I embraced the adventure—humidity, bugs, and all. Central America was like living inside a moist terrarium, with colors of green I'd never seen. And Cuba was like a round-the-clock vaudeville show, all noise and spice and laughter. Together we tried everything: from savory *ropa vieja* to dancing the rumba and sharing a fine cigar at a café on El Prado.

In late January we returned to New York, lean and tan and slightly more learned about this thing called marriage. Now that we were officially man and wife, spending all our days and nights together, I was learning more about Gerald's complicated psyche, prone to the "Black Service." I often had to work to draw him out of his deep, private landscape, while my nature was more direct—every idea and observation escaping from my lips unchecked.

"Not every thought needs to be expressed aloud, you know," he snapped at me one night in Havana, our last port of call before returning to New York. We were at dinner in the grand dining room of the Hotel Inglaterra when I recognized another American couple from our tour of the Panama Canal. I'd greeted them warmly and made a joke about smelling like stablehands for most of our honeymoon in the tropical humidity. They'd laughed, but I caught the look of chagrin on Gerald's face. And once they'd left, he'd chided me.

My eyes welled up and my face flushed as if he'd slapped me with a hand instead of his words. There was a long silence as Gerald sipped his wine, then closed his eyes.

"I'm such a beast," he finally said and reached for my hand. "I think the trip has just exhausted me. I need to be put in a corner facing the wall until I can be among polite company again. Please forgive me, Sal."

I looked out the window at the streetlights below, then glanced around the room, my gaze unable to land. Finally my eyes found his face again, looking sad and repentant. He was so contrite, so forlorn, that I burst into giggles and gave his hand a playful slap. It would take a while, but we would find our way. I refused to consider the alternative.

Likewise, our explorations in lovemaking were tentative and sometimes confusing. I was definitely more curious and adventurous in that department—I had to coax Gerald away from his lifelong practice of being a gentleman, but he gradually learned to relax. "Does it really matter what affectionate people do?" Mrs. Patrick Campbell once said. "So long as they don't do it in the streets and frighten the horses."

I repeated this quote to Gerald and he laughed. "Really, darling, it's okay to leave a light on," I said one night in Montego Bay. "I'm your wife now. There's no shame in making love to me."

"It's not you I'm ashamed of," Gerald said. But I tilted his chin up to kiss him and soon we weren't talking anymore, our bodies following their instinctive dance. I was learning that I just had to get him out of his head.

---

COMING HOME TO our own place was divine. Here I was, actually living in the Village! Our little brick townhouse sat between Washington Square Park and Union Square Park, surrounded by small storefronts, artists' studios, and the tiny triangular cemetery of the Spanish and Portuguese Synagogue. "The capital of American Bohemia," Gerald called it.

The house itself had a cottagey feel, despite its three stories. On the main floor was a small sitting room that looked onto the street and behind it a dining room and little breakfast area that led to a small garden. Upstairs were two bedrooms, one with a bath, and on the half floor above were rooms for Rose, our cook, and Mollie, the maid. No steam heat, unfortunately, but fireplaces in every room. And we soon installed a telephone.

We'd had the brick facade whitewashed a few months earlier, and soft gray, patterned wallpaper now hung in the hall. From the Dunes, I'd stolen some old hooked rugs, which covered the warm, wide-planked floors. And we filled our new rooms with early nineteenth-century American and English pieces—not currently in fashion but with an authentic charm—that we'd painted or refinished ourselves. On the walls we hung secondhand shop treasures: folk art paintings, gilt mirrors, and tinsel pictures on glass.

"It's shabby genteel," I said. "It looks as if we've lived here forever." It was such a departure from the chintzed and polished rooms I'd grown up in. It felt like a *home*.

That was when I remembered the Baudelaire: *There, all is beauty and symmetry. Pleasure, calm and luxury.* The idea would become a shared ideal between us, an addition to our joint lexicon that we abbreviated to "LCV" for *luxe, calme, et volupté*. The fact that I'd found a man who shared this dream of mine: pure happiness!

From our well-curated home base, Gerald would trudge each day to Mark Cross, where he was surrounded by the shiny paraphernalia we both renounced. To boost his spirits I'd send little notes each day to remind him what awaited at home. We began hosting dinners with new friends and neighbors—small, warm, and fluent with ideas. Our life together was already shaking off the stiff formality of our upbringing—we were reinventing married life. And we were trying to make a family.

---

I BEGAN VOLUNTEERING at St. Vincent's hospital and had caught a lingering cold, which was enough for Mother to insist that I come spend the summer at The Dunes. Gerald could join us on weekends, just as he had before we were married. But now we had our own bedroom, and when he left again on Sunday nights, the loneliness was almost too much to bear. One Monday morning I turned to say something to him as I awoke, when I realized with a pang that he wasn't there. *There was such a strange, unwelcome flatness on your side of the mattress,* my note read.

Come the fall, however, I was glad to have made the effort to spend time in East Hampton. Back in Manhattan, Mother sank into paralysis and then passed away in January 1917. Gone was the pressure I felt from her to conform. Gone was her controlling nature, her lack of compassion for others. But, for all the aggravation she'd caused, I knew I would miss her feistiness and fierce spirit. I marveled at the world she'd shown to us girls: our performing, the global travel, being presented at Court. Although these were done in service to our eventual betrothal, they had also fostered my curiosity and independence. It was a splendid foundation, even if I'd chosen a different life than the one she'd imagined for me.

My greatest regret was that Mother would never witness my own motherhood. I hadn't realized how much I'd wanted to prove myself to her in this role, to show her how differently I would do it. My children would be loved openly and encouraged to find their own paths. After all our struggles, how I longed for her approval!

---

ON THE LAST Saturday in March, I asked Rose to prepare Gerald's favorite dish—pork tenderloin with roasted potatoes—and chilled a bottle of Heidsieck left over from our wedding. Around the stem of his champagne flute I placed my old baby rattle—a ring of sterling silver that I'd polished to a fare-thee-well. He didn't notice until I proposed a toast.

"What's this?" he asked, removing the rattle and twirling it on a finger.

I raised my glass. "It's the rattle we'll be using soon, darling. Sometime in mid-December."

"Sal! Are you sure?" We'd had a couple of false alarms, and we were both on our guard.

"As sure as I can be at four weeks. Otherwise, I've got a nagging case of the stomach flu."

"Oh my girl!" Gerald's hug was tight and, as he held me, I might have heard a muffled sob. He'd wanted a family even more than I did. *Can't you just see them?* he'd written me a while back. *Eager-minded, imaginative, humorous, and lithe.* We spent the rest of the meal making plans for a nursery and talking about names.

Our excitement and hope were tempered by news of what was about to become the Great War, no longer just a conflict on foreign shores. On April 6, 1917, the United States officially declared war on Germany and just ten days later, on Good Friday, American soldiers seized twenty-seven German vessels and imprisoned their crews on Ellis Island. The world felt unstable and chaotic—hardly the climate in which to plan a future for our family.

All the young men of Gerald's age were enlisting. Even Gerald's brother, Fred, with his history of mastoiditis, signed on as a private and was awaiting orders to ship out to France. And Hoytie, still showing no interest in marriage, had volunteered as a nurse in the ambulance corps.

There was no question that Gerald would serve. He was a healthy young man, albeit one about to become a father. In November he signed on as a private, first-class, in order to enlist as soon as possible. In his official military portrait, his face wore a mask of fierce determination, but we both knew how torn he felt to choose country over the new family he'd wanted for so long.

On December 19, 1917, Honoria Adeline Murphy was born at home, named after Gerald's Irish great-grandmother, Honoria Roberts Murphy, and my mother, Adeline.

"Look what we made, G," I said, gazing down at the swaddled red thing in my arms. "Our first real joint enterprise." She squinted up at us, already alert and curious. I couldn't believe she was ours to keep. "Our fragrant garden baby," Gerald called her.

On December 30, our second anniversary, we baptized Honoria at home, with just family in attendance. Because I was still bedridden from the difficult delivery, we held the ceremony in the adjoining bedroom, and I watched its reflection in a handheld mirror. Gerald had installed a tiny Christmas tree in our bedroom, adorned with miniature ornaments he'd found in a shop on Lafayette Street, and he pinned a sprig of mistletoe to Honoria's bassinet—as if we needed a reminder to kiss her. We'd hired a baby nurse, Miss Helen Stewart, who would become a great support for me in the difficult days ahead. And, as an anniversary gift, Father bought our house from Gerald's dad and presented us with the deed.

But the very next day, Gerald left for Kelly Field in Texas for Ground Officers' Training School. In my condition, I couldn't even see him off at Penn Station. When I heard the bedroom door close softly behind him—and a minute later the soft percussion of the front door—I burst into tears and cried for several days afterward.

I'd packed him a traveling medicine chest and one of Honoria's baby shirts. *Its warmth and sweet baby scent was such a gift against the permeating smell of cold steel,* Gerald wrote from the overnight train. *I felt a pang remembering you both in that lovely white room with soft candlelight and flowers.*

Only much later would Gerald confess to me how truly horrible training was. A week after he arrived, a sandstorm turned day into night. Trucks crashed blindly, mules stampeded, and the temperature plunged sixty degrees with snow and sleet mixing with the filthy dust. Four men froze to death overnight and four more killed themselves in desperation. Pink eye and bronchitis were everywhere.

Gerald's experience had never trained him for life beyond boarding school. I poured my worry into practical packages: hand-knitted caps, Brooks Brothers shirts, mufflers, blankets, bran muffins, even squares of cheesecloth to use as disposable handkerchiefs. The blue ink on my anxious letters was usually blurred with tears.

Fortunately, after a month he was shipped to Columbus, Ohio to attend the School of Aeronautics. He called me from St. Louis during a layover on his three-day train journey and the hoarseness in his voice brought me to tears again.

"I can't bear it, darling. I'm so homesick for you, and so worried," I said. "Most days I'm able to be brave, for Honoria's sake, but today I just can't."

"Sal dear," Gerald said. "I'll be fine. After twelve weeks of ground school, they'll send me to flight instruction at Roosevelt Field. That's

Long Island! And then I'll join a flight training unit in England. I need to get over there and help them win this damned war. I want to see some real action. Fred's already on the front lines in France with the Tank Corps."

Gerald's route to England was more complicated than we'd thought. He was commissioned to the 838th Aero Squadron, which took him to three posts around the country. Then finally, some real news: he would be transferred to the Air Service Training Brigade on Long Island, and from there would ship overseas. I tried to feel happy for him. He seemed to need to see action to banish the critical voices of his parents that still echoed in his head. When he managed to come home for a couple of weekend leaves over the summer, we tried to reacquaint ourselves as a couple. Those few nights together were so sweet, but I could feel Gerald's anxiety pulsing just under his fair skin.

I also fought the urge to feel sorry for myself: a wife, a new mother, left entirely to her own devices. At least Gerald had left me this gorgeous little piece of himself: Honoria, whose plump pink mouth mimicked his in miniature. Now I held her in the crook of my arm, sleeping and gently sucking on my finger, as I read the newspaper and frowned. A new "Spanish flu" was quickly spreading across the country. In New York, schools were canceled and public gathering places were shuttered. It was going to be a modern-day plague.

I left Honoria at home with Miss Stewart while I hurriedly ran errands in the neighborhood. People began wearing cloth surgical masks to protect their faces. Between Gerald's absence and our own strange, fearful isolation, I could feel my spirits flag.

And then: Armistice Day. November 11, 1918. The eleventh hour of the eleventh day of the eleventh month. Gerald had spent the past year preparing to go to war as an intelligence officer and had gotten so close to shipping out, only to have the guns go silent and peace declared. I knew he was disappointed—perhaps the only person in the world to be unhappy with the news—but inside I was rejoicing. Because of the pandemic, there were no parades or large celebrations.

You could see it in the faces, though, of everyone on the street: we had survived the worst conflict in human history.

---

WHEN GERALD FINALLY returned home in December, almost exactly a year from the date he'd left, I was on the platform to greet him. He didn't recognize me behind my cotton mask, but I embraced and held him tight for several minutes. Then we took a cab back to Eleventh Street and he tried to explain what was in his head.

"It's not just about missing action," he said, his voice low. We were seated on the divan in front of a fire; through the windows, a light snow fell. Gerald's face looked drawn, older. "I would've been in charge of those soldiers, Sal. All I showed them was a cool civility, a decent interest in their welfare, but now I realize—I really *loved* them!" Gerald turned to me and gripped my hand. "How meagerly I'm equipped for human expression. I should resign from the world of human relationships. I'm just no good at it."

"Darling, Gerald," I said, squeezing his hand back. "You're always so hard on yourself. I imagine your true feelings were more evident than you think. I'll bet those men loved and respected you *back*."

He sighed. "Thank God for you, Sal. It's only you to whom I can show my love in full."

Poor Gerald. So much to give and so, so hard on himself. I already understood that it fell to me to coax him out of his rigid prison of bad self-regard.

But we were a family together again! I dressed Honoria in little smocked dresses and documented her every achievement in a black leather scrapbook. When an expected visit with a neighbor boy had to be postponed because of the virus, Gerald handwrote a little letter of regret from the boy to Honoria. It was barely more than the size of a postage stamp, with a tiny dot of sealing wax and even a miniature cancelation mark drawn by hand. On such occasions I felt another pang for my mother. I wanted her to witness how well we were growing into our new role as parents.

Christmas was coming so, despite the restrictions of the pandemic, we decorated and prepared for another holiday together in our little home—cedar swags at the windows, pomanders of oranges and cloves hanging in the doorways. Instead of lavish presents to each other, we gave gifts in Honoria's name to the Red Cross, the Belgian Babies' Fund, and Fatherless Children of France. And there was another gift: I was pregnant again, expecting our second child.

## Chapter 5
### 1919-1921

"Listen to this," Gerald said, reading from the *Times* as we sat at the breakfast table. "The idea of time is changing dramatically with Albert Einstein's new Theory of Relativity. For many contemporary writers and artists, this discovery is revising the way they see the world."

"What a magical idea," I said, stirring two lumps of sugar into my coffee. "That science can change art!"

How would I revise my view of the world? I was so tired of war and the isolation imposed on us by the flu pandemic. More freedom, I thought. Fresh ideas about art and music and literature. And more room for women to participate in all those things.

We were awaiting Gerald's army demobilization papers and had eagerly begun designing a second nursery for the new baby, who would arrive in the spring. I'd found a pale-blue and cream William Morris wallpaper in a pattern of rabbits, birds, and flowers. Gerald had brought home an Early American bureau and side table, then painted them white and stenciled them with the blue Morris rabbits. When we'd finished the room, we stood back and admired our work. "We're a capital team, you and I," Gerald said, wrapping an arm around my shoulder.

But one day he returned home from Mark Cross in especially low spirits. Working for his father in that commercial environment was always a grind for his creative nature. Before the war, Mr. Murphy had suggested that Gerald try designing an inexpensive safety razor for the company. He'd thrown the full weight of his practical knowledge and visual talent behind the effort and was just about to patent the design when the King Gillette company brought a nearly identical product to market. He'd been crushed, and now he seemed to be reminded anew of what an ill fit he was at the firm.

"Father asked me today what I plan to do when my papers arrive," Gerald said now, slouching onto the sofa. He took off his face mask and loosened his tie. Then he reached up to take Honoria, who'd been squirming in my arms to reach out to him, and bounced her absentmindedly on his knee.

"What did you say?" I asked, sitting down myself.

"I told him I wanted to go to Harvard to study landscape architecture."

"What?" I laughed, because this was the first I was hearing of it.

"I had to say something," Gerald shrugged. "And that's what came out." While he'd been in Texas and Ohio, he'd illustrated his letters with beautiful sketches of the pastoral landscapes and, after he'd returned to New York, he'd been studying at the School of Design and Liberal Arts in the evenings. I was always amazed at what new gifts he was able to unearth in himself. I'd studied painting and drawing for years, and Gerald's work was as good as mine, if not better.

I sat in stunned silence, processing this news. We'd always talked about a bucolic future, perhaps a little farm somewhere, where we'd work as equal partners and create something beautiful, side by side. Something more than just a baby's bedroom.

Now Gerald returned to that scheme, which would somehow grow from a landscape architecture degree. "When we woke up in the morning, the question and work of the day would belong to *both* of us!" he said. "To be able to work together over the same thing? What other husbands and wives can do that? What a thrilling idea."

"Goodness! No flies on you, Gerald Murphy," I said. "But the babies—is now such a good time to uproot ourselves?"

"We don't need to make any sudden moves, do we, dumpling?" he said to Honoria. "I could apply for the fall semester and we would move in late summer. I can go on ahead and find us a perfect house. Think of it, Sal. Cambridge would be a much more suitable place to raise our little tribe."

I thought of our tidy, compressed life on Eleventh Street, the brick townhouses cheek by jowl. How we still had to wear masks out into the street and maintain a safe distance from even our closest friends. Having a larger house with a yard and fresh air would be so wonderful for the children. And we would achieve more distance from our opinionated families. They still asked how we planned to make our way in the world or, more likely, how Gerald planned to support our family. It was less a matter of finances to them, more a matter of American work ethic.

Thus began a pattern that we'd follow for the duration of our marriage: Gerald's restlessness, his ability to see two steps ahead of the status quo, to envision a new chapter for us. And me catching up quickly, understanding his vision and eager to make it real. This was, after all, the very life I'd wanted, wasn't it? I was already becoming the scaffolding upon which Gerald's grand schemes relied.

---

ON MAY 13, 1919, Baoth Wiborg Murphy was born, named for my family and reflecting Gerald's fascination with Celtic history. Father, Hoytie, and Fred were all in London at the time, but you could practically hear the rejoicing from there. You'd think that Father had given birth himself—his unrequited longing for a son was never more apparent. Unlike Honoria, whose delicate features mirrored Gerald's, I could see my own Norwegian stock in Baoth's square face and sturdy body. I marveled at how alike we were in aspect and temperament, and I filled my scrapbook with quick watercolors of our little blond Thor.

It turned out that Harvard's admissions were much easier during the summer semester so, just two weeks later, Gerald was living at the Brattle Inn in Cambridge to begin his studies at the School of Landscape Architecture. He sent me the catalog for women's courses so I could enroll in some classes, too—but I was still in bed nursing a baby and recovering from the delivery. Our dreams of a creative partnership raced ahead of me, out of my grasp.

Within weeks, Gerald was writing about the new world he'd discovered. He'd already met Alice James—widow of William James, the famous philosopher and psychologist—who was helping him find houses for rent: Georgian clapboards with cupolas, Cape Cod shingles, boxy Dutch colonials. And the gardens! Lilacs and hydrangeas and towering elm trees. It was clear that Gerald had found his terra firma.

There was also an intellectual community awaiting our arrival. Gerald tossed around new names like Amy Lowell, who was a leading poet in the Imagist movement; Ezra Pound; Ford Madox Ford; and H. D., which stood for Hilda Doolittle. They were inspired by the poems of ancient Greek lyricists and Japanese haiku poets. "She knows everything about everything," Gerald said of Lowell. "She's like the Bostonian George Sand." He'd found what he was looking for: a blend of off-beat aristocracy and refined intellectualism. And I hoped that I'd recover soon enough from my current role as broodmare so that I could join in.

---

SOON, I BUSIED myself with putting everything we owned into storage, renting out Eleventh Street, and moving our little family plus Miss Stewart to The Dunes for the summer while Gerald stayed in

Cambridge to study. Returning to my old life—especially without Gerald—was especially exasperating. Olga and Hoytie were fighting like cats (Gerald called them Scylla and Charybdis) and Father was running everyone senseless with daily tours, drives, games, and sails. I escaped to the beach as often as I could—the roaring surf and the sand between my toes always restored me to an even keel. Miss Stewart helped me take the children down to the shore, where Baoth would doze in his basket while Honoria and I dug for sand crabs. Such simple pleasures reminded me that, beyond the fractious energy inside the Wiborg house, there were tides and grasses and salty breezes, and I found my balance again.

ONE EVENING FATHER called us three girls into the drawing room for a serious talk. He thrust copies of a pamphlet, "The Safe Keeping of Securities," into our hands and announced that he would be dividing his assets among us within the year. It was King Lear of the Eastern Seaboard. *How do we learn about assessments and amortization and depletion?* I wrote in a whiny letter to Gerald. *Can't we just leave it to God & the Columbia Trust Co.?*

Gerald had always insisted that money wasn't worth fussing over. But our very life together had been built upon the comfortable rock that my family's wealth had provided, and I was usually the one who wrote the checks. Even though I was excited by the independence promised by this abundance, I also knew that no trust fund was limitless. *Nothing, I think, ties one to money as much as disregarding it,* I wrote him now. *Mismanagement is usually what brings it to the fore.* Already I was sensing that money would be my purview in the marriage ahead. Neither one of us wanted to sully our minds with the gritty work of credits and deficits. "Things that smack of the pavement," Gerald had said. But someone had to do it. And that someone would be me.

Soon, though, the vague notion of the money also set me free. In my final weeks in East Hampton, I found myself breathless with the idea of moving to a new town, a new house, a new group of friends. I needed a fresh landscape and a greater distance from my family.

---

IN SEPTEMBER, THE children and I joined Gerald in Cambridge, where we moved into a large white two-story clapboard with green shutters that he'd found for us on Brattle Street. The small front porch was framed with double columns and a lush vine of wisteria, and a broad front lawn would be perfect when the children were old enough to play outside. The house itself was a bit dark, the walls painted in dull and dated colors. But "no matter how ugly any house is, we can make it seem beautiful with sun and open fires and babies," I assured Gerald.

"I defy any house to stay gloomy once we've moved in," he replied, and kissed my cheek.

Once our furnishings had arrived in a caravan of three Ford trucks, Gerald and I set about a ritual that would be repeated in countless houses over the years. He, the methodical architect, would sketch out a room on a pad of graph paper while I would just start pushing furniture around, standing back to squint at my work. Then the negotiations would begin—the best arrangement for the most attractive view, the flow of visitors, the combination of colors. It was when Gerald and I felt most in sync, as if we held an identical vision for the particular life we would create in this house. It was just a matter of finding that vision.

Gerald and I both loved the adventure of a new home more than we hated the tedious task of moving. We were always equally excited by the prospect of creating another chapter of life together in the arrangement of furniture, the choosing of paint colors, the hanging of wallpaper and drapes. It was a mutual fascination that lasted for our entire marriage—and a few times, it may have been all that held us together. Each house promised novel ways of interacting, discovering fresh perspectives, even developing new circles of friends. Until the very end, we used our homes as physical expressions of our manifesto: to find and celebrate beauty in even the smallest things.

---

I WAS ALREADY learning the difference between having one child and two. My leather scrapbook, in which I'd so carefully documented every moment of Honoria's infancy, was now filled with slips of paper hastily recording Baoth's achievements—placeholders for when I could finally find the time to do it right.

Admittedly, one reason for my negligence was our social life. Gerald and I were finding that Cambridge's intellectual and cultural elite welcomed newcomers like us. Besides Alice James and Amy Lowell, art connoisseur Isabella Stewart Gardener and the portraitist John Singer Sargent, who'd created such a stir with his *Portrait of Madame X*, lived there. Gerald had attended several of Sargent's lectures at the Boston Museum of Fine Arts.

Soon after our arrival, we were invited to Fenway Court—Mrs. Gardener's Boston home that also housed a public museum to exhibit her lavish art collection. Outside, the building was a simple brick cube that looked more like a school or office. But once inside, you felt as if you were in one of the great palazzos of Italy. The whole thing was set around an enormous, four-story courtyard in the Venetian style, with lawns and trees and Gothic windows and balconies. And the art! Raphael, Giotto, Bellini, Vermeer. As we walked the corridors peering at the title plaques, Gerald and I turned to each other, wide-eyed. Imagine *owning* these treasures!

At dinner we found the conversation to be as colorful as the paintings. Miss Lowell was a cigar-smoking fortress of a woman. "In science, read the newest works," she was telling Gerald, gesturing with her fork. "In literature, read the oldest. The classics are always modern, don't you agree?"

I was seated next to Alice's son, the painter William James Jr., who drew me out about our reasons for moving to Cambridge. "We're still finding our way here," I told him. "Our families cast a rather long shadow. But we want to do something fresh. Something *creative*."

"My father used to say that the greatest use of a life is to spend it on something that will outlast it," he said. "If you can change your *own* mind, you can change your entire life. Begin now, my dear, to be whatever new person you want to be."

And that was the challenge, wasn't it? What kind of new person *did* I want to be?

Across the table, Mr. Sargent was talking excitedly to Alice. "But portraiture is for the young!" he said. "I've had enough of it. Every time I paint a portrait, I lose a friend!"

After dinner, Mrs. Gardener begged Gerald and me to perform—apparently, he'd shared with her our interest in nineteenth-century American music, and how he'd discovered the sheet music for some old Negro spirituals in the Boston Public Library. We hadn't practiced much, but we harmonized his beautiful tenor with my contralto to sing "Oh Graveyard" and "Sometimes I Feel Like a Motherless Child," both received with rousing applause. I felt embraced by this remarkable community of artistic souls.

---

"HOW BRILLIANT YOU were to lead us here," I told Gerald in the Packard on the way home that night. "It's so stimulating to be surrounded by all this free thought."

Gerald reached over and squeezed my knee. "All we need is a little fertile ground," he said. "Imagine, Sal, what our *own* creative garden will look like!"

Through his classes, he'd become more deeply interested in botany, his notebooks filling with detailed drawings of stamens and calyxes and cross sections of delicate flora that showed their inner mechanisms. On our walks in the neighborhood, Honoria would point out flowers for him to identify. "What this, Dada? What this?" From her two-year-old mouth, the word came out "Dow-Dow."

"That's a bearded iris, Honoria. Look here, this part is the beard." Or "Paper white narcissus. See how the petals look like tissue?" I loved how such details of nature adorned our life as a family. Slowing down, it seemed, to the pace of a small child. I needed to live at a child's pace—in January, we'd learned that I was expecting our third.

---

THOUGH WE RELISHED our newfound freedom from New York, we hadn't renounced Manhattan entirely. Leaving the children with Miss Stewart, we occasionally escaped to the city to see what was new, like the clubs of Harlem with fresh talents like Fats Waller and Bessie Smith. John Sargent brought us to an exhibit of the Russian cubist painter Nicholas Roerich, who'd painted the sets for the *Sacre du Printemps* ballet I'd seen in London.

It reminded me of the avant-garde Armory Show of 1913, which Gerald and I had seen together. We'd stood wide-eyed at Duchamp's *Nude Descending a Staircase*, which one critic described as "an explosion at a shingle factory."

"It's like watching a moving picture, but flattened into a single frame," Gerald had observed.

"I do see the movement," I said. "But who comes down a staircase in the nude? It's that idea I can't quite get over."

The whole show left us breathless. Henri Matisse's red studio, with its inventory of Orientalia crammed onto the canvas. A number of geometrical sketches and paintings by a Spaniard named Pablo Picasso. It took everything we'd thought about art and turned it upside down. As we left, Gerald was quiet and serious. I could almost see the gears turning in his head.

ANOTHER SUMMER LOOMED. Rather than return to The Dunes, with its carousel of visitors and family squabbles, we decided to spend the season in the small town of Litchfield, Connecticut. Now five months pregnant, I'd sit on a wicker chaise in the shade and watch Honoria and Baoth romp about the yard as Gerald caught them with his Brownie camera.

Returning to Cambridge in late August, Gerald bought a bicycle and often came home for lunch with me and the children. It was a welcome relief for both of us—Gerald from his studies and me from the constant demands of managing a house in my third trimester. I was good at it, I realized, and wished that my mother were alive to see how well I was performing without a large retinue of staff. "But this is my final lap," I told Gerald. "Three is all you'll get." Thank goodness there were methods now to control such things.

"Three is enough," he said, kissing the back of my neck. "We'll have enough for a small volleyball team, at least."

I sighed and smiled. The days when we would dance a jig in the sand seemed comically impossible now.

"I want *you* back," Gerald said. "I want you back fully and well-rested for all the adventures that await us."

On October 18, 1920, Patrick Francis Murphy II arrived at a civilized three o'clock in the afternoon. The midwife handed him to me in a blue cotton swaddle and summoned Gerald from the hall. As we gazed into his pink, pinched face, Gerald softly sang an Irish ballad about the dawning of a new day. Patrick peered at us in awe with his blue-black newborn eyes, perhaps wondering what sort of strange family he'd been born into.

Now when Miss Stewart and I took the children to Longfellow Park, we looked like a Silk Road caravan, our two buggies carrying enough diapers and provisions to outfit a legion of babies. When I was the eldest of three children, I doubt I ever went to the park in the company of my mother or even saw her at bath time. How differently my children would grow up. How deeply they would know they were loved!

---

BUT, AS THE new decade wore on, I began to notice a familiar pattern. Gerald no longer came home from school eager to show me his latest drafts and drawings. The landscape architecture program was veering away from botany and designing estates, he complained, and moving toward city planning and engineering. The increased emphasis on mathematics was steering him toward his weakest area, and he'd started skipping assignments. "Unsatisfactory" was a word he began using to describe not his own performance, but the restrictive world around him. With his variety of natural talents, he could become anything or anyone he chose, but the challenge was keeping him interested long enough to achieve that. He was always onto the next idea, the next scheme, and I was always scrambling to keep up.

---

ALTHOUGH I WAS still more preoccupied with nursing and nap times and collapsing into bed by nine o'clock, I too was beginning to feel restless. A recent article in *The Dial* magazine had called out the repressive culture of Puritanism in America. And the passing of the Volstead Act just the year before had definitely struck a blow to our way of life.

"I feel like such an outlaw," I said one evening as we sipped Prosecco in the dining room, drapes drawn. Now we could buy alcohol only from underground sources, the shades pulled down before we could enjoy a cocktail or a glass of wine with dinner. "This country's being run by a group of prudes, who all seem dead set against having any fun."

"I'm so tired of being told what to do," Gerald agreed, and in his tone I heard the boy who'd been sent to cruel boarding schools, who'd been made to walk home with the ice of a Central Park lake freezing to his skin. "First my family and now my country. How can we ever reinvent ourselves in such a cultural straitjacket?"

One day he came in with the paper opened to the second section, pointing to an article with the headline "POST-WAR EXODUS." Americans—especially artists and intellectuals—were flocking to Europe in droves, some with barely more than the price of a steamer ticket in their pockets. They were rejecting the commercial, Puritanical vengeance of American society. And the dollar had grown strong since the war, especially in France.

"What do you think, Sal?" Gerald asked. "What about raising our children overseas? From that vantage point, maybe we'd see all the *best* parts of being American. You know, democracy, industry, forthrightness, a creative ingenuity."

We both loved our country. How could we not? Our families had flourished and we'd been given every opportunity to thrive. But Gerald was right: We needed new terrain. The thought of moving our family of five that far exhausted me, but the ultimate benefits might be worth it.

"I think you're right, darling," I finally said. "We'd be even *more* American there."

We looked at each other for a long minute, each forming an idea in our imagination of what that might look like. Then Gerald strode over to the enclosed cabinet where we kept our liquor to make us a couple of Gin Rickeys. After fetching some ice, soda, and sliced lime, he handed me a chilled cocktail glass, already frosty with condensation.

"To Europe, then?"

"To Europe!"

We clinked our glasses and laughed.

"IRRESPONSIBLE," "ILL-CONCEIVED," "HARE-BRAINED," and "senseless" were just a few of the adjectives that peppered the family letters landing in our mailbox during the weeks that followed. Our moving to Cambridge had been bad enough. Now you'd think we were sailing for the South Pole. *We are still young and this new post-war world is ripe for exploration,* I wrote to my father. *Gerald and I want to do things in a new way. Please understand that it doesn't mean we love you less.* Feeding the envelope into the open mouth of the letterbox, my heart raced a little with this new taste of freedom.

# Chapter 6
## 1921-1922

"You must stay, at least through the spring," Linda Porter was saying. "You can't imagine the parties. Conte de Beaumont reintroduced the ball after the war. His Montmartre soirees are, quite literally, fantastic. *Travestis*, the French call them. Always with the most outrageous theme."

We were sitting at a table outside Le Dôme, watching all of Montparnasse stroll by. I sipped my Pernod and glanced up at the clear autumn sky above the tips of the elms. Gerald once told me that when Louis XIV tore down the medieval city and had Paris redesigned, he'd decreed that the main promenades should be shaded to allow for comfortable strolling. To this day, the street trees had their branches pruned to a height of twelve feet from the sidewalks. I marveled at the simple genius of this country.

Our first stop, England, had been a bust. The summer of 1921 had been the hottest season on record, and all the lush green gardens I'd remembered were brown and parched. London no longer held its allure for me—seeing a big city through the eyes of three young children will do that—and Gerald was equally unmoved by its charms. Instead, we'd set out for the English countryside, settling in Croyde Bay on the Bristol Channel, a flat village of sand and grass and gently rolling surf. One season there was more than enough though, and Gerald and I reluctantly conceded defeat. We would return to America.

But first we'd make a quick detour to Paris, for two reasons: first, because I loved the city, and second, because Gerald hadn't seen it since he was a boy. Besides, our friends from Boston, the Pickmans, were staying here and Gerald's Yale pal, Cole Porter, had rented a lavish flat near the Eiffel Tower. For a few weeks we could enjoy some good dinners and fine museums, and our trip wouldn't have been a total waste.

We quickly found a suite of rooms at the Hôtel Beau-Site near the Etoile in the 8th arrondissement. We hired a new nanny, Mademoiselle Henriette Geron, and began making the rounds. Ed Pickman was working on a book. Cole was writing songs (currently working on a ditty he called "Olga, Come Back to the Volga"), and had married an American "alimony heiress" named Linda Lee Thomas, eight years his senior, who was said to be the most beautiful woman in the world. (Sitting across from her now, I couldn't see it.)

Something else was going on, too. Wandering the same streets I'd walked during so many visits here with my family, I felt something new. The buildings were the same, their neoclassical curves as pretty as ever. The horse chestnuts and the pruned plane trees hadn't changed. But there was an energy now, an edgy spirit that I hadn't felt before. Back in New York, we'd been devastated by news of the war, by seeing our young men return home in pieces, or not at all. Here, the Parisians had lived and witnessed it. The Germans had pushed into France as close as forty-eight kilometers away. Now the city was still traumatized, cleaning its wounds. You could see it in the face of the young boy sweeping the sidewalk in front of the bakery. In the eyes of the woman pushing a rag cart down an alley off the rue la Perouse. In the slouch of a man sleeping off an opium hangover near the Point d'Iéna. "This is a city of ghosts," the florist told me, gesturing to the street from her shop.

But along with the ghosts had come new blood. The franc was less than twenty cents on the dollar, and *everyone* could afford to come to Paris, including artists of every genre—dancers from Russia, painters from Spain, and countless aspiring writers from the States. Serge Diaghilev, who had jolted me awake with his *Le Sacre du Printemps* in London a few years earlier, was in residence with his Ballets Russes. A crazy band of mixed-media artists called Dadaists were presenting *manifestations* at the Palais des Fêtes. And the Fratellinis, a flock of clowns at the Cirque Medrano, packed their tent with audiences from both the bohemian Left Bank and the aristocratic Right Bank. It was the most delicious stew of creative talents and crazy temperaments I'd ever seen. My fluent French and Gerald's rusty command of the language were more than enough to get us by in those early days. After just a few weeks, we felt like we belonged.

A new designer, Coco Chanel, was dressing women in tailored suits, inspired by men's fashion, accessorized with ropes of pearls. It was a trend I wouldn't follow myself, preferring to dress more like the models of Henri Matisse in drapey floral frocks with lots of patterns and layers, but I appreciated the new styles.

Now I watched a woman wearing a gray-and-pink patterned crepe dress approach on the boulevard, walking a black whippet. Her short skirt showed great legs in black suede pumps, and her wide-brimmed cloche framed a dark, pretty face. She stopped abruptly before us and cried out to Linda. "Darling, fancy meeting you here! Never too early for a little Pernod, am I right?"

Linda squealed and reached out a hand. "You wicked thing! We looked all over for you and Harry last night at the Dingo." She gestured to an empty wicker chair across from us. "Sara, it's your lucky day. Polly here is one of *the* most fun Americans in town. Polly Crosby, meet Sara Murphy."

"I was just admiring your dress," I said, extending my hand.

"Don't you *love* a dropped waist?" Polly asked, flouncing the fabric. The dropped waist meant that women could dispose of their corsets, and that's exactly what most of Paris was doing. She flagged a waiter and ordered another round for the table.

"Polly is largely responsible for the death of the corset," Linda said. "She invented something called the *brassière*."

"Really?" I said. I'd never heard the term.

Polly nodded. "Nineteen years old. On my way to a debutante ball. I had the most gorgeous silk gown, but my corset was showing right through it. I asked my maid for a pair of silk handkerchiefs, a cord, some pink ribbon, a needle, and thread." She spoke fast—clearly she'd told this story a hundred times. "When I got to the ball, the girls all lined up to ask me what I'd done with my bosoms—they looked so natural."

"How remarkable!" I said.

"I patented the design, started the Fashion Form Brassiere Company, and a few years later sold the patent to Warner Brothers Corset Company for fifteen hundred dollars. The end!"

The waiter placed new glasses on the table, each filled with two inches of chartreuse liquor. Polly poured a little water into her glass, turning the liquid cloudy and fragrant with anise, and took a long sip. Then she scooped a few peanuts from the dish on the table and delicately fed them to her whippet, whose name was Narcisse Noir.

I'd never known a woman who'd started her own business, let alone at such an early age. "How positively ingenious of you," I said.

"Not that ingenious. Warner Brothers has earned at least five million from my idea so far. I should have held out for more, but oh well." She clinked her glass against Linda's and grinned. "Here we are!"

"Well, I think you're spectacular," I said, and I meant it.

The Crosbys lived on the Quai d'Orléans on the Île Saint Louis and Harry worked at the family bank, J.P. Morgan. Every weekday morning, Polly donned a swimsuit and paddled Harry in a red canoe down the Seine to the Place de la Concorde.

"All that paddling, also good for the breasts," Polly added with a wink.

I couldn't wait to buy some new things and toss my corsets onto the rubbish heap too. Polly promised to take me shopping the following week. And not too long after that, I convinced Gerald that we should stay in Paris for at least a year. Maybe for good.

---

WE HADN'T ESCAPED our families entirely, however. My sister, Hoytie—the difficult one—was ensconced in a fashionable apartment on the quai de Conti, conferred on her for life by the City of Paris in recognition of her services as an ambulance driver during the war. Now an avowed Sapphist, she was as haughty and impervious as ever, pursuing impossible romances with major female players of the demimonde and developing a reputation as a social nuisance. Her total lack of social propriety seemed to strike people as either uncommonly rude or exceedingly charming. I fell into the former camp; she could be so maddeningly oblivious to people's feelings, yet everyone seemed to forgive her, as you would a small child.

Hoytie appeared one day as Hester and I sat in the Café Kléber on the Place du Trocadéro. I heard a furious knocking on the window and looked up to see her in her usual ferocity, one arm weighted with several bags from fashionable shops. Suddenly, there she was at our table.

"I'd heard you were in town," she announced without introduction. "What are you doing wasting your time around *here*?" She meant the Trocadéro, so far from her fashionable Île de la Cité. The garnet brooch on her lapel was the size of a radish.

"Hoytie, this is Hester Pickman, a good friend from our Boston days," I said.

Hoytie gave a tiny nod and proceeded to ignore her. "You've been in town for what, a month now? My dinner invitation must have gone astray."

"We've been so busy getting settled and the children are such a distraction," I said. Dinner with Hoytie was the last thing on my list, and Gerald couldn't stand her.

"Well, I too have been busy with my play," she said. "Have you heard? It's opening in Harlem in April. Cast almost entirely of Negroes!"

"Why, that's marvelous."

"But I simply must run. Á *tout á l'heure!*" And she left us with mouths agape in her wake. A little Hoytie always went a long way.

---

IN OCTOBER WE rented a large furnished flat on the rue de Grueze—a limestone Beaux Arts building with wrought-iron balconies on a leafy street in the 16th arrondissement. The Trocadéro Gardens were just blocks away, and the air was cool and fresh, unlike at the city center. Gerald and I loved to wander the graveled park paths with the children and, at the cafés in the evenings, we were meeting the most intriguing people. Finally, with childbearing behind me, I felt ready to join in the mix—to be part of the action.

One evening Gerald returned home breathless and set his bundle on the dining room table. He'd begun carrying his money and notebook in a small square of silk fabric, like a Japanese bento box, so they wouldn't ruin the lines of his linen suit.

"Sal, I've just had the most extraordinary feeling," he gushed. "Gallery Rosenberg, on the rue de la Boétie. In the window there were paintings like I've never seen. Braque. Picasso. Gris. They're breaking everything apart, down to its most fundamental shapes and colors. It's like looking through a kaleidoscope!"

I reminded him that we'd seen many paintings just like that at the 1913 Armory Show in New York. The same artists.

"Well, I guess I didn't really *see* them then. Maybe I was still too brainwashed by Mark Cross." He was practically effervescing, happier than I'd seen him in years. "Sal, if that's painting? That's *just* what I want to do!"

"Well, darling, I think you should. Why don't we take a painting class?"

"What a brilliant idea. Why are you so brilliant?" He kissed me and we did a little jig, our victory dance.

---

TWO WEEKS LATER, we stood in the bright light of an attic room on the rue Jacob, a square of clear blue blazing through the skylight. Mlle. Goncharova paced between our two easels and spoke forcefully in her Russian accent. "You must boil a thing down to its very *essence* before you even set brush to canvas," she said. "And think *very* carefully about a color before you select it. Color possesses a strange magic and has an effect on one's psyche."

We'd heard about Natalia Goncharova through some art friends. She was an avant-garde painter and costume designer whose guiding principle was *vsechestvo,* which translated to "Everything-ism." On any given day, she might appear dressed as a peasant or a nineteenth-century noblewoman. She'd been deconstructing her style in Russia along similar lines as the Cubists in France. After arriving in Paris just a few years before, she worked closely with Diaghilev.

Although Gerald and I were already fairly accomplished sketchers and painters, Mlle. Goncharova started us off with absolutely nonrepresentational, abstract images. No apple on a dish for her. We showed up at her studio at nine o'clock every weekday morning to paint all day. In the evenings, we received critiques from Mlle. G and her boisterous blond partner—she didn't approve of marriage—Mikhail Larionov. Every time we arrived, he would rush up and kiss us full on the mouth, even Gerald.

It was exhausting and challenging, standing at our easels for hours trying to deconstruct every curve and angle. And we missed the children terribly—by the time we arrived home at night, Mlle. Geron had them bathed and put to bed. But it was such a rich, juicy period for Gerald and me, analyzing form and color and representation. I was reminded of our first weeks together as fiancés, discovering a shared aesthetic.

---

ONE MORNING, MLLE. Goncharova circled our easels and said, "How would you like to work in the theater?" Gerald and I turned to each other, our faces question marks. Goncharova often helped to paint the scenery for Diaghilev, and five of the sets for his upcoming ballet, *Les Noces*, had been destroyed in a warehouse fire. "We need reinforcements. Of course, there's no pay. It would be a sort of apprenticeship," she said, and we agreed on the spot.

For the next few weeks, we took a cab out to Belleville in the 20th arrondissement to work at the Ballets' atelier, on the top floor of a brick warehouse with great louvered windows that could be opened wide to air out the fumes. On the first day, we got astonished looks from the other crew members, all garbed in paint-spattered work clothes. I was wearing a chiffon dress with green kid heels and pearls, and Gerald had fashioned himself a pair of tailored, pressed overalls. He believed that every occasion demanded its own costume.

Laid on the floor like an enormous carpet was an old canvas from a previous production, with new drawings sketched over it in charcoal. We were shown how to paint within the sketch lines with long-handled brooms and Gerald was instructed to climb a thirty-foot ladder to get a proper perspective on our work. It was intoxicating. I'd been to countless plays, ballets, and operas, but had always seen the stage from a velvet chair in a box, looking down on the play from a distance. Now here we were in the actual body of the theater, seeing the blood and organs of a masterpiece being born. I wanted to pinch myself.

On our third day, the set designers showed up. Georges Braque and André Derain wore wool suits and a relatively cordial manner.

They surveyed our work and suggested where we might go heavier with the color or finish a line. Then in walked Pablo Picasso, in a thick gray turtleneck and black peacoat. Since our arrival in Paris, a day hadn't passed without hearing his name. And here he was, in the flesh! His dark hair fell dramatically over a square face and his eyes were like two black bullet holes. I tried to imagine what lay on the other side of those points of darkness, where all those remarkable paintings were conceived. Gerald later compared him to "the bulls of Goya." I simply found him the most masculine creature I'd ever met.

Picasso circled our work like a predator, silently evaluating. Then a burst of staccato French: "More shadow here! And here!" He took my brush and made quick black marks on the canvas, indicating where I should darken it. I nodded vigorously.

"*Apprenez les règles comme un pro, pour pouvoir les enfreindre comme un artiste*," he said, and left. "Learn the rules like a pro, so you can break them like an artist."

It wasn't long before the Ballets Russes began to feel like a kind of madcap family. Picasso had married one of Diaghilev's ballerinas, Olga Koklova ("It was the only way she'd go to bed with me"), and Diaghilev's designer cousin, Vladimir "Vova" Orloff, became a particular friend to us. Before long, we were attending all the rehearsals and premieres, and all the parties afterward. Every night there seemed to be a new spontaneous gathering—at Le Boeuf sur le Toit or the Dingo or at a jam session by Les Six. The air was usually thick with smoke or musky perfume, and I felt like a dart, hurled thirty-six hundred miles across the Atlantic from New York to land right here on the bull's-eye, Paris.

I was beginning to understand that everyone was trying to do the same thing, whether through music or painting or movement or writing: to break a thing down to its most basic components, then rearrange them in unexpected, modern ways to say something completely *new*. Paris was a living, breathing organism in which fresh ideas were floating on the air waiting to be grabbed, like drunken birds. And the theater seemed to be the place where every artistic discipline was coming together. We knew we were becoming part of something important. A *movement*.

---

MEANWHILE, GERALD HAD become good pals with Fernand Léger, a former architect who was creating his own figurative, populist style called Tubism—lots of industrial pipes and shiny round shapes. Fernand and his wife often took us on after-hours tours of Paris's demimonde: opium dens, like cemeteries of ghosts. Homosexual *bals musettes*, where it was impossible to tell the men from the women. Scrapyards illuminated by pale-blue Holophane lamps. Fernand and Gerald would get excited about random, everyday objects that took on a new beauty when viewed with an impartial eye. It was, Gerald said later, "a shock of recognition that put me into an entirely new orbit."

Everything here was art or potential art. Gerald rented a studio in an old horse stable on the rue de Froidevaux, across from the Montparnasse Cemetery, and began buying canvases and paints. He grew out his Irish-red sideburns and started wearing a broad-brimmed black hat like Toulouse-Lautrec. I'd never seen him so happy, so filled with purpose. He began making notes of things he wanted to paint as he wandered the city: everyday objects, particular colors, the way a light illuminated a scene. I pictured a plant, transferred from a pot to a lush garden with irrigation and sunlight. He was finally finding an outlet for his dormant gifts.

But, after a month or two, the novelty of seeing the city's bohemian underbelly began taking a toll on us both. We agreed that, except for an occasional fete, we would quietly leave the party in time to be up for breakfast with the children the next morning. Many was the night when we'd hear a drunken ruckus on the street below and lean out our bedroom window to firmly declare that we weren't to be disturbed. We were older than most of our friends by nearly ten years, and we had a family. I came to realize that these bohemians, as much as I loved them, were like children themselves: no offspring, no responsibilities, nothing to think of except their own art.

---

IT WAS A Sunday, one of those gorgeous spring days in which Paris almost seemed to be showing off. The fruit trees were in bloom and the musky scent of their blossoms filled me with happiness. The sun warmed the limestone buildings while a soft breeze ruffled the air. We'd taken the children to the Luxembourg Gardens and sat by the big round pond, the gravel paths already crowded with families. Gerald had rented three little wooden sailboats from a stand at the café and was showing Honoria and Baoth how to guide them with long sticks around the edge. The boat manager, with pants rolled up past his knees, frequently had to climb into the green water to retrieve a boat that had sailed too far into the middle.

"Abaft the beam! Man the poop deck! Stand amidships!" Gerald cried.

"Abaft! Abaft!" Honoria echoed.

"Poop deck!" Baoth laughed.

Gerald delighted in nothing more than creating enchantment, particularly for our children.

"Permission to board, sir!" Gerald said as his blue boat bumped into Baoth's red one. "Coming athwartship!"

"Aye, aye, sir," Baoth said seriously.

Baby Patrick sat on my lap in the shade of a palm tree, and I spooned strawberry ice cream into his eager mouth—his first taste of it—as he made little hums of pleasure. I couldn't imagine a better day, a more beautiful place, a finer family. How far we had come from New York. Even Cambridge seemed provincial now.

A striking couple approached—two women, arm in arm. One was built like a Buddha, dressed in a voluminous linen skirt and jacket, tailored like a man's with a bowtie at the neck and a homburg hat on her head. The other was attired in a two-piece ladies' suit in a Japanese style, a sort of indigo batik print, with a wide-brimmed black straw hat. They were such an extraordinary pair—one solid and tank-like, the other nervous and fluttery like a bird.

"Ice cream? Somebody's a lucky boy!" They stood beside me now, and Buddha was addressing Patrick.

"Yes, his first," I said. "He seems to like it."

The bird lady smiled and clucked in agreement. "How old is he?"

"Just fourteen months," I said. "If only we could all stay this age, when life is as simple as strawberry ice cream."

"We're always the same age inside," said Buddha. Despite looking so exotic, both women spoke with the broad vowels of the States.

"You're American?" I asked.

"America is our country, and Paris is our hometown," Buddha said. She dug into a pocket of her skirt and pulled out an engraved calling card, which she presented to me. *Gertrude Stein, 27 rue du Fleurus, Paris.*

"Oh Miss Stein!" I said. "Of course I've heard of you!"

"And this is Miss Toklas," she said, to which the dark bird made a slight nod of her head.

"Do you have a husband?" Miss Stein looked around and I pointed to Gerald, who was now mimicking an admiral, with Baoth and Honoria saluting at attention to "Sir Dow-Dow."

"Charming," Miss Stein said. "You must both come to our salon. Every Saturday evening at seven. Everyone comes."

"That's very kind of you," I said. "We'd enjoy that."

They made little bows and continued along the gravel path. That's how it was back then. If you sat in one place long enough, all of Paris would come to you.

That night at dinner I told Gerald of my chance encounter with the Misses Stein and Toklas and their invitation to attend the Saturday night salon.

"I hear they separate the spouses," Gerald said. "The husbands go with Stein to discuss art and philosophy over drinks, while the wives are relegated to small talk with Toklas over tea and cakes."

I gave him a long look. "Well, *that* won't do," I said. We agreed that we'd avoid the experience if possible. Too many other good ways to spend a Saturday night.

# PART II

*Whoever said money can't buy happiness
simply didn't know where to go shopping.*
—Gertrude Stein

*When spring came, even the false spring,
there were no problems except where to be happiest.*
—Ernest Hemingway

## Chapter 7
### 1922

By late spring, we were itching to get out of the city, and summer at the seashore was a family tradition. We headed for Houlgate, a tourist resort on the Normandy coast with a small casino and lots of Calvados. There we stayed at the Hôtel des Clématites and adopted an English spaniel we named Asparagus. The Pickmans and their five children had rented the nearby Villa Germaine.

We'd looked forward to long, sunny days at the shore, with the children playing in the shallow waves and riding the donkeys available for hire. We rented a blue-and-white striped beach cabana. But after a few weeks of this, we hadn't seen a single truly warm day; apparently the French didn't mind the chilly, overcast weather, but it was too cold and melancholy for our American tribe. That's when a letter arrived from the Porters, inviting us to join them at the château they'd rented on the southern Riviera. It seemed a strange choice; while the Côte d'Azur was largely populated by German and English tourists in the cooler months, it was fairly deserted in the sweltering summer. But we were desperate for some heat, so we agreed.

We loaded our fourteen pieces of luggage, plus Asparagus, onto the Calais-Méditerrannée Express, known as *le train bleu*, and settled in for the sixteen-hour overnight journey from Calais to Antibes. It was then that I began my habit of hanging our train cars with sheets I'd washed in Lysol. I had no problem letting my children run wild in nature, coming back covered in sand or dirt. But, after the flu pandemic of four years before, the idea of other people's germs made me fiercely protective.

---

WE AWOKE THE next morning to a new world outside the windows of our couchettes. Rolling hillsides topped with medieval villages, groves of olive trees and lavender, stands of cypress. The yellow light made everything rosy and warm, a Cézanne canvas come to life. We pulled into the Gare d'Antibes, where Cole and Linda were waiting to drive us back to their rented villa, the Château de la Garoupe. The moment we stepped out of the motorcar we smelled lemons and rosemary and salty air. Hard to believe that this was even the same country as gloomy Houlgate.

The tiny village, we learned, nearly rolled up its streets on May first when the tourists all returned home because it was blazing hot, and the French never went into the sea. Even in East Hampton, ocean bathing had been considered largely a health measure. Only recently had swimming become a pleasure activity.

One day Gerald and I headed out to explore the rocky shoreline and came upon the dearest little beach, La Garoupe. It extended only about fifty yards long and was covered with a thick layer of seaweed, but it was sheltered and sat on a beautiful small bay surrounded by umbrella pines, the water calm and clear and the most pristine aquamarine color.

"No big waves or riptides," Gerald said. "The kids could play in the water."

"But the seaweed," I said. The whole beach was covered with it. "The flies will be miserable. And the smell is pretty rank, too."

"Oh ye of little faith," he said, and squeezed my arm.

We found a *quincaillerie* where Gerald bought a sturdy rake, while I stocked up on spades, pails, and a market umbrella. Then we spent the rest of our summer lounging at La Garoupe from ten until two, the children romping in the water and sand, Gerald methodically raking in six-foot quadrants until we had a divine little corner of the beach to ourselves. Cole and Linda occasionally joined us until we all retired for naps before supper.

As the season wore down and we prepared to return to Paris, I turned to Gerald. "I'm almost sad to leave, Dow-Dow," I said. I'd always loved the seashore; it was in my bones. But this family idyll—so relaxed, so intimate—gave me a visceral satisfaction I'd never felt before. It was as if I were watching the childhood I'd always wanted for myself, as our children romped freely like little merfolk in the gently lapping waves.

Gerald wrapped an arm around my shoulder. "I think we've found our spot, Sal," he said, and we instantly agreed we'd be coming back the following year. Before we left Antibes, Gerald spoke to the manager of the Hôtel du Cap, an enormous *fin de siecle* château set in a forest at the tip of the peninsula, and persuaded him to keep it open for us the following summer. It was so unlike him to think that far ahead. But that was the powerful spell that Cap d'Antibes had cast over us.

---

BACK IN PARIS, we returned to a livelier scene. The French, we'd discovered, were mad about anything American, so we were often in demand. Gerald had coordinated with Jack Roth, Jimmy Durante's drummer, to send us a monthly shipment of jazz records—Louis Armstrong, Jelly Roll Morton, Duke Ellington—and there was always a small crowd hovered around our RCA Victor phonograph. They were amazed at the latest gadgets we'd imported from the States; for example, we were the proud owners of the first waffle iron in France.

Other Americana: Gerald and I were often asked to perform our growing collection of Negro spirituals at gatherings. One night Evelyn, our hostess, pressed us to perform "Nobody Knows the Trouble I've Seen" and "Sometimes I Feel Like a Motherless Child." Gerald had worked out a simple arrangement on the piano, and we sat together on the bench singing our usual two-part harmony.

After we'd finished with the second song, Evelyn asked, "Erik, what did you think?" I instantly recognized the man's face from the record we had at home, *Trois Gymnopédies par Erik Satie*. Simple, melodic piano pieces, stripped bare of all unnecessary flourish.

"*Merveilleux, mais il ne devrait pas y avoir de piano*," he said. "Have them turn their backs and sing it again, a cappella."

Gerald and I stood up, turned to the wall, and sang "Motherless Child" again, slow and mournful. The simplicity of it was striking. When we'd finished, still facing the wall, he took my hand and a chill crawled up my spine. There was a minute of silence, then the room erupted into applause.

"Never sing it any other way," Satie said. Then he promptly fetched his coat and left.

As usual, we were also among the first to leave. We both seemed to hit a demarcation point at these gay parties and usually felt a sudden need to sneak out before too much was drunk and too many lines were crossed. It was always a welcome feeling to return to our apartment, with its stillness and routine. We looked in on the children and kissed their warm brows—our most magnificent achievement together. Then we wandered down the hall to bed.

I washed my face, brushed my hair to the count of one hundred, changed into my peignoir, and slid beneath the sheets, where Gerald was sitting and writing in his diary. The bedside lamps cast yellow cones of light on the wall. The linen drapes danced gently at the window.

I turned onto my side and wrapped my arm around his waist. "It's only midnight, darling," I said. "The night is young." I always longed for physical affection from him. To remind ourselves that *this* was our hometown: us.

Gerald smiled and leaned over to plant a kiss on the top of my head. "My mind is still spinning from the day, Sal. It'll take me a while to unwind. Okay if I leave the light on for a bit?"

I sighed. Gerald lived too much in his mind. Lovemaking had lost its urgency, as well as its purpose, since Patrick had been born. But I still needed that union, that physical demonstration of affection. I turned over and switched off my lamp. "Don't stay up too late, Dow-Dow."

Around this time, Gerald and I effortlessly reached the consensus that we weren't going back to the US anytime soon, if at all. We were Americans in Paris now. We sold the house on Eleventh Street for $40,000, which seemed like a king's ransom, and began looking for a place to buy. In October, our agent showed us a place in a sixteenth-century building at the corner of quai des Grands Augustins and the tiny rue Git-le-Coeur. Its charm was buried deep—it probably hadn't been renovated since the French Revolution, and I saw a rat on the stairs. The kitchen was minuscule; food had to be stored in a *garde-manger*—a wooden box that hung outside the window to stay cool. But the northern light was spectacular, and the house sat directly on the banks of the Seine—the view from the front windows extended from the Tuileries to the Île St.-Louis. The work would be massive but, with our windfall from Eleventh Street, we had the funds to pay for it. Most important of all, Gerald and I were at our best when we were building a home together. We signed the deed in a froth of anticipation and new ideas.

Meanwhile, we continued to feed our hunger for the arts. In particular, we were mad about the Kamerny Theater from Russia, an experimental troupe known for such performance art as presenting an operetta on the wings of a parked biplane. We'd attended all ten of their performances of *Girofle-Girofla*, after which we decided to throw a party in the theater's honor at our new place.

"The Russians will make a mess of the house anyway, so why not host them before we've decorated?" Gerald reasoned. "What's another hole or two in the walls?"

We invited the whole troupe over for a late dinner after the last performance of *The Man Who Was Thursday*, and our future home was filled with French and Russian and laughter, the universal language. We had no furniture yet, so we filled the parlor with pillows and mattresses wrapped in yards of brocade that I'd found at an upholstery sale. We fashioned long tables out of sawhorses and planks of raw wood. Lights were acetylene plumbers' lamps, and the walls were festooned with industrial and junkyard finds courtesy of Léger. Dounia, our new Algerian cook, made mountains of nutty couscous and a lentil stew, and for dessert there was a chocolate mousse covered in whipped cream called *négresse en chemise*. Also, of course, many cases of cheap French red wine. A guitar and an accordion appeared and before long the house was filled with song.

Gerald and I sat with Alexander Tairoff, the Kamerny's creative director, on a mattress near the fireplace. Everything had been so gay and festive, but there was a sadness in Alex's smile. The more he drank, the more morose he became. It's the Russian way.

"Everything okay, Alex?" Gerald asked. "You seem a bit *déprimé*."

It didn't take much persuasion to get him to tell us the whole sorry story: that the theater's tour had been a financial failure. He was faced with insurmountable debts and, in fact, the company had no means to return to Moscow. Alex began weeping as he spoke. It was a Russian tragedy.

"Darling Alex," I said, "I'm *sure* there's a solution." And Gerald and I exchanged an important look. Before the night was over, Gerald had written a check loaning him $3,000 which, even with our comfortable income, was a big stretch. As we stood at the top of the stairs bidding everyone good night, we wrapped our arms around each other.

"Well, I guess we're theater backers now," Gerald said.

"They're doing *such* important work, Dow," I replied. "Really, so revolutionary. So avant-garde."

Much later we'd learn that, under the Bolsheviks, no currency was allowed out of the country and foreign debts wouldn't be honored. We'd never see that money again. It was the first time we'd funded an artist we admired, but it wouldn't be the last. We considered it an investment in beauty and novel ideas. Really, was there anything more important?

---

NOW THAT WE'D christened the place with Russian song, we got busy making it our new home. We painted the walls a creamy white and the floors a glossy black, which we covered with white rag rugs. At the tall, front-facing windows we hung red antique curtains I'd found at Les Puces de Saint-Ouen flea market. We had the sofas and chairs upholstered in a black satin fabric, and the side tables were topped with mirrored glass. Throughout the house I placed vases of foliage—anything from a single red rose to stalks of fresh celery. And on the grand piano sat an enormous industrial ball bearing that Gerald had salvaged, which now served as a piece of sculpture.

We moved in during the spring of 1923, then began to welcome *le monde artistique* as word got around that here you could read a new chapter, sing a new opera, display your latest painting, or perform a one-act play. It didn't hurt that free food and wine were usually served. Through our doors walked such emerging names as John Dos Passos, Donald Ogden Stewart, Phillip Barry, and Archibald MacLeish. Aaron Copland and Erik Satie and Bricktop. The Crosbys, who had just formed the Black Sun Press. John and Rue Carpenter, who'd preceded us to Paris and had produced a charming music book for children.

James Joyce—whom we'd once seen downing buckets of oysters with his family at Fouquet's—came in and immediately sat down at the piano. "And now for my Irish repertory," he announced, and sang in his reedy tenor voice for nearly half an hour. His common-law wife, Nora, sat stick-straight on the sofa with a tight little smile. I wasn't sure if she was proud, or mortified, or bored. She was clearly used to playing the role of supportive consort. Between Joyce's literary brilliance and his reputation for sexual adventure, I could imagine she had put up with a lot. Or perhaps she herself was just as wild out of the public eye? Joyce's *Ulysses* had just been published by Sylvia Beach the year before, and when I finally read it—with its titillating final chapter on Molly Bloom said to be closely modeled on Nora—I knew the latter must be true.

---

PARIS WAS A repository for every possible interest, every sensual longing. I spent most days wandering the open-air markets scouting fabrics and fixtures for our home-in-progress. Or gathering provisions for Dounia, who would magically combine them into a meal that even the children loved. Gerald, meanwhile, was usually at his studio, or wandering Paris filling his *cahiers* with ideas for paintings. He'd never been completely content before, but now I saw it in his face, in his step, every day. He was preparing four works to show at the Salon des Indépendants in May, and a frisson of nerves and excitement seemed to bubble out of him.

"The traditional boundaries are gone," he told me one day as we studied several unfinished canvases in his studio. The sun poured in through the tall, dirty windows and the smell of turpentine filled me with a sense of industry and imagination. In addition to oils, watercolors, and canvases, there were ladders of several heights and industrial-size metal rulers. His canvases featured unexpected subjects in fastidious detail: the mechanical elements of machines, the minutiae of human anatomy, little architectural flourishes.

"I seem to see in miniature, but paint in monumental scale," he said. He'd become used to the larger format from our work painting theater sets. His meticulous paintings didn't seem made by hand but rather by machine. He'd sketch out a maquette, then apply a grid transferred onto an enormous canvas of airplane linen or three-ply veneer panels. I'd never seen anything like them, even among the madly innovative cubist abstracts that were now everywhere in Paris.

"Oh, Dow," I said. "Aren't you clever? You're inventing something completely fresh."

"It really *is* different, isn't it, Sal? It doesn't adhere to any particular school."

"It's unto itself. It's otherworldly."

As Gerald was preparing to debut his new paintings, he was also using his daily wardrobe to present himself as a work of art. Here was Gerald as a cowboy, here as a Chinese scholar in silk robes. Here he posed as a Spanish gaucho, or here as an *apache* dancer, with a cigarette dangling from his lip. What might have looked affected or strange on anyone else seemed to suit Gerald naturally—perhaps it was his elegant posture or his diffident expression. "My life has been a process of concealment of the personal realities," he'd written me during our courtship. At the time I hadn't really understood what he meant, but now I was beginning to see that he was always grappling with a true *acceptance* of himself—probably the result of his loveless upbringing. He was now brave enough to experiment with his image to express how he might be feeling on any particular day.

And so I tried to greet each new persona with amusement and enthusiasm. But I found myself returning to that phrase, "concealment of the personal realities." As his fascination with these exotic identities grew, our physical relationship seemed to wane. Who was he trying to be, really? I tried not to dwell on it.

Once again, I was the scaffolding. And, on most days, I was happy with that.

WE ENTERED THE Grand Palais, an art nouveau structure built for the first world's fair. I leaned my head back to take in the vaulted steel and glass roof, which rose like an enormous greenhouse. In its maze of seventy rooms were displayed six thousand paintings by both established artists like Bonnard, Ernst, Léger, Goncharova, and Picabia, and new talent—like Gerald.

He'd avoided showing his paintings to anyone, except occasionally me, because he didn't want any criticism of his work in progress. Now, after six months of reporting every day to his studio, he had four completed works: a drawing, one watercolor, and two oils. We wandered around, scrutinizing the paintings of others and searching for Gerald's pieces. When I spotted them from a distance, rather than in the close quarters of his studio, I could see them for what they truly were: testaments to the man's journey across an ocean and into a new land; the mechanics of a transformed life.

"Darling Dow," I said, squeezing his hand. "You've come home to yourself. Now look at you, here among all these avant-garde visionaries."

"The world is clearer to me now," he said. "I feel as if we've both shucked off the calluses of our puritan upbringing. We've been reborn, don't you think?" He was beaming, and his face had the delighted aspect of a small child.

I looked around at the chic crowd, buzzing with excitement about the brave new things they were seeing. We truly belonged among them now.

"Completely," I said, and gave him a kiss.

The critics agreed. The fancy arts journal, *Shadowland*, gave Gerald a special mention and the *Paris Herald* applauded his "very personal point of view in the study of machinery" and invented a new genre to describe his work: *Centrifugalist*. But the highest compliment came from our dear friend Léger, who said that Gerald was "the only *American* painter in Paris." He would show at the annual Salon for two more years.

AFTER SHARING GERALD'S nervous excitement preparing for the show and helping him with the *vernissage*, I gladly fell back into the domestic routine. Honoria was beginning to read. Baoth was demonstrating a natural athleticism, both on the playground and in any tree worth climbing. And Patrick was forming words and trying to walk. All three were already somewhat bilingual—such an instinctive gift for young children. But as French as they sounded, Gerald and I made sure they knew that they were Americans first.

He was teaching the children to sing songs from the Great American Songbook and act them out. With little to no urging, they happily performed their repertoire for our guests, who were hungry for Yankee culture. To a person—Dos Passos, MacLeish, Stewart—our literary friends were writing not about the France around them but the American experience behind them. It seemed we'd all had to leave the country to see it clearly, and to understand who we were.

Come June, we eagerly awaited the debut of Stravinsky's new ballet, *Les Noces* at the Theatre Gaîeté-Lyrique. As with *Le Sacre du Printemps*, there were delays and disagreements, so Goncharova called us in again to help finish the sets in time. The set designs were all simple shapes in flat white and brown tones, and we spent days laying paint on stretches of muslin in Diaghilev's sweltering atelier.

We simply couldn't get enough of the production, which ignored all of ballet's traditional male and female roles. The message of equality between the sexes was thrilling to me; wasn't that what Gerald and I had been trying to achieve in our own marriage? As we watched the dancers enact their modernist steps in the final rehearsal, I squeezed his hand and he squeezed mine back.

"I feel such a *part* of this, Dow," I said. "A cog in the wheel of this new, spectacular thing."

"It's a special kind of satisfaction," he said. "To be among the *corps*, one of many hands."

"Mmm-hmmm. I wonder . . . I'd just like to do something special. You know, to celebrate opening night."

He turned to look at me. "What did you have in mind?"

"I don't know. A party? Let me think on it."

Gerald was already into a fever of new activity with his painting after the response he'd received from his first exhibition. Now I wanted to find an outlet for my own creativity, to manifest something using my own gifts. This was a chance to define *myself* in our Parisian circle.

The plan came together fairly quickly. I discovered *Le Maréchal Joffre*, a converted barge docked in front of the Chambre des Deputes that served as the deputies' restaurant, closed on Sundays. The chef would be more than happy to cater a private affair.

I ordered an enormous laurel wreath with a banner inscribed *Les Noces—Hommages*, which would be suspended above the banquet table. The morning of the fete, I headed to the flower market on the Île de la Cité with my list of blooms for the table. But as I approached the stalls, my heart sank. It was a Sunday. The merchants were selling birds, not flowers. And live birds were a little too creative, even for me.

So I wandered over to Montparnasse and found a children's bazaar, where I bought bags and bags of cheap toys: fire engines, trucks, dolls, wooden animals, musical instruments, miniature clowns. Then I returned to the barge and arranged them in pyramids along the table. Under the massive wreath, it looked festive and so . . . unexpected. Perfect.

On Sunday, June 17, guests assembled on the barge's upper deck, gazing out at the last shards of sunlight reflected on the Seine. Everyone from Paris's artistic community was there, from the Ballets Russes to the Dadaists to Picasso and Jean Cocteau.

We drank endless rounds of Dom Pérignon and dined on Coquilles St. Jacques as Marcelle Meyer played Scarlatti on the barge's old upright piano and ballerinas danced in the style of Isadora

Duncan. We finished up the meal hours later with individual Grand Marnier soufflés as Goncharova wrapped her silk scarf around her head and began reading palms.

As the night faded into dawn and the guests thinned, Gerald and I began clearing the glasses that sat on every surface. Most of the centerpiece toys had gone home with the guests—adorning hats, stuffed in waistbands, pinned as corsages.

We sat down on a bench near the exit, and I kicked off my shoes. We watched as Cocteau and Tristan Tzara removed the laurel wreath and held it sideways. Then Stravinsky took a running leap and dove nimbly through the center of it, like a tiger through a flaming ring.

"Darling Sal," Gerald said. "Forget paintings that hang on walls. Tonight you created a living, breathing work of art that shall go down in the pages of history."

I smiled and lit a cigarette, exhaling a plume of smoke toward the low ceiling. I had found my métier.

## Chapter 8
### 1923

"When Johnny comes marching home again, Hurrah! Hurrah!" Gerald was marching through the shallow waves followed by Honoria, Baoth, and Mam'zelle Geron holding Patrick's hand, leading his little army along the shore like a flock of ducks. I never tired of watching his delight in his children, and their delight in him.

I reclined on a blanket under the beach umbrella, smoking a Gauloise and trying to read *This Side of Paradise*, which had come out a few years earlier. The lives of Amory Blaine and Rosalind Connage felt only too familiar to my own traditional upbringing. I kept looking up to admire the view, feel the sun on my legs, and watch my family romp in the gentle waves.

As planned the previous summer, we'd arrived at Hôtel du Cap and had the place nearly to ourselves. A Chinese diplomat and his family, hearing that the hotel would remain open with a skeletal staff, had decided to stay on. Otherwise, it was just us, a cook, a waiter, and a chambermaid in the enormous white château. We would smile and bow to the Chinese family when we passed them in the lobby, but otherwise it was a relief not to have to keep our children "seen and not heard" at all hours of the day.

La Garoupe beach was on the opposite side of the Antibes

peninsula from our hotel, in a protected little cove with its own sandy reef. From our spot on the sand, we had a wide view of rocky shore and Aleppo pines, just a few fishermen's shacks and boats at the north end of the beach. After the nonstop activity of Paris, it was divine.

Now Baoth plopped himself beside me and curled into my body on the blanket under the shade of the parasol. "I went all the way in, Mummy," he said. "Dow-Dow said I'm an aqua man."

"I can see that, Bayo. Even your hair is wet! Did you spot any fish?"

"I saw a pretty goldfish," he said. "And a big whale!"

"Goodness! Aren't you the bee's knees? You're *such* a brave swimmer for a four-year-old."

Baoth shivered a bit in the shade, so I covered him with a towel and reached for a paper carton of strawberries. He sat up and quickly began devouring them.

"Don't eat the stems," I said. "You can bury them in the sand like treasure."

I watched him in profile, his chiseled little Nordic face so like mine. I loved all my children of course, but with Baoth I felt a more urgent tug. How alike we were.

There were more of us this year. Before leaving Paris, we'd invited the Picassos to join us for a week or two "or the whole summer!" They took rooms down the hall from us, and we trekked to the beach with religious regularity. Pablo had rented a small studio just up the coast in Juan-les-Pins so he could continue working.

Besides Pablo, his wife, Olga, and their two-year-old son, Paolo, there was Pablo's mother, Señora Ruiz, visiting from Malaga. She spoke not a word of English or French, but we still managed to get along like a house on fire. Every day she arrived in the same black dress and sat in the full sun without complaint. Pablo treated her with a deference I'd never seen him show to any other woman, including his wife, and he cheerfully translated for her when communication was imperative.

For my part, I tried using my French with a Spanish accent,

hoping to land on some middle ground. "How fond we are of Pablo," I tried now in a kind of pidgin language. "What a gift he is!"

Señora Ruiz looked at me as if I were mad and Pablo erupted in his high whinny of a laugh. I have no idea what he said to her in Spanish, but she replied with a smile and a long string of Spanish words.

"When I was very little my mother always told me, 'If you become a soldier, you'll be a general,'" he explained in French. "'If you become a monk, you'll be the pope.'" He grinned in the shadow of the black felt homburg hat that he rarely took off all summer. "Instead I became a painter and voilà!" He gestured to himself. "I became Picasso."

I nodded at Señora Ruiz. "Such brilliance doesn't grow without cultivation," I said in English. "Thank goodness for mothers!"

Meanwhile, there was a kerfuffle down the beach. Gerald had recently found an American canoe at the local yacht harbor and bought it for the price of a good dinner. Now Paolo had fallen as he tried to scramble out of the boat onto the sand. Shrieking, Olga ran over to pick him up. The daughter of a Russian colonel, she was beautiful but a little tightly wound. You never forgot that she was a Ballets Russes *deuxième* dancer, so elegant and erect, but beach life with children was a bit out of her range. The Picassos had previously wintered in the more fashionable St. Raphael, and Olga clearly preferred it.

"My wife likes tea, caviar, and pastries," Pablo once told me. "But it's sausages and beans for me. Good taste is a dreadful thing! Taste is the enemy of creativity."

*Yes!* I thought. In just six words, he'd summarized how I felt about the life of fish forks and finger bowls I'd left behind in New York.

Before long, our "group de la Garoupe" had grown even more. Archie and Ada MacLeish came with their two children, Mimi and Ken. The Count and Countess Étienne de Beaumont, who always brought the party with them. The photographer François Biondo, who documented so many of the good times. Elsie de Wolfe and Sir

Charles Mendl. And Rue and John Carpenter, accompanied by their charming twenty-year-old daughter, Ginny.

The summer stretched out before us with no demands other than gathering at the beach and appearing for supper. Our mornings at the shore were anchored by our familial Murphy routine: we'd arrive around nine thirty, while the air was still cool. We organized our site—blankets, pillows, sand toys, books. We set up umbrellas and later we acquired a small canvas beach cabana for changing. Gerald would rake the beach for an hour or so before friends began arriving down the rocky path from the road. Gerald could swim out for miles, it seemed, and I read or made notes in my journal. Several of us women, having read about Swami Vivekananda at the world's fair, would practice some yoga poses. Gerald would rake the beach some more. And all around would be new ideas and boisterous laughter and songs. The fact that Gerald and I found ourselves in this artistic stew felt nothing short of magic. But somewhere deep down, I credited the girlish vision inspired by a Baudelaire poem. We hadn't merely stumbled upon this life, I told myself; we had willed it into being.

At eleven, I brought out chilled sherry and *petit sablé* biscuits to lighten our hunger. Then, by one or two, we began the slow journey back to the hotel for lunch and naps. Sometimes we'd stay longer, lunching on a baguette with a little cheese and pâté I'd bought at the *charcuterie*. There was a little cinema in Antibes that showed a newsreel and a French feature on Saturday nights, and I found a bar that would stay open for us in the evenings. Just delicious.

---

"*ATTENTION, TOUT LE monde,*" Étienne announced one afternoon. "Tomorrow your presence is requested at a 'Mad Beach Party,' held right here chez La Garoupe. Every guest must come dressed either as their true selves, or as their alter egos. No exceptions!" When several people protested that they hadn't packed costumes, he and Édith assured us that props would also be provided. The de Beaumonts were responsible for the most outrageous *fêtes* in Paris, so we didn't dare disappoint. The next day, Étienne arrived as a primitive South Pacific native and Édith wore a stunning beaded flapper bathing suit; Olga came in full tutu, including her satin toe shoes; and Picasso donned his painter's overalls, along with his black homburg. Señora Ruiz, of course, came in her usual black shroud. Gerald dressed as a French sailor, and I was a gypsy. Then we madly rummaged through an enormous wicker trunk filled with theatrical props: outlandish hats and scarves. False beards and feather boas. Satin skirts and brocade capes.

Once we were fully outfitted, we held a merry parade down the length of the beach led, of course, by Gerald miming a drum major. We posed in the Victorian fashion, seated in our American canoe, and François captured the image for posterity. I'm so glad he did. There would be many times when I'd marvel at that photo—how carefree and madcap our life had been. The innocence of youth, thinking that life would always be so good.

---

"LOOK AT YOU, so lovely and brown!" Rue was rubbing banana oil onto my back, bare in my new wool bathing suit.

"Isn't it funny?" I said. "Until this year, sun-browned skin was considered a sign of poverty." Back in East Hampton, we'd gone bathing in heavy cotton midi dresses, covered nearly head to foot, and we always carried parasols to keep our skin soft and white. But now? Suddenly bronze skin was modern, young, and free—a way to show off your short flapper shift or set off your eyes. We coined a new term for it: sunbathing.

"I heard that Coco Chanel just docked in Cannes on the Duke of Westminster's yacht," Ginny said. "She was very dark in her black tank suit and wore a matching turban. Isn't she just the tiger's spots?"

"Well, there you are," I said. I flipped my opera-length pearls down my back and started to slather oil on my arms. I'd begun wearing them that way so I wouldn't get a white line on my décolletage while sunning my front. I also remembered how chic Lady Headfort had looked when she wore her pearls down her back in London. Now people seemed to credit me with a new beach elegance. "The sun is good for them," I claimed. But secretly, it was my nod to the way I felt about our spontaneous gatherings. Every day *was* a party.

---

*LUXE, CALME, ET volupté.* How often had I thought of that phrase and silently congratulated myself on manifesting the magic of Baudelaire's poem? It was now even the title of a painting by Picasso's most worthy rival, Matisse. It became our code for those soft, luxurious days. Whenever someone would point out a beautiful vista or say something particularly poetic, we would hold aloft one finger and say, *Luxe, calme, et volupté.* Even the children had acquired the habit.

Now Pablo said it and he was looking at me. I'd spread out a pink damask tablecloth with mismatched china surrounding a vase of fresh poppies. In the center I placed a straw-covered Chianti bottle, around which I had twisted a garland of ivy. *"Tu es toujours si festive, ma Sara,"* he said approvingly.

After lunch, I found myself in my favorite spot, propped on an elbow and reclining under the umbrella (Gerald called this "Sara *en repose*"), and there he was, his elbow inches from mine. Between the warm sun, my exposed limbs, and the delicious breeze licking my hair, I always felt more aware of my body at *la plage*. Especially in Pablo's muscular presence.

He wasn't one to perform for others, but if you listened to the things he casually muttered, it was very entertaining. Now, watching the children engrossed in building a sandcastle, he sighed. "It takes a very long time to become young," he said.

"You couldn't be more right about that. I feel twenty years younger now than when I was single." I brushed some hair off my face.

"The key is to find your gift, and then give it away. You do that every day. That's why you're so happy."

"What a lovely compliment, Pablo."

I'd be lying if I said that my feelings toward Picasso were purely platonic. Those black bullet-hole eyes, that brown, compact body. There was something so primitive and masculine about the very energy that surrounded him, as well as a mischievous, puckish quality. (He'd developed a new hobby of capturing people from the rear with his Kodak camera whenever they bent down to pick something up. He'd already acquired quite a collection of derrieres.) I tried not to compare that feeling to the flat mood that had seeped into the bedroom I shared with my husband.

But our growing affection also felt safe. Gerald was right there, cavorting about the beach in his swim briefs, a knitted sailor's cap to protect his receding hairline. And there was Olga, with her pretty bow mouth and predictable bourgeois conversation. Everything just felt warm and relaxed and seductive. I felt entirely comfortable sitting with my bathing suit straps off my shoulders, my pearls draped down my back. If there was a male compliment or two, what was the harm in that?

A week or so later, Gerald and I were driving back to the Hôtel du Cap in our rented blue Renault. Pablo had invited us to his studio—a supreme compliment—to see some of his latest work.

We'd walked into the small, sunny room, with its high windows facing north and south. It was astonishing how prolific the man had been, considering he spent most days with us at the beach. Clearly, he kept late hours. A rumpled daybed sat at an angle in a corner—perhaps he spent some nights there. An easel stood in the center of the room and against all four walls were propped works in progress—oils, watercolors, sketches. While Gerald had been painting productively all year, his method was to outline, to plan, to transfer, to execute. It was a long labor. Pablo, on the other hand, just expelled creativity in every medium, seemingly without much thought. It was as if he didn't create with his mind but channeled some greater power onto the canvas.

"Voilà," he said, and propped a painting onto the easel. "I'm entering a new period." He followed it with several others. If he hadn't been standing there, I'd have thought they were done by a completely different artist. Far from his cubist work, these were realistic and romantic—all done in the classical manner of Greek vase painting. And a recurring theme quickly emerged. There was a portrait of a woman in a white linen dress, her arms crossed and her hair in a loose twist. Another of the same woman holding a child on her lap. There were several ink drawings of a female reclining on a beach, one with a scarf tied as a turban. They all had upturned noses and slightly almond-shaped eyes, like mine. Most wore long strings of pearls—and were naked. Another series depicted several nude women—*Three Modern Graces*—that were clearly Rue and Ginny Carpenter and me.

Gerald was uncharacteristically quiet, so I jumped into the pause. "Well, I guess we should be flattered!"

Pablo's face fell. "You're displeased?"

"Of course not! Not at all. I just didn't realize you were capturing us all this time." *Capturing*. I did feel captured. I just wasn't sure how I felt about it yet.

There were others, too—figures that evoked Gerald and the de Beaumonts and Olga. But I had clearly become something of a muse.

When Gerald finally spoke, his voice was full of awe. "I'm speechless with admiration, man. The way you can pivot from one style to the next—and *master* each new form! You never cease to amaze me." He made a little bow of supplication and Pablo smiled.

Now, as we pulled up to the hotel in our motorcar, I reached for Gerald's arm. "You're not upset, not even a little?"

"Why would I be upset? You've just been rendered for posterity by likely the most gifted artist of our time. I'm proud, and you should be, too."

I scanned Gerald's profile for sincerity in his expression, his voice.

"Even the nudes?"

A pause. "Did you pose nude?" Gerald was looking at me now.

"Of course not." That I would do such a thing without telling Gerald. Unthinkable.

"Well, he has a good imagination then. Anyway, let's be happy about it." He patted my thigh.

I was so relieved. Because now I realized that it *did* feel like a slight infidelity to see myself on those canvases, as if Pablo had correctly read my unspoken attraction to him.

We parked in the circular drive and Gerald turned off the ignition. "There's no doubt, though, that the man *is* in love with you."

I caught myself in a smile. Gerald had never expressed the remotest sign of jealousy in our eight years of marriage. Our mutual fealty—not just physically, but in our absolute acceptance of each other—was the foundation on which our union rested. So why did Gerald's observation give me such a twinge of satisfaction? Though we hadn't strayed with others, I couldn't remember the last time we'd actually made love. My body ached from neglect.

---

SUDDENLY, IT WAS August. Back in February, after the Salon des Indépendents, Gerald had been asked to create the American booth at a charity benefit bazaar to raise money for Russian émigrés. Though all the artistic avant-garde were involved, Gerald's booth stood out: a tableau of skyscrapers, the Great White Way, electric signs that blinked on and off. After that success, Gerald had been invited by the Ballet Suedois to create and design a short ballet to be part of its larger program the following year, and he'd recruited Cole to write the score. Now we were headed to Venice, where Cole and Linda had rented the Ca' Papadopoli, an imposing palazzo on the Grand Canal, to spend a month while Gerald and Cole worked on the project.

We left the children with Mam'zelle and boarded the overnight train across Italy to Venice. Even this far north, Italy in August is a less-than-gracious hostess. All the native Italians decamp to the mountains or the seashore for *ferragosto*, leaving the cities to the foreign tourists and grumpy help. The humidity is appalling. Even so, I was excited to show the city to Gerald, who'd never been this far east in Europe.

Ca' Papadopoli out-*luxed* anything I'd ever experienced, even in my travels with Mother. Carrera marble everywhere, massive Tiepolo classical paintings, and liveried maids and footmen at every turn. Our bedroom looked like something awaiting the pope. We'd barely unpacked when Linda issued us a printed social schedule; her smart-set was in town, and there were parties every night.

"I'm not sure how many more of these burlesques I can endure," I told Gerald on our second morning. "I thought we'd outgrown these people."

"We can always plead food poisoning."

"And give up the dinners? That's all I live for here!" The dinners *were* spectacular: creamed dried cod on polenta. Risotto braised in squid ink. Liver in caramelized onions.

"Perhaps I'll develop a nocturnal migraine," I said. "Say, about nine every evening?"

"Your secret's safe with me."

During the day, we wandered the shadowy alleys of Venice, usually getting hopelessly lost and having to stop for directions or gelato. Or we lay on chaises at the Lido and swam in the lazy Adriatic. Venice was seductive, with her hidden doorways and murky canals. Walking the narrow streets at night, we listened to the echoing calls of gondoliers, like foghorns in the dark.

But as the days wore on, I was struck with a sense of foreboding. Gerald and Cole were best pals, dating back to their days at Yale when neither felt comfortable with the masculine rituals and tribal culture of the typical Yale man. One afternoon I sat in the shade of our Lido cabana and watched as Cole and a group of male friends romped on a large float that was anchored offshore. There was a physical familiarity between them that went beyond mere friendship. "Bent" was the term I'd heard used to describe it. Cole posed and danced on the float to the music from the Lido band, performing with a feminine flamboyance I'd never seen from him in Paris or Antibes. Gerald lingered at the edge of the group but sang along and laughed at Cole's antics.

Living in Paris had exposed me to the full continuum of sexual behavior—the male ballet dancers, the men in drag, the Sapphists—but those were acquaintances, not friends. I'd never given too much thought to the idea of the "lifelong bachelor" but, despite his marriage to Linda, I now fully understood that Cole was such a one. The two were living increasingly separate lives, apart from their formal arrangement. And in Cole's entertaining narrative, I began to discern that he preferred not just the company of men, but a kind of "rough trade." Private parties, unmarked clubs, off-duty gondoliers. That new knowledge was a little hard, but not life-changing. I could still love Cole, despite his peccadilloes.

But tonight the scales had fallen from my eyes. At after-dinner cocktails on San Marco Piazza, Cole jumped up and began playing with the bar's band. He called Gerald up to sing duets and before long they were singing "Yes Sir, That's My Baby" and mugging for the crowd in a coquettish way. This was something Gerald would *never* have done in France—or New York, or anyplace else—but in the exotic Venetian air, under Cole's influence, he seemed to show a different side. Here was a quality I hadn't seen before—or hadn't admitted to myself. Around Cole and his friends, Gerald was lighter, more amusing, a little showier and more extroverted. They seemed to share a subtly coded secret language. It was the first time I'd ever felt left outside of his golden aura of attention.

I sat there, stunned, watching the two men perform. Suddenly, after eight years of marriage, I saw the man I should have seen all along. How different was our marriage from the Porters' "arrangement"? How had I not seen this before? I couldn't move, couldn't even reach for my drink. A glaring spotlight of shame seemed to illuminate me from some heavenly rafter. No one looked my way, but I had the sense that everyone was smirking, averting their eyes. *You foolish, foolish girl.*

---

SOMEHOW, AN HOUR later, I made it back to the palazzo with Gerald. We were in for the night, thank heaven, while the Porters and a million of their closest friends moved on to another social bacchanal. Brushing my hair in the gilded mirror at the garishly rococo vanity table, I studied Gerald's reflection, reclining behind me on the bed.

"I think I finally understand," I said quietly.

"Understand what, my Sal?" He didn't look up. He was busily scribbling in his worn leather notebook—ideas, no doubt, for another painting.

I paused, then exhaled. "I think I understand now what you've meant by your 'defect of character.' All this time, I thought you meant your heightened sensitivity, your depressions. But now I see what's been behind those feelings." I was trying to sound matter-of-fact. But my heart was rattling against my ribs, and I was fighting a quaver in my voice.

Gerald put down his notebook and stared at me from across the room. Our eyes met in the mirror. "Sara," he said, and then went silent.

Nearly twenty years of knowing this man, of feeling that we were twin souls, a united entity. Now I wondered if I really knew him at all.

"*Tell* me," I said finally. "Tell me what you've been hiding from me all these years." I turned to face him, but an enormous marble room still stretched between us.

Gerald's confidence and talent had grown in leaps and bounds since we'd arrived in Paris. He'd *discovered* himself here. But now he looked like an elk seen through the crosshairs of a rifle. His voice was shaking, too.

"I haven't been hiding it. I've been trying to explain it, without ruining everything." He looked so miserable. "Come here, Sal," he finally said. He opened his arms, and I went to lie down beside him, my head tucked into his shoulder.

"I've told you that my life has been a process," he said. Big sigh. "A concealment of the personal realities. I've *tried* to tell you that, at least."

"And now that we're abroad, away from our families, you can let them out?" Apparently, that's what everyone was doing—in Paris, in Antibes, in Venice. Everyone but me.

"I do feel freer here," Gerald admitted. "And spending so much time around Cole and his friends, I guess I unclenched my tight grip on my—" He stopped. "On myself."

I shook my head, and we let those words sink in. "Oh Dow," I said. "What's going to become of us?" The pressure behind my eyes, I knew, was tears. I was trying desperately not to let them escape.

He wrapped both arms tightly around me. "Nothing. Nothing is going to change, Sal. It's *you* I love. You and our three Murphettes. You will always own me, heart and soul."

"But something *has* changed, Dow. I now understand why we don't make love anymore. At least hardly ever." He loved my heart and soul. Just not my body.

Gerald turned and held me to face him. "I'm trying to become the man you fell in love with. I'm working *so* hard at it." He too was fighting back tears.

"I know you are."

He kissed me, and I gave into it. But once we'd turned out the light, I couldn't sleep for most of the night, and I felt Gerald awake beside me too. We both knew something had shifted.

---

THE NEXT MORNING, we took breakfast on the little balcony of our room, sunlight blazing off the canal and into our bowls of caffé latte. We'd been in Venice two weeks, and Gerald and Cole had made little progress on their ballet, for all the partying and fooling around.

I snuffed my cigarette into the garish crystal ashtray. "Well, I'm going to leave you to it," I said suddenly. "I've had enough of Venice in August."

Gerald looked genuinely crestfallen. "Sal, no. We'll buckle down, I promise."

"I hope you will. But I'm serious. I miss the children, and Linda Porter is getting on my last nerve. You stay and work with Cole—and I mean *work*!—and I'll be there with open arms to greet you at the station in September." I stood up and went inside to pack, leaving Gerald speechless on the balcony.

Then I booked a first-class ticket on the afternoon train. I wasn't angry or upset anymore. Just eager to be alone on that rhythmic, pulsing wagon-lit. I made my excuses to the Porters, then Gerald took me to the station and kissed me as we said goodbye on the platform. But once I'd settled into my seat, staring out the window at the Italian countryside and then the wide blue-green Mediterranean, my mind circled back to the hurt. How had this not come up before? How had Gerald thought that he could keep me fooled for our entire marriage? I knew that he was in deep denial about his real feelings and urges, that he hadn't even dared admit it to himself, let alone me. But surely he'd known all along.

I also knew he truly loved me, I did. But I also couldn't help feeling that I'd been played as a fool. The accommodating, supportive wife. Who came with a trust fund! It felt so clichéd. It wasn't until we reached the Italian-French frontier that I was able to calm myself down. Once we passed into France, I gratefully counted the blue-and-white enameled signs at each train station. Menton. Roquebrune-Cap Martin. Villefranche-sur-Mer. Cagnes-sur-Mer. Antibes.

---

I PUT MY key into the door of our suite at the Hôtel du Cap, and the moment I set foot inside I was bombarded by three projectiles—two blondes and a redhead—in matching pajamas. "Maman! Mummy! Mère!" They were followed by a flustered Mam'zelle holding three toothbrushes.

"Madam, you are early! Is everything all right?"

"Everything's wonderful now, Mam'zelle," I said, kneeling down and kissing the tops of three fragrant heads. "I just couldn't stay away from these little savages." My balance felt immediately restored. I was myself again.

"Mummy, look what I did!" Honoria pulled down her lower lip to show a gaping hole in the front of her mouth.

"You lost a *tooth*?" It had barely been loose when we left.

Baoth held up an arm and flexed. "And I've been getting big muscles!"

"Maman!" Patrick, just two and a half, thrust his stuffed toy dog at me.

"I have missed you sooo much," I said, wrapping my arms around all three. "You're just the berries!"

Honoria pulled back from my embrace. "Did you bring us presents from Venice?"

"As a matter of fact, I did. But they're still in my trunk, which Didier hasn't brought up yet. So all *good* children will be patient until the morning, when they'll have a surprise at breakfast."

"Hooray, hooray!" roared the crowd.

"In the meantime, it looks as if Mam'zelle's waiting to brush your teeth. And when that's done, we'll all have a story on Mummy's bed, okay?"

They scampered off like rabbits in flannel.

"'*Tazzywaller, I must have another lion,*' said Mustafa of Mudge, giving his blue whiskers a terrible tweak. '*Another lion, Tazzywaller, at once!*'" I was reading to them from the newest book in the *Famous Oz Stories* series by L. Frank Baum and my audience was rapt. With my arms around their warm bodies, secure in my familiar bed, all seemed well again. Gerald still loved me, and I still loved him. What we'd created together was simply too precious to pull apart.

THE NEXT AFTERNOON, I opened our closet. There were my things on the left—mostly flowing, floral dresses, a few skirts, scarves, and hats. On the right were Gerald's clothes—an abundance of custom-tailored suits with his new Antibes wardrobe that he'd found in a local naval supply: striped sailor's jerseys, duck shorts, canvas belts, knit watch caps. Somehow the striped jersey had already found its way into Chanel's latest summer collection. But that had been Gerald's discovery.

What heterosexual man had such a refined, imaginative sense of style? I fingered the fine linen and looked at the beautiful cut—of course he'd even had the Navy surplus things tailored. How had I not seen it? How had I thought I could have it all—a stylish man *and* a heterosexual husband?

I stood there musing at the evidence of Gerald's true character, which I'd so successfully denied to myself. Then I put on a periwinkle-blue linen shift and my opera pearls and pinned my hair up in a chignon. I went out to the drive where the Renault was parked and drove myself to Juan-les-Pins. I parked on the Avenue Louis Gallet and knocked at number 46.

No answer. I knocked again and waited. Just when I was turning to go, the door opened abruptly, and there stood Picasso looking rumpled in a cotton polo shirt, faded shorts, and sandals.

His face was blank and dark as he took in my appearance. "*Et Gerald?*" he finally asked, looking over my shoulder to the street.

"*Toujours à Venise*," I said.

"*Ah, oui.*"

He led me into the room, pungent with turpentine and new canvas, until we stood in a square of sunlight on the floor. He stared at me for what felt like a long time, those piercing black eyes like one of the African masks hanging on the walls. Then he reached up and slowly undid my chignon, carefully placing the pins in a dish on his worktable and letting my hair fall down my back.

Then he undid the rest of me.

With a rush I could almost hear, a wide, gaping sinkhole of desire opened up and I let myself fall into it. He smelled like sweat with a little vetiver, a surprising note. After that, I didn't think. I just let my body go to some natural, primitive place and followed it obediently. Who knew that it could do such remarkable things?

Back at the hotel, I lay in the bath for a long time, until the water was cloudy and cool.

If I held it in my mind just right, the afternoon's adventure rang with a kind of purity. I knew I should feel as if I'd given something away, something sacred and irreplaceable. But instead, it felt as if I'd restored a sense of balance. Was that only my pride speaking? Was this simply a matter of romantic revenge, a tit for tat? Gerald had sworn that he hadn't been physically unfaithful to me. So why did my own infidelity feel so thrilling? Because Gerald's infidelity wasn't a single affair. It was how he *was*, for life.

I returned to Picasso's studio three more times over the next ten days, and each time I could feel myself inching a little more closely back to Gerald. After that, we both knew I wouldn't be back.

The train pulled to a halt in a combustion of brakes and steam. I stood on the platform scanning the crowd for a familiar silhouette, tall and fair and elegant. When I was just beginning to think that we'd missed each other—was he already at the curb, or had he missed the train entirely?—there he was, in his beige traveling suit, belted at the waist, and his straw Borsalino hat. He ambled toward me, beaming a smile.

"Hello, my darling Sal."

"Hello, my precious Dow."

The kiss that followed contained multitudes: I'm sorry, I love you, all is forgiven, we are still one.

We made our way to the blue Renault at the curb and awaited the porter and wagon carrying Gerald's three trunks. Then Gerald turned the key, and we drove home.

## Chapter 9
### 1923-1924

In late October, I sat in a velvet loge seat at the Théâtre des Champs-Élysées, reviewing the printed playbill for Within the Quota that Gerald and I had designed. The curtain rose to reveal his daring stage backdrop, an enormous reproduction of an American newspaper with headlines that lampooned current events back in the States, from immigration and Prohibition to society gossip.

The ballet portrayed a penniless Swedish immigrant who eventually becomes a movie star. Along the way he meets such American stereotypes as a jazz baby, a millionairess, a cowboy, a colored gentleman, a social reformer, and America's Sweetheart. Gerald and Cole's jazzy spoof on American culture was a triumph—the opening-night audience ate it up with a spoon. By the new year, it would be touring the American provinces.

After the curtain call, as we exited the theater onto Avenue Montaigne, a photographer snapped Gerald in his velvet cape and a reporter from the *New York Herald* stopped us on the sidewalk. "Mr. Murphy! Can you tell us what inspired you to make such a bold statement about American culture?" he shouted. "Aren't you yourself an expatriate?"

Gerald grinned. "It's just an expression of the way America looks to me from over here," he said. "Paris is bound to make a man either more or less American."

I'd never seen him so pleased with himself. And I was pleased, too. In his own way, he was achieving a kind of stardom here in Paris, away from all the family expectations. Perhaps with a little public adulation, Gerald could relax more into a middle ground between exhilaration and black moods. I hooked my arm in his and smiled for the camera.

We took a taxi to Joe Zelli's Royal Box in Montmartre, which had eclipsed the Boeuf sur la Toit as the hottest nightclub of the moment. Donald Ogden Stewart, Dos Passos, Archie and Ada MacLeish, and the Porters all joined us for sidecars and caviar, with music by Eugene Bullard's jazz band. We'd also heard about an exciting new Negro singer named Josephine Baker who was performing a "Danse Sauvage" wearing a skirt strung with papier-mâché bananas and not much else.

I was circling the dance floor with Dos, who was making me laugh in his deadpan way. We felt satisfied—as if we'd really *done* something—although the achievement, of course, was really Gerald's and Cole's. But they'd said something big on behalf of our whole expat tribe.

"And the millionairess, with her golf-ball-sized pearls? She certainly struck a familiar note," Dos was saying.

"I don't know what you mean," I laughed. "We haven't seen Hoytie in ages." We'd heard about her though, stepping on toes all over Paris society. You'd never know she'd attended the finest finishing schools, she was so socially inept.

"Your laugh is one of my favorite things about you," Dos said. "It's how I imagine Louise Brooks would sound, if we could only hear her voice. Husky. Full-throated."

"It's the cigarettes." I laughed again. "You're such a funny egg."

"And you, Mrs. Murphy, are a sphinx. You always look as if you hold the secrets to the universe. Do you?"

"I'll never tell." I smiled and glanced over at our table. Gerald was leaning slightly toward Archie, who was speaking in his ear, but his eyes caught mine before Dos twirled me back to the center of the floor. Since Venice, it seemed, we'd each kept a slightly closer watch on the other. An unspoken agreement that neither of us would stray too far.

The song ended and we were making our way back to the table when there was a loud commotion near the entrance.

"Get your paws *off* me!" a female voice shrieked. "This is a Lanvin!"

A man's voice chimed in. "My good man, don't be such a wet blanket. We're just here to have a good time."

"I believe the Fitzgeralds have arrived," Donald announced to us as we returned to the table. "They always appear with such fanfare."

I looked over and saw a head of glossy blonde marcelled hair, a shimmer of pale-blue beaded fringe, and a man in a tuxedo pushing through the crowd to the dance floor, where the couple suddenly stopped and wobbled a bit, searching for balance. I'd heard of them, of course—expatriate Paris was a very small town. He the author of *This Side of Paradise* and *The Beautiful and Damned*, she the "It Girl" of the flapper set. But I'd never seen them at such close range.

"They're staying at the Ritz, I hear," Donald said. "Apparently they order champagne by the gallon and routinely leave their rooms in complete shambles."

"I guess that's your job when you've been appointed Mr. and Mrs. Jazz Age," Gerald said. "It's got to be quite a mantle to uphold."

"They can be charming when they're not in their cups," Dos said. He'd known them in New York through publishing friends. "I'll introduce you sometime. Before the sun's over the yardarm."

"Get an early start," Donald said. "With the Fitzgeralds, I hear the sun passes the yardarm at about ten in the morning."

I watched, fascinated, as Zelda began dancing alone in the center of the room, either unaware of the bemused stares or encouraged by them. She was utterly captivating with her youth, her golden beauty, her style. There was also something a little sad about her obvious inebriation, her lack of control. In that she was hardly alone in those days, but she commanded more attention than your run-of-the-mill drunken flapper. She had some unnamable quality that compelled you to stare. Scott sat at a nearby table and watched with a sullen gaze.

Before long, the musicians cranked up the volume and we could feel the air shift, as if the moon had entered a new phase, and the party became more charged. We left soon after.

―

IN FEBRUARY WE returned to the Grand Palais for the annual Salon des Indépendents. Gerald had been hard at work on a new painting, and the *vernissage* had been particularly complicated because of its enormous size. Now we milled among the crush of people, looking for his piece.

Passing through a doorway into the American gallery we saw, against the brown walls, countless paintings, dark and small and politely traditional. And at the far end of the room, dwarfing all the others not just in size but in color, was Gerald's work, *Boatdeck*. Twelve feet wide by eighteen feet high, it depicted the bright red smokestacks and black steam pipes of a giant ocean liner. It was so massive and alive, it seemed to glow. A large crowd had gathered at the base of the painting, creating a collective murmur.

I'd seen the painting as a work in progress but not finished and displayed. Now, surrounded by all the dull little peahens of the other paintings, it had become a magnificent peacock.

"Oh Dow!" I said. "It's like something from another century."

Over the next few weeks, Gerald was again sought out by the international press and the crowds kept coming to see his painting. Some said it was immodest, too loud, too commercial.

"After all, it *is* the Grand Palais," Gerald told a reporter. "I'm truly sorry to have caused such a bother with my little picture."

―

*DON'T COME AS you are, come as a car,* the invitation had read, hand-delivered by a uniformed footman. It was early spring and the Comte de Beaumont was holding a new charity gala, the Automotive Ball. Not for the first time, I was grateful for Gerald's flair for design. He wrapped me in yards of aluminum foil with loose rolls of silver wire around my neck and a headdress of fine pewter-colored chains. I carried a round side-mirror on a long walking stick and wore enormous driving goggles on my face.

Gerald's own costume was even more elaborate: a tailored singlet of molded metal panels, including screws and gauges, and a tall toque-style hat that looked like it was made from a car's bumper. It was fantastically impractical, of course—we could barely sit down or dance. But the gasps of approval made the effort worthwhile. I'd never seen such an assortment of outlandish costumes, and ours trumped them all.

As Gerald had helped me to don the fragile costume earlier that evening, I smiled to think of the eighteenth-century white brocade gown I'd worn at my debutante ball in Cincinnati so many years before. I adjusted my goggles and grabbed my stick. Truly, a woman of the future!

In the taxi home, I eased my silver satin heels off my swollen feet. "Well, that was amusing," I said, laying my head on Gerald's shoulder.

"What a spectacle," he said. "If we chose to go into the costuming business, I daresay we could be fully employed year-round in this town."

I turned my gaze out the window, with the Pont de Sully speeding by in a rainy blur of lights. "I'm not sure I can take many more of these fiascos, darling. I'm simply wrung out."

Gerald laughed. "You're not enchanted with the demimonde?"

I pulled back. "You enjoyed it?"

"I'm teasing, Sal. I'm as exhausted as you are. I think the problem is, we don't take our amphetamines."

"Why is it that everyone else will stay out until dawn but we can't wait to get home?" I asked.

"Because we have a home that we love," he said, and kissed the top of my chain-mail wig. "Filled with three stupendous children."

"Let's go in and just stare at their sleeping faces," I said. "It's all the amusement I need."

"That's the best offer I've received all night."

---

AS IT TURNED out, it wasn't Dos who would introduce us to the Fitzgeralds, but Gerald's sister, Esther. Like his brother, Fred, Esther had also migrated to Paris and, like Hoytie, she ran with a crowd of free-thinking women. Her latest obsession was the writer Natalie Barney, whose Rue Jacob salons had become legendary. But Esther was a remarkable talent in her own right; she'd been known as an intellectual prodigy since her adolescence.

We'd invited her to dinner at La Coupole and that afternoon she sent word that she'd be bringing "a very American couple you absolutely *must* meet." Gerald sighed—he always disliked any disruption of the approved plan. But we hadn't seen Esther much in Paris and so wrote back that of course we were *very* excited to meet her friends.

At the appointed hour, Esther entered and approached our table—dressed, as always, from head to toe in black; her short, wiry hair combed severely across her forehead; and her lazy eye taking in the side view. Behind her came the loud couple from Zelli's, but this time they appeared sober and polite. After making introductions, Esther said, "You already know Scott's first two books, I'm sure. Now he's at work on another novel, set on Long Island!"

Over a tower of *fruits de mer* and two bottles of brut champagne, Scott filled us in on the book's theme—the green light across the bay, the disembodied eyes on the oculist's billboard, the valley of ashes.

"It's called *Trimalchio*," Zelda explained. "Based on an ancient satire of a man who pretends to be rich." Zelda's Alabama accent was like butter beans and honeysuckle.

"*The Satyricon* by Petronius," Scott laughed. "But that's the thinnest possible summary!"

"Well, excuse me for trying to be intellectual, Scott," Zelda shot back. "I know you'd prefer me to just be nice and feminine and affectionate." She mimed a stupid smile.

Scott gave her a dark look. "It's a novel about reinvention."

Gerald tried to soften the mood. "I'm intrigued," he said, and Scott suddenly seemed about fifteen as he described his new effort. Unlike the dissipated figure we'd seen at Zelli's, he was determined to write a novel that pierced the very heart of the twentieth-century American experience. He was a Princeton man but seemed to hold some lingering regret about his college experience that clearly reminded Gerald of Yale. Scott had also been stationed at Camp Mills on Long Island, awaiting his orders to ship overseas when the Armistice was declared. Both men were so different, but united by those common regrets and the desire to rise above them.

Meanwhile, I chatted with Zelda, so pretty and vivacious in her peach chiffon dress and rhinestone hair clips. But there was also a lurking intelligence and wit that bubbled up at unexpected moments. She seemed to be trying very hard to be on her best behavior, yet her native smarts kept showing through.

I mentioned the glamorous photo of Scott and Zelda that had recently appeared on the cover of *International Magazine*. Her blue almond eyes looked almost Oriental, surrounded by that curly nimbus of blond hair. "My Elizabeth Arden face," she smirked. "I'm really only myself when I'm somebody else—someone I've endowed with all these wonderful qualities from my imagination."

"But who *are* you when you're not someone else?" I asked. Zelda was like a frothy dime store novel on the outside, an intriguing murder-mystery inside. Her perfect youth, combined with her unexpected intellect, was seductive.

Zelda thought and then sighed. "All I want to be is very young and very irresponsible and to live my life as my own," she said. "And then die in my own way, to please myself."

"Goodness, that sounds like quite an assignment!" I put my hand on her arm, which was surprisingly muscular. "But I think you're well on your way." I'd never been this girl, even in my debutante days. She was the opposite of everything I'd ever tried for, and yet I couldn't help but like her—though I suspected she would make her life more difficult than necessary in the years ahead.

"Thank you, Say-rah," she said in her Southern belle accent. She did look genuinely grateful.

In the taxi on the way home, I turned to Gerald. "What did you think?"

"They're a handful," he said, "but clearly worth the effort." We both agreed that they'd make a wonderful addition to our summer in Antibes.

## Chapter 10
### 1924

We were eagerly making plans for our next season on the Riviera, and whom we would invite to join us. There would be many uninvited guests too: word had gotten out about the pleasures of the Côte d'Azur in the summer, and growing crowds had been traveling south to try them. Le train bleu was becoming crowded with affluent tourists making the trip from Calais or Paris to the Mediterranean. It was becoming, in a term I hate, de rigueur.

"I need to write to Sella about reserving the hotel again next year," Gerald said. We could feel the days in Paris getting a little longer, a little warmer. I could almost smell the salty air of Antibes. "Do we want the same rooms, or should we be higher up?"

"I was thinking of a house," I said. We were sitting on a green wooden bench at Parc Monceau as the children ran circles around us, Honoria and Baoth at full steam, Patrick toddling to keep up. I was *la station service*, the gas station, and every time a child would pass, I would pop a tangerine section into their mouth. "*Service, service!*" they cried. From Patrick's mouth it came out "Saw-*ees!*"

"Hmmm. Renting a house." I could see the wheels turning in Gerald's gaze.

"No, buying a house."

"Buying a house! What an extraordinary idea."

In the distance, framed by willows, a crescent of ruined marble columns circled the pond—one of the park's eighteenth-century "follies."

"We could go as often as we like and stay as long as we like," I said. "Antibes could become our base, with our pied-à-terre here in Paris. It could become a real home. What do you think?" For the first time, *I* was initiating our next chapter. It felt good.

Neither of us had any intention of returning to the States, not for the foreseeable future. And I'd begun feeling crowded by the invasion of all those other pleasure-seekers. For me, paradise was our little family, or a table of friends. We needed a courtyard, not a boulevard of cafés.

"I think you're a woman of big ideas, Mrs. Murphy."

I smiled and popped another orange section into Honoria's mouth. "Let's do find an agent right away, Dow-Dow."

TWO WEEKS LATER, Gerald and I were being led around the hills of Antibes by M. Guy Laurent, a small, officious man with an enormous ring of keys and the manner of a tourist official. We were looking for something large enough for five Murphys plus a few houseguests, a view of the sea. Room for a painting studio. Something we could renovate and make our very own. And a garden. Gerald hadn't lost his passion for landscaping but had never found the right property to put it into practice.

Round and round we drove, peeking into homes both occupied and left behind. Most of them were vacation villas left vacant most of the year. But they were either too expensive, too opulent, or too depressing. Nothing felt remotely right.

By our second day out with Monsieur Laurent, he'd become used to our impossible standards. "I don't think you'll care for this one," he said. "But it does have a garden." Just below the Antibes lighthouse on the narrow Chemin des Mougins, we turned into a gate and down a sloped drive to a small, unpretentious chalet with a pointed roof. It belonged to a French army officer who'd spent most of his career as an attaché in the Near East, Laurent explained. Each year he'd brought back exotic trees and plants—ever-bearing lemons, olives, Arabian maples, black and white figs—all of which were now lush and mature.

We wandered through the terraced garden, sloping toward the sea and traversed by gravel paths. Nearly two acres of plantings: heliotrope, mimosa, jasmine, orange and lemon, lavender. Everything was abundant, Laurent said, because the hillside protected it from the bitter mistral winds. The house opened onto a large brick terrace, in the middle of which sat an enormous linden tree. I could see us eating under that tree all spring and summer long. In the evenings, the fragrance of the citrus would be intoxicating.

I looked at Gerald's face, which now held the expression of a boy who'd just met Babe Ruth.

"We'll take it," I said. We hadn't even stepped inside or asked the price.

By the time we were on the northbound train, Gerald and I were already sketching out ideas for the new house. We would pay the asking price of three hundred fifty thousand French francs, about a quarter of my annual income, and on the deed Gerald would list his profession as *artiste peintre*. It was the biggest expense we'd ever taken on and felt a little scary, but I didn't care. It was the best idea I'd ever had.

"It needs a name," I said. "Something uniquely us."

Gerald fetched some colored pencils from his bag and scribbled for a while. By the time we arrived in Lyon, he held up a sketch. Down half the page was a gold star on a blue field with five white stars along the side. The other half page was red and white stripes. Against this background, all in capital letters, the name Villa America.

"Exquisite," I said. Our family crest.

IN THE MEANTIME, we were outgrowing our apartment on the quai des Grands Augustins. It might have been perfect for a young couple, but add three young children plus Mam'zelle and Dounia, who came in to cook each day, and it was as tight as a gnat's chuff. We decided to keep the apartment for late nights but move the *ménage* to a place with more room and a yard. We settled on a gorgeous brick and gabled house in Saint-Cloud, a suburb just fifteen minutes by train from the Paris center. From its upper windows, you could still see the tip of the Eiffel Tower poking up across the Seine.

ONE NIGHT IN late June, we were back at Theatre des Champs-Élysées, where a one-act ballet by Cocteau, *Le train bleu,* was being performed by the Ballets Russes. The curtain was a replica of Picasso's *Deux femmes courant sur la plage.* The costumes, by Chanel, mimicked the French sailors' outfits that Gerald had appropriated himself. The Cubist sets featured our striped beach cabanas and umbrellas. And many of the movements appeared to be inspired by women doing yoga on the beach. It was official: our summer Riviera had become *à la mode.*

"But Cocteau hasn't even *been* to La Garoupe," I whispered to Gerald.

"Yes, but he and Picasso are thick," he said. "Our secret's out. Thank God we'll have Villa America."

In fact, we wouldn't have Villa America for another two years. We'd hired a couple of brilliant young American architects and renovations had begun, but it would still take time. We'd be bunking at the Hôtel du Cap for another season.

GERALD WAS TAKING the train into Paris every day to paint at his studio. After his triumph at the second Salon des Indépendents, his imagination and confidence were both on the ascendancy. One day, after shopping in the 14th, I stopped in to check on him and his work in progress. I always loved the light and smell of his studio—his brushes meticulously cleaned and standing upright in a jar like a bouquet, his paint tubes arranged chromatically.

He was sitting on a stool in an almost trance-like state, studying his maquette and transcribing his sketch onto a grid on the larger canvas. At my greeting, he looked up and grinned.

"Hello, wife."

"What brilliant things have you been up to, *mon peintre*?" I strolled around the room, taking in various oil paintings in progress, and stopped before one. Against a large box of Three Star safety matches lay an almost heraldic arrangement of a red fountain pen—exactly the sort of thing sold at Mark Cross and a symbol of Gerald's past life—and a silver safety razor, the Gillette model that had usurped his own design back in 1920. He was still making sense of his past.

"You've done something interesting here with perspective," I said, putting my nose close to the canvas to inhale the fresh paint. "The pen and the razor are almost three-dimensional, while the box of matches is flat, from two different perspectives. How clever you are!" I looked again, from a different angle, and squinted. "I'd call it a realistic still life, but with an abstract representation."

"That's just what I've been trying to do," he said, giving my shoulder a squeeze. "*Re*-present real objects that I've always admired, along with purely abstract forms."

The canvas on which he was working was still in its embryonic stage, but I could see his eye for precision already at work. On another, a gold pocket watch—perhaps inspired by the one I'd given him upon our engagement?—had been disassembled across the six-foot canvas, a montage of gears and casings and screws in more than fourteen different shades of gray with occasional accents of gold and brown. The required patience and craftsmanship were astonishing—the precise lines often had to be made with brushes as fine as a single hair.

"Well, at least it's keeping you out of trouble," I said, and he knew what I meant. Why was I joking about this? I still watched Gerald carefully when he was around men like Cole. But Gerald didn't do well under a firmer hand, and I was trying to keep my admonishments light.

"Aw, Miz Murphy, I ain't aimin' for no trouble," he said, and gave me a bashful grin. We were speaking in subtitles. I knew that.

---

THE PAINTINGS WOULD earn Gerald more acclaim from the art press at the spring Salon des Indépendants. During the vernissage for the show, we wandered the galleries and stopped to admire *The Farm* by Joan Miró. All browns and oranges against a flat blue sky, a blend of modernistic and folkloric styles. "It looks like our vision for Villa America," I said. "I hope we can keep that rustic feel."

Suddenly we became aware of a handsome young man—tall and muscular, with thick black hair and a matching mustache.

"It looks like so many places I've passed on the train in Spain," he said. His grin was the smile of cowboys and movie stars.

"Gerald Murphy," Gerald said, extending his hand, "and my wife, Sara. I believe Dos Passos introduced us at the Dingo a few months ago."

Ernest Hemingway took his hand and shook it hard, then we turned back to the painting.

"It's a work of primitive realism with the formal vocabulary of cubism," Gerald explained.

"It's what I'm trying to do with my writing," Hemingway said. "Boil everything down to its simplest geography."

"You should buy it," Gerald said. "It's only twenty-four hundred francs. It'll be worth twice that in a few years."

"Ha! That's more than my monthly rent," Hemingway said.

Gerald later told me that he'd considered buying the painting and presenting it as a gift on the spot but sensed that Hemingway's pride would make that a problem.

"Well, your instincts are correct," he said instead. "It's a very good painting."

---

BEFORE WE LEFT for Antibes, I underwent my own transformation. I'd been stubbornly hanging onto my curly, dark-blond locks, still pinning them up in a classic chignon while every other woman in Paris had long since bobbed her hair. I just wasn't ready to follow the flapper crowd. But one evening as we sat near the bar at Le Select, I watched an androgynous British woman surrounded by a small crowd of fawning men. We were near enough to hear her swearing like a sailor and challenging several to a game of cards. My long floral dresses and my pinned-up hair suddenly felt like a remnant of my traditional upbringing. Miss Spence's finishing school. The girl that Mother wanted me to be.

"I see you've discovered Duff Twysden," Caresse Crosby said, following my gaze. A few months before, she'd decided that Polly was too plain a name for her exotic character and had chosen the motto "Always yes, Caresse." She and Harry had been busy saying yes to everything, including smoking opium and starting a small publishing house. "They say her list of lovers could fill a telephone book."

"She's so lanky and handsome," I said. "She's one degree this side of a boy."

"It's called an Eton crop," Caresse said. "For obvious reasons."

Indeed, her hair was as short as that of a schoolboy. It wasn't a style that would work on me, with my curves. But there was something about her androgyny that heightened her femininity. The way her short hair made her neck as long as a swan's. The way her long, loose sweater fell over her flat chest and no hips. The lack of jewelry or scarf or purse. She was so confident, she needed none of those accoutrements of womanhood.

The next day I came home from the *salon de coiffure* with a breeze on my neck and a halo of wavy hair around my face.

"Mummy!" cried Honoria. "You look like Clara Bow!"

"Do you like it?" I asked and crouched down for the children to run their fingers through my new waves. I felt as liberated as the day I'd abandoned my corset.

When Gerald arrived home, he did a double take. "You'd be a knockout no matter what your hairstyle," he said. I worried he didn't like it.

But getting ready for bed that night, he came over and ran his lips along the back of my bare neck. "Whole new geographies," he whispered.

I turned to face him. "Perhaps you can find a place to plant your flag?"

"Gladly," he said, and raised me up to kiss him. "Mundus Novus, here I come."

Maybe a little androgyny could do us some good.

# Chapter 11
## 1924-1925

June arrived, hot and dry, and we were back at the Hôtel du Cap for another summer with friends on the beach. Stewart was there, and Dos Passos, and the Picassos. Also the MacLeishes, Archie and Ada, who had grown to be our closest friends. Dow had initially avoided Archie because he'd heard that he'd been a Skull and Bones man at Yale. Once they met, however, we two couples became inseparable. Ada, with her gorgeous soprano voice, was pursuing a concert career and was prone to bursting into arias at unexpected moments. I thought she was the tiger's stripes.

Later that month, the Fitzgeralds joined us—not at the hotel but from a villa they'd rented up the coast in Valescure. We couldn't wait, not just for the fun new energy they'd bring to our picnics, but because their two-year-old daughter, Scottie, would fit right in with our children and Paolo Picasso. Between Gerald and me and our four siblings, there was only one other grandchild—Olga's son, Stuyvie Fish. Our own children had met their grandfathers on only a few occasions, and there was no flock of cousins as I'd grown up with. Despite the perfection of our own little family, I missed a larger brood.

So it made my heart swell to see them have an extended family like this. Honoria, now six and a half, delighted in being mother hen and Baoth, five, was happily the oldest boy. Patrick just did his best to keep up with the older kids—always the smaller, quieter child. Under the watchful gaze of Mam'zelle and the Fitzgeralds' nanny, they made our little stretch of sand into their own private playground.

But trouble was brewing this side of paradise. While Scott was feverishly working on his new novel, Zelda had discovered the French airbase in nearby Fréjus and was spending her days on the beach there with a squadron of young aviators. By the time the Fitzgeralds joined us at La Garoupe, something was clearly amiss.

"And this is our very good friend, Edouard Jozan," Zelda said, cupping her palm on the bronzed cheek of the young French god who had accompanied them. "Eddie and I are competing for who's the strongest swimmer. I think he's been letting me win!" Zelda was bronze from the daily sun, her light blue swimsuit showing off her slender body.

I looked to Scott, who seemed blissfully unaware of the energy clicking between his wife and the aviator. "Jozan's been keeping an eye on her while I'm slaving away on *Trimalchio*," he beamed. "The swimming has done her a world of good. And just look at her tan!"

I looked. Zelda and Jozan were now splashing in the shallows, she shrieking with delight. "You are *such* a naughty man!" she cried, after he pulled her into the water, drenching her tight wool suit. "Don't you know what I do to naughty men?"

I turned my gaze back to Scott, but he'd already wandered over to the tray of chilled sherry and biscuits.

---

THE SUMMER UNFOLDED with the arrival of new people and energy. There was an alchemy, we found, in mixing our friends from our different lives and interests. We would introduce a poet like Archie to a playwright like Phil Barry or a musician like David Mannes and wait to see what emerged. Spontaneous poems set to improvised music, interpretive dance, charades of renowned cubist paintings—no evening was the same.

The newly wedded Seldeses, Gilbert and Alice, soon joined us on their honeymoon. One afternoon they showed up at La Garoupe with the Fitzgeralds, looking visibly shaken. "We made it here by the skin of our teeth," Gilbert whispered to me, shaking his head. "We were driving on the Boulevard Maréchal Juin—just as we came to a hairpin turn, Zelda insisted that Scott give her a cigarette, and he took his hands off the wheel for what seemed like an eternity. I swear to you, we came within inches of plunging over the cliff into the sea."

We all knew that the Fitzgerald marriage was on the rocks, quite literally. More than once after parties at the Hôtel du Cap, Zelda had run out to the cliffs of Eden Roc, stripped off her evening dress, and plunged into the seawater forty feet below. Scott, never willing to let Zelda best him, always dove in after her. Repeatedly, Gerald and I admonished them—if not for their own welfare, then Scottie's. "But Say-rah, didn't you know?" Zelda drawled back at me. "We don't believe in conservation. Besides, danger makes people passionate."

Another evening, we convinced Scott and Zelda to spend the night at the hotel rather than make the long drive back to Valescure. We were sound asleep when we heard a frantic knocking on our door and opened it to find Scott, sheet-white and shaking.

"Something's wrong with Zelda," he said. And then, as we padded down the hall after him, he added, "I don't think it was intentional."

We entered the Fitzgeralds' room to find the lights blazing and Zelda tucked into a fetal position on the bed. As I sat her up and tried to rouse her, Gerald scavenged the room and the bathroom cabinet, coming back with an empty pill bottle.

"She was just trying to sleep after drinking too much," Scott tried, but even he didn't sound convinced.

"Zelda," I said loudly, gently slapping her cheeks. "Zelda!"

She opened her eyes a crack and said in a pouty voice, "Say-rah. Don't be angry with me." Her golden curls were in disarray, and her pink dressing gown fell off her shoulders.

"Wake up, then," I said. "What foolish thing have you done?"

"I'm dreaming of utopias," she drawled, smiling. This was a woman who knew that, even incapacitated, she was fetching.

I sent Gerald down to the kitchen for some olive oil to help counteract the pharmaceuticals. When he returned, I poured some into a shot glass and held it to Zelda's lips.

"Come on, drink it," I said.

She was testing my last nerve. I don't care how artistic you think you are, when you become a parent, you must leave such drama and selfishness behind. Even Gerald knew it on the days he had the Black Service—the children came first. But the Fitzgeralds hadn't grown up enough yet to learn this, and I was losing patience with them.

She took a sip and gagged. "Please don't, Say-rah," she whispered in her Southern doll's voice. Her blue eyes widened. "If you drink too much oil, you'll turn into a Jew." Gerald and I exchanged a look.

But her lips remained closed tight against the glass, so we hoisted her up and walked her back and forth along the length of the hallway for several hours until daybreak. When we returned her to the room, we found that Scott had calmed his nerves with an early cocktail. They drove back to Valescure later that morning and none of us ever mentioned the incident again.

Gerald often said that Scott and Zelda were becoming victims of the legend they had built around themselves, like so many of Scott's tragically modern characters. But they were so childish in their wonder about this new world they inhabited, it was impossible not to love them. I remembered the fairytale birthday party they'd once thrown for Scottie and how Scott had presented the "dragon"—a cricket in a tiny bamboo cage. Or the paper dolls Zelda had lovingly painted for Honoria. At their best, they were charming and generous and fun.

IN JULY, ADA MacLeish and I were wandering the open-air marché in Antibes—we'd grabbed the chance to escape for some time together, just us girls. Ada was a pretty, plump woman with a soprano voice that sounded like bells. I used to say she looked like she'd just jumped out of a hat box, because she was always perfectly appointed in the most feminine clothes. But she was also an excellent pianist and mad about knitting, both of which earned her the nickname "Ada of the Flying Fingers."

Now we strolled the aisles of the tented stalls, palming plums or examining a rind of cheese, sniffing a bouquet of basil or admiring buckets of dahlias. At ten o'clock, we could already feel the heat shimmering off the stucco buildings in the square.

"Archie can be such a nuisance," Ada said. "Socks and underwear everywhere—it's as if the man were in grade school! Simone only comes in once a week, he knows that. So I'm apparently the maid when she's not there."

"Oh men," I said. "The moment they marry, it's as if they've gone home to Mother." I inspected an eggplant, a shiny purple amulet.

"Surely not Gerald too? But he's so . . . meticulous! Everything he does is in its place."

She was absolutely right about that. "Well, that's true. But trust me, he has other faults." I could feel myself veering into the deeper waters of honesty and vulnerability. Did I dare go further? If I opened the door a crack, the entire edifice might come crumbling down. I picked up a ripe Anjou pear and sniffed it, inhaling the aromas of summer, imagining *paté sucrée* and caramel sauce.

"Gerald? No. The two of you are like Fort Knox. I've never seen a marriage so unmovable, so unified. You and Gerald are like mustard and ketchup. Or gin and tonic!"

I laughed, a little. This was how we appeared to the world. Gerald and I had built such a wall of solidarity around ourselves, the idea of confiding in a female friend was downright scary. But it was also a little lonely behind that wall. Ada was quickly becoming my best friend in France. If I couldn't tell her, who could I tell?

"Honestly, Sara. It's hard to be married around you two. You're so perfectly aligned. And so loyal to each other."

We were passing the spice stall now, the ground cinnamon and turmeric and paprika perfectly molded into tall pyramids of brilliant color, as you see in Morocco. Their fragile perfection comforted me—I was always soothed by beautiful things. I tried to ignore the obvious metaphor.

"You might be surprised," I said. Our shopping wasn't nearly complete, but I was suddenly feeling restless. I looked around for the flower vendors.

Ada cocked her head and gazed at me full on. She had a handsome square face and startling blue eyes. And she had a brain. She could have practiced law, if she'd been a man. I walked to the next aisle, Ada following closely behind.

"Come on, Sara," she said. "Just give me a hint, a little glimpse, into why the Murphy marriage isn't made of gold."

I sighed and turned to her. My heart still ached from Venice, and from what I'd done to even the score. The truth was, Ada was my best female friend, but my real best friend was Gerald. Despite our rickety feelings around the new understanding of his . . . "temperament," my wagon was hitched to his for life. Gerald had helped me escape from the bleak future that had been prescribed for me; my devotion to him wouldn't waver.

Besides, the risk of sharing our dark secret was too frightening. Being a "fairy" was relatively safe in Paris and among our bohemian crowd. But everywhere else—especially in the States—it was considered outright deviant, even criminal. And once that Pandora's box was opened, well, you could never close it again. Still, the relief of just letting the whole story spill out with another woman, a good friend like Ada, was so close I could taste it.

"You know?" I finally said. "Gerald is actually just the opposite. If his socks aren't arranged by color, he has a little fit!" It was the best foil

I could come up with at the moment.

A look passed between us, and I could see a glimmer of doubt in Ada's bright blue eyes. "It's tiresome," I added quickly. "But how can I not love the man?"

Ada nodded but it was clear she knew I was withholding something. Had I missed my chance to secure this friendship? "Sure, me too," she agreed. "At the end of the day, you just can't help but love them, warts and all."

I pointed to a bucket holding large bunches of coral-colored dahlias. "I'll take three," I told the *fleuriste*.

---

THAT SUMMER CARRIED a lovely, relaxed feeling as more friends joined us for a week or a month and we introduced them to our growing list of delights during long days on the beach. For weeks the air held a smoky fragrance from eucalyptus wildfires in the hills. But each day we noticed more unfamiliar faces as more tourists discovered our little secret: the Riviera in summer.

Our long days on the sand were followed by equally long suppers in local restaurants or on the terrace of the Hôtel du Cap. When we weren't dining with friends, we tried to have a formal dinner with the children. I maintained the American tradition of oatmeal and orange juice for breakfast each morning, but at supper the children were encouraged to try everything; the rule was that they could dislike only one thing per week. Baoth and Patrick still preferred Italian noodles with cheese or roast chicken. But Honoria's appetite was adventurous: she grew to love everything from sea urchins to brains with black butter sauce. "*Tu es une vraie gourmande, ma chere*," Gerald would say.

But there was one thing all three children refused to eat: *mangetout*, the French word for snow peas. With their flat, stringy shells, there was no way I could have them prepared so the children liked them. French children must have had the same response, because *mangetout* means "eat it all." I could just imagine mothers across the country pleading with their offspring to finish the offending vegetable.

I thought back to my own upbringing in Cincinnati and New York, the formal meals at which we were required to eat every course, using the right utensil. My mother thought she was preparing us for life—the rigid, socially proper life she foresaw for all of us. There was no room for free will or individual taste. Our children would grow up with the freedom to make their own choices.

One day that spring, I'd taken seven-year-old Honoria shopping for shoes on Rue Montmartre in Paris. She'd had her heart set on a pair of black, patent-leather Mary Janes in the window of Pierrot. The *vendeur* measured her feet on a metal gauge, then brought out several boxes of shoes in her size. When she tried on the Mary Janes, the man demonstrated how the strap could be swiveled back to the heel, creating flat pumps, and I saw Honoria's face light up in an expression of pure happiness.

"Can I wear them like this, *Maman*?" she asked.

"Of course you can, dear." I'd never seen a girl so delighted. I tried to remember a time from my childhood when I'd felt such elation. It certainly hadn't come from a simple pair of shoes.

"Wrap them up," I told the salesman. Then I let Honoria carry the blue-and-white package all the way home.

That evening, I entered Honoria's bedroom to find her holding a Mary Jane to her nose, inhaling its leathery fragrance.

"Darling, what are you doing?" I laughed.

"I'm breathing in my shoes, *Maman*."

"And what do they smell like?"

She thought for a moment. "They smell like being a grown-up."

*Yes*, I thought. *This is the mother I want to be, and this is the kind of child I want to raise.*

IN MID-JULY, DOS Passos and Donald Ogden Stewart arrived, full of stories from the Fiesta de San Fermín in Pamplona, Spain. Stewart's ribs were taped up and he begged us not to make him laugh, but his recounting of the episode made that impossible.

"That bastard Hemingway forced me into it," he griped. "'It's just a yearling,' he said. 'It's a perfect starter bull,' he said. I'd just removed my glasses so they wouldn't break, and the damned beast took me from behind. I think I made a nice dent in the fence, though."

We shook our heads and made sympathetic noises. "It's the most uncanny thing," Stewart said. "The minute Hem shows up, every grown male feels the need to measure his own manhood."

With Ernest's swashbuckling good looks and his appetite for danger, this didn't surprise me. True, most of the American men in our group were of a more effete, cerebral nature, so it made sense they might feel challenged by Ernest's colossal masculinity. But there was another half of the equation that Stewart left out. How did women compete for his attention? It wasn't long before I'd find out.

THAT SUMMER WE also saw the Misses Stein and Toklas again. They were staying with the Picassos, and to observe Pablo and Gertrude together was to watch some sort of chemical reaction; the air around them felt electrified. Miss Stein would park her monolithic body under the shade of an umbrella. Pablo would recline next to her and the conversations would go on for hours, like two monks saying prayers. These conversations were always about art, but at such an abstract level I couldn't exactly parse what they meant. They spoke a language unto themselves.

"Art isn't everything. It's just *about* everything," Miss Stein was fond of saying. "The subject matter of art is life, life as it actually is; but the function of art is to make life better."

She was like an Egyptian pyramid—immovable and mysterious. While I held my own with our other writer and artist friends, with Miss Stein I felt shallow, insubstantial, and would often clam up. What could I possibly say that would interest her?

One afternoon Pablo joined me as I floated in the shallow water, our hands fluttering like fins to keep us afloat.

"Gertrude just told me that she'd seen one of my paintings at the Rosenberg Gallery in Paris that she'd love to have," he chuckled. "Then she asked if she could have it in exchange for the portrait I painted of her!"

The portrait had required months of sitting and was already fairly renowned. I was aghast. "You *can't* be serious! That's just . . . rude is what it is." There were so many aspects of my upbringing that I'd gladly flung aside. But there was still a place for common courtesy and good manners. Rude behavior topped my list of intolerances, along with racism and money without taste.

He laughed his husky, impish laugh. "Yes, but I love her so much. She is *impénétrable*."

I gazed at him, still wearing his black homburg hat as his head floated above the peacock-blue water. Although I still secretly nursed a lingering guilt about our brief dalliance the summer before, our outward rapport had returned to an easy friendship. There was an unspoken understanding that it had been a momentary lapse in my marriage; besides, Pablo loved Gerald nearly as much as he loved me.

---

WE MADE SEVERAL visits that summer to Villa America, which would be completed the following July. Gerald had already painted a wooden plaque for the front gate based on his earlier sketch on the train. As we wandered around the grounds, I admired the new frame that would soon be covered in fresh off-white stucco. A third story was being added to half the house—the pointed Swiss chalet roof replaced with a flat Moroccan-style one—creating terraces with sun decks on the first and second levels. Tall windows, framed with ocher shutters, would open the house to the light and views of the gardens. Inside, I climbed up the spiral staircase to examine the four bedrooms—one for each child and a master suite for Gerald and me with a balcony that offered a view of the sea. I smiled to myself: We had designed something completely new for the South of France, an Art Deco interpretation of a classic Mediterranean theme.

The children scampered around exploring every nook and shrieking with their new discoveries, while Gerald wandered the seven acres of gardens making notes and I took measurements for rugs and furniture. The "little farm" we'd dreamed about for so long was coming to fruition. And it was so much lovelier than I'd even dared to hope for. Not for the first time, I congratulated myself on realizing this gorgeous vision.

---

WITH SEPTEMBER JUST around the corner, we returned to St. Cloud and Paris, where Gerald resumed his days of painting. And we resumed our social life with a little less gusto, venturing out only two or three times a week with small groups of friends.

One evening we took the group to a new restaurant near the Champs Élysées that had an outdoor dance floor and a gypsy band. The food was excellent, the music charming, and the terrace twinkled with electric bulbs. But Gerald was eager to paint early the next day. "Let's make a discreet exit," he whispered to me. "I've already settled the bill with the waiter."

I gathered my purse and wrap. *Bonsoir, bonne nuit!* Kiss, kiss.

I wasn't halfway across the patio when I heard a commotion behind me. Scott had been well behaved throughout the meal—

he could be very clever while seated but, once he stood up, he'd be falling-down drunk. Now he lay on the dance floor, both arms wrapped around Gerald's leg crying, "Don't leave me here! Take me with you!"

Gerald stiffened and looked at Scott with complete fury. "This is *not* Princeton," he hissed, "and I am *not* your roommate!" Scott let go and we hurried out, leaving him sniffling on the floor.

It was becoming a problem. "It's as if, with each drink, Scott becomes a year younger," I said in the car. "Tonight he was a toddler."

"One minute he's hanging on our every word, the next he's making cutting remarks about our habits or our style," Gerald said.

I recalled the time that Scott had turned to Gerald and, eyeing his tailored three-piece suit and leather satchel, asked, "Are you what they call a fop?"

Unruffled, Gerald explained, "No, I'm a dandy, which is entirely different. I always dress the way I want to, not according to fashion or style."

Poor Scott. He was so intent on being a Jazz Age icon, he couldn't see the forest for the trees. Style was something that just infused how you talked, how you entertained, how you dressed. Every minute was important—but not *too* important. One could be too well dressed or not well dressed enough. Style was being just right. Style was to make every day a festival.

---

THE HOLIDAYS ARRIVED and Gerald was invited to show two of his new works, *Razor* and *Watch*, at the L'Art d'Aujourdhui exhibit. At the show's opening, we ran into Hemingway again.

"I bought *The Farm*," he said, and I could see the pride on his young, handsome face. He laughed. "Literally speaking. Not figuratively."

"You did!" Gerald said. "That's excellent!"

"Yeah, I had to borrow some dough from friends, and I worked as a stevedore at Les Halles for a few months to pay it off," Hemingway said. "But now we have a Miró hanging on our wall. Thanks for the inside tip."

"You won't regret it, my friend. Miró's going nowhere but up. He's got the eye."

This time we exchanged cards—rather, we gave Hemingway our card and he scribbled his address in pencil on a page ripped from the tattered *cahier* he pulled from the pocket of his corduroy jacket. He had a wife, Hadley, and a two-year-old son, Bumby. They lived on a working-class street, Notre Dame des Champs, in the 6th arrondissement.

"We'd love to have you 'round," I said. "And we have children, too! Bring your family."

---

SOON WE DID get together with the Hemingways—for dinner, for nightcaps, or to take the kids to the Luxembourg Gardens, which was just across the rue d'Assas from their street. Bumby was a ruddy, apple-cheeked cherub, as adored by his parents as our children were. But Hadley wasn't what I'd expected of Hemingway's wife. She was like a dull brown hen next to Ernest, in her secondhand clothes and outdated haircut. Like me, she'd married late and was older than her husband. I wanted to like her, but it took effort.

"She's lovely, so plainspoken and genuine, but clearly not in his league, do you think?" I asked Gerald. We were walking back up the Boulevard Saint-Michel with the children in tow. The sun dappled the pavement through the leaves of the elms. "Is that terrible of me to say?"

"Well, he's a corker," Gerald said, using his favorite accolade. "He's on the ascendancy, to be sure. And she seems to be from a previous chapter in his life."

"I just hope she'll be able to keep up once he's truly discovered," I said. "She'll have to start pedaling a little faster."

---

ONE NIGHT OUR telephone rang after nine. "It's Ernest, calling from a cabine just down the street," Gerald told me after he'd hung up. "He wants to read us his new manuscript. I couldn't say no." Ernest's new collection of stories had just come out in the States to good reviews and was now displayed in the windows of many Paris booksellers. He was riding high.

Within minutes, Ernest and Hadley were sitting in our living room, Ernest reading aloud and Hadley avoiding our gaze. I could tell she was embarrassed by the uninvited visit at this late hour. I was already in my dressing gown.

Over the next hour, Gerald listened while I fell asleep, straight-backed on the sofa. Written in just ten days, *The Torrents of Spring* was Ernest's first long work—a lampoon of Sherwood Anderson's recent bestseller, *Dark Laughter*.

When they'd finally left, Gerald shut the door softly.

"Well?" I asked. "How was it?"

"It was mean," Gerald said. "Scott and Dos have already advised against publishing it, and Gertrude nearly threw him out once she heard about it. Now he's seeking anyone who will applaud his effort."

"What did you say?" I asked.

"I pointed out that Anderson has been such a good friend and champion of his work," he said. "It was Anderson, after all, who introduced him to Gertrude and Pound and everyone worth knowing in Paris."

"Why bite the hand that feeds you?"

"Exactly. But Ernest said it's meant to be funny, and Anderson should be able to take a joke. Personally, I think he's trying to divorce himself from anyone he might be indebted to."

Much later, we would discover that all too well for ourselves. He published *The Torrents of Spring*, which severed his relationship with Anderson. We brushed it off as the behavior of a young literary colt. Unfortunately, youth had nothing to do with it.

# Chapter 12
## 1925

Les Acacias cabaret what was what we called a "night resort"—a nightclub with showgirls and freely flowing champagne. Its circular stage was surrounded by tables and large trees that gave the feel of a garden, the spotlight twinkling off the women's beaded dresses. It felt like being onstage in a ballet.

Now we sat with Scott, Zelda, and a small group of others off to the side, where the noise was less intrusive. Zelda was as lovely as ever, with her curly blond bob and dark eye shadow. She'd begun wearing a gardenia pinned above her ear, which made her look like a film goddess. But her words were often from some other universe. She seemed to be fraying about the edges.

"My diaries disappeared," she whispered to me as we watched the show. "My letters, too. And do you know? In Scott's latest work there are passages that strike me as vaguely familiar."

In April, Scott's new novel had been published in the States. Fortified by seeing it in print and the initial income it provided, Scott was briefly restored to civilized behavior. But as we gaily made plans for another summer at Antibes, mixed reviews and slower sales had reversed his Jekyll and Hyde personas, worsened by how much he'd had to drink.

"Are you saying that Scott—" I began.

"I'm saying that Mr. Fitzgerald believes that plagiarism begins at home."

"My goodness!" I didn't believe her, not then. We'd seen Scott's work, and his talent jumped off the page. But later that year, Zelda began publishing a few magazine stories under her own name. They were effervescent and clever, just like her. But they were also very well written—and Zelda had a natural wit that Scott lacked. The idea that he could be borrowing her ideas, or even her words, no longer seemed so far-fetched.

I glanced over to where Scott sat with Ernest—heads together, brows furrowed. The two men had met just a week or so before at the Dingo and, while they were full of mutual admiration, Ernest later told Gerald how he'd had to pour Scott into a taxi, he was so drunk. Now they were already solid friends, and already prone to jealousy. Still, Scott was being enormously generous about promoting Ernest's work and introducing him to his publisher.

Les Acacias wasn't the sort of place that Ernest would—or could—normally frequent. It was beyond his budget and too bourgeois for his taste. But I think the chance to visit Scott's world, and the knowledge that the bill would be footed by others, were temptations he couldn't resist. He'd left Hadley at home.

"I don't like him one bit," Zelda said, nodding in Ernest's direction. "He's as phony as a rubber check. A fairy with hair on his chest." She waved at the waiter for another bottle of Moët. "No real man would have to try that hard."

I quickly glanced away to hide any shame that might have crept into my face. As much as I loved Zelda, there would never be a time when I could share with her the complicated nature of my own marriage. Instead, I imagined the theatrics that lay ahead in this litter of outsized egos. Writers and artists are a competitive lot on the best days. Add alcohol and jealousy and Zelda's unpredictable behavior, and well, it wasn't going to be good.

I STOOD ON the sun terrace and looked out over a quilt of pines and palms to the sea. The air was thick with the fragrance of eucalyptus and the rackety pulse of cicadas. It was finally summer again, and this time we'd returned not just to Antibes, but to Villa America—a home of our own. Gerald had taken the children into town to shop for art supplies. Our *bonne à tout faire*, Titine, and the *cuisinière*, Celestine, were at the market. For the moment, I was blissfully alone, and I wandered through the house marveling at what we'd done. I ran my fingers over the mantel, admiring the mirrored fireplace that reflected the sun in shards of light around the living room. The furniture I'd ordered—stainless steel frames with white upholstery—was arranged around a simple rag rug.

We'd unlocked the front door in June to the smell of fresh white paint and waxed black floor tiles. I'd begun shopping for majolica and faience tableware to give it a local flair. On the terrace stood a café table and chairs that Gerald had found in a restaurant supply shop and painted with silver radiator paint. It was so completely modern and unexpected against the Provençal landscape, the perfect marriage of French and American ideals. I felt planted in a way I'd never felt before, as if this were the one true place where I could be my whole self. All of our dreams and sketches and detailed correspondence with the architects had come together in the most beautiful way. Gerald called it "our humble apotheosis."

In July we purchased an adjacent plot with an old *bastide* that we were turning into a guesthouse and converted a gardener's cottage into Gerald's studio. Then there were the grounds, which we both threw ourselves into—Gerald landscaping the terraced hillside into nooks and gardens, me laying out the vegetable, herb, and flower beds. I'd already written to the States for packets of Golden Bantam corn and Brandywine tomato seeds, so that by the following summer we'd be dining on our own produce. We even acquired two cows for fresh milk, because I didn't quite trust what they sold in the local shops.

The villa kept us busy, but it wasn't long before we'd established a lovely routine to our days. We rose early and had breakfast together. Then Gerald retreated to his studio while the children did their lessons with Mam'zelle and I discussed the week's menus with Celestine. I might attend to household accounts or walk the gardens with Giuseppe to discuss plantings.

Around noon each day we'd all carry our things down the little road to La Garoupe beach. Gerald led the children through calisthenics and yoga poses, friends would begin arriving, and we'd settle into a delicious few hours of sunbathing, swimming, and idle discourse.

"During a good conversation, can't you just feel life getting a little denser, chemically speaking?" Gerald once asked. It was true; I could almost see the air thickening with ideas and opinions and clever turns of phrase.

Then we'd decamp back to the villa for a simple lunch on the patio under the linden tree: an omelet and salad, or a plate of roasted baby new potatoes tossed with butter and fresh dill. Or my house special: poached eggs on a bed of fresh corn sprinkled with paprika, a plate of sautéed tomatoes and garlic on the side.

The children chose where they wanted to nap among the garden's little enclaves and we'd set up folding cots for them to doze in the shade. If one of them had to be disciplined for a misdeed, we extended their nap time from one hour to two. After naps, we usually arranged some sort of amusement like a craft project or costume party.

Today we held the Salon de Jeunesse, inspired by Pablo's presence. He scampered around, instructing us as we arranged several folding screens on the patio. Honoria, Baoth, and Patrick excitedly hung all the artwork they'd done over the past few weeks, then stood back as Pablo studied each piece with great seriousness and gently critiqued the technique. He usually insisted that every picture was perfect in its primitive, childish form.

"*Pas un coup de plus! C'est parfait tel quel!*" he said, regarding Honoria's painting of a horse with a rider standing on its back, and she beamed with pride. She knew only that he painted for a living, which was impressive enough to her eight-year-old mind.

Zelda and Scott had rented a nearby villa again and no day was complete without some new drama. No matter how well-behaved they might be during the day, by evening Scott was in his cups and Zelda did her best to compete for attention. Scott had begun working on a new magnum opus, *Tender Is the Night,* named after a line from a Keats poem. Just the week before, we'd watched him row a few yards off the beach and meticulously tear his seventh draft into shreds before scattering them into the Mediterranean.

Now we'd taken a small group to an inn perched on the hills above Nice for dinner, where we sat on a stone terrace overlooking the sea, the moon reflected in pleats on the water below. "Don't look now, but I believe that's Isadora Duncan at the table in the corner," Gerald said sotto voce.

"Who's Isadora Duncan?" Scott asked loudly, craning his neck in the most obvious way.

"The mother of modern dance?" Gerald asked, rhetorically. "Free-form movements and Greek togas?"

We all stole glances at the fiftyish woman surrounded by a gaggle of younger men. She'd clearly put on some weight, and her long, flowing garments made her look like the Statue of Liberty. Holding her head at an angle to display her still-long neck, she waved her hands like pigeons.

Fame of any kind was nectar to Scott, so he promptly walked over and sat at her feet. "Miss Duncan, I have long worshipped you from afar," he said, looking up at her with solemn eyes.

She began combing her fingers through his wavy hair. "My cen-*tur*-ion," she murmured in her throaty voice.

Gerald and I exchanged a look. *Here it comes*, I thought. The whole day had been peaceful, without a scene. But the day wasn't over.

I turned just in time to see Zelda march over and climb up on an empty table, then begin slowly dancing to music only she could hear, much to the amusement of the Provençal men standing nearby. She whirled faster and faster until we could see a froth of lace ruffles under her hem. Then she jumped off the table, ran across the terrace, and plunged herself down a dark stairwell.

I quickly excused myself and ran after her, thinking that this time her rash behavior might have actually killed her, but found her about halfway down the staircase with only bloody knees.

"Are you all right?" I asked, pulling her up.

"I can dance too, you know," she moaned.

"Of course you can, you pretty fool. But not everything has to be a competition."

She began to cry in earnest. "It's over this time—it's really finished," she sobbed. "Don't you know? Scott has betrayed me with a dirty streetwalker!"

"That doesn't sound at all like Scott," I said. "Did he tell you that?"

We were sitting on a cold, stone stair as I tried to calculate how to calm Zelda and return her to the party. We'd just ordered our entrées, and I could picture my Dover sole congealing on the plate. The darkness of the stairwell and the chill of the steps seemed like a metaphor for Zelda's gloomy mind. I wanted to return to the bright lanterns of the terrace where the real grown-ups sat.

Zelda sniffed. "I found a packet of 'French letters' in his pocket and we had a nasty row. He said he was just trying to prove to me that he was a real man."

"Now, why would he need to do that? You're his wife, after all."

Zelda's lower lip poked out. "I may have accused him of being a fairy with Hemingway," she said. "It's not natural the way those two conspire and compete and then fight like cats. That's how lovers behave!"

I sighed and adjusted her hair. Scott and Zelda's world was like something from a dime novel, all tears and tantrums and violent passion. While Gerald's and my ideal for life was an intimate, quiet luxury, the Fitzgeralds' seemed to be deafening chaos. No peaceful gathering went undisturbed. I thought gratefully of Gerald who, despite his complicated mind, was always there when I needed him. He was a constant for me, as I was for him. How exhausting it was to be so young and passionate!

"Zelda, dear. Why must you make life so difficult for yourself? Scott adores you."

"Things just haven't been the same since my little fling with Jozan," she said. On several occasions with friends, Scott had falsely implied that the aviator had killed himself—a tragic fairytale ending to Zelda's earlier indiscretion.

"Let's get back to our dinner, darling. The *soufflé au citron* here is legendary." I hoisted her up and we limped back to the table, disaster averted. But the curious thing about Zelda was that no matter what she did—even the wildest, most terrible acts—she always managed to maintain her dignity. Perhaps because she truly didn't care what other people thought of her. Deep down, a part of me envied her innate ability to throw caution to the wind. Maybe once in a while you just needed to toss yourself down some stairs.

---

ON ONE OF our last days in Antibes, we sat on La Garoupe with Gertrude Stein and Miss Toklas. Fall was in the air, and our clan had dwindled to just a few stalwart souls.

"Good heavens," I said, reading from the *Herald Tribune*. "Isadora Duncan was killed last night in Nice! She was riding in the backseat of an open-air roadster and her long silk scarf got tangled in the back axle. It pulled her from the car and broke her neck." I put down the newspaper and stared at Miss Stein. "She was nearly decapitated. Honestly, can you imagine a more horrible way to die?"

Gertrude didn't look up from her book. "Affectation can be fatal," she said, and turned the page.

# Chapter 13
## 1925-1926

Back in Paris, we found that our American tribe had dwindled as well. The value of the franc had doubled against the dollar, and you could no longer find a four-course meal for the price of a gallon of milk back in the States. But Gerald and I now owned two properties on French soil—this was, quite literally, our terra firma. We were growing particularly thick with the Hemingways, who also stayed on.

The all-night party atmosphere had died down, which was fine with me. The streets seemed quieter, the cafés and bars less crowded. Now it was just the dedicated expatriates who gathered for a meal or a drink. It was like the calm of a Sunday morning after a raucous Saturday night.

---

"SHE WAS SO . . . *VOLUPTUEUSE*," Jeanne said. I'd been telling Jeanne Léger about my impression of Isadora Duncan, how she seemed to hold men in her sway, her raw sensuality in public. As Jeanne said the word, she acted it out by running her hands over her own breasts. We laughed a bit and I thought nothing more about it. But after she'd left, it suddenly struck me: I'd been misinterpreting my lifelong credo—*luxe, calme, et volupté*—all these years. When I'd first read Baudelaire's poem as a young woman, my schoolgirl French had defined the word simply as "pleasure." But now I glimpsed a more nuanced meaning. I dug up my Larousse dictionary and found the definition: *Volupté: the pleasure of the senses, especially sexual pleasure.*

All this time, I'd been priding myself on such niceties as a fragrant garden, a well-set table, an amusing conversation among friends. But I'd been missing the point of the word: lusty, passionate sex. Had Gerald and I been living in the States, perhaps our nearly platonic relations in bed would have been routine in a marriage as old as ours. But here in France, it felt like an absence. A shortfall. My younger self felt chastised. Or perhaps the better word was disappointed. I could count on one hand the times we'd made love in the last few years. We both understood why: I wasn't Gerald's gender of choice. But there was still a genuine love between us, and I kept hoping that he did it out of more than obligation.

---

WE'D BEGUN TAGGING along when Ernest and Hadley went to the races at Auteuil, with Ernest coaching us on the horses and their odds. He seemed to put genuine stock in our thoughts about his writing and briefed us on the details of his negotiations with publishers. It was an odd, changing chemistry: sometimes we were parents, sometimes I felt a distinct physical energy between Ernest and me, and often I saw Gerald hold him in a kind of awe, like an older brother.

"He's such an enveloping personality, so physically huge and forceful," Gerald said, spreading his arms wide. "He talks so graphically and with such conviction that you just find yourself agreeing with him."

With his thick black hair and heavy mustache, Ernest evoked a pirate mixed with a little Gary Cooper. I found his undiluted masculinity impossibly attractive. And he was an actual war hero, with shrapnel still embedded in his thigh—a fact that, deep down, must have tormented Gerald.

But as a foursome we were entirely congenial. So when the Hemingways invited us and Dos for a skiing trip to Austria in late March, we readily agreed to go, leaving our children in the care of Mam'zelle.

To get to the Hotel Zum Rössle-Post at Gaschern we took a miniature electric train up the mountain, the car crammed with our bags, boots, and skis. The alpine landscape felt clean and bracing and healthy—I'd never seen snow so white or firs so green. But the skiing itself was an ordeal: we'd strap sealskins to our heavy wooden skis, climb to the top of a small mountain, remove the skins, and try to make it to the bottom without breaking our necks.

Ernest was a superb skier, of course, and Hadley was nearly as good. Gerald had skied the Adirondacks a few times when he was younger, but Dos and I were hopeless. I carefully followed Ernest's instructions on the Christiana and Telemark turns, stopping after each one to catch my breath and calculate the remaining distance to the base. But Dos figured that, with his terrible eyesight, technique was pointless. So he'd point himself straight down the hill and, when he saw a shape that looked like a tree, just sit down. By the end of the first day, not only were his pants torn to shreds, but his derriere was missing several layers of skin.

The nights were the best. After a dinner of cheese dumpling soup or sausages and fried potatoes with applesauce, we'd gather at the stone fireplace with a bottle of kirsch, feeling exhausted and virtuous after the day's exertions, our faces hot and pink. That first night, Dos couldn't sit at all but leaned against one of the thick pine columns that supported the overhead beams of rough logs.

Ernest relished the role of what Dos called "the alpha male"—in fact, he insisted on it. He automatically took the lead in every new athletic event, every story, every anecdote. But he was so generous in spirit and so patient in teaching us new things, we all fell behind him like ducklings.

One night Gerald and I lay in bed, the moon shining bright as lamplight onto our goose-down duvet. The alpine air, the strenuous exercise and, no doubt, Ernest's masculine influence had done something to revive Gerald's interest in lovemaking and we'd been having a regular honeymoon again. I'd finally given up on the skiing and spent most days wandering the village or reading back at the lodge. But Gerald had doggedly kept up with Ernest on the slopes, even after we learned about a deadly avalanche on a nearby mountain two months before.

"The forest was so thick, we were slaloming between tree trunks," he was saying of that day's efforts. "Ernest would stop every twenty yards or so to make sure I was all right. When we got to the bottom, he asked if I'd been scared, and I confessed that I had. Then he said the most exquisite thing."

I'd been looking out the window at the moon and the snow, which seemed embedded with diamonds. But now I turned to see Gerald's bronzed face in the moonlight.

"He said, 'I know what courage is. It's grace under pressure.'"

"Oh, that's lovely," I said. "And so true. That's why we love him so. His gift with words is extraordinary."

"I know it was childish of me, but I felt absolutely elated." We both understood that, with Ernest, there was always some sort of test. Gerald had apparently passed.

"How's it going with Hadley?" he asked.

"There's a kind of vagueness about her that's worrisome," I said.

"He told me that he hasn't allowed her to know how poor they really are," Gerald said. "But she *should* know, so she can help carry the burden."

"She's not the one spending the money," I said. "It's always Ernest planning these wonderful trips, and she comes along as a good sport."

"Well, that's a point," he said, and rolled over. "Goodnight, my own true Sal."

"Good night, Dow."

I momentarily wondered: how would *our* marriage fare without my inheritance to ease the way? Then I pushed the thought out of my mind and fell into a snowbank of sleep.

Another night, Ernest pulled out the manuscript of his work in progress about Pamplona, for which he'd already received an advance from Scribner's. We'd been hearing about the novel for months, so were eager to get a preview.

"Robert Cohn was once middleweight boxing champion of Princeton," he began, and proceeded to read several chapters without pausing, clearly as delighted with his words as we were. I closed my eyes and let the narrative take me to New Jersey and Spain even as I felt the heat from the roaring Austrian fire on my legs.

Ernest's brilliance on the page had become even brighter than the short stories he'd let us read. The story of Jake Barnes and Lady Brett Ashley, told so tightly in dialogue without adjectives or other embellishments, had us in his grip. We could practically see the bulls in the ring, feel the sun on our heads, taste the wine. And in Lady Brett Ashley, I recognized that extraordinary boyish woman I'd seen at Le Select the year before. Then Ernest pulled out a few photographs of some bullfights they'd seen the previous year, and we were hooked.

"We're going back in July," he said. "Hadley's friend, Pauline Pfeiffer, is coming too. Why not make it six?" Dos wasn't sure he could, but Gerald and I said yes immediately. We couldn't wait to see Ernest's Spain.

---

THAT SUMMER, THE Hôtel du Cap was filled to capacity and a row of cabanas lined La Garoupe beach. Now we arrived early and tried to leave before the shore, which Gerald had so carefully raked, was blanketed with oil-slathered bodies. But the town of Antibes still retained some of its sleepy charm: telephone service stopped for two hours each afternoon and shut down for the night at seven o'clock.

The scrappy local cinema showed one movie a week on Saturday nights. We welcomed the surrounding muffle of only local accents.

Our life in Antibes had already shifted to Villa America. We now had two guest houses, and they were rarely empty. Our days were filled with sails on our new sailboat, the *Picaflor*, games with the children, and long, fragrant dinner parties under the linden tree. We kept these affairs small—usually eight or ten people, just enough for several lively conversations. I called these evenings "Dinner-Flowers-Gala," a phrase I'd taken from captains' dinners on ocean liners. They'd begin with cocktails on the terrace. (When asked what went into his meticulously mixed drinks, Gerald famously replied, "just the juice of a few flowers.") The children would come down, bathed and robed, to perform a song or dance they'd prepared before marching up to bed. Then we'd sit down to candlelight and a simple supper brought out in leisurely courses.

A pulsing song of cicadas. The aroma of jasmine mixed with eucalyptus. Francis Poulenc might perform Bach's variations on the piano or Ada MacLeish might sing an aria. It was heaven on earth. I'd never dreamed I could feel so content. Here it was: the Baudelairian ideal, fully formed. Gerald and I had manifested it ourselves, and it was so much more satisfying than I'd ever imagined. We'd made this new life from scratch. I'll admit it now—my feelings of pride often veered into smugness. Years later, I would rename that feeling *hubris*. "Pride goeth before destruction, and a haughty spirit before a fall." One of my mother's favorite sayings.

One afternoon I was reviewing the evening's menu in the kitchen. Stacks of colorful linen napkins and faience plates awaited their placement on the outdoor table. Small vases of poppies and sweet peas, and a row of hand-blown wine goblets also stood ready to be carried outside. In a flash, I suddenly saw my mother with new eyes. For all her insistence on social propriety, for all her rigid adherence to tradition, she'd been enormously creative when it came to entertaining. I remember seeing her name often in the society columns, with detailed descriptions of her decor, her menu, her glittering guest lists. I now understood that her over-the-top parties were her only means of proving her talents. She didn't have the freedom, as I did, to buck the tide. And for all my supposed rebellion in creating a new kind of life for myself, I now realized where I'd learned to do "Dinner-Flowers-Gala."

---

OUR MEDITERRANEAN BLISS was briefly interrupted by a visit from Hoytie, who always arrived just in time to ruin everything. Now she wanted to bring a horde of her pretentious friends to stay with us.

"You've clearly got the room," she said, waving in the direction of the guest quarters. "What makes you think you're too good for them?"

"It's not that I'm too good for them," I said. "I just don't like them. This is my house, and I'm not going to be a hotel for your fancy friends from Cannes—titled or otherwise." Hoytie ran with the kind of crowd that Gerald called "*sheer* society."

The argument lasted an entire day before Hoytie left in a huff. But it took her so long to get her fourteen monogrammed trunks to the station that she missed her train. She returned to the villa for three more days, refusing to speak to me or Gerald, sending us messages through the children. "Tell your mother she needn't set a place for me at dinner" or "Please have your father call me a taxi."

We all exhaled a sigh of relief when she finally left, a cloud of Shalimar perfume in her wake.

That spring and summer of 1926, our core group included the Hemingways, the MacLeishes, and the Fitzgeralds. Hadley and Ernest were solid and fun, and we were so knocked out by his writing, which Gerald and I felt was redefining the American voice. But Scott and Zelda were still deteriorating. Scott was drinking even more heavily than usual—just two drinks could make him "ossified," in Zelda's patois. And Zelda was coming unstrung herself—at the age of twenty-seven, she'd decided to become a ballerina. Gerald had introduced her to Honoria's ballet teacher in Paris, and she'd been practicing until she was clearly spent, both physically and mentally. Her erratic behavior was increasingly disturbing.

"It's as if she's having a completely different conversation in her head," Gerald said as we drove home from La Garoupe one afternoon. "This ballet thing was a bad idea. I've just added fuel to the fire."

"Fire? What fire?" Baoth piped from the back seat.

"It's an expression, Bayo. It means making something worse."

"Aww," Baoth said. "Why must adults always say things they don't really mean?"

"And why must children always interrupt the adults when they're speaking?" Gerald said, his eyes fixed on the road.

"My personal hunch is that she's obsessed with the idea of becoming as great a dancer as Scott is a writer," I said. "It's a fool's errand. She's just so *compulsive*." Now Zelda flounced about the beach practicing her *jetés* and *assemblés*, counting out loud as she tried to master the jumps. She'd lost her sense of humor, too, which was one of the things I'd most loved about her.

"It's not going to end well," Gerald said as we pulled into the drive.

---

IN EARLY MAY, Ernest had gone to Madrid to see the San Isidro bullfights, so we invited Hadley and Bumby to join us in Antibes—but when they arrived, the poor boy had a bad croup with a horrible, wheezing cough. Gerald arranged for our English doctor to come to the house to take a look at him and when he came downstairs, Dr. Babcock looked serious.

"It's pertussis, I'm afraid," he said, and prescribed a Vapo-Cresolene humidifier to heal Bumby's inflamed lungs. "In the meantime, he should be quarantined. Whooping cough is highly contagious, to adults as well as children."

Hadley blanched. We knew she hadn't the money for treatment or other accommodations.

"What rotten luck," Gerald said, and walked Dr. Babcock to the door. By the time he returned to the living room, he had a solution. (That was my husband, clean through: he knew that the best qualities—like chivalry, civility, and courtesy—didn't announce themselves. They were *enacted*.)

"Look here, Hadley," he said. "Scott and Zelda's lease is up at the end of the month, and they're moving to a new villa. We'll put you up at their old place, have groceries delivered daily, and arrange for all of Dr. Babcock's follow-up visits. How does that sound?"

"That's so kind," Hadley began, "but I simply can't afford—"

"You won't see a bill," I said. "It's all arranged."

"But I couldn't . . ." Hadley tried again. We all knew that Ernest hated feeling beholden to others for money. Especially Gerald.

"We insist," I said. "And I'm sure that Ernest would spare no expense when it comes to Bumby. Go pack up your things and we'll get you all settled."

So for the following week Hadley and Bumby lived at Villa Paquita in isolation, but in great luxury. Every evening at "yardarm time" we brought a full cocktail bar to their gate and sat outside to visit from a safe distance. Honoria, Baoth, Patrick, and Scottie entertained Bumby with puppets and songs. Over the weeks, Hadley's face changed from drawn and pale to happy and tanned. For the first time, she struck me as pretty. At the end of each evening, we'd leave our empty bottles overturned on the iron fence pikes and by the end of a few weeks the place was covered with multicolored bottles in the prettiest array. The trophy wall of a great party.

One evening as we were preparing to leave, Hadley pulled me aside. She seemed positively giddy. "Our nanny's coming down on Monday," she said. "I could use a bit of a break from Bumby's care."

"What a good idea," I said, smiling.

"Better yet, my friend is coming down, too. Pauline Pfeiffer.

You'll love her, she's great fun!"

"Well, how lovely," I said, and tried to hide my surprise. Word had floated around that Pauline had grown close not only to Hadley but to Ernest when she'd joined them in Schruns before our own trip there. "Is that the best idea, though, with Bumby's cough?"

"Oh, it's fine!" Hadley said. "Fife had whooping cough as a child, so she's immune."

I suspected that Pauline was more than happy to join the *ménage* in anticipation of Ernest's arrival. Perhaps Hadley wanted to keep an eye on her or, more likely, she was simply too naive to see where things were headed.

Although originally from St. Louis like Hadley, Pauline was a career girl—an editor at Paris *Vogue*—and she'd clearly learned a thing or two from the fashion world. She was as chic and well appointed as Hadley was plain. The moment she stepped off the train, decked out in a stylish traveling ensemble with her hair freshly bobbed, my antennae went up. "What on *earth* is Hadley thinking?" I whispered to Gerald behind my hand.

Ernest returned from Spain in June, his face glowing with the news that the writing had gone well. By now the nanny had moved with Bumby into a guest cottage, so Ernest, Pauline, and Hadley had the main house to themselves. I could only imagine the complicated goings-on in there. Pauline's wit was sharp. She and Ernest bantered and flirted and laughed while Hadley looked increasingly miserable. It was a bad sign.

SOON AFTER ERNEST'S arrival, we decided to throw a small party in his honor—champagne and caviar on our terrace at Villa America. I'd begun to notice a pattern—that Scott's drinking and behavior became even worse when he was around Ernest—and that night was no exception. As Titine brought our glasses and plates, Scott started in.

"Champagne and caviar?" he mused. "Are there any other clichés you'd care to exploit? Where are we, in a Cole Porter song?"

"Don't, Scott," Gerald said, and I could see his jaw beginning to work.

"Is there anything *more* affected than caviar and champagne?" Scott sang out in a made-up tune.

"Well, I think it's *ambrosial*," Pauline said. That was her favorite word.

Scott left the table and the party proceeded, but we soon heard the tinkling of shattered glass. By the time we identified the source of the sound, we found him gleefully tossing onto the flagstone pavement, one at a time, my hand-blown goblets from Venice. My set of twelve was now down to nine.

Gerald grabbed Scott by the arm and sternly escorted him and Zelda to our front steps to await a taxi. We then banished him from our home for three weeks.

*Gerald & I can no longer tolerate the rude and disruptive behavior you displayed so foolishly last night*, I wrote the next day. *After all that we've done to demonstrate to you and Zelda how much we value your friendship, it feels mean-spirited indeed that you would constantly insult us and our hospitality. I know that you probably consider it passé to observe something as common as good manners—I suspect it's probably some Theory you have—but at your age you should know that you can't simply have Theories about friends.*

"He's growing increasingly antagonistic of me," Gerald observed. "It seems the more we do for him, the less he likes me."

I couldn't disagree. We sat outside drinking our café Americanos, the last of the summer sun warming our shoulders. Autumn was just around the bend; you could smell it on the breeze.

"You, however . . ." Gerald gave me a wan smile. "He's become infatuated. You can't deny it."

"Oh, that's just Scott," I said. "He's in love with all women."

"Remember the time he tried to kiss you in a taxi?"

"He's a bit of a masher," I agreed.

"And if you don't pay enough attention to him at dinner? 'Sara, look at me. Sara, look at me.' Or 'Sara's being mean to me.' He's like a small child."

"That's an insult to small children!" I laughed. "At least *our* children are better behaved." I thought of the time that Scott, knowing my habit of washing coins to rid them of germs, began stuffing franc notes into his mouth just to provoke me.

But under my humor lay real grief at Scott's steady decline. Under his drinking and churlish behavior lay an extreme insecurity—about himself as a man and as an author—that was inflamed by Ernest's growing success. While we thought of Scott as an immensely successful commercial writer, we'd been more lavish in our praise for Ernest's *newer* style of writing.

When sober, Scott was actually the strongest advocate for Ernest's work. He refused to hear a negative word about him—even from Zelda, who couldn't stand the man. But when the drink was on him, all his demons rose to the surface. Along with Zelda's increasingly bizarre behavior, he was clearly becoming undone at the dissolution of his sparkling Jazz Age life.

Nearly as disturbing was Scott's scrutiny of us. He'd ask all kinds of probing questions about our finances, our sex life, our history together. He seemed particularly fascinated that when Gerald or I told each other a joke, we "told it as if to a stranger." Our mutual high regard seemed a mystery to him. More than once we suspected he might be studying us for a future novel.

But we couldn't renounce the Fitzgeralds for good. "What I cherish is that region in him where his gift comes from," Gerald said. "And try as he might, he can't bury that gift. In those quiet, sensitive moments, you see the beauty of his natural mind. That's what compels me to love and value him."

He was right about Scott. But "those quiet, sensitive moments" were becoming few and far between. We were having to try harder to love the Fitzgeralds, our problem children.

# Chapter 14
## 1927

We were glad to leave the Fitzgeralds behind in July and accompany the Hemingways to Spain, where Ernest had set his new novel amid the Fiesta de San Fermin in Pamplona. After our years in France, Spain was a delicious jolt to the senses. The air was drier. The wine was spicier. The people were warmer. And everywhere the smell of sweat and frying grease.

Ernest had been to Pamplona twice before; Hadley had been once, but Pauline and Gerald and I were novices. We checked into the Hotel Quintana on the main square and Ernest briefed us on the events of the coming week and how to comport ourselves *como las españolas*.

I tried to keep my focus on the festive mood and not give way to my increasing concern about the state of the Hemingways' marriage. Pauline never missed a chance to insert herself between Ernest and Hadley, showing up to every event in a chic outfit and with freshly coiffed hair. She was consistently awed by Ernest's athletic prowess and intellect, and she always seemed to have a witty retort at the ready.

Hadley looked tired already. But Pauline said she was up for anything; she couldn't *wait* to see Ernest in the ring. I thought of the early days of my courtship with Gerald—had I been so openly coquettish? In any case, Gerald hadn't been a married man.

As we approached our second-floor room, Gerald and I noticed the doors to the rooms across from ours were open, inviting a peek. Inside, the matadors and their *subalternos* were resting on their beds surrounded by candles, flowers, and statues of their saints.

"They look like effigies," I whispered. I suddenly realized how serious this bullfighting business was, how dangerous. These boys looked barely older than twenty.

"They seem to be living somewhere between art and life," Gerald whispered back. "It's like a kind of religion."

Although neither of us believed in formal religion, there was something pure and godly about the men in repose. For the first time, I briefly wondered if we might be missing something. Was there power in prayer like that? Were they more protected by God because of their candles and saints?

---

AT EIGHT O'CLOCK the next morning, we three women gathered on the balcony of the Quintana to watch the bulls run through the street from the cattle yard to the bullring. Dressed in white with red kerchiefs, the men ran ahead of them, desperately trying to avoid horns and hooves. Some fell and were trampled. Every morning all week, the same chaos, the same fool-hardy game.

Our two men stood on the street below. Ernest normally ran with the bulls each day, but today he suggested that they stand in a recessed doorway, sensing that this was outside of Gerald's expertise. We all knew that he'd have preferred to attend a ballet or play rather than stand amid that dust and violence. Earlier that morning, he'd worried over what to wear and chose an old wool golfing cap over his usual Brooks Brothers hat. I could see he wanted to impress Ernest in the worst way.

"I'm sorry you didn't run," I said later. "It would have been a great feeling afterward." I don't know why I said it. Perhaps, in the company of Ernest, I was wishing that Gerald could try just a little harder to be more masculine.

He looked a bit crushed. "I was afraid of looking like a fool," he said. "But Ernest said my cap was just right." His face brightened. "He said I looked tough."

I smiled. "I'm sure you did, darling." I hated myself for how I was feeling. At home I could see Gerald in his element and admire the qualities that were so attractive in that context: his skills as a generous host, his eye for elegant decor, his obvious love for his children. But here, in Ernest's world, he seemed awkward and uncomfortable. Beside Ernest, he seemed weak. I banished the thought from my mind with shame.

---

AFTER LUNCH WE headed to the bullring, where amateurs could face the bulls again. Perhaps spurred on by my earlier comment, Gerald gamely volunteered to go in. Ernest was in the middle of things, but I could see him keeping Gerald in his line of vision, making sure he was all right. Suddenly, a young bull charged toward Gerald, who stood frozen holding his Aquascutum raincoat squarely in front of him. My heart stopped beating, I'm sure of it, as I watched the bull aim his horns at Gerald's nether regions.

"Move it to the side! To the side!" Ernest yelled and, at the last possible moment, Gerald complied. The bull passed to his right, grazing his head on the raincoat.

"That's a goddamn *veronica*, Dow!" Ernest cheered. Gerald grinned up at me and I applauded. Then Ernest, bare-handed, attracted another charging bull. Just as it seemed about to strike, he grabbed its horns and vaulted himself onto its back, held on for a minute, then brought the animal to its knees.

"*Olé!*" cried the entire arena, on its feet.

"HAVE YOU EVER seen anything like it?" Pauline was saying. "Such calm! Such dexterity and strength!"

We were seated outside at Café Iruña in the late afternoon sun, eating salted almonds and tart green olives and drinking very dry sherry in shot glasses. Hemingway sat between Pauline and Hadley and every few minutes the admiring local men would come to squirt red wine into his mouth from their leather *botas*. "*Torero Americano!*" they cheered.

"Thanks, daughter," Ernest said to Pauline. "Daughter" was what Gerald had long called Honoria, a term he also extended to any familiar young woman. Since we'd come to Pamplona, Ernest had started using the term as well. And everyone had begun calling him Papa, including Gerald. Now when Gerald called Pauline or Hadley "daughter," Ernest looked annoyed.

"You were magnificent, Tatie," Hadley said quietly, as a bootblack approached and offered to polish Ernest's shoes without charge. Throughout the week, I watched as Pauline subtly moved into their marriage and Hadley took it with downcast eyes. I wanted to pull her aside and offer some support, but the very fact of her passivity somehow annoyed me. Why didn't she at least try to assert her place as Ernest's wife? Couldn't she just once put on some lipstick? Here, twelve years into our marriage, I still made sure I was always tidy for my husband.

Then Ernest turned his heroic gaze on me. "Say, Sara," he said, "why do you only wear your good jewelry after dark? That's such a bourgeois thing to do. Those diamonds of yours would look magnificent in the Spanish sunlight. Think of how beautiful you'd be, sitting in the stands with all your diamonds blazing in the sun!" Ernest didn't normally pay attention to such things as diamonds. But here in Spain he was El Cid. He grinned his pirate smile.

I demurred. As if Ernest didn't have enough women on his hands without also flirting with me. But sure enough, the next day I donned a yellow silk dress and all my diamonds to sit beside Ernest at my first corrida. We were in the barrera—the posh seats—which of course Gerald and I had paid for. We hadn't been there long, however, before the bulls' goring of the picadors' horses made me angry and ill. I held my tongue but thought, how could this slaughter be considered entertainment? I soon found my way to the aisle and stomped back to the hotel, diamonds and all.

After a brief lie-down, I came to my senses. We were here to experience a foreign culture. Who was I to judge a twelve-hundred-year-old tradition? The next day I was back at the corrida. And the next, and the next. Ernest coached me on the three *tercios*, or acts, of the bullfight. How the matador gradually wore out the bull through exhaustion and loss of blood. And how skillfully he executed the estocada, the coup de grâce that quickly ended the bull's life.

"The red cape is just a bow to tradition," Ernest told me. "Bulls are actually color-blind."

Each day I wore my diamonds to the ring. On the fourth day, the matador gestured to me and bowed low. "He's dedicating the fight to you," Ernest said, patting my leg. "I told you those diamonds were the ticket!"

Gerald was right: Ernest's approval was like standing in the glow of a thousand-watt spotlight. You felt like you were on the stage of Carnegie Hall with roses falling at your feet. I smiled and bowed my head back at the matador, then waved to the crowd. I felt like Miss America.

———

THE REST OF the week was filled with bullfights, parades, and folk dancing. On Saturday night, the crowds gathered in the square at midnight for *El Struendo*, "the Roar," making an ungodly din with pots and pans until morning. Gerald and I called it a night around two, hearing the ruckus through a fitful half-sleep but, between the noise, the crowds, and the copious amounts of red wine, our heads were throbbing.

On our last day we prowled the shops, and I bought a small guitar for Baoth, an embroidered shawl for Honoria, and a toy bull for Patrick. After dinner, there was a fireworks display, and the locals gathered at city hall to sing "Pobre de Mí" by candlelight as all the men formally removed their red kerchiefs until the following year. The crowd formed circles to dance the traditional sardana and we followed along as best we could.

Suddenly, the little brass band broke into the "Savoy Hop" and the crowd began chanting *"Dansa Charleston! Dansa Charleston!"* Gerald and I were confused until we saw the look on Ernest's face: knowing we'd learned this newest dance craze, he'd tipped off the band. Gerald took my hand and led me to the center of the crowd, where we giddily swung our arms and kicked our feet in time to the beat. I caught his eye and we both grinned. After a week of trying so hard to fit into Ernest's world, it felt good to be ourselves.

"What a splendid week we've had, Papa," Gerald said as we stumbled back to the Quintana after midnight. "You just keep outdoing yourself with the *best* experiences."

Ernest smiled, but even he looked tired. Pauline had taken off her red T-strap heels and was limping barefoot on the cobblestones. Hadley walked with us, but she seemed to be apart somehow, somewhere else.

From Pamplona, Gerald and I returned to Antibes, Pauline returned to Paris, and Ernest and Hadley moved on to San Sebastian and Valencia. But in August they stopped back at Villa America to tell us they were separating. Rather, Ernest told us while Hadley remained in the guest cottage. When they arrived back in Paris, they'd be looking for two apartments. Although I can't say it came as a surprise, it hurt. Piece by piece, couple by couple, our Paris tribe seemed to be splintering apart. Perhaps we weren't as gifted at everything as we'd thought.

"It's an awfully hopeless business to lose someone you've loved and made your life with," he said, twirling his aperitif glass. From where we were seated on the patio, we could see the wide blue platform of the sea through a scrim of pine trees, and it seemed hard to reconcile all that beauty with such sad news. I felt doubly bad because I'd never really accepted Hadley as much as I should have. The truth is, what we cared most about was Ernest's talent and what would be best for its growth. Now we jumped a little too quickly onto the moving train of his romantic life, wanting to support him however we could.

"Hadley's tempo seems a little slower and less intuitive than yours," Gerald ventured. "Perhaps remaining in the marriage might be a dangerous betrayal of your own true nature."

Ernest's sad eyes seemed to be begging for such words of encouragement.

"You and Hadley are after two different kinds of truth in life, I think," Gerald continued. "I hold in sacred respect the thing you two have enjoyed, but your heart will never be at peace until you clean up and cut through." His hand sliced gently at the air.

I jumped in. "We *so* believe in what you're doing, Ernest, and the way you're doing it. I admire your refusal to accept any second-rate things. Or places, ideas, or human natures."

Gerald offered him his studio in Montparnasse as a place to land until he found a real apartment. And, after they'd left, Gerald deposited $400 in Ernest's bank account. *When life gets bumpy, you get through to the truth sooner if you're not hand-tied by the lack of a little money,* he wrote. *Sara said just to deposit this and talk about it after.*

Decades later, I would marvel at how quickly we'd supported his decision to leave his wife and child. We, who believed so fully in the principle of marriage. Who would fight to stay together through much greater adversities than one's "tempo." I would come to regret how quickly we'd thrown Hadley over in our rush to support Ernest's work. Even he would eventually condemn us for it, finding it easier to blame others than accept responsibility himself. Until then, everything around us had seemed blessed with youth and charm and talent. But this was the first sign that lives were beginning to fall apart. Although we soon came to adore Pauline, I always felt remorse for our part in his divorce from Hadley.

---

BEFORE THE SUMMER was over, we summoned the children for a confidential family meeting. Eight-year-old Honoria, seven-year-old Baoth, and five-year-old Patrick sat breathlessly around the dining table. It wasn't often we were so serious with them.

"I've received an anonymous letter in the post today," Gerald announced, and gravely placed the letter on the table. "Apparently, there's an ancient map hidden in our *very own* garden that leads to pirate treasure, buried somewhere between Antibes and the Spanish border."

We led the children to the lawn where, miraculously, a large X was marked in chalk under the hydrangea bush. After very little digging, they unearthed a rusty metal box containing an old key and an ancient parchment map with faded brown ink.

"It's written in blood!" Baoth whispered.

Gerald scrutinized the map. "Good news, comrades! The treasure looks to be buried in a cove near St.-Tropez, just ninety-seven kilometers from here. It'll be faster if we take the *Honoria*." The year before, Gerald had traded in the *Picaflor* for a longer, fancier sailboat now named after our daughter.

The next day, we loaded the boat with provisions and shovels and, with Vova at the helm, we set sail. With a full heart, I watched the children scampering confidently across the deck. Honoria was still a bit tomboyish, with her short-cropped hair and dungarees. Patrick followed Baoth's example and direction, clearly deferring to his older brother's leadership. For once, there wasn't a single quarrel or fuss.

By the time we'd dropped anchor at the sheltered cove, rowed ashore, and made camp, dusk was falling. Vova built a fire while the children and I made a stew, and Gerald opened an excellent bottle of old Bordeaux red. After dinner, I played Debussy on the windup phonograph as Gerald told ghost stories. Under a sky full of stars and the rhythmic pulse of the surf, we fell soundly asleep in our flannel bags. I thought of that first night when Gerald and I had slept under the stars on Wiborg Beach. Still two young strangers.

Baoth was up with the sun, of course, and the other two quickly followed.

"Patrick, you're in charge of the map," Gerald said, then nudged them in the right direction when they veered off course. Honoria was the first to find another X, marked neatly in stones. Equipped with child-sized shovels, the kids tired after a few minutes, so Gerald and Vova continued the job. They'd gotten about three feet down when we spotted it: the battered lid to an old leather chest.

*Trésor! Trésor! Trésor!*" the kids chanted, stomping their feet. We pulled it up with difficulty, then I inserted the key into the lock and lifted the lid.

The expressions of disbelief and delight were so enormous, I won't forget the sight as long as I breathe air. Twinkling in the early morning sun were piles of gems, jewelry, coins, compasses, and spyglasses.

"We found pirate treasure! We found pirate treasure!" they sang as they grabbed hands and danced in a circle of victory.

Gerald, Vova, and I exchanged conspiratorial smiles. The chest, found by Vova in a thrift shop on the Left Bank. The map, carefully drawn in Gerald's exquisite hand then soaked in tea to age it. And I'd bought the faux coins and paste jewelry at the Clignancourt flea market. The escapade had been months in the planning and execution. All more than amply rewarded by this moment of pure glee and magic, the look of awe on the three young faces we loved most. Once again, I secretly congratulated myself on this magical life we'd created. It would be years before they'd learn the real story.

"It was so beautiful, sometimes I question whether it really happened at all," Gerald told me much later, a faraway look in his pale eyes. In fact, it would live like a fairy tale in our collective memory, long past the time when we understood that not all fairy tales end well.

# PART III

*Show me a hero and I'll write you a tragedy.*
—F. Scott Fitzgerald

*No tears in the writer, no tears in the reader.*
—Ernest Hemingway

# Chapter 15
## 1928-1929

The previous two years had been a string of pearls: cocktail parties on the terrace, the moon reflecting off the sea. Gay mornings on the beach, the children brown and hardy in their matching sunsuits. Our guest house, la Ferme des Orangers (or, as Bob Benchley called it, "la Ferme Derangée"), was usually occupied. Ernest had quickly married Pauline. Charles Lindbergh had flown solo across the Atlantic. ("It tightens the main spring," Gerald said when he read of the crossing.)

There were times when I couldn't help myself. I would look around at our brilliant friends, our beautiful children, our sublime surroundings, and think, *Aren't we clever?* We'd set out to achieve this life, and we had achieved it. We could do anything.

---

SCOTT, ALWAYS THE fly in the butter, had revealed that he was modeling the two principal characters in his work in progress, *Tender Is the Night*, on our marriage, interrogating us in an intrusive way about the most private details of our lives.

"How much is your annual income *really*?" he asked me *alto voce* one night at dinner, in front of all our guests. I usually gave him some preposterous answer, just to shut him up, and I did so again now.

"Eleventy million American dollars—after taxes," I said, and turned to pass the platter of mussels to my left.

Scott was obsessed with our financial status, resenting us as inherently privileged while he'd had to labor so hard for his income. But I wasn't even a lesser heiress compared to some of our expatriate crowd. We were getting three and a half percent on a fund of less than $200,000, with an occasional gift from Gerald's father. Rather than receiving a monthly income, we just spent what we wanted and had our man at the Loomis-Sayles investment firm write a check to cover it.

Now Scott glowered at me with reddened eyes and thin lips. "Seriously, Sara mine. Would you say it's more than twenty-five thou a year?"

What he didn't grasp was that taste can compensate for means. For our entire marriage, Gerald and I would always be perceived as wealthier than we actually were, because we had a daring sense of style. "We're not that *kind* of rich," Gerald once said. Scott and Zelda, meanwhile, threw money away on fleeting fashion, free-flowing booze, and generally living beyond their means.

"Scott," I said now, not trying to disguise my irritation, "you think if you just ask enough questions, you'll discover what people are like, but you won't. You really don't know anything at all about people. You just don't."

Scott stood up and glared at me. Then, pointing his finger inches from my face, he said, "Nobody has *ever* had the temerity to speak to me like that!"

"Would you like me to repeat it?" I looked across the table at Zelda, who seemed mildly amused in her new, glazed way. She didn't say much these days, just fiddled with a button or muttered something under her breath. Except for her fevered study of ballet, she'd withdrawn into herself.

But Scott's face was white, his body shaking. Yes, I was being rude too. I couldn't help myself. When someone acts so vulgar, so common, sometimes you just find yourself down there on the floor with them. Refined manners were completely lost on Scott. My patience was used up.

"You really don't know anything at all about people," I said again, and he stormed off in a rage. The next day, as I so often did after these gaucheries, I wrote him a sternly worded letter explaining the basics of human company and behavior. It was tiresome, this job of mothering a fully grown man, and I began counting the days until we could return to Paris and have more distance from him.

---

THAT FALL, GERALD launched his first one-man show at the Galerie Bernheim. One of his latest paintings, *Portrait*, was a montage of his own body parts, down to his actual fingerprint. I could see his spirit opening up like the lens of a camera: curious, sensitive, vulnerable. Whenever he stumbled upon a new plan or idea, he'd make a little yelp, like a hiccup. In those moments, my heart bloomed and I remembered that he was the only man I'd ever loved.

But our eyes were already on new horizons: American ones. That summer, King Vidor had come to France to promote his latest picture, *The Crowd*. He'd heard about Gerald's expertise in Early American Negro music and wanted to talk to him about his first talkie film, *Hallelujah!*, set in the South with an all-Negro cast. And by the time Vidor left five days later, he'd made Gerald an irresistible offer to become a music consultant on the new film.

"I want to talk about it first," I said. "No more impulsive moves. This affects the whole family."

We were sitting at a café in Antibes' main square, the weak autumn sun casting longer shadows on the black cobblestones. We'd never stayed this late in the season before. The bandstand was empty, the plane trees' stubby branches becoming bare. After a summer of constant guests, having a *café complet*, just the two of us, felt precious. The pungent scent of the date palms mixed with the marine air gave off a salty-sweet, caramel smell.

"The first all-Negro talkie, Sal! What an opportunity to say something big! Besides, none of us has ever been to the West Coast. It'll be such an adventure!"

I sighed. "I know. But it feels like we're always chasing after the next big thing. Here we've created the exact life we always dreamed about. Why can't we just stay put and enjoy it?" A breeze flew by, skittering the leaves on the pavement.

In the end, I capitulated, as I usually did. It was so hard to resist Gerald when he got inspired.

---

WE BOOKED PASSAGE to New York on the SS *Saturnia* in October and from there boarded a Pullman Palace car on the train to Los Angeles. We moved as our own little town: in addition to Gerald, me, and the three children, there was Mam'zelle and Vova, who'd come to assist Gerald with his work on *Hallelujah!*

As we stood on the platform at Grand Central Station awaiting more porters to help us load our luggage, I checked and counted our trunks and valises, each color-coded with its own stripe according to its owner. Our spaniels, Porthos and Fideau, whined in their wooden crates. And I made sure I spotted my leather "bottle bag," which contained rubbing alcohol, Vichy pastilles for stomach troubles, witch hazel, Dobell's solution for sore throats, and several other remedies. I'd also decanted some good whiskey into perfume bottles, should we be stopped by customs. The 1918 pandemic was still fresh in my mind, and I'd be damned if my children were going to catch a filthy virus or a rash. All three wore the white gloves I insisted upon for traveling, and I continued the practice of lining our train car with sheets washed in Lysol.

As I sat in the parlor car watching the flat prairie landscape roll past, it sank in that this was the farthest west I'd ever been. So far we'd passed Cleveland, Chicago, Omaha, and Denver en route to San Francisco and from there to Los Angeles. Who knows, if I'd married anyone else, this might have been my life by now. Instead, Gerald and I felt like foreigners in our own country of birth.

I couldn't imagine looking at this terrain every day. The people we saw outside our train windows all seemed to conform to the same type: ill-fitting suits and practical shoes. Drab colors. Everyone in a hurry to get somewhere else. Sinclair Lewis had written *Babbitt* a few years earlier, and this dreary populace seemed to spring from its pages.

At night we lay in our bunks, rocking with the pulse of the speeding train, propelling us through the darkness toward some new chapter in the book of our lives. Gerald had taken the lower bunk, I the upper; now, when I dangled my arm over the side, he gently took my hand.

"You okay?" he whispered.

"I can't help wondering why we're always on the move like this," I whispered back. I was suddenly tired of all the trains, all the trips, all the houses. "Wouldn't it be lovely to just stay home for a while?"

"But we agreed this would be a wonderful new adventure," he said.

"And it is," I said. "I'd just forgotten how enormous this damned continent is. It's such a long trip. We're so far from everything and everyone we love."

"It's only a few months," he said. "We've never seen California. It's a chance to show the kids their own history."

And that was true. Although we'd always impressed upon the children that they were Americans first, they now spoke in a patois we called "Franglais." Perhaps some time on American soil would do them good.

But I couldn't shake the feeling that we were taking our family in the wrong direction. We were hurtling away from all the happiness we'd worked so hard to build, all the beauty we'd created. We were returning to the very place that Gerald and I had run away from, and for good reason. It was a vague feeling of impending misfortune, but I resolved to put it away and not give it room to grow.

---

"WHAT IF THERE'S an Indian raid, Dow-Dow?" Patrick asked, sitting on Gerald's lap at breakfast in the dining car. "Will the cowboys come to rescue us?" We *had* seen a few Indians out the windows of our train, and a few men in cowboy hats, too. But the Indians were usually selling crafts on blankets near the train stations.

"There aren't raids anymore," Gerald said. "In fact, the Indians are now confined to places called 'reservations' by order of the American government. They've been treated like prisoners on their own land. It's terribly unfair." Patrick's blond brows furrowed over his pale-blue eyes. The magical life we'd created for our family on the shores of the Mediterranean now seemed far away indeed. America was a harder place to explain.

We arrived in Hollywood just before Christmas and installed ourselves in a rented stucco bungalow in Beverly Hills. Our usual wintry, white holiday was replaced with swimming pools and roller-skating and visits to movie sets. The kids loved it, of course, but to me it felt bizarre. Everything was pretending to be something else.

"I don't demand good art of a country," Gerald was saying, "but when they can't cook a decent meal or sell a vegetable with any taste to it, then something's up." We were attending a lavish party at Marion Davies's faux eighteenth-century "beach house" in Malibu, which was the size of a resort fit for hundreds. The kids were ecstatic because they'd heard they'd be meeting Charlot—or Charlie Chaplin, as he was known in the States. He was completely charming, performing a magic trick for them with his hat, but they later confessed disappointment because he was missing his mustache and cane and baggy pants. The real Charles Chaplin looked nothing like Charlot.

The rest of the guests were too fancy for our blood. Dressed to the nines and drinking too much (and we were used to a *lot* of drinking), saying the first thing that entered their heads, laughing too loudly. Although Prohibition was still in effect, it didn't seem to apply to Hollywood's elite.

Fortunately, Dottie Parker was in town to write scripts for MGM and Bob Benchley was doing a few movies for 20th Century Fox, so we had some kindred company. Dottie and Gerald had known each other since grade school in New York, when she was Dorothy Rothschild, and I considered her one of the greatest gifts of our marriage. She'd introduced us to Benchley.

Now we stood on an upper terrace looking out at the Pacific Ocean, so flat and vast it almost seemed possible to see to the Hawaiian Islands. Unlike the beaches at East Hampton, with their hillocks and dunes and sea grasses, the shoreline here was just one long expanse of empty sand. How I missed our rustic little stretch of beach at La Garoupe, seaweed and all.

"The whole place is pretentiously quaint," I complained to Dottie. "The waitresses are costumed like shepherdesses or Dutch girls with wooden shoes. We're surrounded by the Hippedy-Hop Cake Shop, the Storknest Hospital, the Rite Spot, or the 'Home of the Aristocratic Hamburger.'" A burst of raucous laughter sounded from inside the mansion. I took a sip of my gin fizz and reached for another cigarette. I'd begun smoking Lucky Strikes. "The other day in the grocery, I asked for Saltines and the clerk handed me a box labeled 'Cupid Chips'! Can you imagine?"

"Don't forget the Naughty Waffle Sandwich, Buddy Squirrel's Nut Shop, or Ye Bull Pen Inn," Gerald chimed in. "How about that monstrous Brown Derby, where you eat in a hat? Really, where does it end?"

"Philistines, all of them," Dottie agreed. "The other day a director bragged to me about his hundred-and-fifty-thousand-dollar 'liberry' with a first edition of *Edith* St. Vincent Millay."

We gasped and giggled.

"Meanwhile, I'm so desperate for company, I posted a 'Men's Room' sign on my office door. Nobody stays for long, fortunately." She lit a cigarette off mine.

I sighed. "At least we've discovered the Mexican quarter. Olvera Street has practically saved our lives with its crafts and food. Dottie, you haven't *lived* until you've tasted a fresh tortilla."

"Well, consider me dead, then." Dottie was adorable in those days, with her dark almond eyes and her short black bob. I always loved watching men meet her for the first time, assume she was an ingenue and then quickly deflate in the face of her wicked wit. "The first thing I do in the morning is brush my teeth and sharpen my tongue," she was fond of saying.

---

WITH MAM'ZELLE ON hand to tutor the children, our days in California followed a similar routine to our days in France, except that Gerald went to the studio every day to work on the picture. In addition to the two dogs, we'd acquired a turtle for Patrick and a canary for Honoria, though I explained that the creatures would have to remain in California when we returned home.

Naturally, I'd already engaged a family doctor to be on call for any emergencies and, during our first consultation, he recommended tonsillectomies for all three children. It was a relatively new medical discovery, he said, one that was increasingly in vogue with American families.

"The tonsils are portals of infection," Dr. Weiss advised. "Their risk certainly outweighs their benefit. Should the tissue become infected, it can lead to systemic disease in other parts of the body." He was a small man with a tidy mustache and a blue bowtie.

His fingernails were neatly trimmed. "That's why we recommend removing them as a prophylactic measure during childhood, and your three fall in the perfect age range: eleven, nine, and eight." Of course I was sold on it immediately.

Cedars-Sinai Hospital offered a level of care far beyond what was available in France, he assured me, so I made arrangements for Honoria, Baoth, and Patrick to have the operations the following week. *It seems the most favorable time, in a mild climate like this,* I wrote my father. *And it's really most necessary—they have glands and things which will only make trouble later.*

"It will hurt to swallow at first," I told them. "But the good news is that you can eat ice cream all week!" I allowed them to request whatever flavors they wanted, as long as they contained no nuts to scratch their tender throats.

The tonsillectomies went according to plan and all three were looking forward to coming home from the hospital. But a few days later, I received word that Honoria was calling for me.

"My throat hurts so much, Maman," she said, "but the nurse just told me to go to sleep." Her face was red against the starched white pillowcase. Her forehead was aflame. And when she opened her mouth, it was filled with blood.

I picked up the phone on the bedside table and called the nurses' station.

"Dr. Weiss isn't on duty, but I can send the attending physician, Dr. Crozier," the nurse said.

"Right away, please!" I stroked Honoria's cheek and gripped her hand.

Within minutes, Dr. Crozier rushed into the room and examined Honoria's throat. He ordered a nurse to pack her with gauze and immediately transferred her to the operating room to suture a ligation. Gerald met me in the waiting room, and we paced the floor for an hour until the doctor emerged.

"It's a very good thing you called when you did," he said. "Ten more minutes and that child would've died." He assured me that the previous nurse would be promptly dismissed.

Back at home, I cried and balled my fists. "This was an *elective* procedure!" I wailed. "I put my own daughter at risk! How close we came to losing her!"

Gerald sat calmly on the leather sofa. "Sal. You did the best you could. You were trying to protect them from future harm." His face was concerned, but his voice was even. One of the greatest blessings of our marriage was that we could trade places in the blink of an eye, one of us measured and mature when the other was in a freefall. "And you *saved* Honoria! Stop berating yourself."

To come all this way to unnecessarily lose a child. I couldn't get the horror of it out of my mind.

Several days later, all three children came home, bundled up in the back seat of our Plymouth sedan. Baoth and Honoria were able to walk into the house, but our chauffeur, Jocko, carefully carried Patrick inside and upstairs to bed. We were happy to think that the worst was behind us.

Many years later, I would identify that moment—Honoria's near death—as the place when our life began to shift. It was as if we'd reached the summit of some finite universe and tumbled over the edge into a new way of being. Then falling, falling, from a dream world to a life of mere survival.

---

GERALD HAD BEEN at work on *Hallelujah!* for six weeks, and it wasn't going well. "Thalberg's a bully, making executive demands," he said. "Now the picture's losing its soul." The opening scene was now set on a cotton plantation, and the authentic Negro spirituals had been replaced by Stephen Foster songs. "Can you believe it? He's objecting to the lead actress as 'too Negro-looking!'" He shook his head.

One evening, Gerald returned home even more dispirited than

usual. I took one look at the pallor of his face and promptly opened a bottle of chablis, then handed him a glass and we sat down on the sofa, with its view out to the back lawn: date palms and cypresses. A flat blue sky.

"They have it so full of scenes around the cabin door, with talk of chitlins and corn pone and banjos a-strummin', it's about as authentic as Lew Dockstader's Minstrels," he said, shaking his head. "And today came the ultimate insult: they hired Lionel Barrymore to coach the actors on the use of Negro dialect!"

"You can't be serious, Dow," I said, pouring myself a glass to keep up.

"King considers it the most daring, original, planet-displacing thing to not have one single white person in the cast. But they're treating these people as caricatures. Buffoons!" He ran a hand through his thinning sandy hair. "I've been working for six weeks on a picture that should've been surefire stuff: eighty Negroes cast from the Southern states. It was a chance to say something truly original."

"Is there nothing you can do? After all, they hired you to coach them on an authentic sound."

"Oh, it's way beyond my coaching them. It's as if they've never heard of the Civil War."

"So what do you plan to do?"

"I already did something. I resigned today. My god!"

I stopped, my glass halfway to my mouth. "You resigned?" *Again?*

"I did. I'm sorry, it was untenable." He jumped up to pour himself another glass.

I sat for a minute, completely mute. He was always so quick to leave an uncomfortable situation and move onto the next thing. And I always followed. For one tiny moment, I felt foolish for hitching my wagon to this mercurial man. Perhaps I was *too much* of a good sport.

"I just wish we'd talked about it first."

"There was no time. I went onto the set today prepared to make the most of it, but when I heard about Barrymore, a door just slammed in my head. There's no way to stand up to Thalberg. There's no reasoning with him."

How often had this happened? Gerald would get inspired by some whim—to study landscaping, to move to England, to buy a new boat—and the whole family had to uproot itself and follow him blindly. I suddenly felt angry, not only by the news of his resignation, but by the fact that we'd come all the way to California in the first place. What did he know about filmmaking? Such a risky endeavor, only to be tossed away when the going got tough.

"But we've leased the house for three months." I crossed my arms. My head was already calculating the packing, the moving, the rescheduled tickets, the travel. I stared out the window, where the date palms were swaying in the breeze, as if already waving goodbye.

"I'll talk to the leasing agent in the morning; perhaps we can get some of our deposit back. And we could go visit Olga's family in Carmel-by-the-Sea before heading back across country. It'll be a lark."

Of course it *was* a lark. We managed to make everything a lark in those days. We traveled north to visit my sister, Olga, with her husband, Sidney, and her son, Stuyvie. Then we stopped to visit my father in New York, who only wanted to talk about the stock market. "I advise getting out sooner rather than later," he said. "Times are uncertain right now."

But the market had been rising higher and higher, I argued, and Olga had been working with a more aggressive broker. Why not strike while the iron was hot? It was March of 1929, and we were still young and optimistic.

# Chapter 16
## 1929-30

After the disappointment of California, returning to Villa America was like heaven in a teacup. The authentic—not imitation—Mediterranean architecture terraced along the hill of the cap. The warm embrace of intimate dinners with friends in place of loud parties for hundreds. The scent of gardenias and heliotrope—what I called "cherry-pie flower" with its notes of vanilla and almond—wafting from the garden.

One afternoon it was just Honoria and me, sitting in the dining room for high tea with a platter of crêpes and a saucer of lemon curd. Gerald had taken the boys into town for some canvas and garden supplies. It was a rare chance to be alone with my daughter.

Honoria was wearing one of my floral chiffon dresses with about eight necklaces of pearls and crystal beads. I wore a striped sundress with rows of Bakelite bangles on each arm. As we'd observed ourselves in the full-length mirror, I offered Coco Chanel's classic advice: "Before you leave the house, always look in the mirror and take one thing off."

I'd forfeited one bangle. Honoria gave up her dangling earrings.

"Good taste means knowing when to stop," I said. "Whether it's jewelry or conversation or cocktails. Remember that, darling."

Honoria was an athletic girl, forever competing with her brothers in any physical feat, but she had an inherent femininity that always shone through. Even in coveralls, with her hair bobbed short like a boy's, her delicate features and rosebud mouth often brought comparisons with Renoir's female subjects. Now, in her eleventh year, I could see her furtively studying me and the other women in our group on the beach. She could become anything, any kind of person she wanted to be. That was the gift Gerald and I had given our children—the idea of infinite possibility.

Now she chattered on, delighted to have my undivided attention. I thought back to my eleven-year-old self. What I would have given for one afternoon like this with my own mother! As I watched Honoria, bubbling with *boneur*, I marveled at this magical creature and my good fortune to call her my own. She could become anything, this girl. Her future held so many prospects—and not just marriage proposals.

---

GERALD AND I lay in bed as the first rays of sun peeked through the gauzy curtains. From behind, I felt his hand circle my waist, then find its way to my breast. He snuggled closer and I could feel the suggestion of his interest. I rolled over and looked at him.

"Yes?" I smiled.

"We have returned to ourselves, Sal," he said. "And my self loves your self."

"Aren't we lucky, Dow? Let's never leave again."

"Mmm, never." He was brushing his lips on my cheek, my brow, my mouth. I opened my arms to him, and we slid into each other, a coupling I never tired of. Like everything else Gerald did, our lovemaking was done meticulously, consciously, deliberately. And when it was over, the expression on his face always conveyed relief and gratitude. Our mutual satisfaction was always ensured, despite the predictability of our methods. I could be happy with that, I told myself. I knew he loved me, and that would suffice.

As our marriage aged, I came to think of myself as a meadow—flat and exposed to the light, easily surveyed, accessed by straight roads. But Gerald was a forest—deep, dark, and mysterious, with narrow winding paths. When a black mood came over him, he became absolutely unreachable. And when he angered, he could turn icy cold. On the occasional days he was under the spell of the Black Service, I knew to keep others at bay and let him retreat to his dark places. He would come back, in a few hours or a day, full of remorse and contrition. He was like the tide; he would go out, but I always knew he would come back in again.

---

IT WASN'T LONG before our life returned to normal, which meant full of visiting friends. Bob Benchley came down from Paris with his wife and two boys, along with Dottie Parker and her insufferably yapping dog, Timothy. She was recovering from her latest failed American romance and spent much of her time in the garden, smoking Gitanes and staring out to sea with Timothy on her lap. No matter how often I envied her razor wit, I knew that it came with a dark counterpart: a deep, suffocating sadness, much like Gerald's.

Ernest and Pauline came for a brief visit from the States with their new baby, Patrick. When Gerald heard his name for the first time, I saw him flinch. First Ernest had appropriated his use of the term "Daughter" for young women, and now this. There was always some kind of competition between Ernest and other men, and even Gerald fell prey to his game.

Relations between the two of them were becoming noticeably tense. Over the years Gerald had often played father figure to Ernest—supporting his work, paying Bumby's medical bills, approving of his decision to leave Hadley for Pauline, even loaning him his studio during the separation. But now, after the success of *The Sun Also Rises* and a new novel ready for publication, Ernest almost seemed to resent him.

"Doesn't it bother you? After all your kindnesses, he tends to brush you off," I said one day after Ernest had retreated to the *bastide*.

"Ah, the human psyche is a complicated thing," Gerald said. "Remember, his father recently took his own life. Perhaps instead of remorse, he feels he needs to kill off any other paternal relationships as well. I try not to take it personally."

Scott and Zelda also came briefly on their way to Paris, and the spit and shine was fully off their marriage. What had tethered us to them was the sweetness and brilliance they exuded when sober. But Scott was rarely sober now, his face ghostly and drawn, his hands shaking. And Zelda had turned into someone else altogether. Instead of the clever, mischievous girl we'd first met, now she could talk of nothing but her ballet lessons and her futile aspirations to become a prima ballerina.

"Say-rah, did I tell you? They invited me to join the ballet school of the San Carlo Opera Ballet." She spoke in the lower registers now, her voice full of wistfulness. Her hair and dress had become something of an afterthought. "But Scott says we can't go. We only do what's good for *him*. Now he's my lord and master." She gave him a doleful look.

"Oh, don't go all Lillian Gish on me again," Scott shot back. "I'm the one who's killing myself to keep the money coming in, and you want to move to Naples to *dance*? I think not. Your job was Flapper Girl, the embodiment of the world I'm writing about. It's been a pretty good life, I'd say. But all you can think about is *your* artistic ambitions. Such a waste of time."

In more sober, private moments, Scott had confided that he really was worried about Zelda. And I could see he was driving himself too hard to complete his next elusive novel. But being in their presence together was like living with two snapping turtles.

One afternoon the Fitzgeralds joined us with all the children at the little Antibes cinema off the square. As we walked up the street I took in the salty smell of the fishing boats, the warm glow of the blond stones, the gentle plink of the steel *boules* in the pétanque court. It was so good to be back in France, where life went on as it had for centuries.

Once inside, we let the children take their popcorn and sit down in front, while we adults sat in back for a short movie about sea life. The film clattered through the projector and the screen filled with schools of parrotfish, crowds of sea jellies. Suddenly an enormous image of an octopus crawled across the screen. We'd seen plenty of octopuses off the shore of La Garoupe or laid out on ice in the fish market. But the enlarged image in black and white was a little startling. Now Zelda began screaming. "What is it? What is it?" she sobbed into Gerald's chest, clinging onto him for dear life.

"Zelda dear, it's just an octopus," Gerald said, but by now the entire theater had turned to glare at us.

We waited for her sobs to subside, but they didn't. And Scott looked increasingly distressed.

"You take her home, Scott," I finally said. "We'll bring Scottie back after supper."

The Fitzgeralds left Antibes the next day, and we wouldn't see Zelda again for a very long time.

---

THE CHILDREN WERE growing like Midwestern corn. The signs of childhood seemed to drop off them by the day—gone were the dimpled hands, the pudgy limbs, the full cheeks. At twelve, Honoria was beginning to show an adolescent self-consciousness, and the walls of her room displayed magazine photos of movie stars like Rudolf Valentino and Greta Garbo. Baoth's jaw was growing chiseled, and he was developing an athleticism that reminded me of my father. And Patrick—always the slighter and fairer child—was still delicate, but I could see him growing into *his* father. "More Gerald than Gerald," I liked to say. They still loved to romp in the sea, but Honoria frequently migrated to the umbrella where the adults gathered, occupying herself with a book or journal. I could almost see them slipping away from me, growing into lives of their own. I comforted myself with the thought that one day there would be grandchildren, whom I could love as much as my own offspring.

---

IN JUNE GERALD took off on his sailboat race, and I looked forward to a quiet month with the children. But just one week later I wired him to return home immediately: Patrick had developed an intestinal bug and was increasingly feverish and listless. Dr. Babcock had been around to examine him but could make no diagnosis. In the meantime, my eight-year-old son seemed to grow sicker by the day. His normally rosy skin now sallow. His white-blond hair pasted against his skull with sweat. Never a robust child, his frame seemed even slighter than usual. Suddenly our summer plans—Venice, Spain—evaporated.

By the time Gerald arrived home, I'd already taken Patrick to see a doctor at the clinic in Antibes, who concluded it was bronchitis. Now our son had a rumbling, wet cough that threatened to turn him inside out with its spasms.

Here we were, back in the doctor's tiny office with old lace curtains at the windows and a single, faded diploma on his wall from Université d'Aix-Marseille.

"I recommend Villard-de-Lans in the Cévennes *massif*," he said. "It's a high-altitude ski resort with thin, cold air. Get him outside every day. Take him trout fishing."

"I can do that," I volunteered. "Dow, you stay home with Honoria and Baoth. I'll take Patrick to the mountains."

But after three weeks of glacial air, Patrick was not one whit better. I wired Gerald that we'd be coming home; we were expecting Pauline

Hemingway's sister, Jinny Pfeiffer, and she could stay with the older children while we took Patrick to a specialist in Paris.

---

PARIS IN THE fall is usually dramatic in the waning autumn sunlight, the bell towers of Notre-Dame casting long shadows across the *Île de la Cité*. But I saw none of this in our haste to get Patrick to the office of Dr. Armand De Lille at the Hôpital Pitié Salpêtrière. Instead, I memorized every detail of the antiseptic room, first as Dr. De Lille examined our son and a few days later when he called us back in, just Gerald and me, to give us the news. I stared at the eye chart posted against the mint-colored wall, the white enamel cabinets, the pneumatic tubes hanging from the ceiling, the sharp implements in a metal pan on a side table. The horror of our experience at the hospital in Los Angeles came back with a pang.

Dr. De Lille stood before us, fingering his stethoscope and clearing his throat. "It is not good news, I'm afraid," he began in English. We would have understood him in French—the use of our native language made his tone feel even more serious, as if he were telling us that Patrick was already dead.

"Your son has contracted tuberculosis, and it is now firmly entrenched. His left lung is seriously compromised, and the right one is menaced." He paused and Gerald grabbed my hand. Someone was sobbing loudly from the next room. *Menaced?* It was as if a dark, noxious cloud had suddenly descended on our family.

"Sal," he said, stroking my hand, and I realized that the sobs were my own. What little I knew of TB was that it was ultimately a death sentence.

Dr. De Lille began talking again, but I couldn't make out his words. A small animal was scrambling around inside my chest, and my mind was watching a magic lantern casting images of our family over the past decade: the houses, the gardens, the gay dinner parties.

The three gorgeous children, playing innocently in the sand or riding tricycles on the tiled terrace of Villa America. I could hear their voices now, like church bells. We'd thought we were the architects of our enchanted life, which we'd assumed would last forever. What fools we'd been.

Gerald was studiously taking notes in his pocket *cahier* and the doctor was saying that, if Patrick was to stand a chance at survival, he'd need to begin pneumothorax treatments immediately and be taken to a sanatorium.

"The *plombage*, or pneumothorax technique, collapses the infected lung to allow the lesions to heal," he said. "They're injections of three hundred cubic centimeters of gas, which immobilizes and stops the spread of the infection."

"How is it administered?" Gerald asked. "Is it painful?"

"A needle under the arms, between the ribs," the doctor said. "And yes, it is quite a thick needle. One every fifteen days to maintain the pressure, for two years."

I began weeping again. Patrick, my most delicate child. The baby, always trying to keep up with the older children on their tricycles or at the beach. The tiny blue capillaries in his tender eyelids.

As we left, Dr. De Lille handed us a brochure for Montana-Vermala, a health resort on the Plaine Morte glacier in the Swiss Alps.

In the taxi on the way back to Quai des Grands Augustins, I watched as Paris passed by, the city completely oblivious to how our earth had just shifted on its axis. I remembered a day at the East Hampton shore decades before, when I swam out farther than usual. In those days, girls were discouraged from swimming at all, but this was Wiborg Beach, the vast shoreline extending from the Dunes, and we Wiborg girls could do what we pleased.

I'd paddled out to where my feet couldn't touch bottom and soon felt the weight of my thick cotton swim costume begin to pull me under. As I turned around to swim to shore, a big wave caught and tumbled me around underwater until I was sure I would drown.

When it finally spit me back onto the sand, I was scraped and bruised, with salt water pouring from my mouth and nose. I looked around for someone to rush over and make a fuss, but Mother never came down to the shore with us. There was only Hoytie standing a few yards away.

"That's what you get for swimming past the rocks," she'd laughed.

Now I shook my head and continued to stare out the window at Paris. Such a fickle town. So breathtakingly beautiful to look at, but such a breeding ground for bad behavior. I thought of all the time and energy we'd indulged in our Paris life, our Antibes life. The love I'd put into the piles of thick Turkish towels in the guest baths. The vases of fresh flowers in every room. The best Roquefort to accompany the fresh-baked baguettes, the perfectly brined olives. How focused we'd been on such superficial matters when we should never have taken our eyes off our children, not for one second, especially our most delicate child. We'd been good parents, I knew that. But apparently you could never be good enough.

I was gripping Gerald's hand so fiercely that he gently pulled it away.

"Sal," he said. "It's not a *fait accompli*. We're going to take him to Switzerland and apply all our ingenuity to curing him."

He gently took my chin and turned my face to look at him.

"We're being called upon to do something new," he said. "We've always been good at that."

I nodded mutely. But we both felt it. Gerald would be the strong one now.

---

FOR THE NEXT two days, my mind tumbled around the injustice of life. How on *earth* had this happened?

Then one morning, as the sun began seeping through the curtains of our bedroom, I sat up straight and turned to Gerald.

"Jocko!" I said.

"What's that?" Gerald was already up, lathering his shaving foam in a mug.

"Jocko, our chauffeur in California. Don't you remember that awful cough he had?"

"Hmmm, remotely."

"He had a cough the entire time we lived there. And he was the one to carry Patrick into the house after the hospital." I got up and found my dressing gown and slippers.

Wheels were turning behind Gerald's eyes. "I think you may be right."

I groaned. "What a price we've paid for that miserable trip."

He began lathering his face with a sable brush. He didn't want to egg me on or fuel my fury.

I'd had such a bad feeling about that trip, from the very start. Gerald's goddamned Negro spirituals, which had led us to the catastrophe of Hollywood. He hadn't meant to, but his impulsive nature had led us to this possible death sentence for our son. It was so clearly one "adventure" we shouldn't have taken—I couldn't shake the feeling that we'd turned left when we should have turned right. Or better yet, just stayed put! Why did we always have to run after the next shiny thing? If I mentioned it, Gerald would add it to his already long list of things to feel tragic about. So it became a wound I would hold inside for a very long time.

Now I was opening and closing drawers with a little too much force. My anger was bubbling out of my heart and into my hands, my feet, the set of my jaw. I tied the sash of my robe and stomped downstairs for a cigarette.

---

THE REST OF October was a blur. On the eighteenth, Patrick's ninth birthday, Gerald took him directly to Montana-Vermala. Jinny Pfeiffer brought Honoria and Baoth up to Paris from Antibes because Honoria had also been running a fever. Her X-rays showed no evidence of TB bacilli, but her bronchioles were spotty, so De Lille advised three months of bed rest for her as well.

Back we went to Villa America to pack up and move indefinitely to Switzerland, an elevation of five thousand feet above sea level. We also brought Mam'zelle, the tutor, and Dottie Parker came along too, after helping me to pack up the villa. Dottie wasn't someone you'd normally call upon in a crisis, but through this ordeal she was an absolute rock.

After an endless train journey through northern Italy and over the Alps, the last leg of which was on a tiny groaning funicular, we made it to the Palace Hotel, our many trunks following in the next gondola. The place operated both as a sanatorium for patients and a hotel for their families, but a palace it was not. Everyone had to observe quiet hours every afternoon and after eight in the evening. The windows and doors were kept ajar all day to keep the air frigid and the hotel well-ventilated. No fresh flowers or greens were allowed, as allergies could add to the already compromised lungs.

Upon our arrival, Dottie scanned the sparse and antiseptic lobby, which smelled of floor wax. "Kindly direct me to hell," she said.

It wasn't long before she was casually referring to the sanatorium as the "Death House at Sing-Sing." Patrick's day nurse was "Frau Schadenfreude" and Montana-Vermala was "this goddamned Alp." Her razor wit was one of the few things that could make me laugh in those terrible days.

That evening when the adults all met in the dining room, she appeared looking like Nanook of the North. "I've dressed for dinner," she said, showing us her layers: a tweed suit, an overcoat, a woolen muffler, a knitted cap, and mittens. "But good news! When I go outside tomorrow, I'll take off either the coat or the muffler." She was hardly exaggerating. For the next seven months, we would dress like Siberians at all hours of the day.

We'd taken a suite of five rooms on the second floor that opened onto a balcony with a fine view of the lake and mountains, and Patrick's room at the far end. We wore cloth masks all day except in the dining room and on the balconies. I shopped in the village for little touches that might make our rooms feel gayer, but there's only so much you can do with red felt and miniature cuckoo clocks.

Oddly, the hotel had allowed us to bring our four dogs as well as a naughty monkey, Mistigris, we'd picked up somewhere along the way. And Dottie gave us a parrot named Coquotte, whom she had taught to squawk, "What fresh hell is this? What fresh hell is this?" The bird took to sitting on Gerald's shoulder as he scurried about attending to Patrick's needs.

Between the chaos of our household and the round-the-clock care of Patrick, I was grateful to be constantly occupied, to distract my mind from how dreadfully off course our lives had veered. And I could see in Gerald—his obsessive attention to Patrick's every need—how he was trying to make up for what had brought us here.

While Honoria and Baoth grew fuller and rosier with the hearty Swiss food and the Alpine climate, Patrick just looked older and more drawn. I bought a thick goose-down comforter to layer over the hotel's thinner one to keep him warm in his frigid room at night, and today I tucked it around him before I wheeled him onto the balcony to inhale the glacial air. He resembled a little old man as he scowled out from his nest of eiderdown quilts, his blue eyes faded in their sockets.

The sight of my youngest child, my baby, in a wheelchair never ceased to clutch my heart like a claw. We'd always taken such good care of our things. My Venetian goblets wrapped in tissue in a wooden cabinet. Gerald's silver cocktail forks stored in a felt bag. The annual application of clear varnish to the hull of the *Honoria*. Why could you never fully protect your children in the same way?

*Melankolly skenery*, Patrick jokingly captioned one of his landscape drawings, a view across the lake to the jagged white Alps.

The lake was nearly black, much darker than the aquamarine blue of the Mediterranean, and to swim in its icy waters would kill you in a matter of minutes. Such was my outlook most days on the goddamned Alp.

"My poor little Pook." I patted his scrawny arm under the quilt. It felt like a wishbone.

"I miss the seashore, Maman. How can all this cold air do anyone any good? I miss the umbrella pine trees and the stinky smell of seaweed. I want to swim and sail and eat *pomme frites* at the café."

We *all* wanted to be back at the seashore, I thought, where life had been so simple and lovely and warm. I could practically smell the pommes frites myself.

"We'll be there again, dear. We just have to get you better first." The thought of Villa America, now so empty and quiet, made my heart pinch. My mind's eye went to the wall of the kitchen, where we'd meticulously marked the children's growing heights in pencil. Back when we were so confident they'd all grow taller and older.

I went inside and returned with the case of good Swiss art supplies I'd found in town. Patrick—like a miniature version of his father—had always been an excellent sketcher, and now he spent hours each day filling a notebook with drawings and watercolors. It was all we had to distract him from the tedium of his regimen and the pain of his pneumothorax treatments.

---

ON THE MORNING of October 30, Gerald and I came down to breakfast with Baoth—Honoria and Patrick received their meals on trays in bed, although Honoria was well on her way back to health. We found Dottie at the table with a copy of the *International Herald Tribune* and a face even darker than her usual deadpan.

"Goodness Dottie, the day's hardly begun," Gerald said as he poured our coffee and placed the sugar bowl next to my cup and saucer. "What can you possibly have found already to merit your displeasure?"

She merely turned the paper so we could read the headline in large block type: "BLACK TUESDAY." Gerald took it and we read together. Some sixteen million shares had been traded on the New York Stock Exchange the day before. Billions of dollars were lost, wiping out thousands of investors. Many had already jumped to their deaths from Manhattan's skyscrapers.

"Let's wire Mr. Amory at Loomis-Sayles," I said. "I'm sure he'll tell us there's nothing to worry about."

"We're invested in securities, Sal," Gerald said, still reading. "Not much Amory can do for us now. There's plenty to worry about."

My eyes roamed around the dining room—its white tablecloths and dark red carpet, its stern waiters walking briskly to and from the kitchen, the constant smell of consommé. I wanted to be anywhere but here.

"Well, I have no more worry to spare," I said. "Wall Street can go hang itself."

"Apparently half the city is already walking about with nooses around their necks," Dottie said, scraping a film of butter on her toast. "So consider it done."

By now our waiter was standing to my left, ready to take my order. "I'll have the *omelette aux herbes*, wheat toast, and the fruit compote," I said with conviction. Damn tuberculosis and the stock market to hell. We would still eat.

"I'll cable Loomis-Sayles straightaway," Gerald said. "He'll give us the real story."

The news from America felt faraway and unimportant. Everything would turn around before we really needed to worry, I told myself. It would be three years before we truly understood how life-changing Black Tuesday had been.

---

GERALD HAD BEGUN tending to Patrick himself—sleeping at his bedside, taking his temperature, emptying his chamber pot, escorting him to his injections. We'd both been doting parents, but now Gerald surpassed me. His manic side took over, and I was grateful for it. He threw himself into our son's medical care the way he'd thrown himself into everything else—with passion. Back at Villa America, his studio sat gathering dust. He would never paint again.

At Christmas, reinforcements arrived. Scott came, and the Hemingways, and John Dos Passos with his lovely new bride, Katy. Ernest brought a goose he'd shot himself, which I asked the kitchen to prepare along with mashed chestnuts and a flaming pudding. We sang some Christmas carols. And we turned one of our rooms into a *gluhwein* parlor with a little bar, where Gerald revived his talents as a bartender. We all sat around and spoke in whispers, tiny clouds in the chilly air.

That's how we celebrated our fourteenth anniversary on December 30. Gerald and I entwined our arms and drank the spicy wine from heavy mugs in a sad echo of our wedding day back in New York, when everything was so glossy and promising and unknown. Gerald was no longer that Gerald and I was no longer that Sara. We had to find a new way of being together, as our new selves. Strength and patience now had to replace levity and imagination.

"To better days," Gerald said.

"To better days," we all echoed.

We kissed a lovely, tender kiss. The room fell silent for a minute or two.

Then Gerald broke the pall. "And here's to the czar," he said. "When the people were penniless, the czar was Nicholas!"

We laughed as quietly as we could. For a moment I saw the old Dow-Dow—the raker of beaches, the priest of cocktails, the boulevardier of Paris.

Not that our life before had been effortless. We'd worked hard for it, but our focus had been on amusements. Long, leisurely dinners with witty banter. Sailing excursions along the coast. Gay parties for the children. The question was always: how can we make this moment even more beautiful? What a superficial folly that all seemed now, when we were faced with matters of life and death. Once again, I stifled my urge to blame Gerald for the fiasco of California.

---

AT NEW YEAR'S, Ernest began taking Honoria and Baoth up the mountain for skiing lessons. They'd return home with red faces and bottomless appetites, and I felt a little hope that we would be a healthy family again. Patrick rallied, then faltered, then rallied again. We saw gradual improvement in his weight and temperature as we fed him good meats and cereals, fruit compotes, fresh vegetables. We absolutely refused to consider any future other than the one in which he recovered completely.

Somehow we endured eighteen months of "the goddamned Alp." By May of 1930, Patrick had recovered sufficiently for us to rent a nearby chalet, La Bruyère. What a relief to get out of the Palace Hotel! But just two days after the move, I received a cable that my father had died of pneumonia in East Hampton, so I booked passage and took Baoth back to America for the funeral, where I briefly saw Olga and Hoytie.

We didn't speak much of it then, but the general black mood was deepened by our knowledge that our bank accounts had been hit hard by the crash. We weren't yet ready to admit it, but the old life was already gone.

## Chapter 17
### 1930-1931

We were desperate for some diversion. Although La Bruyère was leased, we bought another house in nearby Montana-Vermala and fixed it up as a nightclub. We hung the windows with red-and-white-striped awnings, and I decorated the interior with mirrors and red stars. Then we found a good chef, Gerald hired a dance band from Munich, and I had little leather-bound pocket diaries printed as souvenirs.

The place was open on Fridays and Saturdays and even charged admission. We called it Harry's, after Harry's American Bar in Paris and, as usual, the locals flocked to anything American like ants to a picnic. After the last set finished, Gerald and I would often sit at the piano and sing. It was a noble attempt to remind us of gayer times—we were determined to show that we were still the magical Murphys, at least on the weekends.

Now I sat at a table with Dottie, drinking Cinzano in pretty little green glasses. We watched as Gerald stood at the bar chatting with a guest, acting out some amusing charade and charming all within earshot. His public persona. The happy atmosphere relaxed me into a confessional candor that I didn't often allow. Now I found myself sharing details of our lives that I usually protected.

"He's so stalwart and responsible about Patrick's care," I said. "He holds himself to *such* a high standard. But that's caused his black moods to return. And he doesn't have his painting to pour himself into anymore."

Dottie nodded. "Mr. Gormerly, he's a complicated man," using Bob Benchley's fond name for the gloomy version of Gerald. "He has that Irish morbid, turned-in thing."

"Patrick's illness has triggered all his old self-doubts," I said. "We all naturally love him, but he simply can't love himself in the same way." Once again, I'd felt the burden of responsibility shift to me. Gerald and I were relay runners, passing the baton back and forth between us across the years of our marriage.

---

WE HAD ANOTHER occasional visitor in those days. Scott was living in Geneva because Zelda had been committed to the care of one Dr. Forel in Prangins, while Scottie stayed with friends in Paris. After we'd last seen her in Antibes, Zelda had plunged into a level of madness from which no doctor had been able to extract her; the diagnosis was schizophrenia. We could see the growing devastation on Scott's face with each visit, but after a few drinks he'd become mawkish and offensive, just as he always had.

One night we were sitting with Scott and Dottie at a corner table. Scott was already past his limit, his elbows splayed on the table, his sentences slurred. Gerald and I exchanged the look that said we needed to find a way to transport him back to his room before he said or did something unforgivable—which we would invariably forgive later.

"She's telling that idiot Forel every goddamned thing she ever thought about me," Scott slurred, "and you know how her imagination works. She says I plagiarized her journals, for one. Can you imagine? As if I needed to read the diaries of a mad flapper for material!" On his last word, a drop of spittle flew across the table and landed on my glass.

"Okay, Scott," Gerald said. "Don't get yourself into a lather."

"Oh, that's not all, sir! My good sir, Gerald Murphy. Do you know she called me a *pansy*? Me, the Arrow Collar Man of the nineteen twenties?" Scott propped his head with a wobbly arm and let out a drunken giggle.

"You've *both* had such a hard time," I said, using my "now-it's-time-to-go" voice. But before I could rise from my seat, Scott turned his sodden gaze on me.

"Ah Sara, my lovely, lovely, lovely friend." He stared at me with red-rimmed eyes. "So sympathetic. So supportive. So goddamned cheerful all the time. I don't suppose *you've* ever known despair."

The whole table froze in shock as we absorbed the cruelty of his words. For perhaps the first time in my life, I was speechless.

"That's enough, Scott!" Gerald stood up so fast his chair keeled over.

It took Dottie mere seconds to load her verbal Tommy gun. "You sniveling, drunken, insulting *sot*!" she said. "You don't even know the *word* despair until you've watched your child linger at the periphery of life for a year and a half. You don't deserve to lick the heel of Sara's well-soled *boot* of despair, you cowardly, self-absorbed clown."

She took my arm and escorted me from the bar, leaving Gerald to deal with the puddle left of Scott. "Remind me again why we're still even friends with that fool?" Dottie asked, lighting a Gauloise.

As we walked down the empty street to our car, I couldn't find an answer. I felt like an old dog that had just been kicked by his master for the hundredth time but knew he would be back at his feet by bedtime. Why did we continue our friendship with such a mean-spirited, undisciplined man? But under the question, I already knew the answer. We'd seen the pure white light of Scott's talent—and Zelda's. We'd seen them at their shining best. The drink and the madness were just layers of tarnish over the beautiful young souls we'd once known. Besides, loyalty was a signature trait for me. It wasn't anything I prided myself on or aspired to. It's just how I was. Once I decided I liked you, you were stuck with me.

MOVING TO LA Bruyère had restored us as a family. Once again, we had our own house, with the privacy of four solid walls. It was a four-story, half-timbered stucco perched on a steep hill with views of forested slopes and the Rhône Valley below. On a clear day, we could make out Mont Blanc in the distance. Now we could laugh or act up without being hushed by a passing nurse. Now we were five Murphys plus Patrick's nurse and our growing menagerie—a monkey, a rabbit, a parrot, two mammoth tortoises, and several dogs. Vova Orloff also joined us from Paris. I thought I'd missed the pandemonium of Villa America until the day that Mistigris, the monkey, got into a bottle of ink and did her best Picasso impression on several of the bedroom walls. Gerald nearly threw her out a window until Vova offered to build a cage for her.

At La Bruyère, we tried our best to restore the *luxe, calme, et volupté* of Villa America. I placed fresh flowers in every room. Gerald had the latest phonograph records sent, including an astonishing new voice from Germany named Marlene Dietrich. On Wednesday nights we showed newsreels and movies in the library. Most days, I successfully banished the term *TB* from my thoughts.

The heightened privacy and lack of hotel regimen also allowed Gerald and me to return to a single bedroom, to become reacquainted with each other in the old way—no grand passion, but a physical closeness that we both desperately needed. But I also saw, beyond the veneer of composure he donned in public, that inside he was coming undone. The pressure of keeping up his witty, elegant demeanor was beginning to dull the sheen.

In September, as he planned to make a trip to New York, I said I'd cable the MacLeishes to meet him at the dock. He refused. We were standing in our upstairs bedroom, Gerald wearing a worn gray linen bathrobe as he packed his suitcase. The house was quiet, except for the sound of the maid working the carpet sweeper downstairs.

"Well, what about Bob Benchley then? You can't go all the way to New York and not see your friends." I found his shaving kit in the bathroom cabinet and tossed it on the bed.

"That's exactly what I intend to do. I'm in no frame of mind to see anyone." Gerald took a stack of undershirts from a drawer. "I can't risk disfiguring my friendships with them, among the many phantom realities of my life."

A couple of thrushes bobbed in the enormous blue spruce tree outside our window, and the summer sun illuminated everything. We had so many reasons to feel hopeful now that Patrick was finally on the mend. But here inside, we were all living with the regular spells of darkness cast by Gerald. I'd reached my limit. I felt something pop in my head, like a blown gasket on an old Buick.

"Gerald Murphy, stop being such a child!" I spun around to face him, my heart racing. "You're a grown man, for God's sake. You might be used to skulking around like a shadow at home, but you can't just ignore your good friends because of your constant moods."

He was sitting on the edge of our bed now, his chin in his hands, but now he looked at me with alarm. We so rarely fought.

Once I'd lost my temper, however, I couldn't catch up to it. "And stop using words like 'phantom realities'!" I shrieked. "Why must everything come out of your mouth with pomade on it?"

Gerald's chin was quivering. "I just can't keep up the convivial Dow-Dow show much longer. You know, I don't think I've had one real relationship or one full experience in my entire life."

"*Excuse* me? Not *one* real relationship?" I gaped at him, incredulous.

"Excepting you, of course. But even our marriage has been crippled by my defects. You know that as well as I do. I've held life at a remove from the time I was fifteen."

"You know what I think?" I yelled. "I think you're just afraid to have people like you. You use your charm to keep them at a distance. You've made the world so flat, you can't breathe in it."

Gerald bathed in his misery. "You're entirely right, of course. As always."

"I'm so damned tired of your pitiful festivals of self-sabotage," I continued, on a roll. "I really am, Gerald. We've all been through the wringer these past eighteen months, all of us. But do you see me moping about or flying into rages? It's time you put your tragic childhood behind you, Mr. Murphy."

We said nothing for a few minutes while I paced and tried to calm down. To our children, to our friends, to the whole world, we always presented a united front. And knowing how hard Gerald could be on himself, I'd rarely allowed myself to confront him so violently. But, as good as it felt to unleash my anger, now I hated it. I sat down beside him on the bed and sighed, then gently rubbed the nape of his neck. "Please don't be so hard on yourself, Dow."

"You, Sara. You're able to give people exactly who and what you are. You've no idea what a gift that is. It's a rare alchemy of nature for which I've always taken too much credit. Instead, I feel impoverished. Spiritually, I mean." He palmed his face.

"Oh, that's not true. We've created our own alchemy. Bea Stewart says we're everyone's models for the Happy Life."

"And it's usually so. Just not always." He gave my knee a squeeze and we sat for a while looking out at the different blues of the spruce tree and the sky beyond. The goddamned forever push-pull of this marriage. It's what I'd asked for; it's all I'd ever wanted. I *still* wanted it. But goodness, it took work.

"No matter how hard I love you, it means nothing if you can't love yourself," I said. I stroked his back, the fabric of his bathrobe soft with age, and could feel his still-strong spine underneath. "It falls on deaf ears."

Gerald turned and gave me a sad smile, then brushed my cheek with a kiss.

He finally agreed to cable Archie to meet him at the pier. Just Archie, no one else. Small victories.

ONE AFTERNOON I brought Patrick's bed tray—fresh milk, soft cheese, some apple slices—into his darkened room after his nap. His color was returning and he'd gained several pounds. Our determination was paying off—we were becoming hopeful enough to plan for the day when we could all return home to France.

"Here you go, darling," I said, as I propped up a pillow behind him and laid the tray on his lap. "Are you ready for a little surprise?"

"Yes, ma'am, I sure am!"

I opened the curtains to the afternoon outside. Patrick's second-floor bedroom looked down onto the chalet's broad, flat lawn and there, in white lime chalk, was an aerial view of a sailboat's deck, drawn to scale.

"What is it?" Patrick asked.

"It's our new boat, darling. It's being built in Normandy, ready to launch next year."

Gerald appeared in the doorway, his hands still white with lime, Honoria and Baoth grinning behind him. We'd all conspired together to create this moment.

Patrick's face looked like every Christmas and birthday he'd had in his ten-year life. "Will I be well enough?"

"The doctors say so, if you continue eating well and putting on weight and taking your treatments." I brushed the straw-colored hair off his forehead. "Won't that be lovely?"

"What's she going to be called?"

"The *Weatherbird*."

It had been my idea. After the *Picaflor* and the *Honoria*, Gerald and I both knew what we did and didn't want in a boat. We named her for one of our favorite jazz songs—a Louis Armstrong recording of it would be sealed in her hull.

This boat contained not only every modern convenience, but

a growing sense of hope for the future of our family. We briefly entertained the notion that we could give the children a classical education by taking them along the coasts of Greece, Africa, Italy, and Spain. The important thing was that we had a new plan—Gerald was always buoyant when there was a plan. We were trying our hardest to make life feel golden again, even if it meant ignoring our plummeting bank balance.

---

THE STRAIN OF the past two years had taken a serious toll on my body; I was spending hours in bed each month from intense cramping and abdominal pain. At Gerald's insistence, in October I traveled to Paris for some medical tests and the diagnosed condition—a gallbladder disorder—would plague me for the rest of my life.

When I finally returned to Switzerland in November, both Gerald and I were in a somber mood. His father had just died of pneumonia and his mother was seriously ill; by the following April, she would die too. With my own father's death the previous year, we were now only parents, no one's children anymore. Life felt weighty and serious. We had flung ourselves so hard at having fun, but now we seemed to be pursued by gloom and responsibility.

"I've been corresponding with Amory at Loomis-Sayles," Gerald said one evening after dinner. We sat alone at the table; Honoria was draped over an armchair reading *Those Thornton Girls*, while Baoth built a match-box car track on the coffee table. Patrick, of course, was upstairs in bed.

"Hoover says the States are headed for a great depression. And the exchange rate here is doing us no favors." He twirled his empty wine glass, making circles on the damask cloth.

It wasn't our first discussion on the subject—we'd skirted around it since we'd first read of the stock market crash two years before. Our dollars were dwindling—Patrick's medical treatments had been jaw-droppingly expensive, and we'd sent Baoth to an expensive German boarding school and hired a tutor for Honoria.

"I'm afraid the idyll is truly over, Sal," Gerald said. He looked as tired as I felt. Suddenly, it seemed, our youth was gone.

I sighed. "How much do we need to cut back?"

"As much as we can."

"Well, we can sell the *Honoria* immediately," I said. "But I'm not selling the *Weatherbird*."

"We can give up the Paris apartment. We're hardly ever there."

"The Paris avant-garde has grown stale, anyway—don't you think?" I said. "Everyone's gotten fat and rich, or else moved on. And we outgrew that scene years ago."

The truth was, Patrick's health crisis had beaten us down and now neither of us had the strength to maintain such an international life. All the houses, the animals, the parties, the travel took so much energy and organization. A simpler life would be a relief, I told myself. The Riviera had become a playground for the very rich, anyway. La Garoupe was now lined with fancy lunch places and beach cabanas that charged by the day.

But it was about more than scaling back. Our closest friends—the Hemingways, the Dos Passoses, the Fitzgeralds, the MacLeishes, Dottie Parker and Bob Benchley—all lived in the States now. Even Zelda had been moved to a hospital in Baltimore. Germany was increasingly under the spell of the frightening new Nazi Party—when we'd arrived to pick Baoth up from boarding school, we learned that he'd been made to stand in the snow performing "Heil Hitlers" in his underwear. Later, when we'd docked at Portofino, we'd found the buildings plastered with the glaring face of an autocrat named Benito Mussolini. A shadow of fear and evil was spreading across the continent. And, as the dollar continued to plunge, Europe was becoming more expensive with each passing week. At some point, I'd already begun referring to our past decade as "the era."

I don't remember who spoke of it first. But within a week or so, we'd reluctantly decided to return to America. Perhaps we could also find better care there for Patrick's TB. But Honoria and Baoth would need more convincing.

"Will we keep Villa America?" Honoria asked through tears. "Will we ever go to La Garoupe again? What about Mam'zelle and Titine and Celestine?"

While I put on a brave face for the children, inside I was crumbling, too. Villa America, "our humble apotheosis," was the crowning manifestation of everything I'd dreamed of since I was a girl. Antibes had been the most stable home our children had ever known. It felt like a death in the family, a chamber of my heart closing up.

"We'll have a new house with wonderful new help," I said. "And you and Baoth will go to real school and make friends your own age!" This was a powerful attraction. Our children had been living in a fantasy kingdom with few young peers, and they were eager to know people other than our adult friends.

"Will we get to wear uniforms, like in the *Jolly* books?" Honoria asked.

"Definitely uniforms, probably plaid," Gerald said. "Lots and lots of plaid."

In anticipation of the move, we made arrangements to renovate a small house on my father's East Hampton property. We would call it Hook Pond Cottage.

Now I loaded our books onto the dining room table to sort and decide which ones to take with us. "It was lovely while it lasted, huh Dow?" I said.

"It was extraordinary. Now a new adventure awaits. We've always been Americans, after all." But there was resignation in his voice.

Our feelings of good times lost were compounded when we read in March of the kidnapping and murder of Charles and Anne Lindbergh's twenty-month-old son at their New Jersey home. I found myself crying for an entire day. What kind of a place were we returning to?

"HAIL THE CONQUERING hero!" we all sang as Patrick and his nurse entered the gate of Villa America in May. We'd returned to Antibes for one last lovely summer on the Mediterranean before sailing for the States. Honoria and I had strung paper lanterns around the patio and the garden was at its fragrant height with citrus and mimosa. I served Patrick's favorite lunch of roast chicken with Gerald's Mysterious Noodles (which was just fettuccine drenched in butter). As I watched our family gathered together around the table under the linden tree, my heart swelled and my eyes teared up. Never again would I take this sight for granted. Even Honoria and Baoth's adolescent bickering was welcome. In a symbolic gesture of optimism, I'd tossed out all the medicines in my leather travel case, except for Patrick's prescriptions. I was done worrying about all that.

The next two months were like a victory lap of our previous life in the South of France. Long, leisurely sails on the *Weatherbird* to St. Tropez and Portofino. Evenings in Monte Carlo at the ballet or casino. We were packing it all in, and I tried to memorize every moment like a crisp Kodak photograph. Goodbye, France. Goodbye, Italy. Goodbye, *luxe, calm, et volupté*. We'd have to invent a new, American version of that credo now.

We spent July packing up the house, the carefully chosen linens and china and paintings. We gave away the well-used childhood toys—scooters and kites and the contents of Honoria's playhouse. The monkey, Mistigris, and the parrot, Coquotte, went to an old woman who kept exotic animals. Vova would stay, living on the *Weatherbird* and keeping it ship-shape at an Antibes dock—we could come back for school vacations.

The day arrived too soon, of course. Our valet, Arnaud, had loaded our many valises into the Renault, which he would take to the station. A taxi sat, its motor running, on the graveled drive. Inside, furniture lay draped with dust covers. Beds were stripped, cabinets wiped down. The staff had said their goodbyes the day before, Titine and Celestine weeping loudly. Arnaud would stay on as a part-time caretaker.

Now Gerald quietly shut the door, then turned the brass key in the lock and pocketed it. "Well, I guess that's it, then," he said.

We five stood on the stone front steps and said nothing. Honoria finally broke the silence.

"*À toute à l'heure,* Villa America," she said.

"À plus tard, alligator," Baoth said.

Gerald and I locked eyes. The children were stoic, but we two were tearing up. For some reason, I thought of my kitchen garden, where the eggplants and sweet peppers and green beans were still ripening. I would normally be planting squash and onions about now.

"We'll be back at summers," I said. "No need to get maudlin about it." I dabbed an eye. "Let's get to the station before the train leaves without us."

As we turned onto Chemin des Mougins, I looked back at the plaque hand-painted by Gerald a decade before: Villa America, with its five gold stars and half an American flag. Yes, we would return, but I knew it would never be the same.

## Chapter 18
### 1932-1934

I sat on a teak deck chair on the SS *Aquitania*, a worn woolen blanket tucked around my legs. The ocean had always been a kind of church for me—the salty air my incense, the cries of gulls my choir. These languid days at sea gave me time to sink into my thoughts, to reflect on the past decade and what those years had really meant. I'd been so eager to leave behind the life my parents had envisioned for me and, in that respect, it had been an unqualified success. We'd created a new, beautiful world, more exciting than anything I could have imagined when we'd sailed for Europe in 1921. Costume balls! Theatrical debuts! Mad beach parties! International art salons! Somehow Gerald and I had managed to raise our family within the very pulse of twentieth-century culture.

But I couldn't help feeling as if we were returning to American soil in some kind of defeat. The dream had faded. Our bank account was dwindling. And our youngest child was recovering from what could have been a mortal disease. We were, in many ways, on our heels.

A small but sturdy figure clumped toward me on the promenade deck and plunked down in the chair beside me. Baoth. I glanced at his noble profile, the Nordic lines of my own face so strongly etched on his. How he reminded me of myself: a stoic, cheerful, brick of a child.

"Hello, Bayo," I said. "What news?"

He squinted out at the flat blue Atlantic, a ruffle of whitecaps at the surface.

"Mama? What are boys like in America?" he asked in his husky voice. "What kinds of games do they play?"

"Well, let me see. They play marbles and hide and seek, just like you do. There's a game called 'kick the can,' which you'll be *excellent* at. And you'll want to learn a *lot* more about baseball."

"Can Dow-Dow teach me that?"

I thought for a minute. "No, probably not. But Uncle Ernest can, I'm sure."

---

AS IF OUR feelings about returning to America weren't already ambivalent enough, Hoytie surprised us by meeting us at the dock. She talked during the entire drive in her hired car, Gerald and I exchanging pained glances the whole way. "You know I lost my absolute *shirt* in the crash," she was saying. "Built and developed a large property at Park Avenue and 72nd . . . personal bankruptcy . . . The Dunes . . . shell corporation . . . unpaid taxes." On and on she went, an endless ribbon of complaints and bad decisions. Classic Hoytie.

"What in God's name are you getting at?" I finally blurted out. "What is it you need *now*?"

Hoytie had always been a handsome woman: tall and stately with a strong jaw and aristocratic nose. I'd often look at her and think, *If only she'd keep her mouth shut, she could be quite attractive.*

"About twenty-five thousand dollars," she said. "I've already gone to everyone else in the family, but they're of no use whatsoever." She'd always thought of herself as a successful businesswoman, and she kept proving herself wrong.

Hoytie had purportedly "sold" the entire Dunes property, all twenty-seven oceanfront acres of it, to Aunt Mame for one dollar, then transferred the deed to Trex, her shell corporation. Now she owed an enormous sum in back taxes. If I'd ever wanted to throttle my younger sister with my bare hands—and I *had* wanted to, many times—that paled when compared to this moment. As we unloaded ourselves at the entrance to the Savoy Plaza, I could barely muster a goodbye.

But by the time we'd gotten settled into our suite and were decompressing over Gerald's expertly mixed Bloodhounds, I'd given it some more thought. Was I going to let Hoytie's headstrong behavior rob our family of its beloved estate? My parents might be gone but our children adored that place, and so did I.

"I've been thinking, Dow," I said. "Mightn't it be more prudent to get involved now instead of later, when Hoytie may well have lost The Dunes altogether?"

Gerald quickly summarized our financial obligations, both in France and in the States, which we both already knew too well. He and Esther, still living in France, would be receiving some income from Mark Cross but, to his outrage, control of the company had been left to their father's mistress, so that inheritance was uncertain. And my own capital, like Hoytie's, had taken a beating in the crash and current depression.

"I can't see us taking on such an enormous expense at a time like this," Gerald said, reasonably. "The heating costs alone on that pile of bricks could break us."

I knew he was right, but the idea of losing my family's home was too much to bear. "We could try renting it," I said. "Perhaps there's still a millionaire or two out there who can afford to live in grand style."

In the end, it was my money. So I instructed Mr. Amory to sell some more stock and I bailed Hoytie out. Now The Dunes was ours, for better or worse.

We continued to live at the Savoy Plaza Hotel, weekending at East Hampton. Our new Hook Pond Cottage was a single-story saltbox of brown shingles and bright white trim. It was a tight squeeze when all the children were home, but that would be rare because Gerald and I had finally realized it was time to attend to their educations. We'd enrolled Baoth at the Fountain Valley School in Colorado Springs and Honoria would be attending the Convent of the Sacred Heart in Connecticut, just across the Sound. Patrick, poor thing, was still stuck at home until he was well enough for school.

During the week, Gerald dutifully returned to Mark Cross, managing the company he'd so eagerly fled thirteen years before. If I'd felt a sense of defeat at leaving our carefully crafted life in France, I think Gerald felt it by a factor of two or three. Here he was, back in *commerce*, handling tedious issues like profit margins and employee performance. It made my heart swell a little to see him return to that life so stoically. He was willing to do what was best for our family, and right now that was to become a merchant again.

WE SOON RENTED another house in Bedford, New York, where we could be closer to much of the old Paris gang again. Archie had just won the Pulitzer for his long poem *Conquistador* and was working on a new ballet, called *Union Pacific*, about the building of the Transcontinental Railroad. He pulled in Gerald to help create the score.

Suddenly I could see glimpses of the Paris Gerald again—creative, inventive, and excitable. The project would occupy him for months, and I was grateful for the newfound distraction. Of course we also invested in the production and threw several parties for such new friends as Aaron Copland and Virgil Thomson. Tightening our belts didn't mean we had to live like complete paupers, did it? After the last few years, we all deserved a little fun.

"ALL THIS PLACE has been missing is a couple of swell dames like you!" Ernest had picked up Ada and me at the station and was driving us to his new home at 907 Whitehead Street, the largest house in Key West, Florida. The top was down on his emerald-green Chevrolet Phantom convertible and the air was warm and humid in my hair.

In February of 1933, we'd taken the train down from New York; Gerald and Archie were still too preoccupied with the production of *Union Pacific*; besides, Gerald's current view was that "a little Ernest goes a long way." Pauline had taken their two young boys back to Arkansas to visit her family, and Ernest seemed overjoyed to see Ada and me. For a man who'd fashioned himself into the masculine ideal, Ernest certainly was helpless without a woman around.

We pulled up to the curb and Ernest turned to grin at me. "It's a far cry from the place above the sawmill, huh?" When we'd first met him in Paris, he and Hadley were living in near squalor above a mill on Rue Notre-Dames-des-Champs. Now his pride at his new home was infectious. He and Pauline had renovated the place in keeping with his new reputation as America's greatest living writer.

"Ernest, it's lovely!" I said. The French Colonial had a two-story, wrought-iron wraparound porch and arched windows with green trim and bright yellow shutters. Rolling lawns and palm trees covered the surrounding acre.

He grabbed our bags from the trunk and took us inside to a central room with high ceilings, dark wood floors, and bright white walls lined with books and paintings. Through the French doors we could see to the lush yard out back, equipped with a raised boxing ring.

"The humble estate of the Great American Novelist," Ada said.

Ernest grinned and carried our suitcases to the guest rooms upstairs. "I'll give you an hour to get unpacked, and then we're going to Sloppy Joe's!" he said.

SIX HOURS LATER, we were back in the living room, and we were tight. Over conch fritters and the bar's namesake sandwiches, plus about eight rounds of rum-based cocktails, we'd met most of Ernest's Key West friends as well as a goodly number of autograph seekers. Now Ernest was mixing us the house specialty, called the Bacardi Flip, made with an egg, powdered cinnamon, and rum that he'd had personally shipped over from Cuba. Along with his acclaim as a writer, it seemed, his capacity for drinking had grown.

"Here's mud in your eye," he said, raising his glass. "May you live all the days of your life."

Ada and I were now seated on the Victorian sofa, struggling to stay upright.

"You gals just need a little movement to revive you," Ernest said, and laid one of the new vinyl records I'd brought from New York onto the phonograph.

"Come on Sara, dance with me." He pulled me up and I was suddenly supported by the muscular scaffold of his torso. He slowly circled me around the floor, humming off-tune in my ear. I giggled and let him support me, rocking gently to the jaunty beat of Fats Waller singing "Honeysuckle Rose."

After the past five years of us living like gypsies and chasing a cure for Patrick's disease, my heart and my body were tired. It felt so good to be wrapped in Ernest's strong, tanned arms, following his lead across the glossy wood floor.

When the song finished, Ernest rummaged through his collection. "Ain't Misbehavin'" continued the rolling Waller beat—so easy to dance to, even for a big man like Ernest. With his cheek next to mine, he gently maneuvered me around the room. He smelled of sweat and soap and all the rum he'd consumed that night. He smelled like pure man. Ernest tightened his hold around my waist and nuzzled his nose into my hair. "Lovely, lovely Sara," he whispered. I hoped the song would never end.

THE NEXT AFTERNOON, after we'd recovered from our "rum flu," Ernest took us out on his new fishing boat, the *Pilar*. We sailed out into the strait and Ada and I lounged in the sun as Ernest caught a few snapper and amberjack for supper. The sky was a bright blue parasol with a fringe of lacy clouds on the horizon. The water was the same bright turquoise I remembered from Antibes. I pulled the straps of my suit off my shoulders and closed my eyes, letting the boat rock me to sleep; it was the most sun I'd felt on my body since La Garoupe years before.

Once we returned to the house, Ernest gave the fish to his housekeeper to clean and prepare for supper. Then we gathered in the living room, where he mixed us drinks and began sorting his mail.

"God damn," he snorted. "Have you seen this?" He held out a copy of *Scribner's Magazine*, its trademark orange-and-black cover listing the issue's contents. "The Last Installment, *Tender is the Night* by F. Scott Fitzgerald," it read.

"I'd heard it was out, but I haven't read it," I said. I glanced over at Ada, whose expression said she already had.

"Not the last chapters, though," she said.

"*Should* I read it?" I asked. It was common knowledge that Scott had based the two main characters upon Gerald and me for the first half of the book, and upon himself and Zelda for the second half. Most of America would have read the whole series by now.

"I think you'd better," Ada said. Was that worry or pity on her face?

Ernest pulled some other issues from off the shelf and handed me all four. "Save it for the morning, when you're not so tired," he said. "It's not very good."

The next day, I took all four issues to the shaded back porch and read them in one sitting, the ashtray next to me slowly filling with crushed butts. I hadn't made it to page three before I felt the bile rising into my throat as I read the description of Nicole Diver.

> *. . . a young woman lay under a roof of umbrellas making out a list of things from a book open on the sand. Her bathing suit was pulled off her shoulders and her back, a ruddy, orange-brown, set off by a string of creamy pearls, shone in the sun. Her face was hard and lovely and pitiful.*

The next paragraph introduced her husband, Dick.

> *. . . the man in the jockey cap was giving a quiet little performance for this group; he moved gravely about with a rake, ostensibly removing gravel and meanwhile developing some esoteric burlesque held in suspension by his grave face. Its faintest ramification had become hilarious, until whatever he said released a burst of laughter.*

Scott had described Gerald and me wholesale, without even the slightest attempt to disguise us. It felt like having the life sucked out of me by a vampire. Nicole also harbored fantasies of leaving Dick for a dark, dashing "adventurer" that sounded just like Ernest. And, by the end of the book, she was institutionalized for mental illness and Dick was a raging alcoholic.

By dinner that evening, I was so livid I could barely speak. "He may have appropriated our outward appearances," I said. "But I reject categorically any *real* resemblance to us or to anyone we knew." The sautéed shrimp sat plump and pink on my plate, but even they made me angry. Scott had been at work on this tripe for nearly a decade. He'd known all along what he was doing, even as he accepted our many generosities.

Ada nodded. "He went too far," she said.

"If you're going to write about someone, you need to stay true to their character," Ernest said, holding his fork and knife in both fists. "It started off with that marvelous description of you and Gerald, but then he started fooling around, changing your characters into other people."

"What infuriates me is that Scott seems to think of Gerald and me as the *same* people as him and Zelda," I said. "Nothing could be *further* from the truth!"

"He only wishes that were true," Ernest said. "He has remarkable powers of observation, but in this case his blinders are a foot thick."

"Have you already spoken with him about this?" I asked. Everything suddenly felt like a conspiracy. There was nothing I liked less than being talked about—to my face or behind my back.

"Not yet. I wanted to finish the last installment. But I plan to write and tell him what I think. He can't be so careless with his character development." Ernest reached out and squeezed my hand for so long that I finally pulled back.

It would be a very long time before I wanted to see Scott again.

---

THAT WAS OUR last evening in Key West. Ada and I planned to take the morning train back to Miami and then the overnight to New York. I was sitting in bed with the bedside lamp on, writing in my diary, when I heard a soft knock. "Yes?"

Ernest poked his head in. "Are you all right, Sadie?" That was Archie's nickname for me. It sounded strange coming from Ernest.

"Oh, of course I am," I said. "Just indefinitely steamed at Scott is all. I'll be fine."

Ernest nudged the door open farther and came into the room, then sat down on the bed. He'd clearly continued his drinking in the hour since we'd said goodnight.

"I don't want you to leave, Sadie," he said. "Life feels so wholesome and good with you and Ada here. But especially you." He leaned back on the pillow and put his head on my shoulder.

"Aw, that's very sweet, Ernest. We've had such a *wonderful* time. And we'll come again next year." I patted his leg in what I hoped was a wholesome way. The attraction I'd felt while dancing with him was gone now without Fats Waller in the background and with the rum on Ernest's breath.

"I'm going to miss you so," he said, and suddenly his big head was lolling toward me in a sloppy kiss. "I've always loved you, Sara, you know that, don't you?"

"Now, Ernest," I said, trying to push him upright. "I know you love me. And I love you. We'll always be such dear, dear friends. We just don't want to make a mess of it, now do we? Think of all the people we'd hurt." The truth was, I'd often felt attracted to the man, with his muscular bravado and his athletic skill. But my infidelity with Picasso ten years before still felt like a tiny, secret scar in my marriage, and I didn't want any more secrets. Besides, in his current condition, Ernest made it easy to resist. There'd be no misbehavin' tonight.

---

I RETURNED TO East Hampton—and Gerald—with relief. I stood in our bedroom and studied the top of his bureau, where his tank watch, his cufflink box, his money clip, and his pocket notebook were laid out in perfect right angles. Inside the drawers, I knew, his clothes were folded and sorted by color. Sometimes his meticulous behavior annoyed me. But now I saw how much I depended on his sense of order, the safety and reliability I felt with him.

Ernest was like a cabin built from rough-hewn logs, and staying with him was like looking up at a night sky packed with stars. But coming home to Gerald was like sleeping in a bed with soft sheets that has molded itself to the curve of your body.

A week later, I received a letter from Ernest, a reminder of that last night:

*Dearest Sara, I love you very much, Madam, not like in Scott's Christmas tree ornament novels but the way it is on boats, where Scott would be seasick. Don't let's go so long without seeing each other again. We really do something against the world when we're together, and the world is always trying to do all these things to us when we're apart.*

What woman wouldn't be flattered to be loved by Ernest Hemingway, "the way it is on boats"? Still, it was like being adored by a friend's handsome younger brother, whose ardor was genuine but not to be taken seriously. The very best thing about flirting with

Ernest was the way I loved Gerald even more afterward.

"I suspect Scott thinks he's paid us a tribute," Gerald said, once he'd read the *Scribner's* pieces. "He used the two of us to depict the glamorous side of the Divers, then used himself and Zelda to show the damaged, broken parts."

Occasionally, Gerald could be the more compassionate, forgiving one; this was one of those times. He just didn't take it as personally as I did. I stared out the window at Hook Pond, its grassy edges and green water offering exactly the same view as twenty years before. Here we were, so far from the crazy life in Paris and Antibes, but the vaudeville act continued.

"Is that just the writer's way, scavenging your friends' lives to sell a book?" I asked. Ernest had done something similar with *Sun Also Rises*, barely disguising the bad behavior of his friends in Pamplona. Now Scott was doing it too.

"You and I are much more guarded when it comes to our personal lives," Gerald said.

"Thank goodness! If you ever wrote a 'semiautobiographical' novel about us, I'd murder you myself."

Gerald laughed. "All our sordid secrets are safe, Sal. Anyway, you have much more dirt on me than I have on you."

"That's what you think," I said, winking. It was a safe joke to make. My dalliance with Picasso was firmly in the past.

Of course I would still love the Fitzgeralds in the fierce way I loved all our talented, flawed friends. But for the rest of my life, I would never fully forgive Scott for *Tender is the Night*.

# Chapter 19
## 1934-1935

Soon after my return from Key West in March, we got the best possible news: Patrick's doctor said he was sufficiently recovered for us to return to France for the summer. After five years of living in fear of each new diagnosis, this was beyond wonderful. Suddenly the whole ordeal felt like an important lesson, a test that we'd passed with our hard work and our dedication to the cause of healing our son. We'd done it! My sails were full again.

I went into a frenzy of shopping and packing for the trip, as well as for school in the fall. It had been so long since Patrick had been properly out in public, I threw myself into buying him some new togs.

"I'm fourteen, Mama. You can stop dressing me like Buster Brown," Patrick scowled as we stood among the racks at Young Man's Fancy on Main Street. "And my clothes don't need to match Baoth's anymore."

"Now that's a slight exaggeration, Pook," I said. "I haven't dressed you boys alike since you were in grade school."

"We were never in grade school, Ma. I've never been to school at all!"

"You know very well what I mean, Patrick. Just because you're an old man of fourteen is no excuse for not putting some thought into your appearance. You're such a handsome young buck." I combed his blond hair back off his forehead with my fingers. "You'll soon be beating the girls away with a stick!"

Patrick frowned and pulled away, and it made my heart swell. For five years he'd been so quiet and stoic, taking his raw eggs and painful pneumothorax treatments like a soldier. Now he was still skinny and frail, but he was showing the gumption of a typical adolescent boy. He was back among the living.

Later, loaded down with shopping bags and shoe boxes, we sat in a red leatherette booth at the ice cream parlor down the street. To be doing something so normal together, just a healthy son and his mother, felt like a miracle.

"Butter Pecan for me and Neapolitan for the young man," I told the waitress. "In a coupe, not a cone."

"No, I want a cone," Patrick said. "Please."

"Are you sure, darling? A waffle cone?"

"Yes, please."

When the waitress had left, he said, "Mom, stop treating me like an invalid. I'm fine."

"Of course you are. I've just been so worried about you for so long, it's hard for me to remember how it used to be."

We sat for a moment in silence and I stared at my beautiful boy. "You did it, Patrick," I said. "You beat it, you survived the white plague. I couldn't be prouder of you." Then I gave him a big squeeze and Patrick smiled, despite himself. I blinked back tears.

Our ice cream arrived and Patrick tipped his cone toward me in a little salute. "It's going to be great seeing France again, isn't it, Ma?"

"Better than great. You have *so* many things to look forward to, young man!"

---

THEN, JUST BEFORE our departure, Hoytie managed to rain on our parade once more.

"She wants The Dunes back!" I wailed to Gerald, holding her letter for him to see. "She's insisting that my purchase back in thirty-two was merely a loan secured by the property. Now she wants to repossess it!"

I scanned the bedroom, where our suitcases and trunks were arrayed, half-packed. So close to making our escape, to revisiting the good life we remembered. But my sister had reared her ugly head once again. Hoytie was like a bunion, nothing but pain and inconvenience.

"Relax, Sal," Gerald said, skimming the letter. "We've got Hamilton on retainer. He can look into it while we're away."

Hamilton was our family lawyer. We'd had him on retainer since we returned to the States, largely because of Hoytie's habitual crises. He wrote back to her immediately, reminding her that I had actually purchased The Dunes from her. I sighed and pushed the matter to the attic of my brain, where all other financial and legal concerns were stored. I refused to be worried about one more thing when we had so much to be hopeful about, and continued packing.

"The blue or the aubergine?" I asked Gerald, holding up two dresses on hangers.

Gerald studied my choices with a sober look. He took these matters seriously.

―

BUT JUST AS we were boarding the SS *Conte di Savoia* for our crossing, we received an ominous telegram.

> YOU WILL NOT HAVE A LUCKY JOURNEY
> FOR WHAT YOU HAVE DONE
> IN BREAKING FATHERS PLANS FOR US -(STOP)-
> ALL HIS REPROACHES WILL BE WITH YOU -(STOP)-
> HOYTIE

If I could have burned it then and there, I would have. Instead, I crumpled up the yellow paper and threw it into a litter basket on the pier. But Hoytie's threatening words lodged in my brain, where they lingered for the entire crossing. That woman was like a malignant tumor.

---

LÉGER MET US in Gibraltar, where he'd arrived on the *Weatherbird* with Vova and the crew, and presented us with a book of his watercolors. He'd inscribed it *To Sara and Gerald from their very devoted cabin boy.*

"What a lovely gesture, Fernand," I said, squeezing his hand.

"Just a small *reconnaissance* for all your generosities," he said. "The trip to America. The many gifts of money."

"They were *very* small checks," I said. "Already forgotten."

We departed for a month-long cruise of the Mediterranean coast with our friends the Myerses, and it was almost enough to make us forget the despair of the previous five years. Honoria and Fanny behaved like typical young ladies of eighteen, whispering between themselves and smiling shyly for Gerald's new Kodak movie camera. Baoth and Patrick were rambunctious brothers again, scrambling up and down the rigging, always clowning around. We had our family back. I had never been happier, or more grateful. My gaze landed on each of my golden children, and Gerald, and our friends, and it was like rereading a favorite book. One with a happy ending.

Then we spent two glorious months at Villa America with side trips to St. Tropez, Monte Carlo, and Juan-les-Pins. I often found myself strolling in the terraced garden, trying to take in the beauty of it all. The air was thick with jasmine and citrus. The view to the sea was all pastels. And the peacefulness! Extraordinary. We had saved ourselves. I kept repeating it like a kind of mantra. We had saved ourselves.

But by early July of 1935 there was ominous news about Chancellor

Hitler and, by mid-August, he'd declared himself Germany's "führer." Mussolini and his Italian Fascist Party were also making headlines. Even in sleepy Antibes, we knew it was just a matter of time before France was in Hitler's sights too.

"Even if we hadn't already planned to, we'd be packing up now," Gerald said. "Let's get out while we can."

When we boarded the SS *Aquitania* to return to New York in September, it felt not a day too soon. The ship's manifest was filled with the surnames of Jewish families, already fleeing the escalating persecution.

We had no idea, of course, of the scale of what was to come. But there was a sense of foreboding, like a dark shadow growing across Europe. That shadow seemed to follow us across the Atlantic, darkening our path across the water.

---

BACK AT HOOK Pond, it was a flurry of activity as we prepared the children to go to school: Honoria would be starting at Rosemary Hall in Greenwich, while Baoth and Patrick would go to the Harvey School upstate. All three were percolating with the excitement of being among other kids their age, making new friends.

But before we packed the children off, Gerald took Patrick into the city for a routine check-up. The moment they walked back into the house, I sensed something was amiss. Patrick stomped to his room without even saying hello. Gerald came in and sat down at the window. I'd never seen him look so deflated. I sat down across from him, holding my tongue, afraid to ask.

"He's had a *rechute*," he finally said, palming his hair back with a tired hand. "There's a spot on his good lung. The one that's been keeping him alive."

*NO!* I wanted to shout. *I refuse!* But I sat in silence. All that hope. Patrick's new chance at life. Instead, the infection had been growing, spreading. It was as if the world were sneering at us. *Those ignorant Murphys, always thinking they could win at life.* The image of Icarus fluttered through my mind.

"What a fool's paradise," I finally said, shaking my head. "That whole, delicious summer. Thinking we were out of the woods." Our eyes met and we both tried hard to smile.

Then Gerald was up, his long arms around me. "No more doom and gloom," he said, kissing the top of my head. "Now our shoulders go back to the wheel."

---

IN LATE SEPTEMBER, after dropping Honoria and Baoth off at their schools, we brought Patrick to Doctor's Hospital on the Upper East Side. His symptoms were already back: a high fever, no appetite, labored breathing. He wasn't even allowed to sit up in bed so he couldn't etch or paint, the things that had kept him occupied until now. Gerald gave me news from the doctors only when necessary and I kept up an encouraging tone in my daily letters to our friends. Here again was that delicate dance we did together: one of us rising to the challenge, instinctively knowing when the other needed shoring up.

And that wasn't the only bad news: Cross's president resigned, leaving Gerald responsible for the store and all its employees. He took over in December with a steely resolve to redeem the company. But in the current climate—what was now called the "Great Depression"—how many people could afford fine leather luggage or crystal martini glasses? The company was $1 million in debt, perched on the verge of bankruptcy. It pained me to see Gerald trapped in a role he'd always loathed, but this seemed to be the new theme of our lives: hunkering down and getting serious about life.

For the next twenty-two years, Gerald would tighten and manage the company responsibly. And though I could occasionally see a spark of delight when he sketched out an idea for a new product—a key case based on one he'd seen in a dime store, or a leather satchel inspired by a bicycle messenger's bag—I overheard him confiding to Phil Barry that his new job felt "like sleepwalking."

Now we were truly living the life we'd long rejected, with Gerald working long hours to pay for three houses, two schools, and a hospital. I tried not to think how stunned my parents would be to witness this new life of ours, had they been alive. We were now "in the trades."

It wasn't the reduced social status that bothered me. It was the fact that we'd always held ourselves above issues of money, and being in commerce was all about money. My mind kept bouncing to a single punitive thought: that we wouldn't have found ourselves in this mess if we'd handled my trust more responsibly. The Baudelairian ideal, I now realized, had been wildly feckless. Though I wouldn't have traded those years for anything, my father was probably twisting in his grave.

---

CHRISTMAS 1934. ANOTHER holiday of forced gaiety as we tried to ignore the obvious: that our youngest son was fighting a mortal disease. Had we been celebrating at Villa America, we would have been sitting around a fragrant spruce tree, its branches decorated with strings of kumquats and tin trinkets I'd found in the open-air market. I wiped the image from my mind.

"Here's one for you, Pook," I said, as I passed Patrick a flat gift wrapped in red foil. We'd carried a small tree into his hospital room and decorated it with garlands and baubles. Now we opened our presents sitting around his bed, exclaiming with false delight over things that any of us would have happily traded for a healthy diagnosis.

"Oh! *Cigars of the Pharaoh*, I've been wanting this one," Patrick said as he unwrapped the latest Tin Tin book. But as he lay back on the pillow, his skin was as white as his bedsheets. His weary expression made him seem older than all of us.

The week before, Baoth had returned to Manhattan on the Fall River steamer with a group of school friends. We now had an apartment on East 51st Street that overlooked the East River. As the boat approached, I stood on the balcony, where I'd hung a sheet painted with the message "Welcome Home, Baoth!" I could see him jumping on the prow, his blond head bobbing with delight when he saw the sign. Such gestures reminded me that I still had two healthy children. I had to hold fast to that thought.

---

"I WANT *YOU* to go," Gerald said. Ernest and Pauline had invited us down to Key West again for the annual gathering in February. Ada would be going, and Dos and Katy. "You need some cheering up," he said. "I can't go anyway because of this new lease negotiation for Cross. I'll keep a watchful eye on Patrick. Go get some sun on your face and some rum in your belly."

So I dug out my floral frocks and I went, and Gerald was right: seeing the old friends again and being in the rambunctious company of Ernest was exactly what I needed. The only difference this time was that Ernest's literary celebrity had grown still greater after his last bestseller, which was evident in the larger crowds of fans in town—Katy dubbed them the "Old Bohemians."

I remembered the first time I'd met Ernest in Paris, when he was still so young and eager about life. He'd held up a forearm and pointed to his elbow to show me where his hometown of Oak Park lay on the map of Lake Michigan. Now his already outsized ego had grown, too. He was never more comfortable than when he was pontificating on the right way to mix a drink, cast a fishing line, or swim a stroke. We began calling him "the Oracle."

Like the year before, there were plenty of good times: fishing on the *Pilar*, dancing on the patio, and drinking, drinking, drinking. Such jollity was countered by Gerald's regular letters from home:

Patrick had been allowed to sit up and draw, and he was consumed with the radio broadcasts of the "Trial of the Century" of Bruno Richard Hauptmann, who was finally convicted for the kidnapping and murder of the Lindbergh baby. *All quiet on the western front,* Gerald wrote.

Then came another, less comforting letter: *Baoth's down with measles but, sturdy specimen that he is, he's recuperating nicely in the school's infirmary. Not to worry.* This was shortly followed by a letter from Baoth himself, full of his usual jokes and bravado. He signed it *The leaning tower of Baoth.* I returned to the revelry.

But a week later, Ernest summoned me to the living room for a long-distance telephone call. "Person to person from Gerald Murphy," the operator said. The connection crackled and spit.

"It's Baoth," Gerald began, and beyond the static I could hear trouble in his voice. "Measles . . . double mastoiditis." Fred, Gerald's brother, had been rushed to the hospital with the same condition years before. He hadn't died, but we knew it could be fatal. "We're at Massachusetts General in Boston," Gerald said. "He'll be going into surgery tomorrow morning."

I put down the receiver and sat back on the sofa with a thud. I simply couldn't wrap my arms around this news.

"What's happened?" Katy asked, and I looked up to see five concerned faces staring back at me.

"It's Baoth," I said. "Mastoiditis. He's going to be operated on tomorrow." I kept looking around the room, waiting for someone to tell me I'd misunderstood. "But he's the *healthy* one!" I wailed.

Ernest flew into action, ever the hero. "There's no overland connection until Thursday," he said. "You'd have to take a car ferry to Havana and fly back to Miami. That's thirty-six hours, at least."

He quickly hatched a plan to motor Ada and me aboard the *Pilar* that very night to the Miami airport, where we'd board the next available plane to Boston.

We packed in about ten minutes flat and then Ernest was at the wheel of the boat, speeding over the swells in pitch darkness, looking very much as he must have looked twenty years before as a young Red Cross ambulance driver on the Italian front.

Twenty-three hours later, Ada and I rushed into the upstairs ward where we found Gerald, pale and pacing in the hallway. "I'll find us something to eat," Ada said, and headed off to find the dining commons. Then we sat and waited for word from the operating room. Nearly two hours later, it arrived.

Dr. Snavely's ashen face announced that the news was bad. "During the surgery, some bacteria invaded Baoth's spinal fluid," he said. He stood there for a moment, rubbing his hands. "He's now developed meningitis."

I slumped against Gerald.

"What is that exactly, meningitis?" Gerald asked. "How serious?"

"Very serious, I'm afraid," Snavely said. It seemed like the past ten years had been narrated by a parade of stern doctors and their very bad news. "It's an inflammation of the brain and spinal column. It can cause blindness or brain damage."

We waited.

"Or death."

A small moan escaped from somewhere in my chest. Two sons in two hospitals? I heard pain in Gerald's voice as he inhaled and formed his next question.

"So . . . what's to be done?"

"He's scheduled for a spinal tap tomorrow morning," Snavely said. I could feel Gerald's body tense under my weight. "I recommend that you both go back to your hotel and get some sleep. It's going to be very touch-and-go from here."

And it was. For the next ten days, we waited through five brain surgeries. Baoth was sedated or unconscious through it all, but that didn't mean he didn't suffer. A legion of family and friends flew or drove in to be by our sides: Honoria from school, my cousin Sara Sherman Mitchell, the Myerses, the MacLeishes, and even the

Pickmans. We were a slowly moving cortege, from hospital to hotel and back again.

By Saturday, March 16, Gerald, Honoria, and I had moved into Baoth's room to sit vigil at his bedside. He was in and out of consciousness and his entire body was burning with fever, trying to fight off the deadly germs that had invaded his spine and his brain.

I sat holding his hand, coaching him, pleading with him not to leave us. "*Breathe*, Bayo," I repeated over and over again. "Please breathe." I was his mother. As a child, he'd always done what I asked, eventually.

I surveyed the beautiful landscape of his face: the sharp cheekbones, the thick brown lashes. The silhouette that looked exactly like my father's. The short blond hair now stiff with dried sweat. I tried to focus only on the present moment, the power of my will to revive my son. But another voice whispered in the back of my mind. What kind of god would allow this to happen? How on earth was this permitted to happen to us?

And another thought was emerging, too: Hoytie's telegram. *Had she actually placed a curse on our family?*

"Breathe, Baoth. Please breathe."

I passed the whole night that way, vaguely aware of Gerald and Honoria in my periphery. And then, the next morning, I awoke from a half-sleep to hear Baoth take a shallow breath. One breath. And then, nothing.

I have no idea how much time passed after that last breath. It was as if all the air were sucked out of me as well, and I sat by the bed, my head still lying on Baoth's chest. I couldn't move. No tears. Just a blank numbness, a void. Soon I became aware of movement behind me, and a nurse gently tried to raise me up from the bed.

"Mrs. Murphy, the doctor has something to help you rest." I gladly let her sit me up and roll up my sleeve. People in white whispering, a needle, a prick in my arm. So I was still alive, apparently. Each holding an arm, the doctor and nurse helped me walk to an adjacent room and an empty bed. Removing my shoes. Placing a soft blanket over me. I looked up and saw Gerald talking to Honoria. I strained to make sense of his words.

"Don't leave her side. Sit by her bed, because when she wakes up, it's going to be rough." Then he left the room. Was he leaving to call Patrick, to tell him his older brother was dead?

The last thing I remember is the morning light pleated through the blinds. I would sleep for weeks, and perhaps when I woke up it wouldn't be so awful.

---

WHEN I DID awaken, it was like coming to the surface of a deep, dark well. There had been no dreams, thankfully, just darkness and quiet. It took me a moment to orient myself to the strange white room. Then I saw the sunlight through the blinds again. The memory of that awful morning. How many days had passed?

Honoria was suddenly sitting next to me on the bed. "Mama. How are you feeling?"

"How long have I been out?" I asked. I wanted to sleep for the rest of my life.

"Just about an hour," she said.

An hour? It was the same morning of Baoth's death? I hadn't escaped a single day? His lifeless body might still be in the next room. Or perhaps by now it was lying on a cold table in the morgue. My beautiful, robust, healthy boy. Snatched away like the Lindberg baby.

I felt like I was about to throw up and waited for the heaves to come. But instead of vomit, I erupted into tears. Wave after wave of sobs, coming as strong and regular as the Atlantic surf at Wiborg Beach. Honoria held me tight and we cried together, long and hard. How unfair life was, how cruel.

---

GERALD MADE ALL the arrangements for the service at St. Bart's on Park Avenue. In the taxi on the way to the memorial, he broke down—the only time I'd seen him so distraught. Of course he dwelled on the times he'd lost his temper with Baoth, blaming himself for everything. I could only sit, frozen and mute. I'd lost my ability to speak three days before. Under any other circumstances, I would have rushed to comfort him, to tell him how hard he was on himself. But I was too distraught to care. I could comfort no one.

Gerald walked Honoria and me up the aisle and sat us in a front pew among what seemed like hundreds of guests. I barely registered their faces. Then I tried to listen as the priest read from the Book of Common Prayer:

> *I am the resurrection and the life, saith the Lord;*
> *he that believeth in me, though he were dead, yet shall he live;*
> *and whosoever liveth and believeth in me shall never die.*

We had blissfully ignored the church for our entire marriage, attending just weddings and funerals. We'd baptized our three children only to appease our families. Gerald had a lifelong disgust for the Catholic Church, having experienced its hypocrisy and cruelty firsthand as a child. And I'd seen no need to observe my Episcopal faith; we were creating our own church of beauty and friendship and the love of our children. Was this the punishment for our sin of negligence?

*What* had we done so wrong?

I felt Gerald's strong hand gripping my gloved one. I suspected that, in the days and years ahead, he would be better equipped to deal with Baoth's death; he was already so well acquainted with sorrow and despair from the Black Service, it was a feeling he'd lived with often. But I had spent the past thirty years *insisting* on happiness—now I didn't know what to do with my grief. On the outside, I was mute. But inside my head, I heard shrieking, wailing, keening.

Now the priest was saying, "O God, whose beloved Son did take little children into his arms and bless them, give us grace, we beseech thee, to entrust this child, Baoth, to thy never-failing care and love, and bring us all to thy heavenly kingdom."

I felt the nausea rising in my throat. To bless Baoth's death, to picture him cradled in the arms of Jesus? The saccharine fallacy of it made me want to scream out loud. This wasn't a blessing! This was a goddamned tragedy! It felt like a public act of disrespect to our son.

I rose and ran down the aisle, ignoring the faces that turned to watch. I pushed against one of the heavy wooden doors and burst out onto Park Avenue, then ran to the corner, where I looked up beyond the tops of the Midtown apartment buildings to the layer of gloom above.

"How *dare* you?" I screamed at the sky. "He was just a child!"

I heard footsteps approach, then two strong arms encircled me. I turned, expecting Gerald, but it was Archie. I collapsed into him, sobbing.

"Dearest Sara," he whispered into my hair. "You're right, there's absolutely nothing fair or noble about this."

I listened to the sounds around us—traffic, taxi horns, the voices of newspaper vendors. Up above, hanging from a telephone wire, dangled a pair of old shoes. Their lifelessness seemed to be a symbol designed for me alone. Perhaps they were Icarus's shoes, I thought, tangled there when he fell to earth. God, or the universe, or whatever folly you chose to believe in—was entirely indifferent to my feelings. Life continued on, oblivious to my pain. And I simply could not imagine a time when I'd be able to return to that life.

# Chapter 20
## 1935-1937

We returned to East Hampton and Gerald and I both shut down, in our own ways. Years later, when my mind had cleared, I saw how—despite our equally desperate grief and our love for each other—we were unable to grieve in tandem. We just couldn't be the exact person the other needed in that bleak, confusing time. Perhaps that's true for all grieving parents.

As usual, Gerald was able to take his feelings and wrap them into some meaningful outward expression. I know that his grief was no less than mine, but he could channel it, articulate it, name it. He poured himself out in letters to friends, trying to find some sort of meaning in Baoth's death.

*I know now that what you said in* Tender is the Night *is true,* he wrote to Scott. *Only the invented part of our life has had any scheme, any beauty. Life itself has stepped in now, and blundered, scarred, and destroyed. How ugly and blasting it can be, and how idly ruthless. In my heart I dreaded the moment when our youth and invention would be attacked in our only vulnerable spot, the children.*

My own grief covered me like a shroud, making me mute and nearly blind to the life around me. The tears came every day at the most unpredictable moments. Hanging laundry on the line in the yard.

Seeing a great blue heron alight from Hook Pond. Hearing Gerald's car pull up on the graveled drive. Friends called with baskets of food or fresh flowers, but I wasn't up to even the most basic conversation. Their words receded into a muffled Greek chorus, the sorrow in their faces a single mask of pity.

I wandered around the house and found myself in one room or another, staring idly at random objects. I tried to occupy myself with small daily tasks, such as ironing napkins or polishing silver, but who cared if the napkins were wrinkled? When would I ever feel like using the good silver again? It all seemed so pointless, now that my heart had been ripped from my body, now that Baoth's ashes lay buried in the South End cemetery under a marble stone.

---

ONE DAY IN June, I stood in the hallway and stared at the closed door to Baoth's room. I hadn't wanted to see his ghost hunched at the desk or lying on his bed with a book. I saw that ghost enough places as it was. But it suddenly seemed essential that I open that door. I stood for the longest time, studying the brass knob as if it would turn itself. Then, like leaping off a diving board, I twisted it, rushed into the room, and stood there, absorbing the leftover world of my lost son. His smell—sweaty wool and cotton. His teenage chaos—a wrinkled blue jersey hung over the desk chair, a few stuffed toys tossed on the bed, a small hill of shoes gathered in a corner.

I lowered myself onto the bed and sat there, the gaping hole in my heart pulsing with grief. "Oh, Bayo," I moaned, and the tears came flooding.

I picked up the jersey and inhaled the smell of him. I held his old stuffed pony, the ear scarred from chewing. I moved to the desk and stared at an old photo of Baoth and Patrick with Gerald, arms around his two little boys, their matching rompers. Through the window, the sun reflected off the old wood of the desktop, revealing scratches and marks. My eye caught a series of deliberate loops: Baoth, it said, in a childish cursive. He'd always pressed too hard with his pencil, nearly tearing the paper of his homework. And here was his boyish signature, impressed into the desk itself. A chill ran through me. The idea that his physical body had left this imprint, and now this was all that was left behind.

Not for the first time, I thought of my mother with real gratitude, with a softer heart. In this moment of desolation, I just wanted to cry into her ample chest, a heartbroken, confused girl.

I'm not sure how long I sat there, crying and shaking my head, but by the time I roused myself, the sun had traveled to the other side of the house and the room was in shadow. I sighed and walked to the kitchen, but now I left the door open behind me.

———

BY JULY, I was enough myself again to realize how much I'd been neglecting Patrick. Honoria was at boarding school during the week and when she returned home, she brought a living energy through the door with her like a rush of brisk air. But Patrick had come home from the hospital and was still bedridden in his room. I needed to attend to his spirits, not just feed and bathe him and do his laundry.

We soon learned about the Trudeau Institute on Saranac Lake in the Adirondacks where, instead of a hospital environment, there were cottages where patients could receive their care and get plenty of fresh air. The town was very quiet with little to do, since the entire population was either current TB patients or those who'd been recently "cured."

I found a small Adirondack lodge to rent, and we lived there with a nurse for the next two years. Steele Camp was built of whole redwood logs with oak paneling, a screened porch, and a stone fireplace big enough to stand up in. Its rolling lawn sloped down to a sandy beach on the lake, with a detached boathouse and a guesthouse nearby. Patrick and I moved there in August, with Gerald making the seven-hour drive from Manhattan every other weekend and Honoria coming up for the whole summer. It was the longest I'd ever been apart from Gerald, but I vowed to turn my full attention to Patrick and enjoy what I could of life.

To stave off loneliness, I renewed my correspondence with good friends. Chief among these was Ernest, who became a staunch source of emotional support. Our letters revealed a mutual vulnerability that neither of us was used to showing.

*This has been a hell of a year or maybe it is just that they are always as bad but your numbers only come up on the wheel all in one season,* he wrote. *I've gotten the feeling that maybe I am bad luck and that I should not have to do with people.*

I wrote back, *Please don't say that again, about being bad luck. It isn't true. When have you been anything but good to people? I've been thinking that perhaps I was a jinx for my family—or worse still, that I was negligent in not seeing that they were ill in time, or how ill they were. But we must not any of us think those thoughts, because that is destructive. I won't if you won't.*

The real negligence I felt wasn't about not acting in time. I couldn't say aloud where I feared the fault really lay: in the germ phobia that had prompted me to overprotect my children, weakening their immune systems to germs they might otherwise have resisted. The lining of our train cars. The washing of coins. And most of all, those tonsillectomies in California. The thought that I had unwittingly caused Patrick's TB and Baoth's death was simply too awful to admit.

---

WHENEVER POSSIBLE, I wheeled Patrick out onto the lawn to get some sunlight and fresh air. I bought a pair of good binoculars and an ornithology guide, and we identified as many birds as we could from our little piece of shore. He made paper airplanes, decorating them with his colored pencils, but he didn't have the strength to cast them into the air to see how they flew. I kept looking for signs of his improvement, and I could rarely find any.

By October 18, when Patrick turned sixteen, he weighed just fifty-nine pounds. Between the isolation and his slow decline, despite our best efforts and the medical treatments of the Trudeau Institute, I was quite desperate for some jolly company.

My letters took on a frantic quality as I invited friends to come visit. *I have such a good wine cellar & lots of new music . . . Our guests are housed apart and all of Patrick's dishes and laundry are done separately so there isn't the slightest danger . . . It will be my pleasure to cozen & feed you & make you little drinks and whatnot . . .* I'm sure those who did visit came out of pure pity because I sounded so pathetically eager.

My affectionate correspondence with Ernest continued, and I confess I was comforted—or perhaps seduced—by his attention. Instead of the charm offensive he used to direct at both Gerald and me, now he didn't bother writing to Gerald at all. And as his marriage to Pauline began to deteriorate, his tone took on a surprisingly tender and sentimental quality. He deplored becoming a double personality: one the puritanical, hard-working writer, the other the drinking and partying man of the hour. *Only place these rival skyzophreniacs agree on is they don't like to sleep alone,* he wrote. When he learned that I wouldn't be coming to Key West for the usual winter visit, he sounded truly despondent and signed off *With very much love much love and love also with love, Ernest.* I wish I could say I rebuffed his affections, but that wouldn't be true. I welcomed them.

---

MEANWHILE, WE'D GIVEN up our Bedford house and New York apartment and rented a suite for Gerald at the New Weston Hotel in Midtown. Here he entertained small groups of friends and occasionally went to the theater. But his most regular friend had become Alexander Woollcott, the *New Yorker's* rotund drama critic. I called him Woolly, but Gerald had several affectionate nicknames for him, including "Alexis, Prince of the Heavenly Flocks." Woolly was as witty as Dottie Parker, and also a member of the Algonquin Round Table, but he was louder and more vulgar. He was also very public about his homosexuality. He just didn't give a damn about what people thought of him. I tolerated the man but worried about what Gerald saw in him.

"Why do you encourage him, Dow?" I asked one night by telephone—he in Manhattan, me at Steele Camp. "Everyone says he's a legend in his own mind. I thought you cultivated a more respectable crowd."

"His blast and bombast are just a shield," Gerald said. "When you get him in a quiet moment, he has a remarkable gift for making the people he loves feel valuable."

That caught me off guard. "And are you one of the people he loves?"

There was a long pause. "He's been an essential support to me over the past year, Sal," Gerald said somberly. This was a tender spot for both of us; we'd both done what was necessary to cope with the loss of Baoth, and sometimes that meant turning to others outside our marriage for emotional support.

"So is this going to be like it was with Cole?" I asked, referring back to Venice in 1924. "Do we need to go through that again?" Over the years, Gerald had repeatedly assured me that nothing physical had ever happened in Venice, least of all with Cole Porter—a platonic friend since his Yale days. Still, it was Cole who'd introduced Gerald to the homosexual scene that had made him realize who he truly was inside. It probably would have happened sooner or later in any case, but I couldn't help blaming Cole for it.

"It's a friendship, Sal. A friendship that's helping me find a little bit of joy again. Will you begrudge me that?"

So I didn't argue with him, particularly in light of the tone my letters had taken with Ernest. We knew enough not to pry too deeply.

I'D BECOME FRIENDLY with Dr. Trudeau's family, including his grown son, Albert. At the first good snow, Albert invited me to go bobsledding over at Lake Placid, site of the 1932 Winter Olympics. It had been years since I'd done anything so physically challenging, but I surprised myself by saying yes immediately. We drove up Mt. Van Hoevenberg in his brand-new Chevrolet, an enormous vehicle called a "station wagon." At the summit, Albert parked near a utility shed and pulled out a large bobsled with four rails, front and back. I helped him carry the thing over to the top of the run, and he spent a minute positioning it for takeoff.

"I sit in front and steer," he said, straddling the sled and grabbing the reins. "Now you hop on back. Put each foot on a rail. Then just lean in the same direction as me."

In a fit of giggles, I squatted over the sled and lowered myself down. "Like this? I'm going to fly off at the first turn!"

"There's a handle on each side. Grab those and don't let go. Ready?"

The snowy track ahead of us seemed to fall straight off the mountain. "Just go," I yelled, "before I get cold feet!" Sailing over the side of a cliff was a choice I'd never have made five years ago. Now I knew it was reckless, but didn't really care.

Albert dug in his heels and we pushed off, down the twisting, plummeting track. Birch and pine and tamarack trees flew by us in a blur. It felt like riding a camel at seventy miles an hour. Tears streaked back toward my ears and my hysterical screams became hiccups as we hit each bump. The sled swayed and careened around all ten curves, then suddenly we coasted and came to rest at the bottom—a wide, flat plain of snow.

I was crying with laughter and fright and surprise, all in one uncontrollable stew of emotions.

"Mrs. Murphy, are you all right?" Albert asked, his face a mask of concern.

I tried to answer, but I couldn't stop laugh-crying. We'd landed safely, and I was surprised to realize that I was glad of it. I rolled off the sled and onto the snow, like a fat sea lion in my layers of wool. Then I was sobbing, just for a moment, before I pulled myself together. Those screams had been buried in my body for the past eight months. I hadn't even known they were in there.

I lay flat on my back, panting heavily, staring up at a steel-blue sky encircled by a crown of whispering trees. Everything was muted by a cushion of snow. I felt quiet and still and perfectly at peace. I couldn't remember the last time I'd felt this peaceful.

"Oh Albert, how did you *know*?" I finally said. "How did you know that was exactly what I needed?" We both laughed then. After that, Albert routinely invited me to go bobsledding with him, and I routinely said yes.

---

DECEMBER 30, 1935, was our twentieth anniversary and, it being a Monday, Gerald was working in Manhattan. "Happy twentieth, darling," I said over the telephone.

"Happy anniversary, Sal," he said. "I'm sorry we're not together for the actual day. We'll celebrate properly the next time you come to the city."

But neither of us felt like celebrating. With our physical distance—and with all that had happened in the previous five years—we were both feeling more apart than ever before. I wondered how we might have acknowledged the day had we continued to live at Villa America. A Dinner-Flowers-Gala on the terrace. Jazz records and dancing, or perhaps a solo violin performance by David Mannes. Songs by the children, a romp on the beach.

In a recent phone conversation, Gerald had said, almost casually,

"Just because two people have been married for twenty years doesn't mean that they should need the same thing of life or of people. It's unrealistic to expect any deep relationship to be kept at a constant emotional pressure."

"Aren't warm human relationships necessary to everyone?" I said. "At least, shouldn't they be?"

"You believe in them, Sal. You're capable of them. But I lack your confidence, your need for affection. And no two people show that need in the same degree or manner."

"Oh sometimes I do tire of your dry, analytical discourse when talking about human relationships," I snapped. "I'll just say I love you and leave it at that."

"I love you too, Sal."

A few days later he wrote, *I suppose it's downright tragic when one person who lives by communicated affection should have chosen a mate who is so damned deficient. As early as I can remember, I've known that I lacked something emotionally. Whether this is due to the absence of feeling, or the learned suppression of feelings, distrust and fear of them, I don't know.*

For the length of our marriage, Gerald and I had been two halves of a whole. Now, after weathering so many years and so much misfortune, it seemed our discourse was more about our differences, not our shared perspectives. Were all marriages like that? I'd always thought ours was something above the norm—were we just like other husbands and wives?

---

THAT SPRING, I left Patrick with the nurse and joined John and Katy Dos Passos to visit Ernest in Havana. Once again, Pauline was in Arkansas, so it was just the four of us. We spent long sea days on the *Pilar*—within two days, I'd caught a barracuda, an arctic bonito, and three groupers—then sailed back with our "fish flag" flying. At the Ambos Mundos Hotel, the chef would prepare one of our catch and we would eat very well, accompanied by many drinks and much wine. After dinner, a little trio played rumbas and Cuban versions of our American favorites. Some nights we stayed at the Ambos Mundos, others we'd return to the *Pilar* to bunk down. It was jolly, jolly, jolly. Such a relief after a frigid winter in upstate New York.

Sometimes I wondered, though, if Ernest deliberately invited me only when Pauline was away. He was always a physically demonstrative man, and it felt good to have his big, tanned arm draped casually across the back of my chair. But after too many drinks—which happened frequently—he would cross the line, as he had done in my room back in '34.

One morning, Ernest stumbled into the galley looking particularly battered from the night before. Eyes bloodshot, skin ashen, hair in disarray. He rubbed his hand over his stubbled face and groaned.

"Oh my dear," I said, and quickly got up to make him a hair of the dog. "You sit down."

I poured him a whiskey sour from the pitcher on the counter and mixed him a Bromo-Seltzer chaser, then set the two glasses before him.

"*Salud*," he said, toasting me with the Bromo, then quickly downed both glasses.

When his face had regained a bit of its color, I spoke. "You called me snooty last night," I said. "You don't *really* think I'm snooty, do you?" I lit another cigarette and leaned back in my galley chair, awaiting his answer.

Ernest laughed without smiling. "I just think you pull the plug on a good time a little too often. Your virtue always kicks in at the last minute."

"And *I* think you find me a convenient flirtation when Pauline's absent," I said. "If it weren't for my last-minute virtue, we'd have made an awful mess of things by now."

"It's not just when she's absent," Ernest growled. "I'm sleeping alone now even when she's home." He turned to scowl at the sea outside but quickly shaded his eyes against the glare.

"And we all know how you hate to sleep alone!" I said it as a joke, but he didn't laugh.

"I'm serious," he said. "We're on the way out."

"Oh Ernest," I said. "I'm sorry. But don't resent me for choosing my marriage. One's affections are about all there are. And you and Pauline have made such a good life together."

But later I'd learn that Ernest's eye was apparently already scouting for the next Mrs. Hemingway.

---

I DON'T KNOW if John or Katy said anything to Gerald or if he just sensed my closeness with Ernest, but soon after I'd returned to Saranac, he wrote me a lovely letter.

*I am terribly, terribly sorry that I am as I am. Only one thing would be awful and that is that you might not know that I love only you. We both know it's inadequate, but such as it is, it certainly is the best this poor fish can offer, and it's the realest thing I know.*

As he always did so beautifully, Gerald had put into words not only exactly how he felt about me, but how I felt about him. After all we'd been through together, we could only ever love each other in our very imperfect ways. There would never truly be anyone else for either of us, not for life. I never once worried about that.

---

LATER THAT YEAR, Ernest published a short story called "The Happy Ending"—we would later know it as "The Snows of Kilimanjaro"—that stunned me. In it, he seemed to blame the wealthy wife, Helen, for the death of her husband. Helen was an American heiress who had lost a child. While I did see parallels between Helen and Pauline (who was also an American heiress), one phrase caught me off guard.

*She looked at him with her well-known, well-loved face from* Spur *and* Town & Country, I read, and stopped. It was *my* engagement photo that had appeared on the cover of *Town & Country* magazine. Once, Ernest had been hunting in the Rockies and found that cover photo pinned to the wall of an abandoned mountain hut. He'd taken it and mailed it to me. We thought it was so funny at the time, but now it felt as if Ernest was using it to wound me.

First Scott and now Ernest. It was becoming very inconvenient to have writers as friends.

---

THAT SUMMER, IN a surge of hopefulness, I bought a camp on nearby Lake St. Regis and moved there with Patrick. I threw myself into decorating in a way I hadn't since Villa America: brightly painted furniture, Mexican metalware, and lots of foliage. It was a temple of optimism, and I named it Camp Adeline, after my mother. I even had stationery letter-pressed with "Camp Adeline" on it, a testament to how long we expected to make our home there. There was a small sandy beach, a boathouse, and even a fishing dock with access for Patrick's reclining wheelchair.

On a long-overdue vacation, Gerald joined us for a summer of swimming and fishing and friends and parties. Outwardly, it was as close to the old life as we'd ever come, but inside, I still felt a low boil of hysteria. So we kept ourselves occupied with guests and costumes and all the old tricks. Patrick's room was now filled with fishing tackle, hunting gear, and animal trophy heads sent by Ernest. I insisted on the belief that he would be just like other boys again. I even began dreaming of getting back to Paris again in the fall. Wouldn't it be divine to go shopping at Nicole Groult or sit in a café with Léger or dance into the night at Le Boeuf? Such fantasies were the only way to keep going.

Outside the dream, there were medical realities. Patrick's condition had worsened since his sixteenth birthday, with chills, night sweats, and a convulsive cough. He was still running a high fever and needed transfusions for anemia. His weight continued to drop.

Gerald had to return to work in the fall, but condensed his week into three long days so he could spend the rest of the time with us. Honoria came up nearly every weekend, calling on the other days to check on Patrick's condition. Even I had to admit that he was deteriorating.

Still, I continued to make little devotionals to some vague god, gestures intended to prolong Patrick's life. For Christmas, I gave him a five-year diary, his name imprinted in gold on fine red leather. On January 1, he wrote, *At Christmas, we pulled some little gifts out of a paper Santa Claus. I am greatly inconvenienced by having to breathe out of an oxygen tank, due to breathlessness.*

After a few days, he was too weak to write in the book itself, but scribbled his random thoughts on paper scraps, which I saved to paste into the diary later. He resumed his pneumothorax injections. We all wore surgical masks in his room to prevent infection.

Soon, friends began to arrive, but not in the usual festive mood. Even our beloved "Titine" visited from France. There was no pretense that they had come for anything but a crisis.

On January 30 Patrick fell into a coma. "He won't be coming out of this one," Dr. Hayes said, shaking his head. "I'm so sorry."

Gerald and I gathered in Patrick's room and removed the oxygen mask. We each sat on one side of Patrick's bed, holding his hands and speaking softly to him.

"We're right here with you, Pook."

"You're fine. Just relax. We're here."

"We love you so much."

I looked up to see Gerald's face shiny with tears, matching my own. My mind whirled a picture show of my youngest, most delicate son, toddling around the tiled patio of Villa America. Always watching his older brother to see what to do next, how to behave like a big boy. Growing into a thoughtful teenager, quietly drawing in his wheelchair. How his face would light up when Ernest came to visit. Such memories already felt like ghosts to me.

Outside, the winter daylight gradually leached out of the sky. The lake sat cold and still, everything in dreary hibernation. Inside, the light of a desk lamp cast a weak halo onto the bed where our youngest child lay slipping away. We were a garland of love, joined by hands: Gerald, Patrick, me. For some reason, the words "holy trinity" came to me. It felt like we were in a private chapel of pure love and grief. Three hearts beating, soon to be two.

As with Baoth, we watched his breaths become shallower and farther apart. But this time we didn't fight it. We didn't beg for him to stay. It had been seven long years, and Patrick had fought like hell. It was time to let him go.

When it was over, Honoria came in and we sat and cried together. The next day, we received a letter from Scott, who'd heard the news from mutual friends and mailed it express. *Fate can't have any more arrows in its quiver for you that will wound like these*, he wrote. *The golden bowl is broken indeed but it* was *golden; nothing can ever take those boys away from you now.*

———

IT WAS A few days before the pain really sank under my skin and into my heart. *Both* of our boys. Although Patrick's illness had taken seven years to do its nasty work, now the shock and unfairness of it really struck me for the first time.

I went to my bedroom and shut the door. I eased myself down onto my knees and propped myself on the bed with my elbows. Then, clasping my hands, I tried to pray.

"Please," I began. "Please, God." What came next?

I had never been a religious woman. I was raised in the Episcopal tradition—the Book of Common Prayer and holiday services—but as an adult my practice, compounded by Gerald's antipathy toward his Catholic upbringing, was to enter a church only on necessity. Our children were taught instead that the divine lived in beauty, in friendship, in nature.

Now, instead of a graceful appeal to God, I found myself defending my lack of spiritual attendance to Him.

Had I lived my life as a Christian? In hindsight, I would say yes. I was sensitive to the feelings of others. I treated both friends and strangers with generosity. I advocated compassion and equality among the races. But did I say formal prayers and put money in the basket on Sundays? No. Now I wondered: was that the problem? Was the arc of my life a cautionary tale about the dangers of ignoring the church? Was God punishing me for my paganism by taking away nearly everything I ever loved?

I wrestled with that question as I shifted on my knees. The carpet was a thin rug, its uneven surface pressing into my bones as if demanding penitence.

If anyone's life was an example of religious truancy, it was mine. And yet, I couldn't believe in a God so vindictive that He would torture me for merely ignoring the church. But what other explanation was there? How could one live so generously, so creatively, so filled with love, and be rewarded with such tragedy and heartbreak? I wanted to believe there was a greater lesson, but I couldn't guess what it was. I struggled to make sense of it.

"Please, God," I said again. "Just give me a way forward. Show me how to continue living. I can't do this alone."

I stayed there for a while on my knees and waited for a response, for some glimmer of grace that would ease my grief. I felt nothing. Instead, I heard voices from the front room—Dos had shown up that afternoon on our doorstep unannounced, straight from South America. After another minute or so, I stood up and went to join them. My salvation would need to come from somewhere else. My body wasn't used to kneeling.

# PART IV

*There is only one thing more painful than learning from experience and that is not learning from experience.*
—Archibald MacLeish

*Life is to be used, not just held in the hand like a box of bonbons that nobody eats.*
—John Dos Passos

## Chapter 21
### 1938-1940

After a lonely little service for Patrick at the Church of St. Luke, the Beloved Physician, in Saranac; after Alice Myers had helped me pack up his room and belongings; after I sent the hunting and fishing equipment and the mounted animal heads to the Hemingway boys—it seemed like life was only about "after" now—I said goodbye to Lake St. Regis with nothing but relief. I didn't have the energy to sell Camp Adeline, so I simply gave the deed to the Kip's Bay Boys Club of New York with the proviso that it be used as a summer camp for underprivileged youth. Perhaps they could fill those cabins with the boisterous laughter that had been all too rare for us there.

For Gerald, it was his soul that felt broken, and he sought to find relief in philosophical ways. But for me it was more visceral. When we lost Baoth, it honestly felt as if I'd lost a part of my body. An arm, perhaps. Now, with Patrick's death, I'd lost another arm. I wandered around each day, my actual arms moving out of habit but with no direct connection to my brain. They were like ghost limbs, behaving according to an old life, now gone.

I JOINED GERALD at the New Weston Hotel in Manhattan, trading his small suite for a penthouse with wraparound views of the city. Instead of going to dinner or the theater as he had when he'd lived there alone, now I noticed that he rarely went out in the evenings, unless I felt like going too. I could tell he was keeping an eye on me, never leaving me alone at night.

One evening I'd persuaded him to take a rare night out, so he insisted that Dottie Parker come over to keep me company. Since she was unable to boil water without incident, I figured a home-cooked meal would do her good.

"You spoil me, Mrs. Murphy," she said. "I feel as if I've gone home to Mother."

Dottie's ingenue days were long gone. Her dark bob had been replaced by a hasty bun with an unkempt fringe at the front. Under her eyes sagged two dark saddlebags, the left one more pronounced than the right. Dottie wore her hard life in a visible mask.

"Have you alerted 21 that your usual table will be vacant this evening?" I set down two simple plates—just pork chops and a green salad—on the small table near the window. A half bottle of Saint-Emilion sat breathing, ready to pour. Although Gerald and I had eaten many meals together without the children over the years, suddenly setting the table for two felt like a slap in the face, a painful reminder of how our family had shrunk.

"Oh, they won't even notice I'm gone," Dottie said. "Besides, I'm boycotting 21. They have a new bartender there who hasn't memorized my martini recipe."

"You mean he actually puts vermouth in your glass, instead of just waving the bottle over it with a benediction?"

"Everyone knows that vermouth just taints a martini," she said. "It disgraces it."

Outside, the sky gradually darkened to indigo and we watched the lights of neighboring skyscrapers wink off. On the streets far below, taxi horns honked and a siren wailed.

"So Gerald enlisted you to babysit me tonight?" I asked, reaching for the remoulade sauce. I considered Dottie to be one of my closest friends, but Gerald had known her since grammar school. She was devoted to both of us.

"He does worry about you, Sara. I wish I'd just once meet a man who cared for me as much as that man does for you."

"But you have that handsome young Alan Campbell."

"I rest my case."

"Oh come on, Dottie," I said. "He's your husband, your screenwriting partner, your aide-de-camp. That's a full marriage!"

"More days than not, it's a paid arrangement," Dottie said. "His devotion is salaried. But Gerald's is heartfelt. He loves you to his core."

"Yes, I know I'm lucky in that respect."

By now, our long marriage was gospel among our circle of friends. "Like Fort Knox," Ada had said, way back when. That was our default: our united front, the one thing I could count on through the serial catastrophes of the past ten years. How many times had I held my tongue, not wanting to contradict Gerald in front of others? But under the glossy damask of that image, we were two unique people who felt and responded to things in very different ways. Sometimes it was downright lonely to be in a marriage perceived to be so perfect. Still, Dottie was right: Gerald did love me and I loved him. And now we were bound even more tightly together through the common geography of grief and memory.

As we lingered over cigarettes, coffee, and butter cookies from the little bakery on 48th street, Puppy, my Pekinese, gave an outburst of yips and Honoria breezed through the door. "Aunt Dottie!" she squealed, and gave her a big smooch.

"Stand back and let me look at you, you gorgeous thing. Are the young men lined up around the block trying to get into your knickers?"

"Dottie!" I said. "Enough of that."

Honoria tried to brush the comment off, but I saw her face flush. Surrounded by actors, musicians, and dancers for her entire young life, she'd set her own sights on an acting career and was now living at home with us, a ray of joy and light in our new situation. She was twenty, with bronze-gold hair and plump red lips—perfect for ingenue roles.

"Honoria's been practicing her diction and her carriage," I said. "With the right break, we think she might make it on the stage."

As I watched my lovely daughter smile and laugh with Dottie, I felt two things: First, I realized how much I'd neglected her in my obsession with the health of her brothers. Second, I began to fear that she too might fall sick. Would the curse continue until we were robbed of our entire brood? I vowed to give my only child all the love and attention she'd missed during those bleak years. And I tried not to smother her with worry as she led her normal, twenty-year-old life.

---

GERALD AND I tried to muster some of our old enthusiasm for life, but we felt like week-old balloons, puckered and bobbing around the floor with only distant memories of the big party. Tightening our belts was still an issue; we were down to about $200,000 in investments. Had we been average Americans, we could have lived on a fraction of that, but that had never been our style. So we quietly sold off a few parcels of my family's property at about $3,000 an acre, and that cash flow afforded a fresh distraction: a new home. On our weekends in East Hampton, we'd found that Hook Pond Cottage was a constant reminder of our two lost boys.

I still thought of them every day, now two brass urns lying under marble headstones. One of them taken quickly, violently; the other given a lingering, painful death sentence. They would never know the joy of falling in love or having a child. They would never go to college, get a job, buy a house. The unfairness of it still takes my breath away.

OUR NEW PLAN was to renovate an old dairy barn on the The Dunes property. Then we studied curling blueprints and debated over ceiling heights, paint colors, wood stains, and room dimensions. I imagined the small, quiet parties we would host on the flagstone patio. The new living room would have seven windows, giving excellent views onto the saltwater pond. And we would name it "Swan Cove," for the flocks of swans that nested there.

We also resumed traveling to Europe every summer, though I couldn't face a return to Antibes without our boys. The echo of those happy days, now gone, was still ringing in my ears. So that year, 1938, we went to Carlsbad, Czechoslovakia where, at the Park Hotel Pupp's health spa, we were herded like cattle in a rotation between baths, gymnasium, dining room, water fountains, and mountain hikes.

"In the face of what's happened, it feels pointless to take care of our own health," Gerald mused one day as we sat in chaises on the terrace, wrapped in thick white robes and towels like mummies. "On the other hand, we might as well feel as well as possible. We'll be better company for others."

I sighed. "I think I'd feel more well with a cigarette and an occasional cocktail." The spa's gastronomic tyranny dictated "no alcohol"—just two small glasses of red wine at night. And I'd vowed not to smoke for the duration of our stay, but it was an oath that haunted me several times a day.

The hotel orchestra struck up a waltz from the balcony and we both hummed along half-heartedly. Then a nurse came by with a pair of wooden tongs to place astringent-soaked cotton pads over our eyes. Perhaps it was this enforced blindness that allowed me to venture into a subject we never spoke of.

"Dow," I said, "do you ever wonder if we got it wrong? What if there really is an all-powerful God, who needs to be obeyed and prayed to? Could it be possible that we've sinned in some way?"

Gerald said nothing for a minute and I fiddled with the lapel of my robe. Would he pooh-pooh my naivete?

"After twenty years of agnostic bliss, you're not going to go all Sister Mary Orthodox on me, are you?"

Good, humor. "Well, it wasn't my intention," I said. "But losing two children is enough to make one sit up and take notice, don't you think? We were so convinced we were mastering life in our own way. Creating a poetic ideal. Perhaps someone, or something, thought we needed to be taught a lesson."

Gerald made a scoffing noise. "You'll never convince me that the Catholic Church—or *any* church—is closer to getting it right with all its rules and penances and judgments."

"I don't mean the church, Dow. I mean some larger, undefined spirit that has ultimate control over our lives."

"I believe in bacteria, Sal. It's science that killed our boys, not spirit."

I knew that Gerald credited unseen forces when it came to creating art, to forging friendships, to listening to one's inner voice about the road ahead. More than once he'd referred to "our better angels." But on this tender, painful point, he was immovable. The notion that a divine justice was behind our most devastating loss was too much for him and I didn't blame him one bit. Still, it weighed on me, that there was a larger force at work. That there was some scheme whose rules we had misunderstood. A line that we'd blundered across.

---

AS OUR TRIP wound down, Gerald detoured to London for business and I took Honoria and Fanny Myers for a final celebratory lunch at Brasserie Lipp, where we were given a nice table in the center of the dining room. I loved this room, with its high ceilings and rich mahogany paneling and tall mirrors. The art nouveau murals were exactly the same as they'd been back in the early '20s. I could almost remember the young woman I'd been then, when eating at Lipp had been a weekly affair. Where was she now?

We were scanning the long menu when Fanny whispered, "Look

there, at the banquette against the wall. It's Picasso!"

Honoria gave a little squeal. "Mother, turn around, it's Oncle Pablo. Let's go say hello!"

But I continued reading the menu as if I hadn't heard. Suddenly the chance to revisit my past was less of an idea and more of a dare. I felt every bit of my fifty-four years. The last decade hadn't been kind to me, with my digestive issues and my grief. I simply couldn't face that man, that phantom from my youth, in my current state. An hour later, as we got up and left the restaurant, I didn't even look in his direction.

---

WHEN WE RETURNED to East Hampton, Swan Cove was nearly finished and I happily turned my attention to decorating the place with a new look—dark, old-world furniture; heavy brocades; and *objets* we'd bought in Czechoslovakia. It looked and felt like a lovingly aged family estate, full of sentimental artifacts and worn glamour. Gerald designed formal gardens with marble statuary and a shady allée of elms leading to the water. We'd done it again, we told ourselves: we'd created a place of loveliness, where we would host our friends and laugh and sing long after dark. It was the first time since the boys' deaths that I felt the allure of *things* again. There's something about grief that puts a gray film over everything; it's as if beauty ceases to exist. The whole world seems drab and lifeless, when in fact that blindness comes from inside you. Now my eyes were beginning to see color again.

But each night in bed, one of the other of us was usually restless. It had felt so good to pour ourselves into a new house, distracting us from the harsh reality of our shrinking funds. It was in the early hours that the worry set in. How much longer could we ignore the numbers? We just weren't good at being anything but rich.

---

THEN IT WAS back to Manhattan, where we celebrated my fifty-fifth birthday in the New Weston penthouse among such friends as the MacLeishes, the Barrys, Jinny Pfeiffer, and Pauline Hemingway. Amid the records and dancing and champagne and a sheet cake that Gerald had decorated like a telegram wishing me good health, I finally collapsed onto a loveseat in the corner, watching this crowd of my favorite people and wondering how we'd all gotten so old. There were aching feet and teeth complaints and the hint of jowls.

Archie joined me on the sofa with a fresh glass of champagne and we sat back, observing the party.

"It's a marvel that we've all stayed connected over the years, isn't it?" he said. "The friendships we forged back on that little beach have endured, what, nearly fifteen years now?"

"Yes, thanks to the US post office and the makers of Dom Pérignon," I laughed. "But you know who I'm thinking of tonight? Scott and Zelda."

The Fitzgeralds had been missing in action for years and were now like faint ghosts at the periphery of our merry group. Zelda had been institutionalized off and on for the past decade, and the last time we'd seen her was at the New York steamship terminal. We'd brought Scottie to Europe with us for the summer, and Zelda was there, with a nurse, to meet us upon our return. She was drawn and pale, lacking that effervescence that had always been her trademark, and her speech seemed labored. There had always been a kind wisdom under Zelda's wildness—that was now gone. She seemed to be trying to mimic some of her earlier wit.

"The ages have been kind to you," she'd said. "You're both impervious to the passage of time. Do you suppose that Paris is still pink in the late sun and latent with happiness?" It was as if she were reciting an old poem from childhood.

For years, Scott had been living in California, where he'd taken up with a gossip columnist named Sheila Graham. But his drinking had obviously continued, and we only heard from him to complain about his various illnesses and to ask for money, usually to help with Scottie's expenses at Vassar or Zelda's medical bills. His inability to get sober had resulted in a string of firings and canceled contracts, and he hadn't published a book or short story in a very long time.

"In spite of everything, I still love them. I do," I said to Archie.

"You're remarkable, Sara," he said. "Your heart's so blind to your friends' glaring flaws. The Fitzgeralds primarily among them."

"Funny," I said. "Ernest once hurt my feelings by calling me snooty. But I just choose my friends carefully. And, having chosen them, I become addicted to their attention."

"Hmmm. I'd put it more like this," Archie said. "Once you've decided that a person is your friend, you're never tempted to part from that choice. Not out of blind loyalty, mind you, but of a kind of humane wisdom."

Archie's love and poetic way with words always healed my heart and made me see myself with kinder eyes.

I laughed. "I'm a very simple creature these days. I only need a little sun and a cocktail to be as happy as a blade of grass." But even then I knew that I was no longer that sanguine creature. After all that had happened, I would never feel that simple happiness again.

---

THE NEXT SPRING I was down again with my gallbladder, which even sent me into the hospital for several days. Ever since Patrick's first diagnosis, my body had rebelled with pain and chills and nausea. After my surgery, Pauline asked me and Honoria down to Key West for a few weeks to recuperate, but I suspected she had a second, unspoken reason for the invitation. It was clear that she and Ernest were in the final throes; the pretty young war correspondent Martha Gellhorn had insinuated herself into the marriage every bit as doggedly as Pauline had done ten years before. I sensed that Honoria and I were there to enliven the conversation and keep things friendly.

After we left, Ernest wrote me a series of letters, all of which veered into overly affectionate prose: *I never did thank you for the lovely records and I never could thank you for how loyal and lovely and also beautiful and attractive and lovely you have been always ever since always . . . I love you always and please always count on it.*

But by the time they arrived, I was already en route to Europe again.

---

THE NEWS FROM the Continent had continued to alarm us that year, but we took a chance and planned another visit, this time to Sicily and the Italian coast aboard the *Weatherbird* with Honoria and the Dos Passoses. We docked in tiny ports with picnics of tangy sheep's milk cheese and little fried sardines, washed down with the rich red Nero d'Avola wine. We gasped at the Villa of the Mysteries in Pompeii. And Gerald read passages to us from *The Odyssey* as we passed through the Strait of Messina, a.k.a. Scylla and Charybdis.

But when we dropped Dos and Katy off at Siracusa, a little crowd of Italians stood on the dock heckling us. Posters everywhere bore Mussolini's face, and I caught a glimpse of hostile graffiti painted on a nearby wall: *Mare Nostrum*—"Our Sea." As we passed the island of Elba, we could hear the thrum of new factories manufacturing weapons and war vehicles. Within a few months, German troops would occupy the Sudetenland in Czechoslovakia, and Jewish homes and businesses across Germany would be destroyed on Kristallnacht. How naive we were; it wasn't just our own lives deteriorating, but the entire world. Since we'd left our French lives in 1932, it seemed, life had gone to hell in a handbasket.

---

WE DETOURED TO Paris. Rather, I did, with Honoria and the Myerses. Gerald had returned to the States to tend to new financial emergencies at Mark Cross. I'd hoped for one last European idyll before the clouds of war became too thick, but Paris was already being mobilized, the city blacked out at night. The mood was very *angoissante*, a terrible depression everywhere. Impossibly long lines at the banks, at the telegraph office, and at the Cunard travel bureau as tourists scrambled to get out before the city shut down. A few days later, Hitler would invade Poland and two days after that, war would be officially declared by Britain and France.

We met the Myerses for dinner—"the last supper" we called it—at Maxim's. With its plush red interior and gold fixtures the restaurant felt, as always, like the inside of a jewelry box, and the waiters were as formal and meticulous as ever. You'd never know there was a war perched on the horizon or that, just outside, most of Paris was painting over its windows.

I was still steaming from a letter I'd received from Hoytie via the Guaranty Trust several days before. After her ridiculous lawsuit of five years earlier, I wanted nothing more to do with the woman. *At this critical moment,* she'd written, *I think all else should be forgotten and forgiven. You are welcome to stay with me at my apartment on the quai des Conti. I think it is one of the safest places in the city.* I'd never responded. We were still at the Hôtel Lutetia and had made plans to stay in Orsay.

We'd no sooner finished the cheese plate when Dick said, "Don't look now, Sara, but Hoytie's headed our way." That woman was like a bad penny. She turned up at the worst times.

"That's all right," I said. "I'm already prepared for the German invasion. She's not much worse."

I was pretending to be absorbed in the stirring of cream into my coffee as she marched over. The tallest of us three sisters, Hoytie had always been a statuesque, attractive woman, but whenever she opened her mouth, toads came out. Now neither of us even said hello. Instead she just blurted in a shrill voice, "Sara, I'm not going to say anything to you except, for the sake of your child and yourself, you must get out of Paris. I happen to know that they're going to bomb tomorrow night."

It was probably the only time in our lives that Hoytie had tried to do the right thing by me. Perhaps I should have acknowledged it, but I was way past that.

"Thank you," I said curtly, not even looking up. "We've already made our plans."

She turned on her heel and walked stiffly away. I felt the eyes of Honoria, Alice Lee, and Dick upon me, but I said nothing more, just stared into my *café crème*.

How is it that two biologically related sisters can be *so* at odds for their entire lives? Friends often told me, "She's just jealous of you, and the beautiful life you've created."

"Hoytie is jealous of *everybody*," I replied. "She just carries a dark cloud above her, always."

From the time she was born, Hoytie was a contrarian, convinced that the sun rose and set upon her alone. Yes, she did some good work in the Great War, for which France rewarded her for life. But to her family, she'd been nothing but trouble—and to me, especially. The way she tried to take advantage of my kindness to her when she was so in debt with The Dunes. She'd even filed a lawsuit against me to try and get the property back, forcing me to countersue.

But nothing fueled my anger at Hoytie more than the cruel telegram she'd sent us back in 1934 before we'd sailed for Europe: *You will not have a lucky journey for what you have done in breaking Father's plans for us. All his reproaches will be with you.*

The following year, Baoth was dead and two years after that, Patrick. I couldn't help but feel that Hoytie had put a deadly curse on our family, compounding whatever divine justice had already dispensed. I wouldn't speak to her again; she died twenty-five years later. She and I were as opposed as two people could be, let alone two sisters. I'd come to believe that one's true family is the tribe of people you choose to surround yourself with, those with whom you share a genuine fondness. Gerald and I had created an enormous chosen family. I had no room in my life for someone like Hoytie, who brought only pain.

There were no German bombs the next night, thankfully. But we knew we were in harm's way and I quickly booked us passage on the freighter SS *George Washington*. Hardly the luxury of a Cunard steamer, but we didn't care. On September 8, we drove to Le Havre in Honoria's car, with "U.S.A." painted in big white letters on the roof—America was still neutral. The ship didn't sail for two days, with four of us in a tiny cabin listening to air alerts all day and night. We finally sailed for Southampton, where we took on twelve hundred more passengers to fill us beyond capacity. That night we left England and watched them lay mines across the mouth of the harbor once we'd passed through. America had never looked so good.

# Chapter 22
## 1940-1950

At Cheer Hall, I loved nothing better than to tend my rose garden and wave to the passengers on the ships of the Hudson River Day Lines as they passed. By 1949, Gerald and I had bought a new home in the Hudson Valley, overlooking the river in the quiet little village of Sneden's Landing.

The place felt every bit as removed from city life as our earlier homes in East Hampton but, instead of the three-hour drive from Long Island, this was a mere thirty minutes from downtown—a difference that changed our daily life with Gerald's shortened commute to the city.

We threw ourselves into the renovations; for Gerald and me, a new house was always a new lease on life. And when the place was finished, we revived our party-giving with a new fervor: fancy cocktails, elegant meals (Gerald was taking classes at the Cordon-Bleu), musical evenings (we'd started singing together again), and lots of laughter on the stone terrace. The war had been over for five years. President Truman had launched the Fair Deal. And Gerald and I were no longer held hostage by grief.

Now I stood on the lawn, my leather gloves up to my elbows, and looked for the V formation between branches thinner than a pencil. A pile of thorny stalks was gathering at my feet, dead blossoms lolling off the stems. What I loved about roses: they were so damned particular. You either played by their rules or they'd sulk and refuse to bloom.

The late afternoon sun illuminated the opposite shore and the village of Dobbs Ferry; the view over the Hudson was so dramatic, it always inspired reflection. I surveyed the broad river and looked south, where Manhattan lay forty miles away. Another decade gone.

We'd celebrated New Year's 1940 with a small, quiet party at the apartment, but I hadn't welcomed a new decade with such enthusiasm for twenty years. Goodbye to the 1930s, and good riddance. The country had suffered the Great Depression and, while we had fared financially better than most, those years had robbed us of our chosen life, much of our estate, and, of course, two of our precious children. Perhaps a decade with the number four would bring some better fortune. Little did we know what lay ahead: a second World War. Hitler's occupation of much of Europe. A Jewish genocide. It was as if our personal heartbreak had infected the entire world.

But back to 1940: later that year, a young man named Alan Jarvis appeared at the door of our Manhattan apartment promptly at seven, extending a small bouquet of ranunculus. Had I mentioned they were among my favorite flowers? Alan was tall and blond, with a wayward forelock that often obscured one eye. He was currently in town on a scholarship with the Institute of Fine Arts at New York University and beginning to inquire about publishers for a book he was writing. I was practically planning Honoria's wedding to him before he'd even sat down.

"How lucky we are that Fanny bumped into you at the World's Fair!" I gushed. "It's kismet that our paths should cross again."

Gerald, meeting Alan for the first time, greeted him warmly. Honoria gave him a big hug and stood back, her cheeks flushed with pleasure. In her black velvet bodice and white tulle skirt, her hair tied back with a blue ribbon, she looked like a Degas painting come to life. After a couple of cocktails we settled down to eat, filling Gerald in on the way Honoria, Fanny, and I had serendipitously met Alan in

Europe the summer before. As was so often the case with my father, Gerald had stayed home to tend to business at Mark Cross.

"Fanny and I met Alan and another boy at the University Hall commencement ball," Honoria bubbled, "and Mother liked them so much she invited them to join us in Monte Carlo for a cruise on the *Weatherbird*."

"We only crossed Sara one time," Alan said. He gave me a careful look as if checking to see if my anger had lasted.

"I wanted to show them my childhood home, so we snuck over to Villa America in the middle of the night," Honoria said. "But when we came back to the boat at dawn, there was Mother at the stern, completely furious!"

"Not furious," I said. "Worried sick is all."

"And you were very upset at where we'd been, as I recall."

"It felt like disturbing ghosts," I said. I never could bring myself to go back to the villa after we'd last left it in 1934. I had no desire to see the empty shell of our dream, so carefully built, that no longer existed.

Over the appetizer, the conversation soon veered to art. "She rejects the label, but her work is technically aligned with the Surrealists," Alan was saying of Frida Kahlo. "She draws upon the private world of her mind and uses dreamlike imagery. It's automatism, it's Freudian. It's Surrealism."

We all feigned fascination. No one mentioned that we Murphys knew *actual* Surrealists. Ernst. Tanguy. Breton. Man Ray had taken our family portraits. We didn't need this darling young man to define Surrealism for us.

"And may I say, Sara, that this crab cake is a work of art unto itself!"

Sigh. With his good looks and his charm, he overrode the faux pas.

"I know some people at Phaidon," Gerald said about Alan's art book. "And I can introduce you to Archie MacLeish."

By the time I'd served dessert, Honoria's enthusiasm had waned. Gerald and Alan, however, were leaning close, exclaiming over their shared passions for the Bach cantatas and Gerard Manley Hopkins.

"His prosody—that sprung rhythm—so precise, like Bach himself!" Gerald exclaimed.

"*Margaret, are you grieving/Over Goldengrove unleaving?*" Alan quoted. "Like a metronome ticking off the seasons toward our own death! The internal rhythm reminiscent of a nursery rhyme. So brilliant."

Honoria and I rose to clear the table as the two men spoke, oblivious to anything outside their golden circle of conversation. At times like this, we were freshly aware that our educations had ended at Spence, while Gerald had gone to Yale.

"I'm sorry, dear," I said, as I placed a pile of plates in the sink. "I know the evening didn't exactly go as planned."

"There's no competing with Dow when his high beams are on," Honoria smiled. "I couldn't possibly have kept up on the poetry alone, so I'm relieved to be excused."

Gerald had frequently mentored young male friends, and I couldn't blame him. He was clearly drawn to those who reminded him of the young men Baoth and Patrick would be now. I thought it was sweet. He often counseled them on what he called "spiritual matters"—good food and wine—or how to have their trousers tailored to get the perfect break in the crease. But none of those had elicited this sparkle in him. And none of them had been as good-looking as our Mr. Jarvis.

Over the next few years, Gerald and Alan would see each other frequently for lunch and corresponded regularly. I once stumbled upon a stack of letters from Alan that Gerald had tied with a thin green ribbon and stashed in his writing desk. I still couldn't begrudge him the friendship; it seemed to give him a renewed zest for his daily life. He'd even become more passionate about work, and the Black Service went on hiatus. If there was more going on than friendship, I was reluctant to know.

But one day I glanced down at a letter Gerald had written to Alan, left nakedly open upon his desk. There, at the top of the page in his floral hand, he'd addressed Alan as *A. amatus*. Latin for "beloved." Had he *ever* called me that? I stood there, eyes burning, hands shaking. When Gerald walked in, I didn't even try to hide my distress.

He saw the letter in my hand and then my face, now wet with tears. "Sal," he said, trying to take my hand, but I pulled away.

How many other letters like this had there been over the years, ones I'd never stumbled upon? As I looked at Gerald, the space between us seemed to expand and compress. Were we soul mates or were we strangers? I turned to face him full on, my shoulders back.

"I thought this was behind us," I said, my voice low and hurt. "You promised me, Gerald, that you wouldn't."

"I *haven't*," he said. "It's an affair of the mind, Sara. That's all. *Nothing* happened."

"If he's your 'beloved,' then something has indeed happened," I said. "What does it matter if it's an affair of the mind or the body? Either way, it's an infidelity."

Gerald sighed. "He lost his father and his brother early in life. I think he's looking for a father in me as much as I'm seeking a son in him."

"You don't call your own son *amatus*," I said. "Especially when he's twenty-six years old and looks like Adonis."

"You're right, it's more complicated than that." He was silent for a minute. "You've known there are parts of me that I can't speak about without causing you pain. Alan is struggling with the same defect as me. It's helped me enormously to be able to share that secret with him, one who understands exactly how I feel."

He sat on the bench at the foot of the bed and pulled me down next to him.

"And what does that make me?" I asked. "The foolish wife who naively looks the other way?"

"You are *not* the naive wife. You are my better half, far beyond the common expression of it. I've *always* felt that we are one, indivisible for life. Especially after what we've been through together. No one else will *ever* break that bond, Sara." He wrapped an arm around me. "'Let no man put asunder.'"

The truth was, I knew that Gerald would never leave me, nor I him. We both knew it. We truly were a single unit, till death us did part. But how I'd tired of this shadow feeling, this nagging little doubt, that had lived in the back of my mind for the entire life of our marriage! Gerald was simply a more complicated person than I was. There was no black or white with him, only many different grays.

He was a forest and I was a meadow. It would ever be thus.

---

IT EVENTUALLY BECAME a moot point when Alan sailed to England with the Canadian army. Gerald's moods slipped downward for a week or two. He'd sworn to me that the friendship had never crossed over into the physical realm, but I also knew that Gerald wanted, above all, to protect me from hurt feelings. Perhaps it was possible that the only physical infidelity had been my own, with Picasso back in 1923. Still, if you counted all of Gerald's emotional affairs over the years, he'd far outpaced me. It was something I'd learned to live with. It was the price of keeping the peace, of keeping our boat afloat. Nothing was worth losing the marriage over.

---

JUST BEFORE THE holidays of 1940, on December 22, we awoke to read of Scott's death in the headlines. He'd been trying to revive his career as a screenwriter in Hollywood, but the drinking had caught up with him and he was frequently ill.

"What a sad end to a sad life," I sighed. Just forty-four years old.

The idea that Zelda had outlived Scott was another surprise. Five years later, she came with Scottie to visit us in New York, and I didn't recognize her. Honoria, then twenty-nine, had joined us for the visit, and she and Scottie escaped to Honoria's old room to catch up on their young lives.

But Zelda and I sat stiffly in the living room—her tea untouched, her face a stone. I couldn't get over how her appearance had changed. In place of the bubbly blond beauty I remembered was this shadow woman, dressed in an ill-fitting black suit with dark, unwashed hair cut in severe bangs. I tried to draw her out with memories from happier days, but she didn't seem to be that person anymore.

"Honestly, Zelda, you and Scott were incorrigible," I teased. "Do you remember the night you kidnapped the waiter at the casino?" I was forcing a smile, trying to charm her out from behind her mask. "Or the time you both collected everyone's shoes and boiled them on the stove?"

She looked at me blankly. "I don't remember much about that anymore." Her voice sounded hollow, wistful. She held her hands in her lap like a lady sitting in church. Where was the madcap flapper girl? Was she still under there somewhere, buried in all that sadness?

"What about Ernest and Hadley, with Bumby? How we put all the little ones in our canoe and Ernest pulled it around by a rope in his teeth?"

"Oh, they were lovely people," Zelda said, staring out into a middle distance.

The whole visit was painful. I couldn't guess at why she'd come if she had so little memory of us. I reminded myself that she'd undergone extreme treatments like electroshock and insulin therapies to subdue her wild and unpredictable mind.

As she was leaving, Zelda turned to me and said, in a ghostlike whisper, "The ashtrays are full, and the glasses are empty." It was one of those brilliant little turns of phrase that she used to utter back when she was so witty and captivating. Now, it was such an apt postmortem on the Jazz Age itself. Perhaps the day's memories had jiggled something loose in her brain, a tiny remnant of that golden girl.

I tried to embrace her, to impart some gesture of warmth or

affection, but it was like hugging a mannequin.

After Zelda and Scottie left, I went into my room and had a little cry.

---

THERE WAS ONE bright spot, in 1943. Honoria had spent time in London and had come back with a handsome English naval officer named John Shelton. They were married on a Monday afternoon at St. Luke's Episcopal in East Hampton, and I thought my heart would explode from happiness.

As we nibbled canapés and drank Moët & Chandon at the reception, I leaned my head against Gerald's shoulder.

"You looked very dignified and proud walking her down that aisle, Dow. Did you ever think this day would come?"

"Finally, to usher one of our children into adulthood," he said. "What an exquisite relief."

He'd spoken aloud the feeling I'd been suppressing all day; I'd been trying not to picture Baoth and Patrick as the groomsmen they might have been, with Windsor knots and hair slicked back. The jocular toasts they would have made at their sister's expense. The photographs of us all as a single, smiling family.

Instead, we watched as Honoria posed for photos with John. She looked so happy! This being wartime, she'd foregone the lacy white gown for a tailored cocktail dress in salmon-colored silk that brought out the rosiness in her lips and cheeks. Her copper-colored hair wore a tall crown of roses with my own wedding veil draped down the back.

"Isn't she exquisite?" I sighed. I wanted to preserve the vision in an oil painting, not a black-and-white photo. "Soon, with any luck, there'll be grandchildren. We'll make up for all the lost celebrations and rituals. We'll squeeze the dickens out of every birthday, every holiday."

"*Luxe, calme, et volupté,*" Gerald said with a little salute, then gave me a squeeze.

SO MUCH OF the '40s had been about letting go. We sold Hook Pond and Swan Cove for about $50,000 each but, by 1941, we had to admit that The Dunes, my family's beloved estate, would have to be destroyed. It was costing us over $1,200 annually in taxes, $500 a year in fuel costs, and we couldn't find a buyer or renter for a property of that size. Gerald called it "the big bad house." That pile of bricks was far beyond our own needs, but when I thought of the parties, the capers, the family celebrations that those walls had witnessed, I couldn't bear it. Demolition was scheduled and we stayed away from East Hampton for the entire week. Even so, when the day arrived, I cried for about eight hours straight. The long, private shoreline would continue to be called Wiborg Beach.

"I THINK IT'S time to sell the *Weatherbird*, Sal," Gerald said one day, in his usual pragmatic tone. He was affixing new cast-iron hardware to the kitchen cabinets, the sleeves of his plaid shirt rolled up, a pencil over his ear. I looked at him with alarm—he'd loved that boat like a member of the family. I thought back to the way he'd drawn a scale model of the ship's hull in chalk on the lawn for Patrick to see from his bedroom at La Bruyère, how he'd labored over every inch of its design. How many summers had we spent on that craft, traversing the coasts of Italy and France?

"It's either that, or get rid of the servants, and I think we both know which is more critical to our daily existence."

"We can't fire Theresa or Jake," I said. "They have families. And we'd be hopeless without them."

"Exactly. The service stays."

Vova soon found a buyer for the boat, a Swiss count who retained him as captain. It would be years before we would see the proceeds, smuggled from Vova to Fanny Myers to Gerald in a sleeve of hidden gold coins during the last years of the war. It felt as if everything that connected us to France was now being severed and tossed away, like a gangrened limb.

---

BUT FINALLY, IN 1944, another piece of good news—I'd won my lawsuit against Hoytie. Now, ten years after all her bad real estate dealings, the statute of limitations had run out and she was free to buy property again. So she'd recently waged another legal battle against me over ownership of the family property, even though the house had been torn down.

That my worst enemy in the world was my own sister caused me endless anguish. How could I be related to one who was so selfish, so blind to the needs of anyone but herself? But Hoytie had been that way since she was small.

I remembered a day in the early 1930s, when we were headed back to Paris from Antibes by automobile. Honoria had begged to ride with her Aunt Hoytie in her chauffeured sedan, and I relented. But after we arrived, Honoria recounted how they'd had a minor collision with another car and Hoytie had rolled down her window and cried "*Jüde! Jüde!*" at the other driver. She'd always been terribly anti-Semitic but, as the Nazi sentiment fermented, her behavior became even more reprehensible. My own sister. I was mortified.

The court eventually ruled in my favor, finding that Hoytie's lawsuit was "conceived in fraud and bad faith." It was a relief, but the whole nightmare had cost me $5,200 and years of distress. My gallbladder problems appeared again and stayed.

The decade had, of course, been dominated by the war. Even in East Hampton, we'd been instructed to black out our windows at night for fear of German U-boats off the coast. We read the papers and listened to FDR's "fireside chats," but our best source of news was Ernest's letters from Europe, where he'd covered the action in France for *Collier's*, including the liberation of Paris. He loved nothing more than being on the front lines of any action, and he proudly reported that he'd incurred three concussions.

Another casualty was his marriage to Martha Gellhorn, who'd turned out to be as intrepid a reporter as Ernest himself. That kind of equal partnership was doomed in a Hemingway marriage—we all knew that—and before long he wrote that he'd met a new girl, Mary Welsh. *She wants to quit work and have children and look after me and I need that plenty,* he wrote. *Also she is the only woman besides you who really loves a boat and the water.* For all his flaws, I still lapped up his flattery like a saucer of milk.

---

IMAGINE MY SURPRISE when, one evening in 1946, I opened the door of our Manhattan apartment to find Alan Jarvis standing there, as beautiful as ever in a navy suit and yellow tie.

"Alan!" I said. "I'm afraid Gerald's not home yet."

He looked so disappointed, I added, "But he should be back any minute. Won't you come in and wait?"

We sat awkwardly in the living room and reflected on the war as the streetlights came on outside the windows. I'd felt such mixed feelings about this dashing young man—he'd been my nemesis, but also a balm to Gerald's sensitive spirit. And he'd just served the Allies overseas—I couldn't begrudge him now the way I once might have.

I heard the upstairs entrance open; Gerald often came in that way and went straight to the bedroom to change. The door led onto a little landing with a half stairway down to the living room.

I paused, waiting. Surely Gerald had heard our voices from the landing, but the footsteps halted and then proceeded to the bedroom, where the door closed. He hadn't even come to the top of the staircase to see who'd called on us. After about ten minutes, it was clear he wasn't coming down.

"I'm sorry, Alan. I guess Gerald's been held up at the office," I said, flushing. We'd both heard the footsteps upstairs.

Alan quickly rose to go. "It's my fault for calling unannounced," he said. "I should have given you more notice."

After he left, I went upstairs and entered the bedroom without knocking. "Your good friend shows up after five years abroad, and you can't even be bothered to come say hello? What on earth, Dow?"

Gerald had donned a cotton Japanese kimono over his slacks, a pair of Moroccan leather slippers on his feet, and stood looking out the window at the street far below. I walked over and wrapped my arms around his shoulders. One of the things I loved about Gerald was that he smelled just as good at six o'clock as he did when he left in the morning. Vetiver and Pearl Bar soap.

"You left me there to soldier on alone," I said. "He's not even *my* friend."

"I'm sorry, Sal. You know how I hate to revisit the past. The reopening of old relationships."

"Even when they're right here sitting on our sofa?"

"I wrote Alan, when he was overseas, that our chapter was over. That I was constrained to protect the past from the present. I returned all his letters. You know, my faulty 'instrument of precision.'"

"Ah yes. The old faulty instrument again."

"People should never be themselves, least of all their *old* selves," he said. One of his favorite expressions.

But loyalty to our friends was an essential credo to us. We were loyal to a fault, even when our friends disappointed us or asked us repeatedly for money. Now Gerald's reticence underscored how different this relationship had been for him. Well, it was done. I wasn't going to spend any more time puzzling over it. Gerald was here with me, and that's all that mattered.

ONE EVENING IN September 1947, I sat reading in the living room of Cheer Hall. The war had been over for two years, but now, with *The Diary of a Young Girl* by Anne Frank, my eyes were opened to the abject cruelty of the Nazis. Anne's optimism, her belief in the basic goodness of people, despite everything her family had been through, made me ashamed. We'd suffered, but not like this.

Gerald was leaving the next day for a buying trip to London, so he was in the bedroom packing. Honoria was visiting for the weekend and, when the telephone rang, she answered it. I could hear her voice from the kitchen, her delight in the person who'd called.

"Aunt Ada! How nice to hear from you!" Honoria had come to the doorway, grasping the candlestick base in one hand, holding the earpiece to her ear with the other. She nodded to me and smiled. We hadn't heard from Ada or Archie in months.

"Yes, she's right here. Oh?" Her face clouded and she turned her back toward me. "Why, what's wrong?" By the time I reached her, Honoria was crying.

"You can't be serious. Are you sure? Where's Dos?"

At Dos's name, Gerald was suddenly in the kitchen as well. Honoria looked at both of us, trying to choose the better recipient of whatever awful announcement sat on the other end of the line.

*More bad news?* was all I could think. Honoria shoved the phone at Gerald and sat down at the table, weeping.

"Ada, it's Dow," he said. "What on earth happened?" I watched as he nodded and made little sounds of distress. "Will there be a service?"

By now I was sitting down, too. I waited for Gerald to hang up and give me the awful details.

"It's our Katy," he finally said. "They were driving to Connecticut from the Cape, Dos at the wheel. He was blinded for a moment by the late afternoon sun and ran into a truck on the side of the road."

"Is she . . ." I could barely form the words. "Has she . . ."

"She was essentially decapitated by the windshield. And Dos has lost an eye. He's at Massachusetts General."

The kitchen spun around me. Katy, always such clever, good company. Her chatty letters. She called me "Mrs. Puss." Gone in the blink of an eye, because of the goddamned sun! The entire decade seemed to evaporate and I was suddenly overwhelmed by the same feeling of doom that had plagued me after the deaths of my boys. The unfairness of life. You could do *everything* right, you could be a lovely wife and friend, and it counted for *nothing*. The angle of a sunbeam and a stalled truck, and your time was up. Once again, I sensed a punitive God.

"How is Dos doing?" I finally asked.

"Ada says he's still knocked out from the surgery on his eye."

We three were quiet for the rest of the evening, each shedding a few private tears. But as we readied for bed, I turned to Gerald. "However will Dos go on after this?" I asked. We both knew too well the road ahead of him.

"I know, I keep wondering what he'll do," Gerald said. "Where will he put this nightmare? Where can he go that Katy won't be, and his knowledge of how she died?" Then he looked at me and shrugged. "He'll just stand it, I guess." Exactly what we'd been doing for ten years.

"Well," I said. "Honoria and I will go back to the city with you. You'll fly to London, but I'll be by Dos's side, just as he was with us after Baoth and Patrick. There's a funeral to organize. We can't let him down."

---

BUT THE DECADE wasn't finished with us. In March 1948, we read of Zelda's death, every bit as tragic and undeserved as Katy's. She'd been living at an asylum in Asheville, locked in her room and sedated in preparation for a shock treatment the next day. A kitchen fire raced up the dumbwaiter and reached every floor. Nine victims in all, including our Zelda.

I don't think I've ever known a creature who embodied such contradictions as Zelda Fitzgerald. Her life had been one extreme example of how all our fortunes had peaked in the twenties and crashed in the decades since. As the firemen weeded through the ashes the next day, they could identify her body only by her slipper.

I thought of our beautiful little group on the beach at Antibes—so young, so talented, so full of life and promise. Yet not a single one of us had escaped tragedy; we'd all been broken by life in one way or another. Were we all doomed by our vanity and ambition, or was that just how life worked?

## Chapter 23
### 1950-1960

The post had brought a small stack of letters, and I sorted through them to pull out the single air-mail envelope, its pale-blue tissue paper bordered by red and blue stripes, and a scrapbook's worth of colorful stamps from République Française. My name and address written in Gerald's elegant hand. Return address: Hôtel du Cap, Antibes. Just the sight of the hotel's emblem made me queasy.

I wandered through Cheer Hall looking for the perfect spot to digest Gerald's letter, finally settling on the living room couch with a view out the window to the lawn and, beyond it, the river. This was a fine house, a perfectly lovely house, and we'd remade it with our usual eye for modernity accented with collectibles. It even had an electric dishwashing machine, something our neighbors had never even heard of before spotting it in our kitchen.

I had absolutely nothing to regret; so why did seeing the name *Antibes* make my heart ache? Because, after being listed for sale since the 1930s, Villa America finally had a buyer. We'd asked $40,000, but were letting it go for $27,000—between our still-lavish life and the renovations on Cheer Hall, we really needed the money. Now Gerald, back in Europe on another buying trip for Mark Cross, had traveled to Antibes to finalize the sale and clean out our old things.

The idea of him unlocking the barn and finding our furniture—so unexpected and new in 1925, now outdated and shrouded in sheets—made my mouth dry. The vision of him wandering through the empty house, scene of so many magical evenings, stung my eyes with tears. I saw the children, freshly bathed and in their pajamas, dancing the Charleston for our guests. I heard the echoes of Gerald and me sitting at the piano harmonizing. The feeling of the Mediterranean sun on my back as I reclined on La Garoupe beach and made a shopping list, the clicking of Ada's knitting needles beside me.

I took a breath and ripped open the envelope with my thumb nail. *Let's get it over with.* Gerald described the twisty ride along Les Corniches from Nice to Antibes, how the rest of the Côte d'Azur had been spoiled by too many tourists, too much money, and badly conceived architecture. But about the villa, instead of feeling distraught, as I might have, Gerald seemed to have gained something as he toured the house and grounds.

*One is immediately caught up by the compelling beauty of it,* he wrote. *That shining transparent sea, the high palms, the smell of oleander and laurier rose. The stillness and peace and the air stirred constantly by the sea. I had come with misgivings, prepared to be saddened, but no! The house is untended, but the garden is as healthy as it ever was. Life goes on.*

I sat back and, for a moment, tried on Gerald's sunnier view of things. But it was hopeless: I couldn't see the place as anything but a house of ghosts. I felt taunted by how happy we'd been there, our blind faith that life would always be that good. I couldn't shake myself of the belief that we'd tempted fate with our hubris, our solid belief that we were in control of our lives. We'd thought we were our own little gods. We took so many things on faith—our health, our wealth, our happy family—and then faith betrayed us completely. Sure, we'd soldiered on, creating new homes and new memories, but the loss clung to the edge of my mind like a stubborn black mold. If we hadn't lived such a lofty life, would we have fallen so hard?

AFTER WE'D SENT Honoria to Britain with John, she found secretarial work in London while he shipped off to the Pacific. Though I worried about her starting a new life alone abroad, I knew she was strong and had pluck. But, as the war was coming to an end, we received a wire that she was headed home.

When we met her Pan Am Clipper at the gate, she arrived alone. And over the next day or two, the story spilled out.

"It's over, Mother. War marriages are *hard!*" She gripped her mug of tea with both hands. Her gaze landed everywhere but into my own eyes. "I've filed for a divorce."

"But that's just it, Honoria. War marriages *are* hard." I thought back to my own early marriage, with Gerald halfway across the country. Crying myself to sleep at night, worrying sick about him. And *he'd* never even seen action.

"*All* marriages are hard," I continued. "They take a lot of work. But it's so worth it."

There was a long silence. Then: "He met a girl in Japan. When he came back, he said it was just a fling, that he knew I'd understand." Tears flowing now.

Ah. And what was I supposed to say to that? On the one hand, I wanted to personally string this rogue up by his thumbs, he who'd dared to be unfaithful to my daughter. On the other: I knew about infidelity. How could I possibly explain to her about Gerald's "intellectual affairs," his "*amata*"? How could I tell her about my week with Picasso? Gerald and I had always presented a united front to the children, to the whole world. Our indiscretions were known to no one but ourselves.

"You wouldn't understand, Maman. You and Dow-Dow have always been such a perfect pair. I didn't realize *how* perfect until I tried it myself."

"Oh, Honoria." I covered her hand with my own. Perhaps we'd gotten it wrong, this image of us as a single unit. Perhaps everyone would have been better off if we'd just been honest about our own marital struggles. But in those days, people didn't talk openly about such things.

"Anyway, I'm happy to be back. A girl can take only so many warm beers and beef pasties. I'll just get a new job and an apartment. I'll be a career girl!"

At those words, my heart pinched. It took me a moment to realize why. The term "career girl" reminded me of that vast, unexplored territory that had never been available to me. What might I have done if I'd been allowed to have a career myself?

---

HONORIA SOON FOUND a job as an assistant at a local production company and an apartment in the West 60s. She was back to being our vivacious, beautiful American girl. And then she traveled to California to visit her cousin, Stuyvie Fish. Instead of coming back after two weeks, as planned, she stayed on all summer. We soon learned why.

"His name's Bill Donnelly," she told us over the telephone, and I could hear elation in her voice. How they'd met at a party and then talked all night. How they'd become "great good friends" and the friendship had quickly grown into something more. After Honoria's heartache over her first marriage, I wanted to tell her to slow down, get to know him better. But she was breathless with excitement.

Gerald was on the extension in the bedroom while I was on the kitchen wall phone, so I couldn't see his face, but I heard his trepidation, too. "We'd love to meet him, Daughter," he said. "Suss him out."

"Too late for that!" she laughed. "Dow-Dow, he's a war hero. Five major campaigns, including Normandy and Bastogne. But to talk to him, you'd never know. He's just funny and warm and so smart. You'll both love him!"

"I'm *sure* we will, darling," I said. "He sounds lovely!"

"But, well, here's the thing. He was injured pretty badly. His jeep was blown up by a land mine. The men on both sides of him were killed."

"A hell of a shame," Gerald said.

"Anyway, he's in a wheelchair. But he's getting better every day. The doctors say he'll graduate to crutches soon."

By the time they came to New York together, Bill was, as promised, walking very slowly with the aid of crutches, attached by metal braces to his arms. Also as promised, we quickly fell in love with him—his humor, his quiet intelligence, the way he gently hovered over Honoria. By the second time we met him, Honoria could keep their secret no longer: They planned to be married on November 14.

She waited until Bill had gone to get the car and she was alone with us to deliver the bombshell: "He's a practicing Catholic," she said.

"Okay," I said. I didn't dare look at Gerald. We all knew his feelings about Catholicism.

"And we want to be married in the chapel at St. Patrick's."

Gerald let out a little gasp. We'd agreed, for the sake of his parents, to baptize the children in the faith, but we hadn't set foot in a Catholic church since.

"I'm asking you, Dow-Dow. Will you please come and give me away?"

There was a long silence. Then he said, "Of course I will, Daughter. Just don't mind the sound of my grinding teeth as we walk down the aisle. *Hoc est corpus meum.*"

Once again, Honoria chose a silk cocktail dress in lieu of a white gown, this one a pale green. Once again, she wore my veil. She looked every bit as beautiful as she had on that other day, just a little older and wiser.

We hosted a small reception at the New Weston apartment, only the closest of friends, for passed hors d'oeuvres and cake and champagne. As we sat on the sofa and rested our feet after the long day, I turned to Gerald.

"I'm thinking the most horrible thought, Dow," I whispered.

"You know what Alice Roosevelt Longworth said," he said. "'If you can't say something nice about someone . . .'"

"'Come sit by me.'"

"Righto."

"But this is really dreadful. Someone should smite me."

"I'm all ears."

"I love Bill, so much. I honestly do."

"But?"

"But we don't know how serious his war injuries really are. I can't bear the notion that there might not be grandchildren."

"Mmm-hmm." Gerald looped his left arm over my shoulder and took a sip from the flute in his other hand. This was a familiar theme, for both of us. We were dying for grandkids.

"I'm so ashamed. But I was really counting on having them, Dow. The sound of babies in our house again!" I began to tear up, dabbing at my eyes with my napkin.

"I know, Sal. I want them too. But this is what Honoria's decided *she* wants. We must focus on being thrilled for her. And for Bill. They're going to be very happy together."

I sighed. "I know."

"Remember how our parents felt about *our* marriage. If they'd had their way, none of us would be here now."

"But that's totally different. That was about money; this is about babies, of having something more to love."

He patted my thigh. "All shall be well, and all shall be well. And all manner of things shall be well."

I needn't have worried. Just seven months later, our first grandchild would be born.

Apparently, Bill and Honoria had already figured all of that out.

WE SAT HUDDLED around the tiny blue screen of the Barrys' RCA television: a blurry, staticky image of a bunch of politicians shuffling papers and whispering into each others' ears. The second round of House Un-American Committee hearings had reopened the investigation into Communist activity in Hollywood and was being televised across the country.

"We've barely recovered from the war and now this," I said, shaking my head. "Why can't we just enjoy peacetime without all this *Sturm und Drang*?"

"It's as if these guys just can't bear not having an enemy of some kind," Ellen said. "Now they're spreading paranoia about Communists hiding in our closets and under our beds."

The majority of witnesses called by the committee had admitted past involvement with the party or leftist causes and were naming names. In all, 324 people had been blacklisted and prevented from working again in Hollywood—including people we knew, like Charlie Chaplin, Dalton Trumbo, and Ring Lardner Jr. Our good friend, Lillian Hellman, was on the list and her man, Dashiell Hammett, had just been arrested for contributing to the Civil Rights Congress, which posted bail for four Communists. Dottie Parker and Donald Ogden Stewart were out of work as screenwriters. At the helm of this moral shipwreck was an angry-looking man with a permanent five o'clock shadow named Joseph McCarthy.

"How's Lill doing?" Phil asked. "She certainly stood up to HUAC with her usual cojones."

She'd stated, "I will not tailor my political beliefs to satisfy those currently in fashion," and the IRS then charged her with not paying back taxes, costing her hundreds of thousands of dollars.

"Last I heard, Hammett's bail was somewhere around a hundred thousand dollars, and his health was declining," Gerald said. "Lill mortgaged her brownstone and pawned her mother's jewelry, but she only came up with about seventeen thousand." What he didn't mention was that she'd called him in desperation and he told her to meet him at Mark Cross. Then he gave her everything in the safe and wrote a personal check for $10,000. That's one of the things I admired most about my husband: he was always a savior of underdogs.

"This attitude of intolerance was why we left America in the first place, wasn't it, Dow?" I said. "Prohibition, the Motion Picture Production Code, the Smith Act—it seems this country never tires of making rules and punishing people."

Post-war Europe was on its heels and we couldn't move back there again even if we wanted to. Gerald's business was here, Honoria and Bill were here. And soon there would be a grandbaby. I tried to focus on the happy things now. I stood up and clicked off the television set, the scratchy picture shrinking to a tiny blue dot. "Let's see about dinner," I said.

---

AND THEN CAME the day when my heart truly began beating again. June 20, 1951: the birth of John Charles Donnelly in Carmel. Everything in our garden was green, green, green. Peonies and Oriental poppies blooming to beat the band.

"Daughter!" Gerald cried into the telephone, and I came running in from the terrace. "It's a boy!" he mouthed to me before I grabbed the phone from his hand.

"My darling, darling girl!" I squealed. "Give me name, rank, and serial number."

"Eight and a quarter pounds; just over twenty inches," Honoria said, her voice as placid as if she were giving the measurements for an area rug. "He has a good amount of hair, but it's so light he looks bald."

"How can you be so calm?" I said. "You've just given us a grandchild!" I passed the phone back to Gerald and went running through the house. "It's a boy!" I shouted at Theresa in the kitchen. "We have a grandbaby!" I shouted to the dogs in the foyer. Here, finally, was a real reason to celebrate and feel joyful, after all the trouble of the past few decades. I felt like singing, dancing, laughing, and kissing someone all at once.

When I'd finally calmed down, I collapsed, panting, into the big striped chair in the living room. Gerald came in and sat down opposite me, a bemused smile on his face.

"Isn't it strange how life goes on?" I asked, still panting.

"I know," he said. "This somehow balances the scales a bit, for what was taken away."

"Exactly." I had no idea that I'd needed this kind of exact retribution, I'd only known that my heart had felt deprived for too long.

Almost exactly two years later, I traveled to Carmel in time for the birth of Honoria's second son, William Sherman Donnelly, on June 10, 1953. *How different a dawn than the one we saw in a hospital 18 years ago,* Gerald wrote to me, alluding to Baoth's death in 1935. *Two boys went out from our family, and now two other boys have come into it.*

Fifteen months later, the family was complete with the birth of Laura Sara Donnelly on September 27, 1954. When Honoria told me her middle name, I burst into tears. Two boys and a girl. Our family repeating itself in a brand-new generation. My heart was beating again, under all the old scar tissue.

---

THERE WERE TWO subjects our friends knew never to mention: the deaths of our sons and Gerald's paintings—the abrupt halt of his art was inextricably tied to Patrick's diagnosis. But in 1950, when a man named Arthur Mizener published a biography of Scott titled *The Far Side of Paradise,* that all changed. Suddenly, our lives in the 1920s had a new cachet. Now people started posing all kinds of questions.

Around this time, two young neighbor girls wandered into the garden as Gerald was pruning a fruit tree and asked if they might play with our pugs, Edward and Wookie. It wasn't long before we met their father, Calvin Tomkins. Tad, as he was known, was a writer and critic for the *New Yorker* magazine, and he was soon joining us regularly for cocktails.

He began asking questions innocently enough. But soon they cracked open the door to an emotional cellar, filled with bittersweet memories we'd stuffed down there for years. Before long, Gerald was like Homer around the firepit, and the Mediterranean was our "wine-dark sea." Once or twice a week Tad would appear and we'd talk long past the dinner hour.

"Dow, those old stories aren't really worth repeating," I'd said at first. I preferred to leave the past alone, at least in polite conversation.

"You're underestimating the worth of your memories," Tad said. I think he had a little crush on me, if you want to know the truth. "These stories belong to our cultural history. You were both part of a *movement*, the very foundations of twentieth-century literature and music and art!"

He turned back to Gerald. "I'm thinking you should write a book about it. I'd be happy to help you, and my contacts would make it an easy sell to a publisher."

Gerald shook his head. "I have too much respect for the craft of writing to take it up as a second-rate practitioner," he said. But the broad smile on his face said he was pleased to be asked.

Eventually, even I opened up and took pleasure in those evenings when Tad would park himself on our sofa with a notepad and a tape recorder and Gerald and I would reminisce. Before long, I'd fetched the photo albums and was pointing out the snapshots of us in Pamplona, in Paris, in Venice. The long, multilingual conversations on the sand of La Garoupe. The ridiculous capers of Scott and Zelda after dark. The magical evenings under the linden tree on the terrace of Villa America.

Tad even got Gerald to talk, in detail, about his paintings. There was a cozy, familial feel to these interviews, and we came to believe that we were preserving our story, and the stories of our friends, in a kind of benevolent amber. Somehow it was agreed that he'd write about us against the backdrop of what was now being called the Lost Generation.

Then, one day in 1956, Gerald announced to our guests at luncheon, "Apparently, I've been discovered." A writer named Rudi Blesh had written a book, *Modern Art USA*, in which he described Gerald's paintings in the 1920s as "meticulous in craft and heroic in size." He cited their wit and complexity and included Gerald among French Purists like Amédée Ozenfant and Le Corbusier.

"Whatever does one wear?" Gerald smirked. He was trying to appear mildly amused, but under that veneer I could see pure delight.

He hadn't even looked at a paint brush since we'd packed up to go to Montana-Vermala in 1929 for Patrick's treatment. And, since we'd returned to the States, all his creativity had been channeled into the inventory and operation of Mark Cross, what he called "that monument to the inessential." But five of Gerald's paintings—which had been smuggled out of France by Alice Lee Myers after the war—stood rolled up in a corner of our attic. Perhaps now that happier, more artistic man could emerge once more. I so longed to see him again.

Not long after the news of Blesh's book, the curator of the Dallas Museum for Contemporary Arts wrote to say he was building an exhibition of "neglected artists of the twentieth century." Would Gerald be interested in participating? I watched as twenty-five years rolled off my husband's face and remembered those early days of wandering the Salon des Indépendents together, feeling so proud to be on his arm.

Gerald had finally retired from Mark Cross at the age of sixty-eight. I'd worried about him finding something new to do, and here it was: a fresh look at his previous achievements, and a new audience to appreciate them. We brought the canvases down from the attic and unrolled them on the dining room table—the linen was in surprisingly good condition. Gerald ordered new frames built and designed shipping crates for the trip to Dallas and the exhibit "American Genius in Review."

Now we strolled around the exhibit's spare white halls to find each of Gerald's surviving paintings—*Cocktail, Watch, Razor, Doves,* and *Wasp and Pear*. Each bore its own little plaque explaining Gerald's technique, his training with Goncharova, and stories of our early life in Paris.

"I feel every bit as proud of you today as I did back then, when these paintings were new," I said, squeezing his arm. He was wearing a pale-blue linen jacket with a rose-colored pocket square and a straw fedora on his head. Still so handsome.

Even Gerald seemed a little astonished by his own prowess. "Would you look at the detail on that cigar label!" he said, taking in *Cocktail*. Then he whispered in my ear, "I'm better than I'd remembered."

"Your style, and your perspective, have held up beautifully," I said.

Perhaps, despite all the damage and hurt of the previous three decades, the same might be said of us.

# Chapter 24
## 1960-1963

Later that year, Ada and Archie returned from Paris. They'd bumped into Picasso on the rue de l'Odeon and shared the news that, once again, he'd started a new chapter with a new woman. Still feeling a little ashamed for not greeting him when I'd seen him at Brasserie Lipp before the war, I sent him a letter of felicitations.

*One remembers so well the beautiful days we all had together back then,* I wrote. *Some people have suggested that we started the summer season in the Midi!* I silently wondered if he also remembered our week together, just the two of us, when I'd left Gerald back in Venice. It still caught in my memory, a cat stuck up a tree. Then I added, *Please accept all our warmest wishes for long life and happiness—which you so richly deserve.*

Picasso never did write back. But the following year another friend visited him at his studio—now located in the posh rue des Grands Augustins—and gave him our regards. "Tell Sara and Gerald that I'm well," he replied, "but now I'm a millionaire and all alone."

It was an odd thing to say, considering he'd just married a much-younger woman who apparently attended to him like a nursemaid. I wondered if it was his way of telling me he missed me. I didn't miss him so much as I missed the woman he saw in me: classic, serene, self-contained. Linen and pearls. Young and beautiful.

THE 1960S ROLLED in on a wave of optimism for our crowd, and for the country. After the trials of the McCarthy era, we'd elected John F. Kennedy president! With his darling wife, Jackie, he made Washington not only elegant, but young and forward-thinking, and artists were celebrated. And civil rights, the space program, the Peace Corps! JFK had wit and Jackie had style. It was the first time I felt real pride in my country. The nation felt young again; even the French admired us.

There had been so much loss in the previous decades that my thoughts frequently turned to old friends with whom we'd lost touch. Picasso had been one. Ernest was another. Between his reporting on the Second Sino-Japanese War and the Allied march through France, we were used to seeing his name in the papers—not to mention his novels on the bestseller list. *The Old Man and the Sea* had even won the Nobel Prize for Literature back in 1952, and we were busting with pride for our dear friend.

The following year, we read of his death after two plane crashes within two days in the African bush with his newest wife, Mary. We'd been shocked, of course, but it was classic Hemingway to go out in such spectacular glory. But leave it to Ernest to make it a double disaster. Several days later, we were relieved to learn that he had, in fact, survived, though with serious head injuries.

As Ernest's fame overshadowed his earlier, more humble life, we heard less and less from him. And we knew Mary not at all. But one day in 1961 I had the strongest urge to write to him. We were reading reports that he'd been admitted to the Mayo Clinic in Rochester, Minnesota for hypertension, but I sensed something more. Ernest would never be troubled by something as common as blood pressure.

*Please write me a card saying it isn't so, or at least that you're recovered,* I wrote. *It isn't in your character to be ill. I want to see you, as always, as a burly, bearded young man with a gun or a boat. I always remember old times with the greatest pleasure, and that you were helpful to me at a time when I certainly needed it. Affectionately, your very old friend, Sara.*

He never wrote back. Ten days after I slipped that letter in the post, *The New York Times* ran a front-page headline:

HEMINGWAY DEAD OF SHOTGUN WOUND;
WIFE SAYS HE WAS CLEANING WEAPON.

I went into the bedroom and shut myself down—pulled the drapes, took a diazepam, and laid myself out on the bed. It was days before I could even speak of it, even to Gerald. Yes, this was just more loss on top of all the other friends we'd lost in tragic, premature ways. But the end of Ernest? I guess I'd always naively believed the myth he'd built around himself: that he was larger than life, stronger than men, destined for immortality. Two plane crashes: entirely Ernest. But accidentally shooting himself? This felt even more tragic than Scott's slow, deliberate self-destruction.

A Kodak slide show ran across my mind of all the Ernests I had known. The young aspiring writer, handsome as a pirate, with Bumby riding on his shoulders at La Garoupe. The outdoorsman in Wyoming, where he showed us how to hunt and fish and skin a rabbit. The successful novelist basking in his own glory at Key West and Havana. It was painful to think of him in recent years—out of shape and racked with paranoia and regret.

I found Gerald outside on the lawn, a hose in his hand and a distant look in his eyes. The Hudson River was the color of bottle glass, the opposite bank a wedge of darker green. Rising behind the hills, cumulus clouds rose like piles of whipped cream. *Chantilly de géants*, Patrick used to call them.

"I can't shake the sadness," I said. "Ernest being gone is like losing a face off Mount Rushmore."

"He lived by the sword and died by the sword," Gerald said,

bending down to turn off the faucet and carefully coil the hose.

We wandered inside and Gerald prepared his "sacred objects": a shaker, a jigger, a muddler, and two frosty glasses from the icebox. He began peeling an orange with his sterling silver channel knife and carefully placed a twisted peel in each glass.

"I know it's unseemly of me, but I need to know what really happened," I said. "The question of his intent is what bothers me most." Gerald placed a glass on the table in front of me and I took a sip. How I cherished this ritual. Among the many things that sustain a marriage, surely cocktail hour is at the top of the list.

"I'll make it easy for you," Gerald said, sitting down across from me. "Ernest had been using guns since he was ten years old. If anyone knew not to clean a loaded shotgun, it was him."

"Poor man," I said. "Can you imagine the pain he must have been in?"

"He always warned us that this might be his way out. He often spoke of his father's suicide, and he said he'd probably go the same way. Think of all the suicides, particularly of fathers, in his stories and novels."

After my sadness had subsided, I was surprised by the anger. This man, who'd spent his whole life proving to the world how strong and brave he was, had taken the coward's way out. Whatever happened to 'grace under pressure'? Gerald and I had been through much worse than his various injuries over the years. Rather than choosing to stand in harm's way, we were dealt blows of fate that had torn our hearts from our bodies. Yet here we were, still putting our best feet forward. I finally reminded myself that there is simply no way to truly comprehend the struggles of another. That's where I had to leave it.

In early 1962, the movie of *Tender Is the Night* came out. I refused to go, but Gerald was curious and drove to Nyack to see it at a Friday matinee.

"Well?" I asked as he came through the door. "I'm hoping they improved the story. What was it like seeing your own apparition on screen—played by Jason Robards, no less?"

Gerald stomped the snow from his shoes, then hung his coat and hat in the hall closet and came over to perch on the back of my armchair.

"I was the only one in the theater," he said. "It was so far from any sort of relationship to us, or the period. I don't know. I couldn't feel any emotion at all except perhaps sympathy for Jennifer Jones, trying her best to play Nicole as an eighteen-year-old. She's forty-three, for heaven's sake. And the opening song was so sugary it made my teeth hurt."

"That sounds painful."

"It was not a good movie."

"Nor a good book."

"Well, most of it, no. But seeing the film did revive Scott for me, just for a brief moment."

Scott had often said he thought it was his best novel. He told Gerald the story "was inspired by Sara and you, and the last part of it is Zelda and me because you and Sara are the same people as Zelda and me." The nerve of that man. He hadn't a clue about the real people in his life.

I had to wonder again: why were we so loyal to our friends, when they careened through life hurting feelings and feeding their own insecurities? Scott had betrayed us with that book. But we never stopped supporting him or believing that he could write another fine book like *Gatsby*. Were we good people? Or just foolish?

―――

THAT JULY, FOUR years after we'd first met Tad, the *New Yorker* published his article, titled "Living Well Is the Best Revenge." We both winced when we read it; I could hear my mother's disapproving dictum that a lady's name should appear in the paper only twice: on her wedding day and in her obituary.

"It feels a bit tawdry, doesn't it?" I asked. "Like being a secondary celebrity, or resting on one's laurels." And of course the piece did nothing to dispel the notion that we were still very wealthy—which was increasingly untrue.

Even Gerald, the raconteur, was a bit abashed. "I never wanted revenge on anyone," he said. "On whom is he implying that we want revenge?"

"I guess we got carried away," I said.

"Well, it's done now, we can put it aside."

But later that year, the article was lengthened into a book. By now, despite our previous protests, I think Gerald and I had become secretly gratified to have our own story preserved in some small way. This was different from being used by Ernest and Scott as purloined characters in their novels. This showed us at our best: loving and generous and kind. And the best gift of all: Gerald was now being recognized as a noteworthy painter.

---

WE STILL SPENT our summers at the cottage in East Hampton. Honoria and Bill had relocated their young family to McClean, Virginia for Bill to take a job with the Interior Department. So now we were together much of the time and Gerald and I could bask in the company of our growing grandchildren.

After all these years, it was surprisingly easy to recreate some of the magic of our own young family. There were picnics on Wiborg Beach, which Gerald would rake as carefully as he had La Garoupe. There were games and calisthenics on the sand, with "Captain Dow-Dow" in command. There were flower garlands for Laura, and folded paper hats for John and Sherman.

One day Gerald called the children in to gather around the hi-fi. "Now, pay attention," he said. "These young men are going to be very, very big." Then he placed the needle onto the black vinyl of "Meet the Beatles" and gave a short lecture on the classic influences—Fats Domino, Motown, Chuck Berry—that had brought contemporary music to this special moment.

Another night, after dark, Gerald piled the three grandkids, along with sundry visiting children, into his vintage Pontiac, which had a searchlight mounted on the roof—he called it his "Black Maria." They all returned about an hour later, the kids shrieking like a pack of hyenas.

"Goodness, Dow-Dow, did you have to wind them up so much right before bed?" Honoria complained, but she knew the drill. With Gerald in the right mood, it was never a bad time for a spontaneous adventure.

"What on earth did you do to them?" I asked, as Honoria rustled them off to the bedroom.

Gerald's grin spread across his whole face. "I started by telling them the story of the haunted house out on Jericho Lane," he said, pouring himself a glass of milk. "Then I suggested we all get out to investigate. They still pretended not to be scared, so I dared them to walk through the gate. Then I hopped back in the car and squealed off. I could hear their screams behind me."

"Dow. That's so cruel!"

"I only left them there for about fifteen minutes."

"Fifteen minutes! That's an eternity to a child!"

"Ah, but they'll never forget it! It takes a little drama to consign a story to family legend." As Gerald always said, "In order to educate children, you must keep them confused."

—

AMID THE HIJINKS and revelry, though, were some grim realities. One night, we sat Honoria and Bill down to set the record straight. I fidgeted in my chair; I always loathed any talk of money.

"We don't want you to be alarmed," Gerald began. "But we do

want to be frank with you."

My gaze floated outside to the garden, to the pond, to anywhere but here in this room.

"When I retired from Mark Cross in fifty-five, I gave up my annual salary," he said, as he consulted his ledger. "Since then, the income from our funds has been sixty-seven thousand annually, but our withdrawals have been totaling about twenty-three thousand."

Honoria and Bill nodded, their faces stoic.

"People have always thought us richer than we are because we've always spent freely," Gerald said. "Anyway, simple math will tell you that our resources can't last indefinitely."

"We're always here to help," Bill began, but Gerald waved him off.

"Not necessary. But we *will* be making some adjustments." He turned to me to take over.

"We've decided to sell Cheer Hall," I said, my throat suddenly thick. *Don't be ridiculous*, I thought. *Don't cry*. "That house has gotten to be too much for us, anyway. Too cold in winter, the roads too icy. And it's a bit remote for us at this age."

Long pause. "So what's next?" Honoria finally asked, and I felt a surge of optimism.

"We're going to renovate the cottage here in East Hampton!" I said, clapping my hands together at the thought. "We're already drawing up plans, and we're calling it La Petite Hutte."

Bill looked visibly relieved. "So you'll stay here year-round instead of just summers," he said. "Honestly, I think it's an excellent idea. Honoria and I will still be a drivable distance away."

---

WE SOLD CHEER Hall in April but would rent it back until November, which gave us plenty of time to host a few last fetes, including a grand seventy-fifth birthday celebration for Gerald and a rollicking Fourth of July party with fireworks over the river and Gerald dressed as

George Washington in a white wig and knee breeches.

Those last eight months also allowed us to sort through the accumulated possessions of nearly fifty years of marriage.

"Good god, Dow, have we thrown *nothing* away? Where do we begin?" In the slanted, dusty light of the dormered attic, we were surrounded by cartons and chests and baskets of ephemera. Clothing from decades before. Photographs never pasted into albums. Lampshades without bases. Linens and place-settings from France. Even the rocking chair in which I'd rocked all three babies. Everything covered in a fine layer of dust.

"Do you think Honoria would want any of this?" I tried again, holding up a lace pillowcase. The air was warm and thick with the scent of mothballs.

"Perhaps, with the popularity of Tomkins' book, we can simply donate it all and have someone else archive it for us," Gerald said, surveying the room and scratching the back of his head. "Or perhaps we could just drown ourselves in the Hudson, our bodies borne downstream to Manhattan on a barge. Like Tennyson's Lady Shallot, *blown shoreward; so to Camelot.*"

"Goodness, Dow. That's an extreme solution just to avoid a little clutter."

He said nothing, but feigned interest in an old leather chest near the stairs. I knew this was painful for him. It was one thing to tell the old war stories about our famous friends to Tad; it was quite another to touch these personal keepsakes, like human bones from an archaeological dig.

"All right," I said. "I'll invite Honoria up next weekend. Anything she doesn't want, we'll donate to Goodwill. They can come with a truck."

But Gerald had opened the trunk and found some costumes from France. "Look, Sal! My *apache* outfit!" He held up a pair of leather pants, creased from years of storage. He suddenly forgot how much he repeatedly renounced our "old selves." Soon he'd unearthed an embroidered silk robe and a bamboo Chinese hat. He put them on and sauntered the length of the attic and back.

"Ah, Dow," I sighed. "That young man still lives on. I can see him!"

Gerald gave me a wan smile. We would get through this together.

———

BY THE SUMMER, we were back in East Hampton again. We were always much happier designing a new house than reflecting on the reminders of past homes. For us, it was always about the *future*. Tucked into the grasslands just behind where The Dunes had stood, La Petite Hutte afforded a delicious view over the property to Hook Pond and as far as the treetops and steeple of East Hampton Village. Neither one of us said the words aloud, but we both understood that this would be our last house together.

Over the past six months, Gerald had been suffering from bouts of intestinal pain and spells of lightheadedness. His appetite dwindled, and he didn't have the energy to swim in the ocean or dig about the garden the way he always had. During our long marriage, I'd been ill many times, but Gerald almost never had been. Between my smoking—the surgeon general had just announced that it could cause lung cancer and emphysema—and my gallbladder issues, I'd always assumed that Gerald would outlive me. He'd been robust to the point of annoyance—the man who, at the age of seventy, could still swim far out past the breakers and return home barely winded.

I brought him to Dr. Abel in town, but Gerald wouldn't let me come with him into the examining room. When I was finally waved in, I found Gerald buttoning up his shirt, and he did most of the talking. "Now, it sounds worse than it is," he said.

I took a chair in the tiny examining room. Of course he'd try and orchestrate this moment.

"Just hush and let the doctor talk," I said.

"I'm afraid the X-rays showed a tumor in his gut, Mrs. Murphy,"

Dr. Abel began, but Gerald interrupted him.

"A benign tumor, Sal. And they'll be able to remove it surgically, isn't that right, Abel?"

Dr. Abel nodded apprehensively. I looked from one man to the other, sensing that Gerald was protecting me from the full weight of his diagnosis. Perhaps he thought that, with all the bad news we'd received in doctors' offices over the years, I couldn't handle any more. He was right about that. I didn't argue.

I took him home and we prepared for his surgery which, he assured me, would make him right as rain. When I dropped him off at Stony Brook Southampton Hospital, I felt completely unmoored, but Gerald's stoutness of spirit kept everyone relaxed. He was so good at presenting well. He'd brought only his best linen pajamas for his hospital stay.

Then came three days of visits and returning home without him. The experience was oddly reminiscent of the days before we were married, when his absence made me long for him in the worst way. We'd lived largely apart while I was in the Adirondacks with Patrick, but we were focused on the future then. Now each day took on a precious density, with the understanding that there weren't an infinite number of them left.

> *Here I am at home without you,* I wrote, *and it is no longer a home, just a place to live. You must know that, without you, nothing makes any sense. I am only half a person, and you are the other half. It is so, and always will be.* Please please *get well soon and come back to me.*
> 
> *With love—all I have, Sara*

Although I refused even to entertain the idea of Gerald's demise, his absence reminded me of two other deaths. Gerald's sister, Esther, had died the year before, and we'd recently received word that Hoytie, back in Paris, had just died in April. When we received Esther's ashes from France, Gerald designed the gravestone himself and buried her remains in the East Hampton cemetery next to Patrick and Baoth. "I wish I'd shown her more affection while she was still alive," was all he said.

Hoytie was another matter entirely—upon word that she'd died, I simply couldn't sort my feelings out. There was relief and anger and sorrow all at once, a rat's nest of emotions with no telltale thread to untangle it. Hoytie had been the only enemy I'd ever had, and even advanced age hadn't shown us a way through. Now our story together was finished. Regret, regret, regret.

---

I BROUGHT GERALD home to recuperate, feeding him puréed fruit at first, then eggs, then meat. Surprisingly, he followed his doctor's instructions to rest, spending his days in an Adirondack chair gazing out across the sea to the horizon. I'd never seen him so quiet and still and remarked on it.

"Has anyone ever accurately described the true nature of old age?" he asked. "No one warns us about how it comes in the night when one's guard is down. I wish I'd known."

"Who's ever ready to get old?" I said. "What I'd give to have my waistline back, or my optimism."

"On the other hand, it's a wonderful thing to reach the irresponsible age of seventy," he said, changing tack. "If only it hadn't come so late in life."

"I know what you mean. I wish we'd been this satisfied with life when we were younger. Not to be in such a hurry to see things, to get things done." Even as I said this, I was mentally calculating how much time the roast chicken had left in the oven. But I was trying to slow down, to meet Gerald's new equanimity. "If we tallied up all the time we've spent moving from one house to another, we'd probably reclaim a few years!"

I leaned back and felt the sun on my face, the salty breeze rustling my hair. The dune grasses were whispering. A flock of honking geese flying overhead reminded me of saxophones at the Cotton Club.

"So many houses. Thankfully, we shared that passion, to create a new world with each new address, like designing our own stage sets."

I squeezed his knee. "Partners in crime."

---

AS GERALD'S STRENGTH returned and his appetite increased, we resumed a habit we'd practiced for years. At cocktail time, as the sun went down, we'd toast Baoth and Patrick, imagining what they might be doing on that particular day. They would have been forty-four and forty-three now. Careers. Children of their own. We decided that Baoth would have become a journalist, Patrick an engineer. How proud they would have made us! Our Christmases would have been even louder and merrier than they were now with Honoria's family. Instead, our lives were populated by ghosts.

---

BACK AT CHEER Hall, our things were almost entirely packed and the house was filled with labeled boxes. But Gerald and I sat huddled in front of the television, stupefied. We were watching the president's funeral caisson roll slowly down Pennsylvania Avenue to the somber beat of a military drum. The idea that this had happened in our newly optimistic country. Just unbelievable. Everything had been going so well!

The cameras zoomed in on Jackie, so elegant in her black Givenchy suit. Through a sheer black veil, her face was a mask of grief and shock. When she leaned down to instruct little John-John to salute his father's coffin as it passed by, I let out a choked wail.

"Easy, Sal."

"I don't think I can take anymore, Dow. For that poor young family. For our country!"

"Total chaos."

In just three days, the assassination of our beloved president, the murder of his murderer, and now a national funeral witnessed by a shocked population. It felt like our private family tragedies had somehow metastasized and infected the entire nation.

"I keep picturing him in his rocking chair, playing with his children," Gerald said. "His family was so young, he had a dog in the fight for our country's future. Our only hope lies with the young."

## Chapter 25
### 1964

The next spring, following the mild success of *Living Well Is the Best Revenge*, Gerald received another request for an exhibition, this time from the Corcoran Gallery of Art in Washington, DC. We were sitting at the little breakfast table when he showed me the curator's letter and I expected to see his eyes light up again, the way they had for the Dallas show. The Corcoran was a nationally known gallery.

"Darling, that's wonderful!" I said. "Your renown is growing—a whole new generation of art lovers."

Instead, he gave me a weak smile and shook his head. "*Je n'en peux plus*," he said. "*Trop tard.*"

"But Dow, this is your renaissance! Your entire métier is being rediscovered!"

The sunlight pooled around him, emphasizing the years inscribed on his face. He looked tired.

"Yes, I felt really alive during those years I was painting," he said. "Perhaps the happiest days of my life. But now it feels as if it's all in a sealed chamber of the past. I can't summon the energy, or the interest, to rise to the occasion anymore."

That was my first sign that something was wrong, that Gerald's miraculous recovery was not as it had seemed.

Two weeks later, we were back in Dr. Abel's office. Gerald had lost his appetite again and seemed weaker every day. This time, as he took Gerald's blood and checked out his vital signs, Abel's manner was more somber. He observed Gerald warily.

"No more nonsense, Murphy," he said. "You can't keep this a secret forever."

"What secret?" I asked, looking at Abel and then Gerald. "Dow?"

Gerald couldn't even return my gaze. He sat, head down, staring at his lap in his thin medical gown. He looked like a truant schoolboy who'd been hauled into the headmaster's office. I turned back to Abel.

"What's going on?" My tone was steely. I'd already sensed what I was going to hear.

"The surgery," Abel began. "It wasn't curative. It was palliative. At this point, we just need to make your husband as comfortable as possible."

I turned back to Gerald. I was so angry, I couldn't even feel sorrow or distress. For now, I focused on pragmatic issues. "How long does he have?"

"If he's lucky, I'd say about six months." Abel looked ready to bolt. He couldn't wait to get out of the room, where this husband and wife had so *very* much to say to each other.

But I couldn't even speak to Gerald for the entire way home, I was still so incensed at his deception. After we'd pulled into the drive and I'd turned off the ignition, I just sat there, though I knew that Gerald needed my help getting out of the car. For now, he was my captive audience. He sat on the leather bench seat like an old stuffed toy. Gone was the perfect posture.

"How *could* you?" I finally blurted out. "All this time I was blissfully thinking that you would return to good health! Once again, I've been played as the ignorant fool."

"Not played, Sal." A palpable sadness was oozing out of him. "I was just trying to spare you as long as I could. I didn't want to give you one more piece of bad news."

I tried to think of the other times I'd ever seen Gerald cry. The deaths of the boys—other than that, never.

"*I* was supposed to go first," I said. "My body has always been frailer than yours. This wasn't the plan."

Gerald smiled weakly. "I don't remember signing any contracts to that effect."

For nearly fifty years, Gerald and I had instinctively known which of us would be the stronger one in any given situation. If there *was* a God, or some mystical force, it had decided that I would be the stronger one now. That I would bear the unbearable: a future without my other half. In that moment, a gear slipped into place and I knew that I would gladly be Gerald's guardian until his death, and to live alone thereafter.

"Let's get you inside," I said with a sigh. "Let's not lose one minute more."

---

IT WAS DOS who sent us an advance galley of *A Moveable Feast* in May—Ernest had been working on it just before he died, and the book would be published in December. Sitting in our deck chairs on the terrace, the sun on our shoulders and the Atlantic surf pounding in our ears, Gerald and I traded the manuscript back and forth, each reading a chapter before passing it back.

At first, we were transported to the Paris we'd loved. Ernest wrote so tenderly of his early years there with Hadley: their scrappy apartment on rue Cardinal Lemoine, his days spent writing in the cheap cafés, their bohemian adventures and rustic travels. It had the voice—that inimitable, simple Hemingway voice—that made you feel the Alpine chill of Austria and taste the dry *tempranillo* of Spain.

Then he began to settle some scores with the very people who'd helped him to be the great American writer he became: Sherwood Anderson. Gertrude Stein. Scott Fitzgerald. He called Dos Passos "a one-eyed Portuguese bastard." It became clear that he was looking back, not with love, but with a ruthless resentment toward his friends. Still, our relationship with Ernest, particularly my friendship with him, had stayed warm and loving until the end. Perhaps he wouldn't mention us at all.

But he did. On page 214 I read, *That year the rich came led by the pilot fish. A year before they would never have come.* And my heart stopped. Dos had been the one who first introduced us to Ernest—now he was the pilot fish.

*When they said, "It's great, Ernest. Truly, it's great. You cannot know the thing it has," I wagged my tail in pleasure and plunged into the every day a fiesta concept of life to see if I could not bring some fine attractive stick back, instead of thinking, "If these bastards like it what is wrong with it?"*

In the end, Ernest blamed us for supporting his decision to leave Hadley for Pauline. He saw us as the enemy, the cause of his most regrettable decision. He rewrote history to absolve himself of his mistakes and assigned them to others. He ignored our unwavering enthusiasm for his new style of writing; our financial support for him and his family in those sad, uncertain days; our gifts of spirit and friendship and things. Now we were just "the rich."

*They were bad luck to people but they were worse luck to themselves and they lived to have all their bad luck finally; and to the very worst end that all bad lucks could go.*

Was it possible he was repeating Hoytie's curse? Was he really saying we deserved the deaths of our sons?

Near the end of the book, Ernest said he planned to write another, called *The Pilot Fish and The Rich and Other Stories*. So he wasn't done with us; only his death had prevented further insults.

I put the manuscript down and said, "Well. He certainly got the last word in." My heart was hurting, but I was still so surprised by Ernest's venom that the pain was numbed a bit. In my view, you had to love your friends no matter what. And failing that, you had, at least, to forgive them.

Gerald quietly waited for me to finish the book. "What a strange kind of bitterness, what shocking ethics!" he said. Then, "But also, of course, how well written."

That was so Gerald. Even his condemnation came with a courtly concession. He'd begun pulling away from Ernest years before, as if he'd seen the potential for this betrayal all along. He'd never come with me to Key West, and he'd never been on the receiving end of Ernest's white-hot adoration. Ernest had written me *love letters*! He'd doted on me like some smitten high schoolboy. And I had secretly welcomed his affections, even as I pushed him away. Now I was just some soulless rich woman. The idea that it could end this way, that he could so easily condemn us after our decades of true friendship. Thirty-five years of golden memories, erased with one book penned from a sick mind.

"This isn't the Ernest we knew," I said. "I don't think he was right in his head at the end. All those plane crashes and concussions from boxing and the bull ring. Not to mention the drinking."

"Perhaps you're right. You certainly saw him more recently than I did."

"What a sad end to a remarkable life. Too bad he had to give us such a mean send-off."

"Remember that line in the *Snows of Mt. Kilimanjaro*?" Gerald asked. "Helen says to Harry, 'Do you have to kill your horse and your wife and burn your saddle and your armour?'"

"Then he says, 'Your damned money *was* my armour.'" I closed my eyes and turned my face toward the sun. "Ernest died with far more money than any of us. The irony was apparently lost on him."

I mailed the manuscript back to Dos the next day and we never spoke of it again.

---

THE MONTHS THAT followed were wide and simple: we spent as much time as we could outdoors on the terrace, or sitting before the fire at night. I made simple broths and fresh juices and coaxed Gerald to consume them. I arranged vases of late-blooming roses and coneflowers on every surface. Friends called or stopped by and we tried to keep the mood as jolly as possible under the circumstances. And of course Honoria and Bill and the grandchildren came as often as they could.

But as I tried to tend to Gerald, I began struggling a bit myself. He sweetly hinted that I'd begun to repeat myself. I frequently had to double-check my work—had I already added the stock to the soup? Had I taken out the wash? One afternoon I spent an hour looking for my purse before stumbling upon it in the ice box.

The old memories, though—those were coming back to me more vividly than ever. The present was fading and the past was rising up to greet it. As Gerald's body betrayed him, my mind was beginning to betray me. What would I do when he was no longer around to keep me straight? I began leaving notes for myself, making lists to cross off. I'd always loved my lists.

―

BY SEPTEMBER, GERALD was confined to his bed, sleeping for much of the day. One day's mail brought a letter from Archie with what would otherwise have been spectacular news: he'd donated *Wasp and Pear*, which Gerald had given to him decades before, to New York's Museum of Modern Art. Honoria read the letter to him in a shaking voice. *Under normal conditions, these acquisitions take years to get approved and administered,* Archie wrote, *but I've convinced MOMA's director to make it official immediately. I wanted you to die knowing how important your work is; to really think of yourself as a painter.*

Gerald just smiled and whispered, "How wonderful."

By early October, we'd hired a nurse, who was able to administer the morphine as needed. Gerald's waking moments were brief. He was mostly lost to me now, but I still had his body, his physical presence, at home with me.

I looked around this, our final house together: the wall of shelves in the little dining area, filled with the blue-and-white faience pottery we'd collected over the years. The little wooden flourishes—which Gerald had found at a carpenter's shop in England—hung at a rakish angle over a door. The mirror-lined window frames looking out onto Hook Pond, magnifying our view. Everything exuded "Gerald and Sara," as each of our houses had. Gerald was right: we were the set designers of our own life together.

On October 15, Honoria and Bill sat by Gerald's side. "Please, Dow-Dow," Honoria said. "Bill knows a priest at St. Philomena's in town, a former Army chaplain in the war. I know you don't believe in it, but he could give you last rites, just in case."

"Just in case I have a last-minute conversion?" Gerald managed a little grin.

"Just to cover your bases, old man," Bill said.

There was a pause. I wasn't sure if he was thinking, or if he'd dozed off again.

"Get me the Army man, then," Gerald finally said.

Honoria let out a little sob. I was surprised that Gerald, so devout in his lifelong rejection of the Church, would agree to a hurried concession like this. But seeing our daughter's reaction, her pure relief, I realized that he'd done it entirely for her. That was so Gerald. Gallant until the end.

Two days later, Dr. Abel said it wouldn't be long now, so Honoria and I sat vigil at Gerald's bedside. I watched this man, who had given me everything I ever wanted plus so much more. How well I knew his body: his long, soft white torso. His muscular legs that looked so good in shorts and espadrilles. His balding pate, always pink from the sun. His look of gratitude and pride after we'd made love. This body belonged to me, even if his mind had been elsewhere at times. We'd initiated each other into sex, so many years ago, and nothing could take that away. He'd given me three children, three astonishingly lovely children. They'd appeared in my life like the lights of a magic lantern projected on a screen, dancing and laughing and occasionally being contrary, as all children do. They passed through my body and left me permanently changed. I was—and still am—a different person because of them.

I suddenly thought of a phrase made famous by Coco Chanel: "Never a button without a buttonhole." No form without function. It also seemed to sum up my nearly lifelong relationship with this man. Throughout our fifty years together, we'd adapted ourselves to each other, giving or taking as needed. What a dance it had been.

In Gerald's weary seventy-six-year-old face, I could still see the young man I'd met that summer of 1904. In many ways, he'd seemed older then than he was now. Gone was the serious, scrutinizing expression, and in its place: acceptance. Peace. Perhaps even bemusement. I wanted to memorize this face, this person who would not be in my life much longer. How would my days pass without seeing this face?

The nurse took Gerald's wrist to find a pulse, and the gesture wakened him. He suddenly looked at Honoria, then me, with more clarity in his blue eyes than I'd seen in weeks.

"Forgive me, Sal," he said softly, and gave me a wan smile. "The things you've put up with."

I squeezed his hand. "Nothing to forgive," I said. "It's been one big, grand adventure. And I would never have taken it without you."

"The *Picaflor*. The *Honoria*. The *Weatherbird*." He was reciting the names of all our sailboats.

"The courses we've charted!" I said. "Remember the buried treasure at St. Tropez?"

Honoria, holding his other hand, gulped down a sob. That had to be one of the happiest days of her life, back when we were five Murphys.

He smiled again and closed his eyes. But by now, Honoria and I were both weeping aloud. We weren't ready to let him go.

Gerald's eyes opened again and he said, as if to the nurse behind us, "Smelling salts for the ladies!" At which Honoria and I laughed through our tears. He was still alert enough to see or hear us. Perhaps we'd have him for another day.

But he closed his eyes again and let out a long sigh. We sat for a moment like that.

"Dow-Dow," Honoria said. Silence. Then, "Dow?"

The nurse quietly came over and took his wrist from my hand, consulting her watch. Then she shook her head.

The wail that came from my throat surprised even me. My head fell into Gerald's lap and I sobbed in a way that I hadn't since Baoth left us. For all the frustration and confusion and anger I'd felt at this man over the past few decades, I had *never* imagined life without him.

The way that cocktail hour was a time of meticulous precision. The way our home was filled with little embellishments that displayed his whimsical eye. The way conversation was never predictable; his knowledge of nearly every subject vast and at times encyclopedic. The way he signed his letters to me "love, d.d." I'd taken those little flourishes for granted every day.

And now . . . gone. My twin soul departed. I would never again see his perfectly sized homburg hat approaching on a Manhattan street or smell his signature scent of vanilla and cedar. Who would I be without him? It was like looking in the mirror and not seeing your reflection—your exact opposite, but quite essential.

At last I sat up and looked at Honoria, whose red eyes matched mine. "The end of an era," she said.

I let out a long breath. "How do we go on, Honoria? We've lost our captain."

"We had two captains, Mother. We still have one."

I smiled at her gratefully. "That's kind of you to say."

"It's entirely true. The ship moves forward, even if it's manned by a woman. You were every bit his equal, don't forget that."

"My darling girl." I blew my nose. The grief would last forever, or at least until I found Gerald again in some other place. But for now we would forge ahead.

We sat like that for a long time, I have no idea how long.

"You know what I'd like to do?" I finally said. "Let's go outside and toast Dow's departure. He's on some grand crossing now, and that always calls for champagne."

I pulled a bottle of Dom Pérignon Brut from the ice box and took it out to the terrace, where we plopped down in two wicker chairs with faded striped cushions. Bill came out and did the honors, sending the cork flying off into the yard. Then he poured the champagne into crystal flutes and we held them aloft.

"To Dow-Dow," Honoria said.

"To Gerald. To Dow," Bill and I said.

And, taking a sip, we all gazed at the treetops.

# Chapter 26
## 1964-1975

It was Dottie Parker's telegram that moved me the most. "DEAREST SARA DEAREST SARA" was all it said. She understood that, in this moment, even the most eloquent expressions of sorrow would be inadequate.

Despite his last-minute Catholic conversion, we held Gerald's service at St. Luke's Episcopal. That little stone church, beside the old windmill, had seen nearly every one of our family's rites; after this, just one more to go. I wore my black crepe Lanvin suit and managed not to cry through the mercifully short Anglican service. Archie read a poem he'd written just for Gerald.

Afterward, there was a small gathering at home—simple passed hors d'oeuvres and a nice young bartender from the Maidstone Club—with the closest of friends and my nephew, Stuyvie. As the guests left, the October sun cast everything in a soft yellow light and I watched them pull out onto the graveled drive in their shiny, finned automobiles.

Dawn Powell gave me a gentle hug. "*What* a lovely party, Sara," she said, and her kiss brushed my cheek. "Courage disguised as taste." I'd fought back tears for the entire day, but that one little phrase brought a knot to my throat and stung my eyes. It seemed to sum up my approach to life over the past thirty years. I thought to tell this to Gerald, before I remembered.

---

THAT WOULD BE my last "lovely party." It wasn't long before I decided to leave La Petite Hutte and move back to the city, where I took a four-room apartment at the Volney Residential Hotel on East 74th Street, two floors up from Dottie. A woman came in every other day to cook and clean, but I relished the days I was alone. Margaret was polite but nosey and, when she cleaned, she set everything back at right angles, instead of gently skewed as I preferred them. This wasn't a gift shop.

I still had our last dog, an old French bulldog named Marceau, and his company was what kept me going in those days. That and Dottie, whom I tried to see nearly every day. She lived on the eighth floor with her poodle, Troisiéme, and her Boston terrier, Woodrow Wilson.

"There are two requirements for living at the Volney," she told me when I announced I'd be moving there. "You must be a woman over sixty, and you must own a dog even older than yourself."

She wasn't wrong. The entire building appeared to be occupied by elderly women and their ancient canines. Waiting for the one tiny elevator could take hours, it seemed, as on one floor or another a tenant would be tangled in a leash or urging her pooch to go in. "Godot showed up sooner than that elevator," Dottie said.

She pretended to look after me, always expressing concern about the fact that Margaret had a key and could let herself into my apartment. "I've come to count the silverware," Dottie would say, then wander around my place with her nose in the air, ready to sniff out a crime.

But it was she who needed looking after, in my opinion. The first time I visited her apartment I was shocked beyond words. "Welcome to Château Skid Row," she quipped, and I could tell she was a little embarrassed.

The living room and tiny kitchen were stacked with books, newspapers, and magazines. The sink was filled with dirty dishes of unknown vintage. Several vodka bottles sat on various surfaces, and I noticed a tumbler that rarely left her hand. Of course, I already knew that Dottie drank.

The worst offense was the smell: scattered throughout the apartment, like Easter eggs, were the *crottes de chien* of her dogs. A few flies, too.

"Dottie!" I finally said, collecting ashtrays and teacups and carrying them to the sink. "You must let me send Margaret down to help you straighten up." The place needed so much more than straightening up, but it was a place to start.

"I'm not like you, Sadie," she said. "I don't need doilies on every surface."

"Take that back," I said. "I don't own a single doily, you know that."

I opened the icebox, which housed a few crusty cartons from Chong Yee's around the corner, a bottle of tonic water, and a carton of milk I was afraid to open. There was also a single, puckered apple that looked as if it had been there since the Civil War.

"Dottie," I said, holding it by the stem, "how old is this apple?"

"Oh, that. I've had it since I was a small child and can't bear to part with it."

I laughed but persisted. "Whatever do you live on?"

"Lettuce and dust bunnies," she said. "I'm on a restricted diet."

---

DOROTHY WAS SEVENTY-ONE and I was ten years older. Our world had shrunk to a tight circumference on the Upper East Side; every Sunday we tried to walk the dogs to the Bethesda Fountain in Central Park, about four blocks away. The beautiful brick loggia there reminded me of Florence.

This day we sat on a bench and watched the young people move at speeds that now seemed positively athletic.

"Look here, Dottie," I said, pulling out a packet of Scottish shortbread from my purse. "Walker's." I was always trying to fatten her up.

"Yes, please," she said and, biting off a piece, pulled out a silver flask of vodka with which to wash it down.

"Remember cartwheels?" I asked, watching a young girl execute a perfect one. "Remember dancing?"

"Don't forget romping and cavorting and gallivanting," she said. "So much gallivanting."

"Oh yes."

"You and Gerald were the most adorable dancers. You could have taken that act on the road."

"We were well suited. And he was a strong lead."

We sat in silence for a while and I watched as a little boy walked along the rim of the fountain, his parents not watching. Surely he would fall in and then they would scold him, when they should have been holding his hand all along.

"I wish I'd had an ounce of your luck when it came to husbands," Dottie said.

"I don't know how we got so lucky either," I said. I stroked Marceau's warm back, his rib cage vibrating with his labored breathing. He turned his flattened face up for my admiration, his tongue lolling out of the side of his mouth. Winston Churchill as a canine.

Dottie had been married three times, twice to the handsome actor and screenwriter Alan Campbell. They'd been fractious marriages, but even we were shocked when Alan had died of a drug overdose the year before, when they were still living in Hollywood. Dottie had insisted to the press that the death was accidental. But we were too old and tired for such secrets now.

"It wasn't actually an accident, you know," she said. "He'd been drinking Bloody Marys all day. When I came home, I found him surrounded by Seconals with a plastic bag over his head."

"Oh Dottie. How dreadful for you!" I knew how it was to watch someone die. But this added another whole layer of hurt.

"He was involved in such tawdry things, at first I thought it might have been a sex caper gone wrong. But then I decided it was his final 'fuck you' to me."

"Oh my!" My life with Gerald suddenly felt like a fairy tale.

"Pardon my French." She took another cookie and another swig. "When the police and the coroner finally left, my nosey neighbor, Mrs. Bachman, came over and asked if I needed anything. I said, 'I could use a new husband.'"

"You didn't!"

"I did. She was shocked and scolded me for my disrespect. 'I'm sorry,' I said. 'Then run down to the corner and get me a ham and cheese on rye. And tell them to hold the mayo.'"

I snorted. "You're incorrigible."

"Apparently so."

"Poor Alan."

Dottie's gift was her irreverence. But her wicked wit was also her fortification, her rampart. Now, with so much life and tragedy behind us, it made everything a little easier to bear—at least for me. Dottie had never found the genuine love I'd had; her humor came from a place of disappointment and pain. That she could make light of such a tragic scene alarmed me a bit. But I think it was her way of distracting others, and perhaps herself, from the deep sadness that had been her true companion for her entire adult life.

"Ah well," she sighed. "I've befriended the vodka bottle which, I find, has never let me down."

Other days, when Dottie wasn't feeling up to it, I'd take Marceau the single block over to the park and the sailboat pond. Here, in the warmer months, I'd watch the children rent model sailboats, which could now be powered by little black remote-control devices. The sight of those miniature wooden boats brought me right back to France.

The *petits voiliers*—rented for two sous and powered only by long sticks— in the Grand Bassin of the Luxembourg Gardens. How often had we taken the children there for an afternoon of ice cream and sailing? How simple and hopeful everything had felt then! Then there were our own three sailboats, each of which had borne us along the Mediterranean coast with Vova and our friends, with music and picnics and dancing. Watching these tiny wooden craft sail circles around the shallow pond, I could almost feel the warm breeze in my hair again.

Which was more painful: to have lived such a full, beautiful life and gradually lost it in bits and pieces? Or to live with the regret of never having had those experiences at all? I knew the answer, but sometimes it felt worse, this loss. Happiness is fleeting. People are mortal. And it's cold comfort to be left alone at the end. I'd tried so hard to savor every moment. Why was I now haunted by the feeling that I hadn't paid enough attention?

---

DOROTHY DIED DOWNSTAIRS in 1967, buried at Woodlawn Cemetery in the Bronx. My little Marceau died in 1970. I hung on as best I could for several more years, increasingly attended by a rotating staff of housekeepers and nurses and the occasional doctor. There was no privacy at all anymore.

A few years later—I couldn't tell you how many—Honoria sat me down and told me it was time.

"Time for what, darling? Time for tea? Have Margaret check the tea box."

"No, Maman. It's time you came to live with us. In Virginia. It's time you lived with family again. The children are all grown and off to college, and the guest room is big and comfortable."

"All right, darling," I said. "Whatever you think is best."

I don't know when that was. A year ago? More?

NOW I SEE our old blue Renault, sitting at the curb of the Antibes train station on Avenue l'Esterel. I take the wheel and turn right on Boulevard Maréchal Juin along the western coast of the Cap. Left on Chemin des Ondes, which takes me up a slight hill, then another left on Chemin des Nielles. Then a right onto tiny Chemin des Mougins, the Street of the Windmills, which gently ascends to the spine of the peninsula. There it is on the right, number 112, and I turn into the drive. The familiar plaque, five stars on a blue background with the American flag, and Villa America rises before me. Inside, I know, are the smells of lilacs and freshly ground coffee. Sunlight streaming through the glass-paned doors overlooking the sea. And three children's voices: singing or laughing or speaking a patois of French and English. How many homes in how many towns over sixty years? Of all of them, this is the one I choose to return to.

# Epilogue
## 1975
### HONORIA MURPHY DONNELLY

It's early October, and outside the leaves of the sugar maple and sweetgum trees are a blaze of red and orange. I sit holding Mother's hand, listening to the ticking of the clock on her bedside table. The blue curtains are pulled open, but the filtered autumn sunlight is weak. Dr. Fitzgerald came by this morning—the fact that his name is Fitzgerald would amuse Mother no end; or perhaps it would annoy her.

"Probably days, if not hours," he'd said.

Now it's just a matter of waiting. She's been mostly unconscious for the past three days. An oxygen mask obscures her face and a morphine drip is attached to the puckered, paper-thin skin in the crook of her arm. Her breath is shallow and ragged from the pneumonia. I can hear the fluid rattling in her lungs.

In the year since we moved her from the Volney Hotel to live here with us, Mother has danced in and out of reality. Her thoughts became intertwined, a montage of images across ninety years. She became a kind of child again. Sometimes she spent whole days just clipping photos from magazines and pasting them into scrapbooks. At bedtime, she would brush her long silver hair over and over. "One hundred strokes, Honoria," she'd say. "That's how you get the sheen."

But on other days, she'd come back to us and we'd sit for

hours reminiscing about the lovely times. The skiing trips with the Hemingways or the painting advice from Picasso. The countless train journeys with our forty-five pieces of luggage (the number of bags increased every time we told the story). The parrot, Coquotte, and the monkey, Mistigris. The magical search for pirate treasure on the beach at St. Tropez. Those memories—it was like counting gold pieces or jewels as we spoke of them aloud again.

One day last week, Mother had a short period of great clarity. She knew this day was approaching and, a great hostess to the last, she wanted to approve all the arrangements for her memorial. "St. Luke's, of course," she said. "Short and sweet. Absolutely no choirs or droning pastors. Ten minutes, tops. Archie can read something, just as he did at Dow's."

And then, in a moment of mystical, mathematical accuracy, she said, "I want the service held on October 18."

I got up and opened my desk calendar. "That's a Saturday, so the church may be booked, but I'll ask."

"Promise me, Honoria. I want the eighteenth."

"What's so special about the eighteenth?"

"It'll be eleven years to the day from your father's service. And also Patrick's fifty-fifth birthday. The very same day!"

"Dow would approve of that precision."

"Wouldn't he?" She giggled, the first time I'd heard her laugh in a while.

The matter of the cemetery plot and the headstone was settled years ago. She'll have a simple, classical stone to match Dow-Dow's, carved from unpolished marble so that it will quickly age and attract moss. Unlike almost all the others in the cemetery, which face east or west, their graves face north. A few yards away, facing south toward them, lie the graves of Baoth and Patrick.

Before Dow died, he'd asked Archie MacLeish to choose the epitaph for his gravestone. Archie selected a phrase from *King Lear*: "Ripeness is all." It was just like Dow: succinct, elegant, and full of meaning.

"One should never choose one's own epitaph," Dow said. "That's just hubris." Then he handed a sealed envelope to Mother. "I've already chosen yours." He instructed her not to open it until after he died.

The morning after Dow's service, Mom retrieved the envelope from her jewelry box and immediately tore it open. In his graceful penmanship he'd written:

*And she made all of light.*

It was an excerpt from the poem "Follow Thy Fair Sun" by Thomas Campion. When Mother read it, she cried and cried.

---

NOW I'VE REMOVED the oxygen mask and I gently grip Mother's hand as her breathing falters. Her hair lies twisted on the pillow, a thin silver rope. The sun has moved from the side of the house to the backyard, casting the room into deeper shadow. Even the ticking of the clock seems slower. When she's gone, I'll be the only survivor of our magical family. I think of the five stars Dow painted on the plaque for Villa America, the many sequences of five in all his paintings. Baoth, Patrick, Dow, Mom. Soon I'll be the only star left.

Suddenly, her eyes open, a glimpse of dark blue in the fading light. She mouths something with her lips, so I lean closer to hear. She's singing: *Dum-dum-de-dum*. It's a familiar melody but I can't quite place it. Then she smiles and stares at something just over my shoulder. I turn around to see if Bill has entered the room, but we're alone. The brass crucifix catches my eye, but her gaze is on something else.

I recognize the tune now. Mom is humming Lohengrin's wedding march and smiling at the groom who awaits her just outside my range of vision. She's a young woman again, wearing a wreath of orange blossoms and her grandmother's veil. She's walking up the aisle to take Dow's hand, to march into a new life beyond her imagination with joy and a sense of adventure.

She'd do it all over again.

# ACKNOWLEDGMENTS

The seed for this book was planted many years ago when I enrolled in a literature course at UC Santa Cruz about expatriate writers in 1920s Paris led by Professor Paul Skenazy. The class syllabus included *Living Well Is the Best Revenge* by Calvin Tomkins—the very first biography of Sara and Gerald Murphy—and, reading it, my fascination with the couple took root and never died over the ensuing decades. So thank you, Professor Skenazy, for that fruitful introduction.

I never thought I'd actually put my admiration into words until I read *The Paris Wife* by Paula McLain in 2011. Seeing how she gave new life to the character of Hadley Hemingway introduced in Ernest Hemingway's *A Moveable Feast*—deeply fleshing out actual events and relationships rather than creating an alternate plot—first inspired the possibility that I could do something similar with Sara. In 2022 I attended the Kauai Writers Conference specifically to meet and work with McLain and serendipitously found myself alone in an elevator with her one morning. She generously listened to my book idea (a *literal* "elevator pitch"!) and, as our conversation continued outside, gave me encouraging feedback. I will never forget that encounter with one of my writing idols.

In 2020, just weeks before we were hit with the COVID lockdown, I was invited to join a writers' group—the need to have a project to workshop gave me the impetus to actually start working on this book. That lovely group of women—Anne Matlack Evans, Rachelle Newbold, and Susan Karr—helped to birth the first few drafts of this novel. I'm grateful for their thoughtful reading and critiques.

Once I'd finished a third or fourth draft, I turned to developmental editor Heather Campbell Martin of MartinInk to help me trim the fat (cutting 10,000+ words) from my lengthy manuscript.

For the next two years I worked with writing coach par excellence Kerry Savage, who not only taught me how to deepen my portrayal of Sara and to find "the golden thread," but believed in this book with her heart and soul.

Finally, thanks to my beta readers—Ilana Sharlin Stone, Robin McMillan, and Robin Allen—and friends far and wide who have expressed real interest and curiosity about Sara and her Lost Generation tribe. It's been my privilege to introduce you to these fascinating folks, and I hope this novel will give you as much pleasure to read as it's given me to write.

www.ingramcontent.com/pod-product-compliance
Lightning Source LLC
LaVergne TN
LVHW041746060526
838201LV00046B/916